NEW YORK REVIEW BOOKS
CLASSICS

# DON'T LOOK NOW

DAPHNE DU MAURIER (1907–1989) was the daughter of the legendary actor-manager Gerald du Maurier and granddaughter of George du Maurier, the author of the vastly successful late-Victorian novel *Trilby* and cartoonist for the magazine *Punch*. She grew up in London and Cornwall, where she would settle as an adult. Du Maurier published her first novel when she was twenty-three and would go on to write seventeen more, many of them best-sellers, including *My Cousin Rachel, Jamaica Inn,* and *Rebecca*, one of the most popular novels of the twentieth century. In addition to her fiction, du Maurier wrote several family biographies, a biography of Branwell Brontë, a study of Cornwall, two plays, and a good deal of journalism. She was married to Tommy "Boy" Browning and was the mother of three children.

PATRICK McGRATH is the author of two story collections and seven novels, including *Port Mungo, Dr. Haggard's Disease, Spider,* (which he also adapted for the screen), and most recently, *Trauma. Martha Peake: A Novel of the Revolution* won Italy's Premio Flaiano Prize, and his 1996 novel, *Asylum*, was short-listed for both the Whitbread and the *Guardian* fiction prizes. McGrath is the co-editor of a collection of short fiction, *The New Gothic*. He lives in New York.

# DON'T LOOK NOW
*Stories*

DAPHNE DU MAURIER

*Selected and with an introduction by*
PATRICK McGRATH

NEW YORK REVIEW BOOKS

*New York*

THIS IS A NEW YORK REVIEW BOOK
PUBLISHED BY THE NEW YORK REVIEW OF BOOKS
435 Hudson Street, New York, NY 10014
www.nyrb.com

"The Birds," "Monte Verità," and "Kiss Me Again, Stranger" first collected
in *The Apple Tree* (1952); "La Sainte-Vierge" and "Indiscretion" first collected
in *Early Stories* (1959); "The Blue Lenses" first collected in *The Breaking Point*
(1959), "Don't Look Now" first collected in *Not After Midnight* (1971); "Escort"
and "Split Second" first collected in *The Rendezvous* (1980).

Library of Congress Cataloging-in-Publication Data

Du Maurier, Daphne, Dame, 1907–1989.
  Don't look now : stories / by Daphne du Maurier ; selected and with
an introduction by Patrick McGrath.
    p. cm. — (New York Review Books classics)
  ISBN 978-1-59017-288-9 (alk. paper)
  I. McGrath, Patrick, 1950– II. Title.
  PR6007.U47D66 2008
  823'.912—dc22

                              2008024188


ISBN 978-1-59017-288-9


Printed in the United States of America on acid-free paper.
10  9  8

# CONTENTS

# INTRODUCTION

DAPHNE du Maurier was born into a distinguished London theatrical family but spent most of her life in Cornwall, where she lived in a large, romantic house near the sea. She shared it somewhat uneasily with her husband, "Boy" Browning, a distinguished military man, and their three children. Du Maurier loved the simple writerly existence she created in Cornwall, and once wrote to a friend that she was only really happy "in the middle of Dartmoor in a hail storm within an hour of sundown of a late November afternoon." But she also lived an intense, unorthodox personal life, and sustained love affairs with various men and women, including the great Nöel Coward actress, Gertie Lawrence. A prolific writer who published more than three dozen works of fiction, history, and biography, du Maurier despaired if ideas would not come, and when her imagination was finally exhausted saw little point in carrying on. She died in 1989.

Despite du Maurier's range, her reputation as a writer is based almost entirely on her historical novels: *Frenchman's Creek, Jamaica Inn,* and *The King's General,* and of course *Rebecca,* which owes much to Charlotte Brontë's *Jane Eyre*; it was to become the basis of Alfred Hitchcock's first American movie. But in her many short stories——there were five collections published between 1940 and 1971—she explored a darker, sexier, more diverse and fantastic fictional landscape than she did in her novels, which despite their gothic atmosphere and distinctly weird touches—think of the evil albino clergyman in *Jamaica Inn*, for example——stayed faithful to a genre template and largely ended well.

In the stories du Maurier was not at all wedded to a happy outcome, and employed a sophisticated range of narrative techniques designed to sustain tension and deliver shocking endings. She was also tantalizingly inconclusive at times, demanding of her readers that we devise for ourselves explanations for the uncanny events she describes. Her imagination is liberated in the short story, where brilliant flashes of originality, pessimism, and even perversity are to be glimpsed.

True to her love of the country and the sea, du Maurier was fascinated by the collision, preferably violent, of humanity and the natural world. This is the central preoccupation of two of the stories collected here ("The Blue Lenses" and "The Birds"), and in each case humanity's prospects look bleak. Du Maurier's vision is a complex one, suggesting on the one hand the antagonistic quality of the relationship of man and nature, and on the other our proximity, even identity, with the animals—our low cunning, our savagery, and not least, our helplessness when subjugated to the appetites of a stronger creature.

In "The Blue Lenses" we come upon a woman recovering in the hospital after eye surgery. Lenses have been implanted. The day comes for the removal of the bandages. To the woman's horror, everyone she sees has the head of an animal. Each has assumed the bestial identity that expresses their true character, a kind of reverse anthropomorphism.

The terrified woman yearns for her husband to come and take her away from this hellish menagerie, but when at last he appears—

And it is here that we get what, from a lesser writer, would be the grim denouement of the tale. But du Maurier is not done yet, and she ratchets the story up a further notch or two before we arrive at the true ending, an instance of narrative ingenuity from this consummate storyteller. Note, too, the theme of *clairvoyance*, the paranormal ability to see beyond the immediate physical world to an otherwise inaccessible realm. It is a theme that recurs in this collection.

Of all the short stories du Maurier wrote, "The Birds" is the masterpiece. Hitchcock also filmed this story, and du Maurier was extremely displeased with the result. It is not hard to see why. Hitchcock shifted the action from rugged, windswept, British cliffs to placid Sonoma County, and invented a sophisticated plot involving a couple from San Francisco caught in a bizarre Oedipal struggle with a dreadful controlling mother. Du Maurier's original tale was far bleaker, far more naturalistic, and as a result, far more powerful.

The story could not be simpler. In a remote area of Cornwall, close to the sea, birds begin to attack humans. One man, a farm laborer, attempts to defend his family; we hold out little hope for them. There is no explanation for the behavior of the birds, though a suggestion is made that Arctic winds are the cause of the attacks. But the power of the story resides, at least in part, in the reader's suspicion that there exist other, less narrowly scientific explanations for what by the end is a scene of apocalyptic violence, perhaps rooted in cosmic punishment for humanity's sins; and this indeterminacy contributes to the story's disturbing potency. What "The Birds" did, in effect, was to anticipate an imminent large-scale ecological catastrophe. It can be seen as a starting point in the popularization of an entire genre devoted to environmental-disaster narratives. It could not be more timely, yet it was written more than forty years ago.

Given the gothic tendency of du Maurier's imagination, it is not surprising that she should have written ghost stories, and in this collection there is one nicely spooky example. Set in the early days of World War II, "Escort" is an oddly stirring tale of the sea. A British merchant ship on her way home from Scandinavia is stalked by a German submarine and her prospects don't look good. A mysterious vessel appears, offering to escort the merchantman home. As to the precise identity of the escorting vessel, and in particular her captain, so deftly does du Maurier withhold this information that only in the last few sentences does an unashamedly patriotic theme strike up. "Escort" is a small gem in the ghost-ship genre.

But clairvoyance was always more to du Maurier's taste than ghosts. In "Split Second," as in "The Blue Lenses," she is concerned with a kind of second sight. In this nightmare of a story a young widow comes home to find that strangers are living in her house, and this is far from the only disruption she discovers in the order of her world. Her appalling sense of dislocation is handled with empathy, no small accomplishment on du Maurier's part, for she made the woman quite insufferable. She foregrounds the intense distress the woman's predicament arouses, and once again supplies an elegant closure to this subtle tale of psychological horror.

Clairvoyance hints at the existence of a supernatural realm, but can only offer glimpses of it. Du Maurier wrote a long story, "Monte Verità," in which she attempted boldly to go deep into this territory, convinced, perhaps, that if we humans share so much with the apes then it's not unreasonable to suppose we have something in common with the angels too. A beautiful woman joins a strange monastic community possessed of extraordinary powers, living in an ancient fortress at the top of a remote mountain. A complicated allegory about purity and renunciation develops, and at the same time a narrative gathers momentum involving two Englishmen, both of whom are in love with this elusive, otherworldly woman. It is an unusual tale in that its success lies in its very ambiguity. And despite the story's intense focus on purity and the rejection of the body, it is in a sense charged with sex, is perhaps all about sex and the unbridgeable distance between those who yearn passionately to be united.

In fact du Maurier wrote well about sex. She was clearly fascinated with the knots and tangles men and women can get themselves into, and three of the stories collected here display this facet of her restless narrative intelligence. "La Sainte-Vierge," one of the earliest stories in the collection, is a delicate and cynical tale of a young Breton peasant girl who prays to the Virgin Mary that her fisherman husband comes to no harm at sea. Her prayer seems to be answered, for she has a vision. The girl remains deluded as to the meaning of her vision, but we do not; and herein lies the pathos of this simple yarn.

A more tortuous tale of sexual duplicity is "Indiscretion," in which the author carries her readers irresistibly forward to the revelation of a shocking truth, one that will prove destructive to all parties concerned. Then she discreetly lowers the veil, allowing us to imagine for ourselves the imminent disastrous implosion. These two darkly pessimistic stories are models of clarity and economy, and each allows the reader to go forward with the characters, after the ending, alone.

Also included here is "Kiss Me Again, Stranger," an even darker tale, part gothic, part *noir*, narrated by a young man who one night goes to the cinema and is powerfully attracted to the usherette. He follows her onto a late-night bus and sits beside her. She asks him to wake her before they get to the cemetery.

There is a fine, macabre humor here. The reader is intrigued as to what sort of cemetery-loving femme fatale this is, and of course by the end we know. The answer is a good example of the sort of perversity of which du Maurier was capable in her fiction. The story was written in 1951, and it is hard to think of any female character in British fiction, before this husky siren, who does what she does and with such cool aplomb: an unexpectedly powerful proto-feminist role model.

Finally, "Don't Look Now." This story was filmed by Nicolas Roeg, and of this adaptation of her work du Maurier strongly approved. Unlike Hitchcock in his celebrated film version of "The Birds," Roeg stayed close to the original material. The setting is Venice, in whose sinister, echoing labyrinth of alleys and piazzas, churches and canals the unwary visitor will quickly be lost. An English couple is on vacation not long after losing their young daughter to meningitis. In a restaurant the mother is told by a blind woman with psychic powers that while she and her husband were eating, their dead daughter was sitting between them. This chilly piece of information is the first in a string of developments in a horror story driven by coincidence, mistaken identity, clairvoyance, and murder. It contains a gloriously uncanny scene in which the husband glimpses his wife in a vaporetto on the Grand Canal, at the very moment when she is supposed to be on a plane on her way back to England.

"Don't Look Now" is a deeply unsettling story, its power a function of the slow, inexorable accumulation of incident and feeling that almost imperceptibly move toward the ultimate tragedy, leaving the reader both shocked when it comes and at the same time relieved, for an intolerable tension has been relaxed. This is narrative control of a very high order.

Daphne du Maurier's work has enjoyed great popular success over the years. But during her lifetime she received comparatively little critical esteem. "I am generally dismissed with a sneer as a bestseller," she once said, for it pained her deeply that she was not regarded as the serious writer she took herself to be. It is true she wrote fast and sometimes carelessly, but even her best work was treated with condescension. Critics dismissed the astute and subtle psychological dynamic in much of her fiction, also the passion with which she wrote. At her best, in a story like "The Birds," there is an exhilarating fusion of feeling, landscape, climate, character, and story. She plotted superbly, she was highly skilled at arousing tension, and she was, too, a writer of impressive originality and range. Not least, she showed real depth of understanding with regard to relationships between men and women, and much as she is celebrated as a writer of romance, suspense, and the supernatural, she is also a perceptive and skeptical interrogator of quotidian human experience.

—Patrick McGrath

# DON'T LOOK NOW

# DON'T LOOK NOW

"DON'T LOOK now," John said to his wife, "but there are a couple of old girls two tables away who are trying to hypnotise me."

Laura, quick on cue, made an elaborate pretence of yawning, then tilted her head as though searching the skies for a non-existent aeroplane.

"Right behind you," he added. "That's why you can't turn round at once—it would be much too obvious."

Laura played the oldest trick in the world and dropped her napkin, then bent to scrabble for it under her feet, sending a shooting glance over her left shoulder as she straightened once again. She sucked in her cheeks, the first tell-tale sign of suppressed hysteria, and lowered her head.

"They're not old girls at all," she said. "They're male twins in drag."

Her voice broke ominously, the prelude to uncontrolled laughter, and John quickly poured some more Chianti into her glass.

"Pretend to choke," he said, "then they won't notice. You know what it is—they're criminals doing the sights of Europe, changing sex at each stop. Twin sisters here on Torcello. Twin brothers tomorrow in Venice, or even tonight, parading arm-in-arm across the Piazza San Marco. Just a matter of switching clothes and wigs."

"Jewel thieves or murderers?" asked Laura.

"Oh, murderers, definitely. But why, I ask myself, have they picked on me?"

The waiter made a diversion by bringing coffee and bearing away the fruit, which gave Laura time to banish hysteria and regain control.

"I can't think," she said, "why we didn't notice them when we arrived. They stand out to high heaven. One couldn't fail."

"That gang of Americans masked them," said John, "and the bearded man with a monocle who looked like a spy. It wasn't until they all went just now that I saw the twins. Oh God, the one with the shock of white hair has got her eye on me again."

Laura took the powder compact from her bag and held it in front of her face, the mirror acting as a reflector.

"I think it's me they're looking at, not you," she said. "Thank heaven I left my pearls with the manager at the hotel." She paused, dabbing the sides of her nose with powder. "The thing is," she said after a moment, "we've got them wrong. They're neither murderers nor thieves. They're a couple of pathetic old retired schoolmistresses on holiday, who've saved up all their lives to visit Venice. They come from some place with a name like Walabanga in Australia. And they're called Tilly and Tiny."

Her voice, for the first time since they had come away, took on the old bubbling quality he loved, and the worried frown between her brows had vanished. At last, he thought, at last she's beginning to get over it. If I can keep this going, if we can pick up the familiar routine of jokes shared on holiday and at home, the ridiculous fantasies about people at other tables, or staying in the hotel, or wandering in art galleries and churches, then everything will fall into place, life will become as it was before, the wound will heal, she will forget.

"You know," said Laura, "that really was a very good lunch. I did enjoy it."

Thank God, he thought, thank God...Then he leant forward, speaking low in a conspirator's whisper. "One of them is going to the loo," he said. "Do you suppose he, or she, is going to change her wig?"

"Don't say anything," Laura murmured. "I'll follow her and find out. She may have a suitcase tucked away there, and she's going to switch clothes."

She began to hum under her breath, the signal, to her husband, of content. The ghost was temporarily laid, and all because of the familiar holiday game, abandoned too long, and now, through mere chance, blissfully recaptured.

"Is she on her way?" asked Laura.

"About to pass our table now," he told her.

Seen on her own, the woman was not so remarkable. Tall, angular, aquiline features, with the close-cropped hair which was fashionably called an Eton crop, he seemed to remember, in his mother's day, and about her person the stamp of that particular generation. She would be in her middle sixties, he supposed, the masculine shirt with collar and tie, sports jacket, grey tweed skirt coming to mid-calf. Grey stockings and laced black shoes. He had seen the type on golf-courses and at dog shows—invariably showing not sporting breeds but pugs—and if you came across them at a party in somebody's house they were quicker on the draw with a cigarette-lighter than he was himself, a mere male, with pocket-matches. The general belief that they kept house with a more feminine, fluffy companion was not always true. Frequently they boasted, and adored, a golfing husband. No, the striking point about this particular individual was that there were two of them. Identical twins cast in the same mould. The only difference was that the other one had whiter hair.

"Supposing," murmured Laura, "when I find myself in the *toilette* beside her she starts to strip?"

"Depends on what is revealed," John answered. "If she's hermaphrodite, make a bolt for it. She might have a hypodermic syringe concealed and want to knock you out before you reached the door."

Laura sucked in her cheeks once more and began to shake. Then, squaring her shoulders, she rose to her feet. "I simply must not laugh," she said, "and whatever you do, don't look at me when I come back, especially if we come out together." She picked up her bag and strolled self-consciously away from the table in pursuit of her prey.

John poured the dregs of the Chianti into his glass and lit a cigarette. The sun blazed down upon the little garden of the restaurant. The Americans had left, and the monocled man, and the family party at the far end. All was peace. The identical twin was sitting back in her chair with her eyes closed. Thank heaven, he thought, for this moment at any rate, when relaxation was possible, and Laura had been launched upon her foolish, harmless game. The holiday could yet turn into the cure she needed, blotting out, if only temporarily, the numb despair that had seized her since the child died.

"She'll get over it," the doctor said. "They all get over it, in time. And you have the boy."

"I know," John had said, "but the girl meant everything. She always did, right from the start, I don't know why. I suppose it was the difference in age. A boy of school age, and a tough one at that, is someone in his own right. Not a baby of five. Laura literally adored her. Johnnie and I were nowhere."

"Give her time," repeated the doctor, "give her time. And anyway, you're both young still. There'll be others. Another daughter."

So easy to talk ... How replace the life of a loved lost child with a dream? He knew Laura too well. Another child, another girl, would have her own qualities, a separate identity, she might even induce hostility because of this very fact. A usurper in the cradle, in the cot, that had been Christine's. A chubby, flaxen replica of Johnnie, not the little waxen dark-haired sprite that had gone.

He looked up, over his glass of wine, and the woman was

staring at him again. It was not the casual, idle glance of someone at a nearby table, waiting for her companion to return, but
something deeper, more intent, the prominent, light blue eyes
oddly penetrating, giving him a sudden feeling of discomfort.
Damn the woman! All right, bloody stare, if you must. Two can
play at that game. He blew a cloud of cigarette smoke into the
air and smiled at her, he hoped offensively. She did not register.
The blue eyes continued to hold his, so that he was obliged to
look away himself, extinguish his cigarette, glance over his
shoulder for the waiter and call for the bill. Settling for this,
and fumbling with the change, with a few casual remarks about
the excellence of the meal, brought composure, but a prickly
feeling on his scalp remained, and an odd sensation of unease.
Then it went, as abruptly as it had started, and stealing a
furtive glance at the other table he saw that her eyes were closed
again, and she was sleeping, or dozing, as she had done before.
The waiter disappeared. All was still.

Laura, he thought, glancing at his watch, is being a hell of a
time. Ten minutes at least. Something to tease her about, anyway. He began to plan the form the joke would take. How the
old dolly had stripped to her smalls, suggesting that Laura
should do likewise. And then the manager had burst in upon
them both, exclaiming in horror, the reputation of the restaurant damaged, the hint that unpleasant consequences might
follow unless... The whole exercise turning out to be a plant,
an exercise in blackmail. He and Laura and the twins taken in a
police launch back to Venice for questioning. Quarter of an
hour... Oh, come on, come on...

There was a crunch of feet on the gravel. Laura's twin
walked slowly past, alone. She crossed over to her table and
stood there a moment, her tall, angular figure interposing itself
between John and her sister. She was saying something, but he
couldn't catch the words. What was the accent, though—Scottish? Then she bent, offering an arm to the seated twin, and

they moved away together across the garden to the break in the little hedge beyond, the twin who had stared at John leaning on her sister's arm. Here was the difference again. She was not quite so tall, and she stooped more—perhaps she was arthritic. They disappeared out of sight, and John, becoming impatient, got up and was about to walk back into the hotel when Laura emerged.

"Well, I must say, you took your time," he began, and then stopped, because of the expression on her face.

"What's the matter, what's happened?" he asked.

He could tell at once there was something wrong. Almost as if she were in a state of shock. She blundered towards the table he had just vacated and sat down. He drew up a chair beside her, taking her hand.

"Darling, what is it? Tell me—are you ill?"

She shook her head, and then turned and looked at him. The dazed expression he had noticed at first had given way to one of dawning confidence, almost of exaltation.

"It's quite wonderful," she said slowly, "the most wonderful thing that could possibly be. You see, she isn't dead, she's still with us. That's why they kept staring at us, those two sisters. They could see Christine."

Oh God, he thought. It's what I've been dreading. She's going off her head. What do I do? How do I cope?

"Laura, sweet," he began, forcing a smile, "look, shall we go? I've paid the bill, we can go and look at the cathedral and stroll around, and then it will be time to take off in that launch again for Venice."

She wasn't listening, or at any rate the words didn't penetrate.

"John, love," she said, "I've got to tell you what happened. I followed her, as we planned, into the *toilette* place. She was combing her hair and I went into the loo, and then came out and washed my hands in the basin. She was washing hers in the next basin. Suddenly she turned and said to me, in a strong Scots accent, 'Don't be unhappy any more. My sister has seen your little girl. She was sitting between you and your husband, laughing.' Darling, I thought I was going to faint. I nearly did. Luckily, there was a chair, and I sat down, and the woman bent over me and patted my head. I'm not sure of her exact words, but she said something about the moment of truth and joy being as sharp as a sword, but not to be afraid, all was well, but the sister's vision had been so strong they knew I had to be told, and that Christine wanted it. Oh John, don't look like that. I swear I'm not making it up, this is what she told me, it's all true."

The desperate urgency in her voice made his heart sicken. He had to play along with her, agree, soothe, do anything to bring back some sense of calm.

"Laura, darling, of course I believe you," he said, "only it's a sort of shock, and I'm upset because you're upset. . . ."

"But I'm not upset," she interrupted. "I'm happy, so happy that I can't put the feeling into words. You know what it's been like all these weeks, at home and everywhere we've been on holiday, though I tried to hide it from you. Now it's lifted, because I know, I just know, that the woman was right. Oh Lord, how awful of me, but I've forgotten their name—she did tell me. You see, the thing is that she's a retired doctor, they come from Edinburgh, and the one who saw Christine went blind a few years ago. Although she's studied the occult all her life and been very psychic, it's only since going blind that she has really seen things, like a medium. They've had the most wonderful experiences. But to describe Christine as the blind one did to her sister, even down to the little blue-and-white dress with the puff sleeves that she wore at her birthday party, and to say she was smiling happily. . . Oh, darling, it's made me so happy I think I'm going to cry."

No hysteria. Nothing wild. She took a tissue from her bag

and blew her nose, smiling at him. "I'm all right, you see, you don't have to worry. Neither of us need worry about anything any more. Give me a cigarette."

He took one from his packet and lighted it for her. She sounded normal, herself again. She wasn't trembling. And if this sudden belief was going to keep her happy he couldn't possibly begrudge it. But...but...he wished, all the same, it hadn't happened. There was something uncanny about thought-reading, about telepathy. Scientists couldn't account for it, nobody could, and this is what must have happened just now between Laura and the sisters. So the one who had been staring at him was blind. That accounted for the fixed gaze. Which somehow was unpleasant in itself, creepy. Oh hell, he thought, I wish we hadn't come here for lunch. Just chance, a flick of a coin between this, Torcello, and driving to Padua, and we had to choose Torcello.

"You didn't arrange to meet them again or anything, did you?" he asked, trying to sound casual.

"No, darling, why should I?" Laura answered. "I mean, there was nothing more they could tell me. The sister had had her wonderful vision, and that was that. Anyway, they're moving on. Funnily enough, it's rather like our original game. They *are* going round the world before returning to Scotland. Only I said Australia, didn't I? The old dears...Anything less like murderers and jewel thieves."

She had quite recovered. She stood up and looked about her. "Come on," she said. "Having come to Torcello we must see the cathedral."

They made their way from the restaurant across the open piazza, where the stalls had been set up with scarves and trinkets and postcards, and so along the path to the cathedral. One of the ferry-boats had just decanted a crowd of sightseers, many of whom had already found their way into Santa Maria Assunta. Laura, undaunted, asked her husband for the guidebook, and,

as had always been her custom in happier days, started to walk
slowly through the cathedral, studying mosaics, columns, panels
from left to right, while John, less interested, because of his
concern at what had just happened, followed close behind,
keeping a weather eye alert for the twin sisters. There was no
sign of them. Perhaps they had gone into the church of Santa
Fosca close by. A sudden encounter would be embarrassing,
quite apart from the effect it might have upon Laura. But the
anonymous, shuffling tourists, intent upon culture, could not
harm her, although from his own point of view they made
artistic appreciation impossible. He could not concentrate, the
cold clear beauty of what he saw left him untouched, and when
Laura touched his sleeve, pointing to the mosaic of the Virgin
and Child standing above the frieze of the Apostles, he nodded
in sympathy yet saw nothing, the long, sad face of the Virgin
infinitely remote, and turning on sudden impulse stared back
over the heads of the tourists towards the door, where frescoes
of the blessed and the damned gave themselves to judgement.

The twins were standing there, the blind one still holding
on to her sister's arm, her sightless eyes fixed firmly upon him.
He felt himself held, unable to move, and an impending sense
of doom, of tragedy, came upon him. His whole being sagged,
as it were, in apathy, and he thought, "This is the end, there is
no escape, no future." Then both sisters turned and went out of
the cathedral and the sensation vanished, leaving indignation
in its wake, and rising anger. How dare those two old fools
practise their mediumistic tricks on him? It was fraudulent, un-
healthy; this was probably the way they lived, touring the
world making everyone they met uncomfortable. Give them
half a chance and they would have got money out of Laura—
anything.

He felt her tugging at his sleeve again. "Isn't she beautiful?
So happy, so serene."

"Who? What?" he asked.

"The Madonna," she answered. "She has a magic quality. It goes right through to one. Don't you feel it too?"

"I suppose so. I don't know. There are too many people around."

She looked up at him, astonished. "What's that got to do with it? How funny you are. Well, all right, let's get away from them. I want to buy some postcards anyway."

Disappointed, she sensed his lack of interest, and began to thread her way through the crowd of tourists to the door.

"Come on," he said abruptly, once they were outside, "there's plenty of time for postcards, let's explore a bit," and he struck off from the path, which would have taken them back to the centre where the little houses were, and the stalls, and the drifting crowd of people, to a narrow way amongst uncultivated ground, beyond which he could see a sort of cutting, or canal. The sight of water, limpid, pale, was a soothing contrast to the fierce sun above their heads.

"I don't think this leads anywhere much," said Laura. "It's a bit muddy, too, one can't sit. Besides, there are more things the guidebook says we ought to see."

"Oh, forget the book," he said impatiently, and, pulling her down beside him on the bank above the cutting, put his arms round her.

"It's the wrong time of day for sight-seeing. Look, there's a rat swimming there the other side."

He picked up a stone and threw it in the water, and the animals sank, or somehow disappeared, and nothing was left but bubbles.

"Don't," said Laura. "It's cruel, poor thing," and then suddenly, putting her hand on his knee, "Do you think Christine is sitting here beside us?"

He did not answer at once. What was there to say? Would it be like this forever?

"I expect so," he said slowly, "if you feel she is."

The point was, remembering Christine before the onset of the fatal meningitis, she would have been running along the bank excitedly, throwing off her shoes, wanting to paddle, giving Laura a fit of apprehension. "Sweetheart, take care, come back..."

"The woman said she was looking so happy, sitting beside us, smiling," said Laura. She got up, brushing her dress, her mood changed to restlessness. "Come on, let's go back," she said.

He followed her with a sinking heart. He knew she did not really want to buy postcards or see what remained to be seen; she wanted to go in search of the women again, not necessarily to talk, just to be near them. When they came to the open place by the stalls he noticed that the crowd of tourists had thinned, there were only a few stragglers left, and the sisters were not amongst them. They must have joined the main body who had come to Torcello by the ferry service. A wave of relief seized him.

"Look, there's a mass of postcards at the second stall," he said quickly, "and some eye-catching head scarves. Let me buy you a head scarf."

"Darling, I've so many!" she protested. "Don't waste your lire."

"It isn't a waste. I'm in a buying mood. What about a basket? You know we never have enough baskets. Or some lace. How about lace?"

She allowed herself, laughing, to be dragged to the stall. While he rumpled through the goods spread out before them, and chatted up the smiling woman who was selling her wares, his ferociously bad Italian making her smile the more, he knew it would give the body of tourists more time to walk to the landing stage and catch the ferry-service, and the twin sisters would be out of sight and out of their life.

"Never," said Laura, some twenty minutes later, "has so

much junk been piled into so small a basket," her bubbling laugh reassuring him that all was well, he needn't worry any more, the evil hour had passed. The launch from the Cipriani that had brought them from Venice was waiting by the landing-stage. The passengers who had arrived with them, the Americans, the man with the monocle, were already assembled. Earlier, before setting out, he had thought the price for lunch and transport, there and back, decidedly steep. Now he grudged none of it, except that the outing to Torcello itself had been one of the major errors of this particular holiday in Venice. They stepped down into the launch, finding a place in the open, and the boat chugged away down the canal and into the lagoon. The ordinary ferry had gone before, steaming towards Murano, while their own craft headed past San Francesco del Deserto and so back direct to Venice.

He put his arm around her once more, holding her close, and this time she responded, smiling up at him, her head on his shoulder.

"It's been a lovely day," she said. "I shall never forget it, never. You know, darling, now at last I can begin to enjoy our holiday."

He wanted to shout with relief. It's going to be all right, he decided, let her believe what she likes, it doesn't matter, it makes her happy. The beauty of Venice rose before them, sharply outlined against the glowing sky, and there was still so much to see, wandering there together, that might now be perfect because of her change of mood, the shadow having lifted, and aloud he began to discuss the evening to come, where they would dine—not the restaurant they usually went to, near the Fenice theatre, but somewhere different, somewhere new.

"Yes, but it must be cheap," she said, falling in with his mood, "because we've already spent so much today."

Their hotel by the Grand Canal had a welcoming, comforting air. The clerk smiled as he handed over their key. The bedroom was familiar, like home, with Laura's things arranged neatly on the dressing-table, but with it the little festive atmosphere of strangeness, of excitement, that only a holiday bedroom brings. This is ours for the moment, but no more. While we are in it we bring it life. When we have gone it no longer exists, it fades into anonymity. He turned on both taps in the bathroom, the water gushing into the bath, the steam rising. "Now," he thought afterwards, "now at last is the moment to make love," and he went back into the bedroom, and she understood, and opened her arms and smiled. Such blessed relief after all those weeks of restraint.

"The thing is," she said later, fixing her ear-rings before the looking-glass, "I'm not really terribly hungry. Shall we just be dull and eat in the dining-room here?"

"God, no!" he exclaimed. "With all those rather dreary couples at the other tables? I'm ravenous. I'm also gay. I want to get rather sloshed."

"Not bright lights and music, surely?"

"No, no... some small, dark, intimate cave, rather sinister, full of lovers with other people's wives."

"H'm," sniffed Laura, "we all know what *that* means. You'll spot some Italian lovely of sixteen and smirk at her through dinner, while I'm stuck high and dry with a beastly man's broad back."

They went out laughing into the warm soft night, and the magic was about them everywhere. "Let's walk," he said, "let's walk and work up an appetite for our gigantic meal," and inevitably they found themselves by the Molo and the lapping gondolas dancing upon the water, the lights everywhere blending with the darkness. There were other couples strolling for the same sake of aimless enjoyment, backwards, forwards, purposeless, and the inevitable sailors in groups, noisy, gesticulating, and dark-eyed girls whispering, clicking on high heels.

"The trouble is," said Laura, "walking in Venice becomes

compulsive once you start. Just over the next bridge, you say, and then the next one beckons. I'm sure there are no restaurants down here, we're almost at those public gardens where they hold the Biennale. Let's turn back. I know there's a restaurant somewhere near the church of San Zaccaria, there's a little alley-way leading to it."

"Tell you what," said John, "if we go down here by the Arsenal, and cross that bridge at the end and head left, we'll come upon San Zaccaria from the other side. We did it the other morning."

"Yes, but it was daylight then. We may lose our way, it's not very well lit."

"Don't fuss. I have an instinct for these things."

They turned down the Fondamenta dell'Arsenale and crossed the little bridge short of the Arsenal itself, and so on past the church of San Martino. There were two canals ahead, one bearing right, the other left, with narrow streets beside them. John hesitated. Which one was it they had walked beside the day before?

"You see," protested Laura, "we shall be lost, just as I said."

"Nonsense," replied John firmly. "It's the left-hand one, I remember the little bridge."

The canal was narrow, the houses on either side seemed to close in upon it, and in the daytime, with the sun's reflection on the water and the windows of the houses open, bedding upon the balconies, a canary singing in a cage, there had been an impression of warmth, of secluded shelter. Now, ill-lit, almost in darkness, the windows of the houses shuttered, the water dank, the scene appeared altogether different, neglected, poor, and the long narrow boats moored to the slippery steps of cellar entrances looked like coffins.

"I swear I don't remember this bridge," said Laura, pausing, and holding on to the rail, "and I don't like the look of that alley-way beyond."

"There's a lamp halfway up," John told her. "I know exactly where we are, not far from the Greek quarter."

They crossed the bridge, and were about to plunge into the alley-way when they heard the cry. It came, surely, from one of the houses on the opposite side, but which one it was impossible to say. With the shutters closed each one of them seemed dead. They turned, and stared in the direction from which the sound had come.

"What was it?" whispered Laura.

"Some drunk or other," said John briefly. "Come on."

Less like a drunk than someone being strangled, and the choking cry suppressed as the grip held firm.

"We ought to call the police," said Laura.

"Oh, for heaven's sake," said John. Where did she think she was—Piccadilly?

"Well, I'm off, it's sinister," she replied, and began to hurry away up the twisting alley-way. John hesitated, his eye caught by a small figure which suddenly crept from a cellar entrance below one of the opposite houses, and then jumped into a narrow boat below. It was a child, a little girl—she couldn't have been more than five or six—wearing a short coat over her minute skirt, a pixie hood covering her head. There were four boats moored, line upon line, and she proceeded to jump from one to the other with surprising agility, intent, it would seem, upon escape. Once her foot slipped and he caught his breath, for she was within a few feet of the water, losing balance; then she recovered, and hopped on to the furthest boat. Bending, she tugged at the rope, which had the effect of swinging the boat's after-end across the canal, almost touching the opposite side and another cellar entrance, about thirty feet from the spot where John stood watching her. Then the child jumped again, landing upon the cellar steps, and vanished into the house, the boat swinging back into mid-canal behind her. The whole episode could not have taken more than four minutes. Then he heard the quick patter of feet. Laura had returned. She had seen none of it, for which he felt unspeakably thankful. The sight of a child, a little girl, in what must have been near danger, her fear that the scene he had just witnessed was in some way a sequel to the alarming cry, might have had a disastrous effect on her overwrought nerves.

"What are you doing?" she called. "I daren't go on without you. The wretched alley branches in two directions."

"Sorry," he told her. "I'm coming."

He took her arm and they walked briskly along the alley, John with an apparent confidence he did not possess.

"There were no more cries, were there?" she asked.

"No," he said, "no, nothing. I tell you, it was some drunk."

The alley led to a deserted *campo* behind a church, not a church he knew, and he led the way across, along another street and over a further bridge.

"Wait a minute," he said. "I think we take this right-hand turning. It will lead us into the Greek quarter—the church of San Georgio is somewhere over there."

She did not answer. She was beginning to lose faith. The place was like a maze. They might circle round and round forever, and then find themselves back again, near the bridge where they had heard the cry. Doggedly he led her on, and then surprisingly, with relief, he saw people walking in the lighted street ahead, there was a spire of a church, the surroundings became familiar.

"There, I told you," he said. "That's San Zaccaria, we've found it all right. Your restaurant can't be far away."

And anyway, there would be other restaurants, somewhere to eat, at least here was the cheering glitter of lights, of movement, canals beside which people walked, the atmosphere of tourism. The letters "Ristorante," in blue lights, shone like a beacon down a left-hand alley.

"Is this your place?" he asked.

"God knows," she said. "Who cares? Let's feed there anyway."

And so into the sudden blast of heated air and hum of voices, the smell of pasta, wine, waiters, jostling customers, laughter. "For two? This way, please." Why, he thought, was one's British nationality always so obvious? A cramped little table and an enormous menu scribbled in an indecipherable mauve biro, with the waiter hovering, expecting the order forthwith.

"Two very large camparis, with soda," John said. "*Then* we'll study the menu."

He was not going to be rushed. He handed the bill of fare to Laura and looked about him. Mostly Italians—that meant the food would be good. Then he saw them. At the opposite side of the room. The twin sisters. They must have come into the restaurant hard upon Laura's and his own arrival, for they were only now sitting down, shedding their coats, the waiter hovering beside the table. John was seized with the irrational thought that this was no coincidence. The sisters had noticed them both, in the street outside, and had followed them in. Why, in the name of hell, should they have picked on this particular spot, in the whole of Venice, unless... unless Laura herself, at Torcello, had suggested a further encounter, or the sister had suggested it to her? A small restaurant near the church of San Zaccaria, we go there sometimes for dinner. It was Laura, before the walk, who had mentioned San Zaccaria...

She was still intent upon the menu, she had not seen the sisters, but any moment now she would have chosen what she wanted to eat, and then she would raise her head and look across the room. If only the drinks would come. If only the waiter would bring the drinks, it would give Laura something to do.

"You know, I was thinking," he said quickly, "we really ought to go to the garage tomorrow and get the car, and do that drive to Padua. We could lunch in Padua, see the cathedral and touch St. Antony's tomb and look at the Giotto frescoes, and come back by way of those various villas along the Brenta that the guidebook cracks up."

It was no use, though. She was looking up, across the restaurant, and she gave a little gasp of surprise. It was genuine. He could swear it was genuine.

"Look," she said, "how extraordinary! How really amazing!"

"What?" he said sharply.

"Why, there they are. My wonderful old twins. They've seen us, what's more. They're staring this way." She waved her hand, radiant, delighted. The sister she had spoken to at Torcello bowed and smiled. False old bitch, he thought. I know they followed us.

"Oh, darling, I must go and speak to them," she said impulsively, "just to tell them how happy I've been all day, thanks to them."

"Oh, for heaven's sake!" he said. "Look, here are the drinks. And we haven't ordered yet. Surely you can wait until later, until we've eaten?"

"I won't be a moment," she said, "and anyway I want scampi, nothing first. I told you I wasn't hungry."

She got up, and, brushing past the waiter with the drinks, crossed the room. She might have been greeting the loved friends of years. He watched her bend over the table and shake them both by the hand, and because there was a vacant chair at their table she drew it up and sat down, talking, smiling. Nor did the sisters seemed surprised, at least not the one she knew, who nodded and talked back, while the blind sister remained impassive.

"All right," thought John savagely, "then I *will* get sloshed," and he proceeded to down his Campari and soda and order another, while he pointed out something quite unintelligible on the menu as his own choice, but remembered scampi for Laura. "And a bottle of Soave," he added, "with ice."

The evening was ruined anyway. What was to have been an intimate, happy celebration would now be heavy-laden with spiritualistic visions, poor little dead Christine sharing the table with them, which was so damned stupid when in earthly life she would have been tucked up hours ago in bed. The bitter taste of the Campari suited his mood of sudden self-pity, and all the while he watched the group at the table in the opposite corner, Laura apparently listening while the more active sister held forth and the blind one sat silent, her formidable sightless eyes turned in his direction.

"She's phoney," he thought, "she's not blind at all. They're both of them frauds, and they could be males in drag after all, just as we pretended at Torcello, and they're after Laura."

He began on his second Campari and soda. The two drinks, taken on an empty stomach, had an instant effect. Vision became blurred. And still Laura went on sitting at the other table, putting in a question now and again, while the active sister talked. The waiter appeared with the scampi, and a companion beside him to serve John's own order, which was totally unrecognisable, heaped with a livid sauce.

"The signora does not come?" enquired the first waiter, and John shook his head grimly, pointing an unsteady finger across the room.

"Tell the signora," he said carefully, "her scampi will get cold."

He stared down at the offering placed before him, and prodded it delicately with a fork. The pallid sauce dissolved, revealing two enormous slices, rounds, of what appeared to be boiled pork, bedecked with garlic. He forked a portion to his mouth and chewed, and yes, it was pork, steamy, rich, the spicy sauce having turned it curiously sweet. He laid down his fork, pushing the plate away, and became aware of Laura, returning across the room and sitting beside him. She did not say anything, which was just as well, he thought, because he was too near nausea to answer. It wasn't just the drink, but reaction from the whole nightmare day. She began to eat her scampi, still not uttering. She did not seem to notice he was not eating. The waiter, hovering at his elbow, anxious, seemed aware that John's choice was somehow an error, and discreetly removed the plate. "Bring me a green salad," murmured John, and even then Laura did not register surprise, or, as she might have done in more normal circumstances, accuse him of having had too much to drink. Finally, when she had finished her scampi and was sipping her wine, which John had waved away, to nibble at his salad in small mouthfuls like a sick rabbit, she began to speak.

"Darling," she said, "I know you won't believe it, and it's rather frightening in a way, but after they left the restaurant in Torcello the sisters went to the cathedral, as we did, although we didn't see them in that crowd, and the blind one had another vision. She said Christine was trying to tell her something about us, that we should be in danger if we stayed in Venice. Christine wanted us to go away as soon as possible."

So that's it, he thought. They think they can run our lives for us. This is to be our problem from henceforth. Do we eat? Do we get up? Do we go to bed? We must get in touch with the twin sisters. They will direct us.

"Well?" she said. "Why don't you say something?"

"Because," he answered, "you are perfectly right, I don't believe it. Quite frankly, I judge your old sisters as being a couple of freaks, if nothing else. They're obviously unbalanced, and I'm sorry if this hurts you, but the fact is they've found a sucker in you."

"You're being unfair," said Laura. "They are genuine, I know it. I just know it. They were completely sincere in what they said."

"All right. Granted. They're sincere. But that doesn't make them well-balanced. Honestly, darling, you meet that old girl for ten minutes in a loo, she tells you she sees Christine sitting beside us—well, anyone with a gift for telepathy could read your unconscious mind in an instant—and then, pleased with her success, as any old psychic expert would be, she flings a further mood of ecstasy and wants to boot us out of Venice. Well, I'm sorry, but to hell with it."

The room was no longer reeling. Anger had sobered him. If it would not put Laura to shame he would get up and cross to their table, and tell the old fools where they got off.

"I knew you would take it like this," said Laura unhappily. "I told them you would. They said not to worry. As long as we left Venice tomorrow everything would come all right."

"Oh, for God's sake," said John. He changed his mind, and poured himself a glass of wine.

"After all," Laura went on, "we have really seen the cream of Venice. I don't mind going on somewhere else. And if we stayed—I know it sounds silly, but I should have a nasty nagging sort of feeling inside me, and I should keep thinking of darling Christine being unhappy and trying to tell us to go."

"Right," said John with ominous calm, "that settles it. Go we will. I suggest we clear off to the hotel straight away and warn the reception we're leaving in the morning. Have you had enough to eat?"

"Oh dear," sighed Laura, "don't take it like that. Look, why not come over and meet them, and then they can explain about the vision to you? Perhaps you would take it seriously then. Especially as you are the one it most concerns. Christine is more worried over you than me. And the extraordinary thing is that the blind sister says you're psychic and don't know it. You are somehow *en rapport* with the unknown, and I'm not."

"Well, that's final," said John. "I'm psychic, am I? Fine. My psychic intuition tells me to get out of this restaurant now, at once, and we can decide what we do about leaving Venice when we are back at the hotel."

He signalled to the waiter for the bill and they waited for it, not speaking to each other, Laura unhappy, fiddling with her bag, while John, glancing furtively at the twins' table, noticed that they were tucking into plates piled high with spaghetti, in very un-psychic fashion. The bill disposed of, John pushed back his chair.

"Right. Are you ready?" he asked.

"I'm going to say goodbye to them first," said Laura, her mouth set sulkily, reminding him instantly, with a pang, of their poor lost child.

"Just as you like," he replied, and walked ahead of her out of the restaurant, without a backward glance.

The soft humidity of the evening, so pleasant to walk about in earlier, had turned to rain. The strolling tourists had melted away. One or two people hurried by under umbrellas. This is what the inhabitants who live here see, he thought. This is the true life. Empty streets by night, the dank stillness of a stagnant canal beneath shuttered houses. The rest is a bright façade put on for show, glittering by sunlight.

Laura joined him and they walked away together in silence, and emerging presently behind the ducal palace came out into the Piazza San Marco. The rain was heavy now, and they sought shelter with the few remaining stragglers under the colonnades. The orchestras had packed up for the evening. The tables were bare. Chairs had been turned upside down.

The experts are right, he thought, Venice is sinking. The whole city is slowly dying. One day the tourists will travel here by boat to peer down into the waters, and they will see pillars and columns and marble far, far beneath them, slime and mud uncovering for brief moments a lost underworld of stone. Their heels made a ringing sound on the pavement and the rain splashed from the gutterings above. A fine ending to an evening that had started with brave hope, with innocence.

When they came to their hotel Laura made straight for the

lift, and John turned to the desk to ask the night-porter for the key. The man handed him a telegram at the same time. John stared at it a moment. Laura was already in the lift. Then he opened the envelope and read the message. It was from the headmaster of Johnnie's preparatory school.

> Johnnie under observation suspected appendicitis in city hospital here. No cause for alarm but surgeon thought wise advise you.
>
> Charles Hill

He read the message twice, then walked slowly towards the lift where Laura was waiting for him. He gave her the telegram. "This came when we were out," he said. "Not awfully good news." He pressed the lift button as she read the telegram. The lift stopped at the second floor, and they got out.

"Well, this decides it, doesn't it?" she said. "Here is the proof. We have to leave Venice because we're going home. It's Johnnie who's in danger, not us. This is what Christine was trying to tell the twins."

The first thing John did the following morning was to put a call through to the headmaster at the preparatory school. Then he gave notice of their departure to the reception manager, and they packed while they waited for the call. Neither of them referred to the events of the preceding day, it was not necessary. John knew the arrival of the telegram and the foreboding of danger from the sisters was coincidence, nothing more, but it was pointless to start an argument about it. Laura was convinced otherwise, but intuitively she knew it was best to keep her feelings to herself. During breakfast they discussed ways and means of getting home. It should be possible to get themselves, and the car, on to the special car train that ran from Milan through to Calais, since it was early in the season. In any event, the headmaster had said there was no urgency.

The call from England came while John was in the bathroom. Laura answered it. He came into the bedroom a few minutes later. She was still speaking, but he could tell from the expression in her eyes that she was anxious.

"It's Mrs. Hill," she said. "Mr. Hill is in class. She says they reported from the hospital that Johnnie had a restless night and the surgeon may have to operate, but he doesn't want to unless it's absolutely necessary. They've taken X-rays and the appendix is in a tricky position, it's not awfully straightforward."

"Here, give it to me," he said.

The soothing but slightly guarded voice of the headmaster's wife came down the receiver. "I'm so sorry this may spoil your plans," she said, "but both Charles and I felt you ought to be told, and that you might feel rather easier if you were on the spot. Johnnie is very plucky, but of course he has some fever. That isn't unusual, the surgeon says, in the circumstances. Sometimes an appendix can get displaced, it appears, and this makes it more complicated. He's going to decide about operating this evening."

"Yes, of course, we quite understand," said John.

"Please do tell your wife not to worry too much," she went on. "The hospital is excellent, a very nice staff, and we have every confidence in the surgeon."

"Yes," said John, "yes," and then broke off because Laura was making gestures beside him.

"If we can't get the car on the train, I can fly," she said. "They're sure to be able to find me a seat on a plane. Then at least one of us would be there this evening."

He nodded agreement. "Thank you so much, Mrs. Hill," he said, "we'll manage to get back all right. Yes, I'm sure Johnnie is in good hands. Thank your husband for us. Goodbye."

He replaced the receiver and looked round him at the tumbled beds, suitcases on the floor, tissue-paper strewn. Baskets, maps, books, coats, everything they had brought with them in the car. "Oh God," he said, "what a bloody mess. All this junk." The telephone rang again. It was the hall porter to say he had succeeded in booking a sleeper for them both, and a place for the car, on the following night.

"Look," said Laura, who had seized the telephone, "could you book one seat on the midday plane from Venice to London today, for me? It's imperative one of us gets home this evening. My husband could follow with the car tomorrow."

"Here, hang on," interrupted John. "No need for panic stations. Surely twenty-four hours wouldn't make all that difference?"

Anxiety had drained the colour from her face. She turned to him, distraught.

"It mightn't to you, but it does to me," she said. "I've lost one child, I'm not going to lose another."

"All right, darling, all right..." He put his hand out to her but she brushed it off, impatiently, and continued giving directions to the porter. He turned back to his packing. No use saying anything. Better for it to be as she wished. They could, of course, both go by air, and then when all was well, and Johnnie better, he could come back and fetch the car, driving home through France as they had come. Rather a sweat, though, and the hell of an expense. Bad enough Laura going by air and himself with the car on the train from Milan.

"We could, if you like, both fly," he began tentatively, explaining the sudden idea, but she would have none of it. "That really *would* be absurd," she said impatiently. "As long as I'm there this evening, and you follow by train, it's all that matters. Besides, we shall need the car, going backwards and forwards to the hospital. And our luggage. We couldn't go off and just leave all this here."

No, he saw her point. A silly idea. It was only—well, he was as worried about Johnnie as she was, though he wasn't going to say so.

"I'm going downstairs to stand over the porter," said Laura. "They always make more effort if one is actually on the spot. Everything I want tonight is packed. I shall only need my overnight case. You can bring everything else in the car." She hadn't been out of the bedroom five minutes before the telephone rang. It was Laura. "Darling," she said, "it couldn't have worked out better. The porter has got me on a charter flight that leaves Venice in less than an hour. A special motor-launch takes the party direct from San Marco in about ten minutes. Some passenger on the charter flight cancelled. I shall be at Gatwick in less than four hours."

"I'll be down right away," he told her.

He joined her by the reception desk. She no longer looked anxious and drawn, but full of purpose. She was on her way. He kept wishing they were going together. He couldn't bear to stay on in Venice after she had gone, but the thought of driving to Milan, spending a dreary night in a hotel there alone, the endless dragging day which would follow, and the long hours in the train the next night, filled him with intolerable depression, quite apart from the anxiety about Johnnie. They walked along to the San Marco landing-stage, the Molo bright and glittering after the rain, a little breeze blowing, the postcards and scarves and tourist souvenirs fluttering on the stalls, the tourists themselves out in force, strolling, contented, the happy day before them.

"I'll ring you tonight from Milan," he told her. "The Hills will give you a bed, I suppose. And if you're at the hospital they'll let me have the latest news. That must be your charter party. You're welcome to them!"

The passengers descending from the landing-stage down into the waiting launch were carrying hand-luggage with Union

Jack tags upon them. They were mostly middle-aged, with what appeared to be two Methodist ministers in charge. One of them advanced towards Laura, holding out his hand, showing a gleaming row of dentures when he smiled. "You must be the lady joining us for the homeward flight," he said. "Welcome aboard, and to the Union of Fellowship. We are all delighted to make your acquaintance. Sorry we hadn't a seat for hubby too."

Laura turned swiftly and kissed John, a tremor at the corner of her mouth betraying inward laughter. "Do you think they'll break into hymns?" she whispered. "Take care of yourself, hubby. Call me tonight."

The pilot sounded a curious little toot upon his horn, and in a moment Laura had climbed down the steps into the launch and was standing amongst the crowd of passengers, waving her hand, her scarlet coat a gay patch of colour amongst the more sober suiting of her companions. The launch tooted again and moved away from the landing-stage, and he stood there watching it, a sense of immense loss filling his heart. Then he turned and walked away, back to the hotel, the bright day all about him desolate, unseen.

There was nothing, he thought, as he looked about him presently in the hotel bedroom, so melancholy as a vacated room, especially when the recent signs of occupation were still visible about him. Laura's suitcases on the bed, a second coat she had left behind. Traces of powder on the dressing-table. A tissue, with a lipstick smear, thrown in the waste-paper basket. Even an old tooth-paste tube squeezed dry, lying on the glass shelf above the wash-basin. Sounds of the heedless traffic on the Grand Canal came as always from the open window, but Laura wasn't there any more to listen to it, or to watch from the small balcony. The pleasure had gone. Feeling had gone.

John finished packing, and leaving all the baggage ready to be collected he went downstairs to pay the bill. The reception clerk was welcoming new arrivals. People were sitting on the terrace overlooking the Grand Canal reading newspapers, the pleasant day waiting to be planned.

John decided to have an early lunch, here on the hotel terrace, on familiar ground, and then have the porter carry the baggage to one of the ferries that steamed direct between San Marco and the Porta Roma, where the car was garaged. The fiasco meal of the night before had left him empty, and he was ready for the trolley of hors d'œuvres when they brought it to him, around midday. Even here, though, there was change. The head-waiter, their especial friend, was off-duty, and the table where they usually sat was occupied by new arrivals, a honeymoon couple, he told himself sourly, observing the gaiety, the smiles, while he had been shown to a small single table behind a tub of flowers.

"She's airborne now," John thought, "she's on her way," and he tried to picture Laura seated between the Methodist ministers, telling them, no doubt, about Johnnie ill in hospital, and heaven knows what else besides. Well, the twin sisters anyway could rest in psychic peace. Their wishes would have been fulfilled.

Lunch over, there was no point in lingering with a cup of coffee on the terrace. His desire was to get away as soon as possible, fetch the car, and be en route for Milan. He made his farewells at the reception desk, and, escorted by a porter who had piled his baggage on to a wheeled trolley, made his way once more to the landing-stage of San Marco. As he stepped on to the steam-ferry, his luggage heaped beside him, a crowd of jostling people all about him, he had one momentary pang to be leaving Venice. When, if ever, he wondered, would they come again? Next year... in three years... Glimpsed first on honeymoon, nearly ten years ago, and then a second visit, *en passant*, before a cruise, and now this last abortive ten days that had ended so abruptly.

The water glittered in the sunshine, buildings shone, tourists in dark glasses paraded up and down the rapidly receding Molo, already the terrace of their hotel was out of sight as the ferry churned its way up the Grand Canal. So many impressions to seize and hold, familiar loved façades, balconies, windows, water lapping the cellar steps of decaying palaces, the little red house where d'Annunzio lived, with its garden—our house, Laura called it, pretending it was theirs—and too soon the ferry would be turning left on the direct route to the Piazzale Roma, so missing the best of the Canal, the Rialto, the further palaces.

Another ferry was heading downstream to pass them, filled with passengers, and for a brief foolish moment he wished he could change places, be amongst the happy tourists bound for Venice and all he had left behind him. Then he saw her. Laura, in her scarlet coat, the twin sisters by her side, the active sister with her hand on Laura's arm, talking earnestly, and Laura herself, her hair blowing in the wind, gesticulating, on her face a look of distress. He stared, astounded, too astonished to shout, to wave, and anyway they would never have heard or seen him, for his own ferry had already passed and was heading in the opposite direction.

What the hell had happened? There must have been a hold-up with the charter flight and it had never taken off, but in that case why had Laura not telephoned him at the hotel? And what were those damned sisters doing? Had she run into them at the airport? Was it coincidence? And why did she look so anxious? He could think of no explanation. Perhaps the flight had been cancelled. Laura, of course, would go straight to the hotel, expecting to find him there, intending, doubtless, to drive with him after all to Milan and take the train the following night. What a blasted mix-up. The only thing to do was to telephone the hotel immediately his ferry reached the Piazzale Roma and tell her to wait—he would return and fetch her. As for the damned interfering sisters, they could get stuffed.

The usual stampede ensued when the ferry arrived at the

landing-stage. He had to find a porter to collect his baggage, and then wait while he discovered a telephone. The fiddling with change, the hunt for the number, delayed him still more. He succeeded at last in getting through, and luckily the reception clerk he knew was still at the desk.

"Look, there's been some frightful muddle," he began, and explained how Laura was even now on her way back to the hotel—he had seen her with two friends on one of the ferry-services. Would the reception clerk explain and tell her to wait? He would be back by the next available service to collect her. "In any event, detain her," he said. "I'll be as quick as I can." The reception clerk understood perfectly, and John rang off.

Thank heaven Laura hadn't turned up before he had put through his call, or they would have told her he was on his way to Milan. The porter was still waiting with the baggage, and it seemed simplest to walk with him to the garage, hand everything over to the chap in charge of the office there and ask him to keep it for an hour, when he would be returning with his wife to pick up the car. Then he went back to the landing-station to await the next ferry to Venice. The minutes dragged, and he kept wondering all the time what had gone wrong at the airport and why in heaven's name Laura hadn't telephoned. No use conjecturing. She would tell him the whole story at the hotel. One thing was certain: he would not allow Laura and himself to be saddled with the sisters and become involved with their affairs. He could imagine Laura saying that they also had missed a flight, and could they have a lift to Milan?

Finally the ferry chugged alongside the landing-stage and he stepped aboard. What an anti-climax, thrashing back past the familiar sights to which he had bidden a nostalgic farewell such a short while ago! He didn't even look about him this time, he was so intent on reaching his destination. In San Marco there were more people than ever, the afternoon crowds walking shoulder to shoulder, every one of them on pleasure bent.

He came to the hotel and pushed his way through the swing door, expecting to see Laura, and possibly the sisters, waiting in the lounge to the left of the entrance. She was not there. He went to the desk. The reception clerk he had spoken to on the telephone was standing there, talking to the manager.

"Has my wife arrived?" John asked.

"No, sir, not yet."

"What an extraordinary thing. Are you sure?"

"Absolutely certain, sir. I have been here ever since you telephoned me at a quarter to two. I have not left the desk."

"I just don't understand it. She was on one of the vaporettos passing by the Accademia. She would have landed at San Marco about five minutes later and come on here."

The clerk seemed nonplussed. "I don't know what to say. The signora was with friends, did you say?"

"Yes. Well, acquaintances. Two ladies we had met at Torcello yesterday. I was astonished to see her with them on the vaporetto, and of course I assumed that the flight had been cancelled, and she had somehow met up with them at the airport and decided to return here with them, to catch me before I left."

Oh hell, what was Laura doing? It was after three. A matter of moments from San Marco landing-stage to the hotel.

"Perhaps the signora went with her friends to their hotel instead. Do you know where they are staying?"

"No," said John, "I haven't the slightest idea. What's more, I don't even know the names of the two ladies. They were sisters, twins, in fact—looked exactly alike. But anyway, why go to their hotel and not here?"

The swing-door opened but it wasn't Laura. Two people staying in the hotel.

The manager broke into the conversation. "I tell you what I will do," he said. "I will telephone the airport and check about the flight. Then at least we will get somewhere." He smiled apologetically. It was not usual for arrangements to go wrong.

"Yes, do that," said John. "We may as well know what happened there."

He lit a cigarette and began to pace up and down the entrance hall. What a bloody mix-up. And how unlike Laura, who knew he would be setting off for Milan directly after lunch—indeed, for all she knew he might have gone before. But surely, in that case, she would have telephoned at once, on arrival at the airport, had the flight been cancelled? The manager was ages telephoning, he had to be put through on some other line, and his Italian was too rapid for John to follow the conversation. Finally he replaced the receiver.

"It is more mysterious than ever, sir," he said. "The charter flight was not delayed, it took off on schedule with a full complement of passengers. As far as they could tell me, there was no hitch. The signora must simply have changed her mind." His smile was more apologetic than ever.

"Changed her mind," John repeated. "But why on earth should she do that? She was so anxious to be home tonight."

The manager shrugged. "You know how ladies can be, sir," he said. "Your wife may have thought that after all she would prefer to take the train to Milan with you. I do assure you, though, that the charter party was most respectable, and it was a Caravelle aircraft, perfectly safe."

"Yes, yes," said John impatiently, "I don't blame your arrangements in the slightest. I just can't understand what induced her to change her mind, unless it was meeting with these two ladies."

The manager was silent. He could not think of anything to say. The reception clerk was equally concerned. "Is it possible," he ventured, "that you made a mistake, and it was not the signora that you saw on the vaporetto?"

"Oh no," replied John, "it was my wife, I assure you. She was wearing her red coat, she was hatless, just as she left here. I saw her as plainly as I can see you. I would swear to it in a court of law."

"It is unfortunate," said the manager, "that we do not know the name of the two ladies, or the hotel where they were staying. You say you met these ladies at Torcello yesterday?"

"Yes...but only briefly. They weren't staying there. At least, I am certain they were not. We saw them at dinner in Venice later, as it happens."

"Excuse me..." Guests were arriving with luggage to check in, the clerk was obliged to attend to them. John turned in desperation to the manager. "Do you think it would be any good telephoning the hotel in Torcello in case the people there knew the name of the ladies, or where they were staying in Venice?"

"We can try," replied the manager. "It is a small hope, but we can try."

John resumed his anxious pacing, all the while watching the swing-door, hoping, praying, that he would catch sight of the red coat and Laura would enter. Once again there followed what seemed an interminable telephone conversation between the manager and someone at the hotel in Torcello.

"Tell them two sisters," said John, "two elderly ladies dressed in grey, both exactly alike. One lady was blind," he added. The manager nodded. He was obviously giving a detailed description. Yet when he hung up he shook his head. "The manager at Torcello says he remembers the two ladies well," he told John, "but they were only there for lunch. He never learnt their names."

"Well, that's that. There's nothing to do now but wait."

John lit his third cigarette and went out on to the terrace, to resume his pacing there. He stared out across the canal, searching the heads of the people on passing steamers, motorboats, even drifting gondolas. The minutes ticked by on his watch, and there was no sign of Laura. A terrible foreboding nagged at him that somehow this was prearranged, that Laura had never intended to catch the aircraft, that last night in the restaurant she had made an assignation with the sisters. Oh God, he thought, that's impossible, I'm going paranoiac. . . . Yet why, why? No, more likely the encounter at the airport was fortuitous, and for some incredible reason they had persuaded Laura not to board the aircraft, even prevented her from doing so, trotting out one of their psychic visions, that the aircraft would crash, that she must return with them to Venice. And Laura, in her sensitive state, felt they must be right, swallowed it all without question.

But granted all these possibilities, why had she not come to the hotel? What was she doing? Four o'clock, half-past four, the sun no longer dappling the water. He went back to the reception desk.

"I just can't hang around," he said. "Even if she does turn up, we shall never make Milan this evening. I might see her walking with these ladies, in the Piazza San Marco, anywhere. If she arrives while I'm out, will you explain?"

The clerk was full of concern. "Indeed, yes," he said. "It is very worrying for you, sir. Would it perhaps be prudent if we booked you in here tonight?"

John gestured, helplessly. "Perhaps, yes, I don't know. Maybe . . ."

He went out of the swing-door and began to walk towards the Piazza San Marco. He looked into every shop up and down the colonnades, crossed the piazza a dozen times, threaded his way between the tables in front of Florian's, in front of Quadri's, knowing that Laura's red coat and the distinctive appearance of the twin sisters could easily be spotted, even amongst this milling crowd, but there was no sign of them. He joined the crowd of shoppers in the Merceria, shoulder to shoulder with idlers, thrusters, window-gazers, knowing instinctively that it was useless, they wouldn't be here. Why should Laura have deliberately missed her flight to return to Venice for such a purpose? And even if she had done so, for some reason beyond his imagining, she would surely have come first to the hotel to find him.

The only thing left to him was to try to track down the sisters. Their hotel could be anywhere amongst the hundreds of hotels and pensions scattered through Venice, or even across the other side at the Zattere, or further again on the Giudecca. These last possibilities seemed remote. More likely they were staying in a small hotel or pension somewhere near San Zaccaria handy to the restaurant where they had dined last night. The blind one would surely not go far afield in the evening. He had been a fool not to have thought of this before, and he turned back and walked quickly away from the brightly lighted shopping district towards the narrower, more cramped quarter where they had dined last evening. He found the restaurant without difficulty, but they were not yet open for dinner, and the waiter preparing tables was not the one who had served them. John asked to see the *padrone*, and the waiter disappeared to the back regions, returning after a moment or two with the somewhat dishevelled-looking proprietor in shirtsleeves, caught in a slack moment, not in full tenue.

"I had dinner here last night," John explained. "There were two ladies sitting at that table there in the corner." He pointed to it.

"You wish to book that table for this evening?" asked the proprietor.

"No," said John. "No, there were two ladies there last night, two sisters, due sorelle, twins, gemelle"—what was the right word for twins?—"Do you remember? Two ladies, sorelle vecchie..."

"Ah," said the man, "si, si, signore, la povera signorina." He put his hands to his eyes to feign blindness. "Yes, I remember."

"Do you know their names?" asked John. "Where they were staying? I am very anxious to trace them."

The proprietor spread out his hands in a gesture of regret. "I am ver' sorry, signore, I do not know the names of the signorine, they have been here once, twice, perhaps for dinner, they do not say where they were staying. Perhaps if you come again tonight they might be here? Would you like to book a table?"

He pointed around him, suggesting a whole choice of tables that might appeal to a prospective diner, but John shook his head.

"Thank you, no. I may be dining elsewhere. I am sorry to have troubled you. If the signorine should come..." he paused, "possibly I may return later," he added. "I am not sure."

The proprietor bowed, and walked with him to the entrance. "In Venice the whole world meets," he said, smiling. "It is possible the signore will find his friends tonight. Arrivederci, signore."

Friends? John walked out into the street. More likely kidnappers...Anxiety had turned to fear, to panic. Something had gone terribly wrong. Those women had got hold of Laura, played upon her suggestibility, induced her to go with them, either to their hotel or elsewhere. Should he find the Consulate? Where was it? What would he say when he got there? He began walking without purpose, finding himself, as they had done the night before, in streets he did not know, and suddenly came upon a tall building with the word "Questura" above it. This is it, he thought. I don't care, something has happened, I'm going inside. There were a number of police in uniform coming and going, the place at any rate was active, and, addressing himself to one of them behind a glass partition, he asked if there was anyone who spoke English. The man pointed to a flight of stairs and John went up, entering a door on the right where he saw that another couple were sitting, waiting, and with relief he recognised them as fellow-countrymen, tourists, obviously a man and his wife, in some sort of predicament.

"Come and sit down," said the man. "We've waited half an

hour but they can't be much longer. What a country! They wouldn't leave us like this at home."

John took the proffered cigarette and found a chair beside them.

"What's your trouble?" he asked.

"My wife had her handbag pinched in one of those shops in the Merceria," said the man. "She simply put it down one moment to look at something, and you'd hardly credit it, the next moment it had gone. I say it was a sneak thief, she insists it was the girl behind the counter. But who's to say? These Ities are all alike. Anyway, I'm certain we shan't get it back. What have you lost?"

"Suitcase stolen," John lied rapidly. "Had some important papers in it."

How could he say he had lost his wife? He couldn't even begin . . .

The man nodded in sympathy. "As I said, these Ities are all alike. Old Musso knew how to deal with them. Too many Communists around these days. The trouble is, they're not going to bother with our troubles much, not with this murderer at large. They're all out looking for him."

"Murderer? What murderer?" asked John.

"Don't tell me you've not heard about it?" The man stared at him in surprise. "Venice has talked of nothing else. It's been in all the papers, on the radio, and even in the English papers. A grizzly business. One woman found with her throat slit last week—a tourist too—and some old chap discovered with the same sort of knife wound this morning. They seem to think it must be a maniac, because there doesn't seem to be any motive. Nasty thing to happen in Venice in the tourist season."

"My wife and I never bother with the newspapers when we're on holiday," said John. "And we're neither of us much given to gossip in the hotel."

"Very wise of you," laughed the man. "It might have spoilt

your holiday, especially if your wife is nervous. Oh well, we're off tomorrow anyway. Can't say we mind, do we, dear?" He turned to his wife. "Venice has gone downhill since we were here last. And now this loss of the handbag really is the limit."

The door of the inner room opened, and a senior police officer asked John's companion and his wife to pass through.

"I bet we don't get any satisfaction," murmured the tourist, winking at John, and he and his wife went into the inner room. The door closed behind them. John stubbed out his cigarette and lighted another. A strange feeling of unreality possessed him. He asked himself what he was doing here, what was the use of it? Laura was no longer in Venice but had disappeared, perhaps forever, with those diabolical sisters. She would never be traced. And just as the two of them had made up a fantastic story about the twins, when they first spotted them in Torcello, so, with nightmare logic, the fiction would have basis in fact; the women were in reality disguised crooks, men with criminal intent who lured unsuspecting persons to some appalling fate. They might even be the murderers for whom the police sought. Who would ever suspect two elderly women of respectable appearance, living quietly in some second-rate pension or hotel? He stubbed out his cigarette, unfinished.

"This," he thought, "is really the start of paranoia. This is the way people go off their heads." He glanced at his watch. It was half-past six. Better pack this in, this futile quest here in police headquarters, and keep to the single link of sanity remaining. Return to the hotel, put a call through to the prep school in England, and ask about the latest news of Johnnie. He had not thought about poor Johnnie since sighting Laura on the vaporetto.

Too late, though. The inner door opened, the couple were ushered out.

"Usual clap-trap," said the husband sotto voce to John. "They'll do what they can. Not much hope. So many foreigners in Venice, all of 'em thieves! The locals all above reproach. Wouldn't pay 'em to steal from customers. Well, I wish you better luck."

He nodded, his wife smiled and bowed, and they had gone. John followed the police officer into the inner room.

Formalities began. Name, address, passport. Length of stay in Venice, etc., etc. Then the questions, and John, the sweat beginning to appear on his forehead, launched into his interminable story. The first encounter with the sisters, the meeting at the restaurant, Laura's state of suggestibility because of the death of their child, the telegram about Johnnie, the decision to take the chartered flight, her departure, and her sudden inexplicable return. When he had finished he felt as exhausted as if he had driven three hundred miles non-stop after a severe bout of 'flu. His interrogator spoke excellent English with a strong Italian accent.

"You say," he began, "that your wife was suffering the after-effects of shock. This had been noticeable during your stay here in Venice?"

"Well, yes," John replied, "she had really been quite ill. The holiday didn't seem to be doing her much good. It was only when she met these two women at Torcello yesterday that her mood changed. The strain seemed to have gone. She was ready, I suppose, to snatch at every straw, and this belief that our little girl was watching over her had somehow restored her to what appeared normality."

"It would be natural," said the police officer, "in the circumstances. But no doubt the telegram last night was a further shock to you both?"

"Indeed, yes. That was the reason we decided to return home."

"No argument between you? No difference of opinion?"

"None. We were in complete agreement. My one regret was that I could not go with my wife on this charter flight."

The police officer nodded. "It could well be that your wife had a sudden attack of amnesia, and meeting the two ladies served as a link, she clung to them for support. You have described them with great accuracy, and I think they should not be too difficult to trace. Meanwhile, I suggest you should return to your hotel, and we will get in touch with you as soon as we have news."

At least, John thought, they believed his story. They did not consider him a crank who had made the whole thing up and was merely wasting their time.

"You appreciate," he said, "I am extremely anxious. These women may have some criminal design upon my wife. One has heard of such things..."

The police officer smiled for the first time. "Please don't concern yourself," he said. "I am sure there will be some satisfactory explanation."

All very well, thought John, but in heaven's name, what?

"I'm sorry," he said, "to have taken up so much of your time. Especially as I gather the police have their hands full hunting down a murderer who is still at large."

He spoke deliberately. No harm in letting the fellow know that for all any of them could tell there might be some connection between Laura's disappearance and this other hideous affair.

"Ah, that," said the police officer, rising to his feet. "We hope to have the murderer under lock and key very soon."

His tone of confidence was reassuring. Murderers, missing wives, lost handbags were all under control. They shook hands, and John was ushered out of the door and so downstairs. Perhaps, he thought, as he walked slowly back to the hotel, the fellow was right. Laura had suffered a sudden attack of amnesia, and the sisters happened to be at the airport and had brought her back to Venice, to their own hotel, because Laura couldn't remember where she and John had been staying. Perhaps they were even now trying to track down his hotel. Anyway, he could do nothing more. The police had everything in hand, and, please God, would come up with the solution. All he wanted to do right now was to collapse upon a bed with a stiff whisky, and then put through a call to Johnnie's school.

The page took him up in the lift to a modest room on the fourth floor at the rear of the hotel. Bare, impersonal, the shutters closed, with a smell of cooking wafting up from a courtyard down below.

"Ask them to send me up a double whisky, will you?" he said to the boy. "And a ginger-ale," and when he was alone he plunged his face under the cold tap in the wash-basin, relieved to find that the minute portion of visitor's soap afforded some measure of comfort. He flung off his shoes, hung his coat over the back of a chair and threw himself down on the bed. Somebody's radio was blasting forth an old popular song, now several seasons out of date, that had been one of Laura's favourites a couple of years ago. "I love you, Baby..." He reached for the telephone, and asked the exchange to put through the call to England. Then he closed his eyes, and all the while the insistent voice persisted, "I love you, Baby...I can't get you out of my mind."

Presently there was a tap at the door. It was the waiter with his drink. Too little ice, such meagre comfort, but what desperate need. He gulped it down without the ginger-ale, and in a few moments the ever-nagging pain was eased, numbed, bringing, if only momentarily, a sense of calm. The telephone rang, and now, he thought, bracing himself for ultimate disaster, the final shock, Johnnie probably dying, or already dead. In which case nothing remained. Let Venice be engulfed...

The exchange told him that the connection had been made, and in a moment he heard the voice of Mrs. Hill at the other end of the line. They must have warned her that the call came from Venice, for she knew instantly who was speaking.

"Hullo?" she said. "Oh, I am so glad you rang. All is well.

Johnnie has had his operation, the surgeon decided to do it at midday rather than wait, and it was completely successful. Johnnie is going to be all right. So you don't have to worry any more, and will have a peaceful night."

"Thank God," he answered.

"I know," she said, "we are all so relieved. Now I'll get off the line and you can speak to your wife."

John sat up on the bed, stunned. What the hell did she mean? Then he heard Laura's voice, cool and clear.

"Darling? Darling, are you there?"

He could not answer. He felt the hand holding the receiver go clammy cold with sweat. "I'm here," he whispered.

"It's not a very good line," she said, "but never mind. As Mrs. Hill told you, all is well. Such a nice surgeon, and a very sweet Sister on Johnnie's floor, and I really am happy about the way it's turned out. I came straight down here after landing at Gatwick—the flight O.K., by the way, but such a funny crowd, it'll make you hysterical when I tell you about them—and I went to the hospital, and Johnnie was coming round. Very dopey, of course, but so pleased to see me. And the Hills are being wonderful, I've got their spare-room, and it's only a short taxi-drive into the town and the hospital. I shall go to bed as soon as we've had dinner, because I'm a bit fagged, what with the flight and the anxiety. How was the drive to Milan? And where are you staying?"

John did not recognise the voice that answered as his own. It was the automatic response of some computer.

"I'm not in Milan," he said. "I'm still in Venice."

"Still in Venice? What on earth for? Wouldn't the car start?"

"I can't explain," he said. "There was a stupid sort of mix-up..."

He felt suddenly so exhausted that he nearly dropped the receiver, and, shame upon shame, he could feel tears pricking behind his eyes.

"What sort of mix-up?" Her voice was suspicious, almost hostile. "You weren't in a crash?"

"No...no...nothing like that."

A moment's silence, and then she said, "Your voice sounds very slurred. Don't tell me you went and got pissed."

Oh Christ...If she only knew! He was probably going to pass out any moment, but not from the whisky.

"I thought," he said slowly, "I thought I saw you, in a vaporetto, with those two sisters."

What was the point of going on? It was hopeless trying to explain.

"How could you have seen me with the sisters?" she said. "You knew I'd gone to the airport. Really, darling, you are an idiot. You seem to have got those two poor old dears on the brain. I hope you didn't say anything to Mrs. Hill just now."

"No."

"Well, what are you going to do? You'll catch the train at Milan tomorrow, won't you?"

"Yes, of course," he told her.

"I still don't understand what kept you in Venice," she said. "It all sounds a bit odd to me. However...thank God Johnnie is going to be all right and I'm here."

"Yes," he said, "yes."

He could hear the distant boom-boom sound of a gong from the headmaster's hall.

"You had better go," he said. "My regards to the Hills, and my love to Johnnie."

"Well, take care of yourself, darling, and for goodness' sake don't miss the train tomorrow, and drive carefully."

The telephone clicked and she had gone. He poured the remaining drop of whisky into his empty glass, and sousing it with ginger-ale drank it down at a gulp. He got up, and crossing the room threw open the shutters and leant out of the window. He felt light-headed. His sense of relief, enormous, overwhelming, was somehow tempered with a curious feeling of unreality, almost as though the voice speaking from England had not been Laura's after all but a fake, and she was still in Venice, hidden in some furtive pension with the two sisters.

The point was, he *had* seen all three of them on the vaporetto. It was not another woman in a red coat. The women *had* been there, with Laura. So what was the explanation? That he was going off his head? Or something more sinister? The sisters, possessing psychic powers of formidable strength, had seen him as their two ferries had passed, and in some inexplicable fashion had made him believe Laura was with them. But why, and to what end? No, it didn't make sense. The only explanation was that he had been mistaken, the whole episode an hallucination. In which case he needed psychoanalysis, just as Johnnie had needed a surgeon.

And what did he do now? Go downstairs and tell the management he had been at fault and had just spoken to his wife, who had arrived in England safe and sound from her charter flight? He put on his shoes and ran his fingers through his hair. He glanced at his watch. It was ten minutes to eight. If he nipped into the bar and had a quick drink it would be easier to face the manager and admit what had happened. Then, perhaps, they would get in touch with the police. Profuse apologies all round for putting everyone to enormous trouble.

He made his way to the ground floor and went straight to the bar, feeling self-conscious, a marked man, half-imagining everyone would look at him, thinking, "There's the fellow with the missing wife." Luckily the bar was full and there wasn't a face he knew. Even the chap behind the bar was an underling who hadn't served him before. He downed his whisky and glanced over his shoulder to the reception hall. The desk was momentarily empty. He could see the manager's back framed in the doorway of an inner room, talking to someone within.

On impulse, coward-like, he crossed the hall and passed through the swing-door to the street outside.

"I'll have some dinner," he decided, "and then go back and face them. I'll feel more like it once I've some food inside me."

He went to the restaurant nearby where he and Laura had dined once or twice. Nothing mattered any more, because she was safe. The nightmare lay behind him. He could enjoy his dinner, despite her absence, and think of her sitting down with the Hills to a dull, quiet evening, early to bed, and on the following morning going to the hospital to sit with Johnnie. Johnnie was safe, too. No more worries, only the awkward explanations and apologies to the manager at the hotel.

There was a pleasant anonymity sitting down at a corner table alone in the little restaurant, ordering vitello alla Marsala and half a bottle of Merlot. He took his time, enjoying his food but eating in a kind of haze, a sense of unreality still with him, while the conversation of his nearest neighbours had the same soothing effect as background music.

When they rose and left, he saw by the clock on the wall that it was nearly half-past nine. No use delaying matters any further. He drank his coffee, lighted a cigarette and paid his bill. After all, he thought, as he walked back to the hotel, the manager would be greatly relieved to know that all was well.

When he pushed through the swing-door, the first thing he noticed was a man in police uniform, standing talking to the manager at the desk. The reception clerk was there too. They turned as John approached, and the manager's face lighted up with relief.

"Eccolo!" he exclaimed. "I was certain the signore would not be far away. Things are moving, signore. The two ladies have been traced, and they very kindly agreed to accompany the police to the Questura. If you will go there at once, this agente di polizia will escort you."

John flushed. "I have given everyone a lot of trouble," he said. "I meant to tell you before going out to dinner, but you were not at the desk. The fact is that I have contacted my wife. She did make the flight to London after all, and I spoke to her on the telephone. It was all a great mistake."

The manager looked bewildered. "The signora is in London?" he repeated. He broke off, and exchanged a rapid conversation in Italian with the policeman. "It seems that the ladies maintain they did not go out for the day, except for a little shopping in the morning," he said, turning back to John. "Then who was it the signore saw on the vaporetto?"

John shook his head. "A very extraordinary mistake on my part which I still don't understand," he said. "Obviously, I did not see either my wife or the two ladies. I really am extremely sorry."

More rapid conversation in Italian. John noticed the clerk watching him with a curious expression in his eyes. The manager was obviously apologising on John's behalf to the policeman, who looked annoyed and gave tongue to this effect, his voice increasing in volume, to the manager's concern. The whole business had undoubtedly given enormous trouble to a great many people, not least the two unfortunate sisters.

"Look," said John, interrupting the flow, "will you tell the agente I will go with him to headquarters and apologise in person both to the police officer and to the ladies?"

The manager looked relieved. "If the signore would take the trouble," he said. "Naturally, the ladies were much distressed when a policeman interrogated them at their hotel, and they offered to accompany him to the Questura only because they were so distressed about the signora."

John felt more and more uncomfortable. Laura must never learn any of this. She would be outraged. He wondered if there were some penalty for giving the police misleading information involving a third party. His error began, in retrospect, to take on criminal proportions.

He crossed the Piazza San Marco, now thronged with after-dinner strollers and spectators at the cafés, all three orchestras going full blast in harmonious rivalry, while his companion kept a discreet two paces to his left and never uttered a word.

They arrived at the police station and mounted the stairs to the same inner room where he had been before. He saw immediately that it was not the officer he knew but another who sat behind the desk, a sallow-faced individual with a sour expression, while the two sisters, obviously upset—the active one in particular—were seated on chairs nearby, some underling in uniform standing behind them. John's escort went at once to the police officer, speaking in rapid Italian, while John himself, after a moment's hesitation, advanced towards the sisters.

"There has been a terrible mistake," he said. "I don't know how to apologise to you both. It's all my fault, mine entirely, the police are not to blame."

The active sister made as though to rise, her mouth twitching nervously, but he restrained her.

"We don't understand," she said, the Scots inflection strong. "We said goodnight to your wife last night at dinner, and we have not seen her since. The police came to our pension more than an hour ago and told us your wife was missing and you had filed a complaint against us. My sister is not very strong. She was considerably disturbed."

"A mistake. A frightful mistake," he repeated.

He turned towards the desk. The police officer was addressing him, his English very inferior to that of the previous interrogator. He had John's earlier statement on the desk in front of him, and tapped it with a pencil.

"So?" he queried. "This document all lies? You not speaka the truth?"

"I believed it to be true at the time," said John. "I could have sworn in a court of law that I saw my wife with these two ladies on a vaporetto in the Grand Canal this afternoon. Now I realise I was mistaken."

"We have not been near the Grand Canal all day," protested the sister, "not even on foot. We made a few purchases in the Merceria this morning, and remained indoors all afternoon. My sister was a little unwell. I have told the police officer this a dozen times, and the people at the pension would corroborate our story. He refused to listen."

"And the signora?" rapped the police officer angrily. "What happen to the signora?"

"The signora, my wife, is safe in England," explained John patiently. "I talked to her on the telephone just after seven. She did join the charter flight from the airport, and is now staying with friends."

"Then who you see on the vaporetto in the red coat?" asked the furious police officer. "And if not these signorine here, then what signorine?"

"My eyes deceived me," said John, aware that his English was likewise becoming strained. "I think I see my wife and these ladies but no, it was not so. My wife in aircraft, these ladies in pension all the time."

It was like talking stage Chinese. In a moment he would be bowing and putting his hands in his sleeves.

The police-officer raised his eyes to heaven and thumped the table. "So all this work for nothing," he said. "Hotels and pensiones searched for the signorine and a missing signora inglese, when here we have plenty, plenty other things to do. You make a mistake. You have perhaps too much vino at mezzo giorno and you see hundred signore in red coats in hundred vaporetti." He stood up, rumpling the papers on his desk. "And you, signorine," he said, "you wish to make complaint against this person?" He was addressing the active sister.

"Oh no," she said, "no, indeed. I quite see it was all a mistake. Our only wish is to return at once to our pension."

The police-officer grunted. Then he pointed at John. "You very lucky man," he said. "These signorine could file complaint against you—very serious matter."

"I'm sure," began John, "I'll do anything in my power..."

"Please don't think of it," exclaimed the sister, horrified. "We would not hear of such a thing." It was her turn to apologise to the police-officer. "I hope we need not take up any more of your valuable time," she said.

He waved a hand of dismissal and spoke in Italian to the underling. "This man walk with you to the pension," he said. "Buona sera, signorine," and, ignoring John, he sat down again at his desk.

"I'll come with you," said John. "I want to explain exactly what happened."

They trooped down the stairs and out of the building, the blind sister leaning on her twin's arm, and once outside she turned her sightless eyes to John.

"You saw us," she said, "and your wife too. But not today. You saw us in the future."

Her voice was softer than her sister's, slower, she seemed to have some slight impediment in her speech.

"I don't follow," replied John, bewildered.

He turned to the active sister and she shook her head at him, frowning, and put her finger on her lips.

"Come along, dear," she said to her twin. "You know you're very tired, and I want to get you home." Then, sotto voce to John, "She's psychic. Your wife told you, I believe, but I don't want her to go into trance here in the street."

God forbid, thought John, and the little procession began to move slowly along the street, away from police headquarters, a canal to the left of them. Progress was slow, because of the blind sister, and there were two bridges. John was completely lost after the first turning, but it couldn't have mattered less. Their police escort was with them, and anyway, the sisters knew where they were going.

"I must explain," said John softly. "My wife would never forgive me if I didn't," and as they walked he went over the whole inexplicable story once again, beginning with the telegram received the night before and the conversation with Mrs. Hill, the decision to return to England the following day, Laura by air, and John himself by car and train. It no longer sounded as dramatic as it had done when he had made his statement to the police officer, when, possibly because of his conviction of something uncanny, the description of the two vaporettos passing one another in the middle of the Grand Canal had held a sinister quality, suggesting abduction on the part of the sisters, the pair of them holding a bewildered Laura captive. Now that neither of the women had any further menace for him he spoke more naturally, yet with great sincerity, feeling for the first time that they were somehow both in sympathy with him and would understand.

"You see," he explained, in a final endeavour to make amends for having gone to the police in the first place, "I truly believed I had seen you with Laura, and I thought..." he hesitated, because this had been the police officer's suggestion and not his, "I thought that perhaps Laura had some sudden loss of memory, had met you at the airport, and you had brought her back to Venice to wherever you were staying."

They had crossed a large square and were approaching a house at one end of it, with a sign "Pensione" above the door. Their escort paused at the entrance.

"Is this it?" asked John.

"Yes," said the sister. "I know it is nothing much from the outside, but it is clean and comfortable, and was recommended by friends." She turned to the escort. "Grazie," she said to him, "grazie tanto."

The man nodded briefly, wished them "Buona notte," and disappeared across the campo.

"Will you come in?" asked the sister. "I am sure we can find you some coffee, or perhaps you prefer tea?"

"No, really," John thanked her, "I must get back to the hotel. I'm making an early start in the morning. I just want to make quite sure you do understand what happened, and that you forgive me."

"There is nothing to forgive," she replied. "It is one of the many examples of second sight that my sister and I have experienced time and time again, and I should very much like to record it for our files, if you will permit it."

"Well, as to that, of course," he told her, "but I myself find it hard to understand. It has never happened to me before."

"Not consciously, perhaps," she said, "but so many things happen to us of which we are not aware. My sister felt you had psychic understanding. She told your wife. She also told your wife, last night in the restaurant, that you were to experience trouble, danger, that you should leave Venice. Well, don't you believe now that the telegram was proof of this? Your son was ill, possibly dangerously ill, and so it was necessary for you to return home immediately. Heaven be praised your wife flew home to be by his side."

"Yes, indeed," said John, "but why should I see her on the vaporetto with you and your sister when she was actually on her way to England?"

"Thought transference, perhaps," she answered. "Your wife may have been thinking about us. We gave her our address, should you wish to get in touch with us. We shall be here another ten days. And she knows that we would pass on any message that my sister might have from your little one in the spirit world."

"Yes," said John awkwardly, "yes, I see. It's very good of you." He had a sudden rather unkind picture of the two sisters putting on headphones in their bedroom, listening for a coded message from poor Christine. "Look, this is our address in London," he said. "I know Laura will be pleased to hear from you."

He scribbled their address on a sheet torn from his pocket-diary, even, as a bonus thrown in, the telephone number, and handed it to her. He could imagine the outcome. Laura springing it on him one evening that the "old dears" were passing through London on their way to Scotland, and the least they could do was to offer them hospitality, even the spare-room for the night. Then a seance in the living-room, tambourines appearing out of thin air.

"Well, I must be off," he said. "Goodnight, and apologies, once again, for all that has happened this evening." He shook hands with the first sister, then turned to her blind twin. "I hope," he said, "that you are not too tired."

The sightless eyes were disconcerting. She held his hand fast and would not let it go. "The child," she said, speaking in an odd staccato voice, "the child...I can see the child..." and then, to his dismay, a bead of froth appeared at the corner of her mouth, her head jerked back, and she half-collapsed in her sister's arms.

"We must get her inside," said the sister hurriedly. "It's all right, she's not ill, it's the beginning of a trance state."

Between them they helped the twin, who had gone rigid, into the house, and sat her down on the nearest chair, the sister supporting her. A woman came running from some inner room. There was a strong smell of spaghetti from the back regions. "Don't worry," said the sister, "the signorina and I can manage. I think you had better go. Sometimes she is sick after these turns."

"I'm most frightfully sorry..." John began, but the sister had already turned her back, and with the signorina was bending over her twin, from whom peculiar choking sounds were proceeding. He was obviously in the way, and after a final gesture of courtesy, "Is there anything I can do?" which received no reply, he turned on his heel and began walking across the square. He looked back once, and saw they had closed the door.

What a finale to the evening! And all his fault. Poor old girls, first dragged to police headquarters and put through an interrogation, and then a psychic fit on top of it all. More likely epilepsy. Not much of a life for the other sister, but she seemed to take it in her stride. An additional hazard, though, if it happened in a restaurant or in the street. And not particularly welcome under his and Laura's roof should the sisters ever find themselves beneath it, which he prayed would never happen.

Meanwhile, where the devil was he? The square, with the inevitable church at one end, was quite deserted. He could not remember which way they had come from police headquarters, there had seemed to be so many turnings.

Wait a minute, the church itself had a familiar appearance. He drew nearer to it, looking for the name which was sometimes on notices at the entrance. San Giovanni in Bragora, that rang a bell. He and Laura had gone inside one morning to look at a painting by Cima da Conegliano. Surely it was only a stone's throw from the Riva degli Schiavoni and the open wide waters of the San Marco lagoon, with all the bright lights of civilisation and the strolling tourists? He remembered taking a small turning from the Schiavoni and they had arrived at the church. Wasn't that the alley-way ahead? He plunged along it, but halfway down he hesitated. It didn't seem right, although it was familiar for some unknown reason.

Then he realised that it was not the alley they had taken the morning they visited the church, but the one they had walked along the previous evening, only he was approaching it from the opposite direction. Yes, that was it, in which case it would be quicker to go on and cross the little bridge over the narrow canal, and he would find the Arsenal on his left and the street leading down to the Riva degli Schiavoni to his right. Simpler than retracing his steps and getting lost once more in the maze of back streets.

He had almost reached the end of the alley, and the bridge was in sight, when he saw the child. It was the same little girl with the pixie-hood who had leapt between the tethered boats the preceding night and vanished up the cellar steps of one of the houses. This time she was running from the direction of the church the other side, making for the bridge. She was running as if her life depended on it, and in a moment he saw why. A man was in pursuit, who, when she glanced backwards for a moment, still running, flattened himself against a wall, believing himself unobserved. The child came on, scampering across the bridge, and John, fearful of alarming her further, backed into an open doorway that led into a small court.

He remembered the drunken yell of the night before which had come from one of the houses near where the man was hiding now. This is it, he thought, the fellow's after her again, and with a flash of intuition he connected the two events, the child's terror then and now, and the murders reported in the newspapers, supposedly the work of some madman. It could be coincidence, a child running from a drunken relative, and yet, and yet... His heart began thumping in his chest, instinct warning him to run himself, now, at once, back along the alley the way he had come—but what about the child? What was going to happen to the child?

Then he heard her running steps. She hurtled through the open doorway into the court in which he stood, not seeing him, making for the rear of the house that flanked it, where steps led presumably to a back entrance. She was sobbing as she ran, not the ordinary cry of a frightened child, but the panic-stricken intake of breath of a helpless being in despair. Were there parents in the house who would protect her, whom he could warn? He hesitated a moment, then followed her down the steps and through the door at the bottom, which had burst open at the touch of her hands as she hurled herself against it.

"It's all right," he called. "I won't let him hurt you, it's all right," cursing his lack of Italian, but possibly an English voice might reassure her. But it was no use—she ran sobbing up another flight of stairs, which were spiral, twisting, leading to the floor above, and already it was too late for him to retreat. He could hear sounds of the pursuer in the courtyard behind, someone shouting in Italian, a dog barking. This is it, he thought, we're in it together, the child and I. Unless we can bolt some inner door above he'll get us both.

He ran up the stairs after the child, who had darted into a room leading off a small landing, and followed her inside and slammed the door, and, merciful heaven, there was a bolt which he rammed into its socket. The child was crouching by the open window. If he shouted for help someone would surely hear, someone would surely come before the man in pursuit threw himself against the door and it gave, because there was no one but themselves, no parents, the room was bare except for a mattress on an old bed, and a heap of rags in one corner.

"It's all right," he panted, "it's all right," and held out his hand, trying to smile.

The child struggled to her feet and stood before him, the pixie-hood falling from her head on to the floor. He stared at her, incredulity turning to horror, to fear. It was not a child at all but a little thick-set woman dwarf, about three feet high, with a great square adult head too big for her body, grey locks hanging shoulder-length, and she wasn't sobbing any more, she was grinning at him, nodding her head up and down.

Then he heard the footsteps on the landing outside and the hammering on the door, and a barking dog, and not one voice but several voices, shouting, "Open up! Police!" The creature fumbled in her sleeve, drawing a knife, and as she threw it at him with hideous strength, piercing his throat, he stumbled and fell, the sticky mess covering his protecting hands.

And he saw the vaporetto with Laura and the two sisters steaming down the Grand Canal, not today, not tomorrow, but the day after that, and he knew why they were together and for what sad purpose they had come. The creature was gibbering in its corner. The hammering and the voices and the barking dog grew fainter, and, "Oh God," he thought, "what a bloody silly way to die..."

# THE BIRDS

ON DECEMBER the third the wind changed overnight and it was winter. Until then the autumn had been mellow, soft. The leaves had lingered on the trees, golden red, and the hedgerows were still green. The earth was rich where the plough had turned it.

Nat Hocken, because of a war-time disability, had a pension and did not work full-time at the farm. He worked three days a week, and they gave him the lighter jobs: hedging, thatching, repairs to the farm buildings.

Although he was married, with children, his was a solitary disposition; he liked best to work alone. It pleased him when he was given a bank to build up, or a gate to mend at the far end of the peninsula, where the sea surrounded the farm land on either side. Then, at midday, he would pause and eat the pasty that his wife had baked for him, and sitting on the cliff's edge would watch the birds. Autumn was best for this, better than spring. In spring the birds flew inland, purposeful, intent; they knew where they were bound, the rhythm and ritual of their life brooked no delay. In autumn those that had not migrated overseas but remained to pass the winter were caught up in the same driving urge, but because migration was denied them followed a pattern of their own. Great flocks of them came to the peninsula, restless, uneasy, spending themselves in motion; now wheeling, circling in the sky, now settling to feed on the rich new-turned soil, but even when they fed it was as though they did so without hunger, without desire. Restlessness drove them to the skies again.

Black and white, jackdaw and gull, mingled in strange partnership, seeking some sort of liberation, never satisfied, never still. Flocks of starlings, rustling like silk, flew to fresh pasture, driven by the same necessity of movement, and the smaller birds, the finches and the larks, scattered from tree to hedge as if compelled.

Nat watched them, and he watched the sea-birds too. Down in the bay they waited for the tide. They had more patience. Oyster-catchers, redshank, sanderling, and curlew watched by the water's edge; as the slow sea sucked at the shore and then withdrew, leaving the strip of seaweed bare and the shingle churned, the sea-birds raced and ran upon the beaches. Then that same impulse to flight seized upon them too. Crying, whistling, calling, they skimmed the placid sea and left the shore. Make haste, make speed, hurry and begone: yet where, and to what purpose? The restless urge of autumn, unsatisfying, sad, had put a spell upon them and they must flock, and wheel, and cry; they must spill themselves of motion before winter came.

Perhaps, thought Nat, munching his pasty by the cliff's edge, a message comes to the birds in autumn, like a warning. Winter is coming. Many of them perish. And like people who, apprehensive of death before their time, drive themselves to work or folly, the birds do likewise.

The birds had been more restless than ever this fall of the year, the agitation more marked because the days were still. As the tractor traced its path up and down the western hills, the figure of the farmer silhouetted on the driving-seat, the whole machine and the man upon it would be lost momentarily in the great cloud of wheeling, crying birds. There were many more than usual, Nat was sure of this. Always, in autumn, they followed the plough, but not in great flocks like these, nor with such clamour.

Nat remarked upon it, when hedging was finished for the day. "Yes," said the farmer, "there are more birds about than usual; I've noticed it too. And daring, some of them, taking no notice of the tractor. One or two gulls came so close to my head this afternoon I thought they'd knock my cap off! As it was, I could scarcely see what I was doing, when they were overhead and I had the sun in my eyes. I have a notion the weather will change. It will be a hard winter. That's why the birds are restless."

Nat, tramping home across the fields and down the lane to his cottage, saw the birds still flocking over the western hills, in the last glow of the sun. No wind, and the grey sea calm and full. Campion in bloom yet in the hedges, and the air mild. The farmer was right, though, and it was that night the weather turned. Nat's bedroom faced east. He woke just after two and heard the wind in the chimney. Not the storm and bluster of a sou'westerly gale, bringing the rain, but east wind, cold and dry. It sounded hollow in the chimney, and a loose slate rattled on the roof. Nat listened, and he could hear the sea roaring in the bay. Even the air in the small bedroom had turned chill: a draught came under the skirting of the door, blowing upon the bed. Nat drew the blanket round him, leant closer to the back of his sleeping wife, and stayed wakeful, watchful, aware of misgiving without cause.

Then he heard the tapping on the window. There was no creeper on the cottage walls to break loose and scratch upon the pane. He listened, and the tapping continued until, irritated by the sound, Nat got out of bed and went to the window. He opened it, and as he did so something brushed his hand, jabbing at his knuckles, grazing the skin. Then he saw the flutter of the wings and it was gone, over the roof, behind the cottage.

It was a bird, what kind of bird he could not tell. The wind must have driven it to shelter on the sill.

He shut the window and went back to bed, but feeling his knuckles wet put his mouth to the scratch. The bird had drawn blood. Frightened, he supposed, and bewildered, the bird, seeking shelter, had stabbed at him in the darkness. Once more he settled himself to sleep.

Presently the tapping came again, this time more forceful, more insistent, and now his wife woke at the sound, and turning in the bed said to him, "See to the window, Nat, it's rattling."

"I've already seen to it," he told her, "there's some bird there, trying to get in. Can't you hear the wind? It's blowing from the east, driving the birds to shelter."

"Send them away," she said, "I can't sleep with that noise."

He went to the window for the second time, and now when he opened it there was not one bird upon the sill but half a dozen; they flew straight into his face, attacking him.

He shouted, striking out at them with his arms, scattering them; like the first one, they flew over the roof and disappeared. Quickly he let the window fall and latched it.

"Did you hear that?" he said. "They went for me. Tried to peck my eyes." He stood by the window, peering into the darkness, and could see nothing. His wife, heavy with sleep, murmured from the bed.

"I'm not making it up," he said, angry at her suggestion. "I tell you the birds were on the sill, trying to get into the room."

Suddenly a frightened cry came from the room across the passage where the children slept.

"It's Jill," said his wife, roused at the sound, sitting up in bed. "Go to her, see what's the matter."

Nat lit the candle, but when he opened the bedroom door to cross the passage the draught blew out the flame.

There came a second cry of terror, this time from both children, and stumbling into their room he felt the beating of wings about him in the darkness. The window was wide open. Through it came the birds, hitting first the ceiling and the walls, then swerving in mid-flight, turning to the children in their beds.

"It's all right, I'm here," shouted Nat, and the children flung themselves, screaming, upon him, while in the darkness the birds rose and dived and came for him again.

"What is it, Nat, what's happened?" his wife called from the further bedroom, and swiftly he pushed the children through the door to the passage and shut it upon them, so that he was alone now, in their bedroom, with the birds.

He seized a blanket from the nearest bed, and using it as a weapon flung it to right and left about him in the air. He felt the thud of bodies, heard the fluttering of wings, but they were not yet defeated, for again and again they returned to the assault, jabbing his hands, his head, the little stabbing beaks sharp as a pointed fork. The blanket became a weapon of defence; he wound it about his head, and then in greater darkness beat at the birds with his bare hands. He dared not stumble to the door and open it, lest in doing so the birds should follow him.

How long he fought with them in the darkness he could not tell, but at last the beating of the wings about him lessened and then withdrew, and through the density of the blanket he was aware of light. He waited, listened; there was no sound except the fretful crying of one of the children from the bedroom beyond. The fluttering, the whirring of the wings had ceased.

He took the blanket from his head and stared about him. The cold grey morning light exposed the room. Dawn, and the open window, had called the living birds; the dead lay on the floor. Nat gazed at the little corpses, shocked and horrified. They were all small birds, none of any size; there must have been fifty of them lying there upon the floor. There were robins, finches, sparrows, blue tits, larks, and bramblings, birds that by nature's law kept to their own flock and their own territory, and now, joining one with another in their urge for battle, had destroyed themselves against the bedroom walls, or in the strife had been destroyed by him. Some had lost feathers in the fight, others had blood, his blood, upon their beaks.

Sickened, Nat went to the window and stared out across his patch of garden to the fields.

It was bitter cold, and the ground had all the hard black look of frost. Not white frost, to shine in the morning sun, but the black frost that the east wind brings. The sea, fiercer now with the turning tide, white-capped and steep, broke harshly in the bay. Of the birds there was no sign. Not a sparrow chattered in the hedge beyond the garden gate, no early misselthrush or blackbird pecked on the grass for worms. There was no sound at all but the east wind and the sea.

Nat shut the window and the door of the small bedroom, and went back across the passage to his own. His wife sat up in bed, one child asleep beside her, the smaller in her arms, his face bandaged. The curtains were tightly drawn across the window, the candles lit. Her face looked garish in the yellow light. She shook her head for silence.

"He's sleeping now," she whispered, "but only just. Something must have cut him, there was blood at the corner of his eyes. Jill said it was the birds. She said she woke up, and the birds were in the room."

His wife looked up at Nat, searching his face for confirmation. She looked terrified, bewildered, and he did not want her to know that he was also shaken, dazed almost, by the events of the past few hours.

"There are birds in there," he said, "dead birds, nearly fifty of them. Robins, wrens, all the little birds from hereabouts. It's as though a madness seized them, with the east wind." He sat down on the bed beside his wife, and held her hand. "It's the weather," he said, "it must be that, it's the hard weather. They aren't the birds, maybe, from here around. They've been driven down, from up country."

"But Nat," whispered his wife, "it's only this night that the weather turned. There's been no snow to drive them. And they can't be hungry yet. There's food for them, out there, in the fields."

"It's the weather," repeated Nat. "I tell you, it's the weather."

His face too was drawn and tired, like hers. They stared at one another for a while without speaking.

"I'll go downstairs and make a cup of tea," he said.

The sight of the kitchen reassured him. The cups and saucers, neatly stacked upon the dresser, the table and chairs, his wife's roll of knitting on her basket chair, the children's toys in a corner cupboard.

He knelt down, raked out the old embers, and relit the fire. The glowing sticks brought normality, the steaming kettle and the brown teapot comfort and security. He drank his tea, carried a cup up to his wife. Then he washed in the scullery, and, putting on his boots, opened the back door.

The sky was hard and leaden, and the brown hills that had gleamed in the sun the day before looked dark and bare. The east wind, like a razor, stripped the trees, and the leaves, crackling and dry, shivered and scattered with the wind's blast. Nat stubbed the earth with his boot. It was frozen hard. He had never known a change so swift and sudden. Black winter had descended in a single night.

The children were awake now. Jill was chattering upstairs and young Johnny crying once again. Nat heard his wife's voice, soothing, comforting. Presently they came down. He had breakfast ready for them, and the routine of the day began.

"Did you drive away the birds?" asked Jill, restored to calm because of the kitchen fire, because of day, because of breakfast.

"Yes, they've all gone now," said Nat. "It was the east wind brought them in. They were frightened and lost, they wanted shelter."

"They tried to peck us," said Jill. "They went for Johnny's eyes."

"Fright made them do that," said Nat. "They didn't know where they were, in the dark bedroom."

"I hope they won't come again," said Jill. "Perhaps if we put bread for them outside the window they will eat that and fly away."

She finished her breakfast and then went for her coat and hood, her school books and her satchel. Nat said nothing, but his wife looked at him across the table. A silent message passed between them.

"I'll walk with her to the bus," he said, "I don't go to the farm today."

And while the child was washing in the scullery he said to his wife, "Keep all the windows closed, and the doors too. Just to be on the safe side. I'll go to the farm. Find out if they heard anything in the night." Then he walked with his small daughter up the lane. She seemed to have forgotten her experience of the night before. She danced ahead of him, chasing the leaves, her face whipped with the cold and rosy under the pixie hood.

"Is it going to snow, Dad?" she said. "It's cold enough."

He glanced up at the bleak sky, felt the wind tear at his shoulders.

"No," he said, "it's not going to snow. This is a black winter, not a white one."

All the while he searched the hedgerows for the birds, glanced over the top of them to the fields beyond, looked to the small wood above the farm where the rooks and jackdaws gathered. He saw none.

The other children waited by the bus-stop, muffled, hooded like Jill, the faces white and pinched with cold.

Jill ran to them, waving. "My Dad says it won't snow," she called, "it's going to be a black winter."

She said nothing of the birds. She began to push and struggle with another little girl. The bus came ambling up the hill. Nat saw her on to it, then turned and walked back towards the farm. It was not his day for work, but he wanted to satisfy himself that all was well. Jim, the cowman, was clattering in the yard.

"Boss around?" asked Nat.

"Gone to market," said Jim. "It's Tuesday, isn't it?"

He clumped off round the corner of a shed. He had no time for Nat. Nat was said to be superior. Read books, and the like. Nat had forgotten it was Tuesday. This showed how the events of the preceding night had shaken him. He went to the back door of the farm-house and heard Mrs. Trigg singing in the kitchen, the wireless making a background to her song.

"Are you there, missus?" called out Nat.

She came to the door, beaming, broad, a good-tempered woman.

"Hullo, Mr. Hocken," she said. "Can you tell me where this cold is coming from? Is it Russia? I've never seen such a change. And it's going on, the wireless says. Something to do with the Arctic circle."

"We didn't turn on the wireless this morning," said Nat. "Fact is, we had trouble in the night."

"Kiddies poorly?"

"No..." He hardly knew how to explain it. Now, in daylight, the battle of the birds would sound absurd.

He tried to tell Mrs. Trigg what had happened, but he could see from her eyes that she thought his story was the result of a nightmare.

"Sure they were real birds," she said, smiling, "with proper feathers and all? Not the funny-shaped kind, that the men see after closing hours on a Saturday night?"

"Mrs. Trigg," he said, "there are fifty dead birds, robins, wrens, and such, lying low on the floor of the children's bedroom. They went for me; they tried to go for young Johnny's eyes."

Mrs. Trigg stared at him doubtfully.

"Well there, now," she answered, "I suppose the weather brought them. Once in the bedroom, they wouldn't know where they were to. Foreign birds maybe, from that Arctic circle."

"No," said Nat, "they were the birds you see about here every day."

"Funny thing," said Mrs. Trigg, "no explaining it, really. You ought to write up and ask the *Guardian*. They'd have some answer for it. Well, I must be getting on."

She nodded, smiled, and went back into the kitchen.

Nat, dissatisfied, turned to the farm-gate. Had it not been for those corpses on the bedroom floor, which he must now collect and bury somewhere, he would have considered the tale exaggeration too.

Jim was standing by the gate.

"Had any trouble with the birds?" asked Nat.

"Birds? What birds?"

"We got them up our place last night. Scores of them, came in the children's bedroom. Quite savage they were."

"Oh?" It took time for anything to penetrate Jim's head. "Never heard of birds acting savage," he said at length. "They get tame, like, sometimes. I've seen them come to the windows for crumbs."

"These birds last night weren't tame."

"No? Cold maybe. Hungry. You put out some crumbs."

Jim was no more interested than Mrs. Trigg had been. It was, Nat thought, like air-raids in the war. No one down this end of the country knew what the Plymouth folk had seen and suffered. You had to endure something yourself before it touched you. He walked back along the lane and crossed the stile to his cottage. He found his wife in the kitchen with young Johnny.

"See anyone?" she asked.

"Mrs. Trigg and Jim," he answered. "I don't think they believed me. Anyway, nothing wrong up there."

"You might take the birds away," she said. "I daren't go into the room to make the beds until you do. I'm scared."

"Nothing to scare you now," said Nat. "They're dead, aren't they?"

He went up with a sack and dropped the stiff bodies into it, one by one. Yes, there were fifty of them, all told. Just the ordinary common birds of the hedgerow, nothing as large even as a thrush. It must have been fright that made them act the way they did. Blue tits, wrens, it was incredible to think of the power of their small beaks, jabbing at his face and hands the night before. He took the sack out into the garden and was faced now with a fresh problem. The ground was too hard to dig. It was frozen solid, yet no snow had fallen, nothing had happened in the past hours but the coming of the east wind. It was unnatural, queer. The weather prophets must be right. The change was something connected with the Arctic circle.

The wind seemed to cut him to the bone as he stood there, uncertainly, holding the sack. He could see the white-capped seas breaking down under in the bay. He decided to take the birds to the shore and bury them.

When he reached the beach below the headland he could scarcely stand, the force of the east wind was so strong. It hurt to draw breath, and his bare hands were blue. Never had he known such cold, not in all the bad winters he could remember. It was low tide. He crunched his way over the shingle to the softer sand and then, his back to the wind, ground a pit in the sand with his heel. He meant to drop the birds into it, but as he opened up the sack the force of the wind carried them, lifted them, as though in flight again, and they were blown away from him along the beach, tossed like feathers, spread and scattered, the bodies of the fifty frozen birds. There was something ugly in the sight. He did not like it. The dead birds were swept away from him by the wind.

"The tide will take them when it turns," he said to himself.

He looked out to sea and watched the crested breakers, combing green. They rose stiffly, curled, and broke again, and because it was ebb tide the roar was distant, more remote, lacking the sound and thunder of the flood.

Then he saw them. The gulls. Out there, riding the seas.

What he had thought at first to be the white caps of the waves were gulls. Hundreds, thousands, tens of thousands... They rose and fell in the trough of the seas, heads to the wind, like a mighty fleet at anchor, waiting on the tide. To eastward, and to the west, the gulls were there. They stretched as far as his eye could reach, in close formation, line upon line. Had the sea been still they would have covered the bay like a white cloud, head to head, body packed to body. Only the east wind, whipping the sea to breakers, hid them from the shore.

Nat turned, and leaving the beach climbed the steep path home. Someone should know of this. Someone should be told. Something was happening, because of the east wind and the weather, that he did not understand. He wondered if he should go to the call-box by the bus-stop and ring up the police. Yet what could they do? What could anyone do? Tens and thousands of gulls riding the sea there, in the bay, because of storm, because of hunger. The police would think him mad, or drunk, or take the statement from him with great calm. "Thank you. Yes, the matter has already been reported. The hard weather is driving the birds inland in great numbers." Nat looked about him. Still no sign of any other bird. Perhaps the cold had sent them all from up country? As he drew near to the cottage his wife came to meet him, at the door. She called to him, excited. "Nat," she said, "it's on the wireless. They've just read out a special news bulletin. I've written it down."

"What's on the wireless?" he said.

"About the birds," she said. "It's not only here, it's everywhere. In London, all over the country. Something has happened to the birds."

Together they went into the kitchen. He read the piece of paper lying on the table.

"Statement from the Home Office at eleven a.m. today. Reports from all over the country are coming in hourly about the vast quantity of birds flocking above towns, villages, and outlying districts, causing obstruction and damage and even attacking individuals. It is thought that the Arctic air stream, at present covering the British Isles, is causing birds to migrate south in immense numbers, and that intense hunger may drive these birds to attack human beings. Householders are warned to see to their windows, doors, and chimneys, and to take reasonable precautions for the safety of their children. A further statement will be issued later."

A kind of excitement seized Nat; he looked at his wife in triumph.

"There you are," he said, "let's hope they'll hear that at the farm. Mrs. Trigg will know it wasn't any story. It's true. All over the country. I've been telling myself all morning there's something wrong. And just now, down on the beach, I looked out to sea and there are gulls, thousands of them, tens of thousands, you couldn't put a pin between their heads, and they're all out there, riding on the sea, waiting."

"What are they waiting for, Nat?" she asked.

He stared at her, then looked down again at the piece of paper.

"I don't know," he said slowly. "It says here the birds are hungry."

He went over to the drawer where he kept his hammer and tools.

"What are you going to do, Nat?"

"See to the windows and the chimneys too, like they tell you."

"You think they would break in, with the windows shut? Those sparrows and robins and such? Why, how could they?"

He did not answer. He was not thinking of the robins and the sparrows. He was thinking of the gulls . . .

He went upstairs and worked there the rest of the morning, boarding the windows of the bedrooms, filling up the chimney bases. Good job it was his free day and he was not working at the farm. It reminded him of the old days, at the beginning of the war. He was not married then, and he had made all the blackout boards for his mother's house in Plymouth. Made the shelter too. Not that it had been of any use, when the moment came. He wondered if they would take these precautions up at the farm. He doubted it. Too easy-going, Harry Trigg and his missus. Maybe they'd laugh at the whole thing. Go off to a dance or a whist drive.

"Dinner's ready." She called him, from the kitchen.

"All right. Coming down."

He was pleased with his handiwork. The frames fitted nicely over the little panes and at the base of the chimneys.

When dinner was over and his wife was washing up, Nat switched on the one o'clock news. The same announcement was repeated, the one which she had taken down during the morning, but the news bulletin enlarged upon it. "The flocks of birds have caused dislocation in all areas," read the announcer, "and in London the sky was so dense at ten o'clock this morning that it seemed as if the city was covered by a vast black cloud.

"The birds settled on roof-tops, on window ledges, and on chimneys. The species included blackbird, thrush, the common house-sparrow, and, as might be expected in the metropolis, a vast quantity of pigeons and starlings, and that frequenter of the London river, the black-headed gull. The sight has been so unusual that traffic came to a standstill in many thoroughfares, work was abandoned in shops and offices, and the streets and pavements were crowded with people standing about to watch the birds."

Various incidents were recounted, the suspected reason of cold and hunger stated again, and warnings to householders repeated. The announcer's voice was smooth and suave. Nat had the impression that this man, in particular, treated the whole business as he would an elaborate joke. There would be others like him, hundreds of them, who did not know what it was to struggle in darkness with a flock of birds. There would be parties tonight in London, like the ones they gave on election nights. People standing about, shouting and laughing, getting drunk. "Come and watch the birds!"

Nat switched off the wireless. He got up and started work on the kitchen windows. His wife watched him, young Johnny at her heels.

"What, boards for down here too?" she said. "Why, I'll have to light up before three o'clock. I see no call for boards down here."

"Better be sure than sorry," answered Nat. "I'm not going to take any chances."

"What they ought to do," she said, "is to call the army out and shoot the birds. That would soon scare them off."

"Let them try," said Nat. "How'd they set about it?"

"They have the army to the docks," she answered, "when the dockers strike. The soldiers go down and unload the ships."

"Yes," said Nat, "and the population of London is eight million or more. Think of all the buildings, all the flats, and houses. Do you think they've enough soldiers to go round shooting birds from every roof?"

"I don't know. But something should be done. They ought to do something."

Nat thought to himself that "they" were no doubt considering the problem at that very moment, but whatever "they" decided to do in London and the big cities would not help the people here, three hundred miles away. Each householder must look after his own.

"How are we off for food?" he said.

"Now, Nat, whatever next?"

"Never mind. What have you got in the larder?"

"It's shopping day tomorrow, you know that. I don't keep uncooked food hanging about, it goes off. Butcher doesn't call till the day after. But I can bring back something when I go in tomorrow."

Nat did not want to scare her. He thought it possible that she might not go to town tomorrow. He looked in the larder for himself, and in the cupboard where she kept her tins. They would do, for a couple of days. Bread was low.

"What about the baker?"

"He comes tomorrow too."

He saw she had flour. If the baker did not call she had enough to bake one loaf.

"We'd be better off in the old days," he said, "when the women baked twice a week, and had pilchards salted, and there was food for a family to last a siege, if need be."

"I've tried the children with tinned fish, they don't like it," she said.

Nat went on hammering the boards across the kitchen windows. Candles. They were low in candles too. That must be another thing she meant to buy tomorrow. Well, it could not be helped. They must go early to bed tonight. That was, if...

He got up and went out of the back door and stood in the garden, looking down towards the sea. There had been no sun all day, and now, at barely three o'clock, a kind of darkness had already come, the sky sullen, heavy, colourless like salt. He could hear the vicious sea drumming on the rocks. He walked down the path, half-way to the beach. And then he stopped. He could see the tide had turned. The rock that had shown in mid-morning was now covered, but it was not the sea that held his eyes. The gulls had risen. They were circling, hundreds of them, thousands of them, lifting their wings against the wind. It was the gulls that made the darkening of the sky. And they were silent. They made not a sound. They just went on soaring and circling, rising, falling, trying their strength against the wind.

Nat turned. He ran up the path, back to the cottage.

"I'm going for Jill," he said. "I'll wait for her, at the bus-stop."

"What's the matter?" asked his wife. "You've gone quite white."

"Keep Johnny inside," he said. "Keep the door shut. Light up now, and draw the curtains."

"It's only just gone three," she said.

"Never mind. Do what I tell you."

He looked inside the toolshed, outside the back door. Nothing there of much use. A spade was too heavy, and a fork no good. He took the hoe. It was the only possible tool, and light enough to carry.

He started walking up the lane to the bus-stop, and now and again glanced back over his shoulder.

The gulls had risen higher now, their circles were broader, wider, they were spreading out in huge formation across the sky.

He hurried on; although he knew the bus would not come to the top of the hill before four o'clock he had to hurry. He passed no one on the way. He was glad of this. No time to stop and chatter.

At the top of the hill he waited. He was much too soon. There was half an hour still to go. The east wind came whipping across the fields from the higher ground. He stamped his feet and blew upon his hands. In the distance he could see the clay hills, white and clean, against the heavy pallor of the sky. Something black rose from behind them, like a smudge at first, then widening, becoming deeper, and the smudge became a cloud, and the cloud divided again into five other clouds, spreading north, east, south and west, and they were not clouds at all; they were birds. He watched them travel across the sky, and as one section passed overhead, within two or three hundred feet of him, he knew from their speed, they were bound inland, up country, they had no business with the people here on the peninsula. They were rooks, crows, jackdaws, magpies, jays, all birds that usually preyed upon the smaller species; but this afternoon they were bound on some other mission.

"They've been given the towns," thought Nat, "they know what they have to do. We don't matter so much here. The gulls will serve for us. The others go to the towns."

He went to the call-box, stepped inside and lifted the receiver. The exchange would do. They would pass the message on.

"I'm speaking from Highway," he said, "by the bus-stop. I want to report large formations of birds travelling up country. The gulls are also forming in the bay."

"All right," answered the voice, laconic, weary.

"You'll be sure and pass this message on to the proper quarter?"

"Yes... yes..." Impatient now, fed-up. The buzzing note resumed.

"She's another," thought Nat, "she doesn't care. Maybe she's had to answer calls all day. She hopes to go to the pictures tonight. She'll squeeze some fellow's hand, and point up at the sky, and say 'Look at all them birds!' She doesn't care."

The bus came lumbering up the hill. Jill climbed out and three or four other children. The bus went on towards the town.

"What's the hoe for, Dad?"

They crowded around him, laughing, pointing.

"I just brought it along," he said. "Come on now, let's get home. It's cold, no hanging about. Here, you. I'll watch you across the fields, see how fast you can run."

He was speaking to Jill's companions who came from different families, living in the council houses. A short cut would take them to the cottages.

"We want to play a bit in the lane," said one of them.

"No, you don't. You go off home, or I'll tell your mammy."

They whispered to one another, round-eyed, then scuttled off across the fields. Jill stared at her father, her mouth sullen.

"We always play in the lane," she said.

"Not tonight, you don't," he said. "Come on now, no dawdling."

He could see the gulls now, circling the fields, coming in towards the land. Still silent. Still no sound.

"Look, Dad, look over there, look at all the gulls."

"Yes. Hurry, now."

"Where are they flying to? Where are they going?"

"Up country, I dare say. Where it's warmer."

He seized her hand and dragged her after him along the lane.

"Don't go so fast. I can't keep up."

The gulls were copying the rooks and crows. They were spreading out in formation across the sky. They headed, in bands of thousands, to the four compass points.

"Dad, what is it? What are the gulls doing?"

They were not intent upon their flight, as the crows, as the jackdaws had been. They still circled overhead. Nor did they fly so high. It was as though they waited upon some signal. As though some decision had yet to be given. The order was not clear.

"Do you want me to carry you, Jill? Here, come pick-a-back."

This way he might put on speed; but he was wrong. Jill was heavy. She kept slipping. And she was crying too. His sense of urgency, of fear, had communicated itself to the child.

"I wish the gulls would go away. I don't like them. They're coming closer to the lane."

He put her down again. He started running, swinging Jill after him. As they went past the farm turning he saw the farmer backing his car out of the garage. Nat called to him.

"Can you give us a lift?" he said.

"What's that?"

Mr. Trigg turned in the driving seat and stared at them. Then a smile came to his cheerful, rubicund face.

"It looks as though we're in for some fun," he said. "Have you seen the gulls? Jim and I are going to take a crack at them. Everyone's gone bird crazy, talking of nothing else. I hear you were troubled in the night. Want a gun?"

Nat shook his head.

The small car was packed. There was just room for Jill, if she crouched on top of petrol tins on the back seat.

"I don't want a gun," said Nat, "but I'd be obliged if you'd run Jill home. She's scared of the birds."

He spoke briefly. He did not want to talk in front of Jill.

"OK," said the farmer, "I'll take her home. Why don't you stop behind and join the shooting match? We'll make the feathers fly."

Jill climbed in, and turning the car the driver sped up the lane. Nat followed after. Trigg must be crazy. What use was a gun against a sky of birds?

Now Nat was not responsible for Jill he had time to look about him. The birds were circling still, above the fields. Mostly herring gull, but the black-headed gull amongst them. Usually they kept apart. Now they were united. Some bond had brought them together. It was the black-backed gull that attacked the smaller birds, and even new-born lambs, so he'd heard. He'd never seen it done. He remembered this now, though, looking above him in the sky. They were coming in towards the farm. They were circling lower in the sky, and the black-backed gulls were to the front, the black-backed gulls were leading. The farm, then, was their target. They were making for the farm.

Nat increased his pace towards his own cottage. He saw the farmer's car turn and come back along the lane. It drew up beside him with a jerk.

"The kid has run inside," said the farmer. "Your wife was watching for her. Well, what do you make of it? They're saying in town the Russians have done it. The Russians have poisoned the birds."

"How could they do that?" asked Nat.

"Don't ask me. You know how stories get around. Will you join my shooting match?"

"No, I'll get along home. The wife will be worried else."

"My missus says if you could eat gull, there'd be some sense in it," said Trigg, "we'd have roast gull, baked gull, and pickle 'em into the bargain. You wait until I let off a few barrels into the brutes. That'll scare 'em."

"Have you boarded your windows?" asked Nat.

"No. Lot of nonsense. They like to scare you on the wireless. I've had more to do today than to go round boarding up my windows."

"I'd board them now, if I were you."

"Garn. You're windy. Like to come to our place to sleep?"

"No, thanks all the same."

"All right. See you in the morning. Give you a gull breakfast."

The farmer grinned and turned his car to the farm entrance.

Nat hurried on. Past the little wood, past the old barn, and then across the stile to the remaining field.

As he jumped the stile he heard the whirr of wings. A black-backed gull dived down at him from the sky, missed, swerved in flight, and rose to dive again. In a moment it was joined by others, six, seven, a dozen, black-backed and herring mixed. Nat dropped his hoe. The hoe was useless. Covering his head with his arms he ran towards the cottage. They kept coming at him from the air, silent save for the beating wings. The terrible, fluttering wings. He could feel the blood on his hands, his wrists, his neck. Each stab of a swooping beak tore his flesh. If only he could keep them from his eyes. Nothing else mattered. He must keep them from his eyes. They had not learnt yet how to cling to a shoulder, how to rip clothing, how to dive in mass upon the head, upon the body. But with each dive, with each attack, they became bolder. And they had no thought for themselves. When they dived low and missed, they crashed, bruised and broken, on the ground. As Nat ran he stumbled, kicking their spent bodies in front of him.

He found the door, he hammered upon it with his bleeding hands. Because of the boarded windows no light shone. Everything was dark.

"Let me in," he shouted, "it's Nat. Let me in."

He shouted loud to make himself heard above the whirr of the gulls' wings.

Then he saw the gannet, poised for the dive, above him in the sky. The gulls circled, retired, soared, one with another, against the wind. Only the gannet remained. One single gannet, above him in the sky. The wings folded suddenly to its body. It dropped like a stone. Nat screamed, and the door opened. He stumbled across the threshold, and his wife threw her weight against the door.

They heard the thud of the gannet as it fell.

His wife dressed his wounds. They were not deep. The backs of his hands had suffered most, and his wrists. Had he not worn a cap they would have reached his head. As to the gannet . . . the gannet could have split his skull.

The children were crying, of course. They had seen the blood on their father's hands.

"It's all right now," he told them. "I'm not hurt. Just a few scratches. You play with Johnny, Jill. Mammy will wash these cuts."

He half shut the door to the scullery, so that they could not see. His wife was ashen. She began running water from the sink.

"I saw them overhead," she whispered. "They began collecting just as Jill ran in with Mr. Trigg. I shut the door fast, and it jammed. That's why I couldn't open it at once, when you came."

"Thank God they waited for me," he said. "Jill would have fallen at once. One bird alone would have done it."

Furtively, so as not to alarm the children, they whispered together, as she bandaged his hands and the back of his neck.

"They're flying inland," he said, "thousands of them. Rooks, crows, all the bigger birds. I saw them from the bus-stop. They're making for the towns."

"But what can they do, Nat?"

"They'll attack. Go for everyone out in the streets. Then they'll try the windows, the chimneys."

"Why don't the authorities do something? Why don't they get the army, get machine-guns, anything?"

"There's been no time. Nobody's prepared. We'll hear what they have to say on the six o'clock news."

Nat went back into the kitchen, followed by his wife. Johnny was playing quietly on the floor. Only Jill looked anxious.

"I can hear the birds," she said. "Listen, Dad."

Nat listened. Muffled sounds came from the windows, from the door. Wings brushing the surface, sliding, scraping, seeking a way of entry. The sound of many bodies, pressed together, shuffling on the sills. Now and again came a thud, a crash, as some bird dived and fell. "Some of them will kill themselves that way," he thought, "but not enough. Never enough."

"All right," he said aloud, "I've got boards over the windows, Jill. The birds can't get in."

He went and examined all the windows. His work had been thorough. Every gap was closed. He would make extra certain, however. He found wedges, pieces of old tin, strips of wood and metal, and fastened them at the sides to reinforce the boards. His hammering helped to deafen the sound of the birds, the shuffling, the tapping, and more ominous—he did not want his wife or the children to hear it—the splinter of cracked glass.

"Turn on the wireless," he said, "let's have the wireless."

This would drown the sound also. He went upstairs to the bedrooms and reinforced the windows there. Now he could hear the birds on the roof, the scraping of claws, a sliding, jostling sound.

He decided they must sleep in the kitchen, keep up the fire, bring down the mattresses and lay them out on the floor. He was afraid of the bedroom chimneys. The boards he had placed at the chimney bases might give way. In the kitchen they would be safe, because of the fire. He would have to make a joke of it. Pretend to the children they were playing at camp. If the worst happened, and the birds forced an entry down the bedroom chimneys, it would be hours, days perhaps, before they could break down the doors. The birds would be imprisoned in the bedrooms. They could do no harm there. Crowded together, they would stifle and die.

He began to bring the mattresses downstairs. At sight of them his wife's eyes widened in apprehension. She thought the birds had already broken in upstairs.

"All right," he said cheerfully, "we'll all sleep together in the kitchen tonight. More cosy here by the fire. Then we shan't be worried by those silly old birds tapping at the windows."

He made the children help him rearrange the furniture, and he took the precaution of moving the dresser, with his wife's

help, across the window. It fitted well. It was an added safeguard. The mattresses could now be lain, one beside the other,
against the wall where the dresser had stood.

"We're safe enough now," he thought, "we're snug and tight,
like an air-raid shelter. We can hold out. It's just the food that
worries me. Food, and coal for the fire. We've enough for two
or three days, not more. By that time..."

No use thinking ahead as far as that. And they'd be giving
directions on the wireless. People would be told what to do.
And now, in the midst of many problems, he realized that it was
dance music only coming over the air. Not Children's Hour, as
it should have been. He glanced at the dial. Yes, they were on
the Home Service all right. Dance records. He switched to the
Light programme. He knew the reason. The usual programmes
had been abandoned. This only happened at exceptional times.
Elections, and such. He tried to remember if it had happened
in the war, during the heavy raids on London. But of course.
The BBC was not stationed in London during the war. The
programmes were broadcast from other, temporary quarters.
"We're better off here," he thought, "we're better off here in the
kitchen, with the windows and the doors boarded, than they
are up in the towns. Thank God we're not in the towns."

At six o'clock the records ceased. The time signal was given.
No matter if it scared the children, he must hear the news.
There was a pause after the pips. Then the announcer spoke.
His voice was solemn, grave. Quite different from midday.

"This is London," he said. "A National Emergency was pro-
claimed at four o'clock this afternoon. Measures are being
taken to safeguard the lives and property of the population, but
it must be understood that these are not easy to effect immediately, owing to the unforeseen and unparalleled nature of the
present crisis. Every householder must take precautions to his
own building, and where several people live together, as in flats
and apartments, they must unite to do the utmost they can to

prevent entry. It is absolutely imperative that every individual stays indoors tonight, and that no one at all remains on the streets, or roads, or anywhere without doors. The birds, in vast numbers, are attacking anyone on sight, and have already begun an assault upon buildings; but these, with due care, should be impenetrable. The population is asked to remain calm, and not to panic. Owing to the exceptional nature of the emergency, there will be no further transmission from any broadcasting station until seven a.m. tomorrow."

They played the National Anthem. Nothing more happened. Nat switched off the set. He looked at his wife. She stared back at him.

"What's it mean?" said Jill. "What did the news say?"

"There won't be any more programmes tonight," said Nat. "There's been a breakdown at the BBC."

"Is it the birds?" asked Jill. "Have the birds done it?"

"No," said Nat, "it's just that everyone's very busy, and then of course they have to get rid of the birds, messing everything up, in the towns. Well, we can manage without the wireless for one evening."

"I wish we had a gramophone," said Jill, "that would be better than nothing."

She had her face turned to the dresser, backed against the windows. Try as they did to ignore it, they were all aware of the shuffling, the stabbing, the persistent beating and sweeping of wings.

"We'll have supper early," suggested Nat, "something for a treat. Ask Mammy. Toasted cheese, eh? Something we all like?"

He winked and nodded at his wife. He wanted the look of dread, of apprehension, to go from Jill's face.

He helped with the supper, whistling, singing, making as much clatter as he could, and it seemed to him that the shuffling and the tapping were not so intense as they had been at first. Presently he went up to the bedrooms and listened, and he no longer heard the jostling for place upon the roof.

"They've got reasoning powers," he thought, "they know it's hard to break in here. They'll try elsewhere. They won't waste their time with us."

Supper passed without incident, and then, when they were clearing away, they heard a new sound, droning, familiar, a sound they all knew and understood.

His wife looked up at him, her face alight. "It's planes," she said, "they're sending out planes after the birds. That's what I said they ought to do, all along. That will get them. Isn't that gun-fire? Can't you hear guns?"

It might be gun-fire, out at sea. Nat could not tell. Big naval guns might have an effect upon the gulls out at sea, but the gulls were inland now. The guns couldn't shell the shore, because of the population.

"It's good, isn't it," said his wife, "to hear the planes?"

And Jill, catching her enthusiasm, jumped up and down with Johnny. "The planes will get the birds. The planes will shoot them."

Just then they heard a crash about two miles distant, followed by a second, then a third. The droning became more distant, passed away out to sea.

"What was that?" asked his wife. "Were they dropping bombs on the birds?"

"I don't know," answered Nat, "I don't think so."

He did not want to tell her that the sound they had heard was the crashing of aircraft. It was, he had no doubt, a venture on the part of the authorities to send out reconnaissance forces, but they might have known the venture was suicidal. What could aircraft do against birds that flung themselves to death against propeller and fuselage, but hurtle to the ground themselves? This was being tried now, he supposed, over the whole country. And at a cost. Someone high up had lost his head.

"Where have the planes gone, Dad?" asked Jill.

"Back to base," he said. "Come on, now, time to tuck down for bed."

It kept his wife occupied, undressing the children before the fire, seeing to the bedding, one thing and another, while he went round the cottage again, making sure that nothing had worked loose. There was no further drone of aircraft, and the naval guns had ceased. "Waste of life and effort," Nat said to himself. "We can't destroy enough of them that way. Cost too heavy. There's always gas. Maybe they'll try spraying with gas, mustard gas. We'll be warned first, of course, if they do. There's one thing, the best brains of the country will be on to it tonight."

Somehow the thought reassured him. He had a picture of scientists, naturalists, technicians, and all those chaps they called the back-room boys, summoned to a council; they'd be working on the problem now. This was not a job for the government, for the chiefs-of-staff—they would merely carry out the orders of the scientists.

"They'll have to be ruthless," he thought. "Where the trouble's worst they'll have to risk more lives, if they use gas. All the livestock, too, and the soil—all contaminated. As long as everyone doesn't panic. That's the trouble. People panicking, losing their heads. The BBC was right to warn us of that."

Upstairs in the bedrooms all was quiet. No further scraping and stabbing at the windows. A lull in battle. Forces regrouping. Wasn't that what they called it, in the old war-time bulletins? The wind hadn't dropped, though. He could still hear it, roaring in the chimneys. And the sea breaking down on the shore. Then he remembered the tide. The tide would be on the turn. Maybe the lull in battle was because of the tide. There was some law the birds obeyed, and it was all to do with the east wind and the tide.

He glanced at his watch. Nearly eight o'clock. It must have

gone high water an hour ago. That explained the lull: the birds attacked with the flood tide. It might not work that way inland, up country, but it seemed as if it was so this way on the coast. He reckoned the time limit in his head. They had six hours to go, without attack. When the tide turned again, around one-twenty in the morning, the birds would come back...

There were two things he could do. The first to rest, with his wife and the children, and all of them snatch what sleep they could, until the small hours. The second to go out, see how they were faring at the farm, see if the telephone was still working there, so that they might get news from the exchange.

He called softly to his wife, who had just settled the children. She came half-way up the stairs and he whispered to her.

"You're not to go," she said at once, "you're not to go and leave me alone with the children. I can't stand it."

Her voice rose hysterically. He hushed her, calmed her.

"All right," he said, "all right. I'll wait till morning. And we'll get the wireless bulletin then too, at seven. But in the morning, when the tide ebbs again, I'll try for the farm, and they may let us have bread and potatoes, and milk too."

His mind was busy again, planning against emergency. They would not have milked, of course, this evening. The cows would be standing by the gate, waiting in the yard, with the household inside, battened behind boards, as they were here at the cottage. That is, if they had time to take precautions. He thought of the farmer, Trigg, smiling at him from the car. There would have been no shooting party, not tonight.

The children were asleep. His wife, still clothed, was sitting on her mattress. She watched him, her eyes nervous.

"What are you going to do?" she whispered.

He shook his head for silence. Softly, stealthily, he opened the back door and looked outside.

It was pitch dark. The wind was blowing harder than ever,

coming in steady gusts, icy, from the sea. He kicked at the step outside the door. It was heaped with birds. There were dead birds everywhere. Under the windows, against the walls. These were the suicides, the divers, the ones with broken necks. Wherever he looked he saw dead birds. No trace of the living. The living had flown seaward with the turn of the tide. The gulls would be riding the seas now, as they had done in the forenoon.

In the far distance, on the hill where the tractor had been two days before, something was burning. One of the aircraft that had crashed; the fire, fanned by the wind, had set light to a stack.

He looked at the bodies of the birds, and he had a notion that if he heaped them, one upon the other, on the window sills they would make added protection for the next attack. Not much, perhaps, but something. The bodies would have to be clawed at, pecked, and dragged aside, before the living birds gained purchase on the sills and attacked the panes. He set to work in the darkness. It was queer; he hated touching them. The bodies were still warm and bloody. The blood matted their feathers. He felt his stomach turn, but he went on with his work. He noticed, grimly, that every window-pane was shattered. Only the boards had kept the birds from breaking in. He stuffed the cracked panes with the bleeding bodies of the birds.

When he had finished he went back into the cottage. He barricaded the kitchen door, made it doubly secure. He took off his bandages, sticky with the birds' blood, not with his own cuts, and put on fresh plaster.

His wife had made him cocoa and he drank it thirstily. He was very tired.

"All right," he said, smiling, "don't worry. We'll get through."

He lay down on his mattress and closed his eyes. He slept at once. He dreamt uneasily, because through his dreams there ran a thread of something forgotten. Some piece of work, neglected, that he should have done. Some precaution that he had known well but had not taken, and he could not put a name to it in his dreams. It was connected in some way with the burning aircraft and the stack upon the hill. He went on sleeping, though; he did not awake. It was his wife shaking his shoulder that awoke him finally.

"They've begun," she sobbed, "they've started this last hour, I can't listen to it any longer, alone. There's something smelling bad too, something burning."

Then he remembered. He had forgotten to make up the fire. It was smouldering, nearly out. He got up swiftly and lit the lamp. The hammering had started at the windows and the doors, but it was not that he minded now. It was the smell of singed feathers. The smell filled the kitchen. He knew at once what it was. The birds were coming down the chimney, squeezing their way down to the kitchen range.

He got sticks and paper and put them on the embers, then reached for the can of paraffin.

"Stand back," he shouted to his wife, "we've got to risk this."

He threw the paraffin on to the fire. The flame roared up the pipe, and down upon the fire fell the scorched, blackened bodies of the birds.

The children woke, crying, "What is it?" said Jill. "What's happened?"

Nat had no time to answer. He was raking the bodies from the chimney, clawing them out on to the floor. The flames still roared, and the danger of the chimney catching fire was one he had to take. The flames would send away the living birds from the chimney top. The lower joint was the difficulty, though. This was choked with the smouldering helpless bodies of the birds caught by fire. He scarcely heeded the attack on the windows and the door: let them beat their wings, break their beaks, lose their lives, in the attempt to force an entry into his home. They would not break in. He thanked God he had one of the old cottages, with small windows, stout walls. Not like the new council houses. Heaven help them up the lane, in the new council houses.

"Stop crying," he called to the children. "There's nothing to be afraid of, stop crying."

He went on raking at the burning, smouldering bodies as they fell into the fire.

"This'll fetch them," he said to himself, "the draught and the flames together. We're all right, as long as the chimney doesn't catch. I ought to be shot for this. It's all my fault. Last thing I should have made up the fire. I knew there was something."

Amid the scratching and tearing at the window boards came the sudden homely striking of the kitchen clock Three a.m. A little more than four hours yet to go. He could not be sure of the exact time of high water. He reckoned it would not turn much before half past seven, twenty to eight.

"Light up the primus," he said to his wife. "Make us some tea, and the kids some cocoa. No use sitting around doing nothing."

That was the line. Keep her busy, and the children too. Move about, eat, drink; always best to be on the go.

He waited by the range. The flames were dying. But no more blackened bodies fell from the chimney. He thrust his poker up as far as it could go and found nothing. It was clear. The chimney was clear. He wiped the sweat from his forehead.

"Come on now, Jill," he said, "bring me some more sticks. We'll have a good fire going directly." She wouldn't come near him, though. She was staring at the heaped singed bodies of the birds.

"Never mind them," he said, "we'll put those in the passage when I've got the fire steady."

The danger of the chimney was over. It could not happen again, not if the fire was kept burning day and night.

"I'll have to get more fuel from the farm tomorrow," he thought. "This will never last. I'll manage, though. I can do all that with the ebb tide. It can be worked, fetching what we need, when the tide's turned. We've just got to adapt ourselves, that's all."

They drank tea and cocoa and ate slices of bread and Bovril. Only half a loaf left, Nat noticed. Never mind though, they'd get by.

"Stop it," said young Johnny, pointing to the windows with his spoon, "stop it, you old birds."

"That's right," said Nat, smiling, "we don't want the old beggars, do we? Had enough of 'em."

They began to cheer when they heard the thud of the suicide birds.

"There's another, Dad," cried Jill, "he's done for."

"He's had it," said Nat, "there he goes, the blighter."

This was the way to face up to it. This was the spirit. If they could keep this up, hang on like this until seven, when the first news bulletin came through, they would not have done too badly.

"Give us a fag," he said to his wife. "A bit of a smoke will clear away the smell of the scorched feathers."

"There's only two left in the packet," she said. "I was going to buy you some from the Co-op."

"I'll have one," he said, "t'other will keep for a rainy day."

No sense trying to make the children rest. There was no rest to be got while the tapping and the scratching went on at the windows. He sat with one arm round his wife and the other round Jill, with Johnny on his mother's lap and the blankets heaped about them on the mattress.

"You can't help admiring the beggars," he said, "they've got persistence. You'd think they'd tire of the game, but not a bit of it."

Admiration was hard to sustain. The tapping went on and

on and a new rasping note struck Nat's ear, as though a sharper beak than any hitherto had come to take over from its fellows. He tried to remember the names of birds, he tried to think which species would go for this particular job. It was not the tap of the woodpecker. That would be light and frequent. This was more serious, because if it continued long the wood would splinter as the glass had done. Then he remembered the hawks. Could the hawks have taken over from the gulls? Were there buzzards now upon the sills, using talons as well as beaks? Hawks, buzzards, kestrels, falcons—he had forgotten the birds of prey. He had forgotten the gripping power of the birds of prey. Three hours to go, and while they waited, the sound of the splintering wood, the talons tearing at the wood.

Nat looked about him, seeing what furniture he could destroy to fortify the door. The windows were safe, because of the dresser. He was not certain of the door. He went upstairs, but when he reached the landing he paused and listened. There was a soft patter on the floor of the children's bedroom. The birds had broken through... He put his ear to the door. No mistake. He could hear the rustle of wings, and the light patter as they searched the floor. The other bedroom was still clear. He went into it and began bringing out the furniture, to pile at the head of the stairs should the door of the children's bedroom go. It was a preparation. It might never be needed. He could not stack the furniture against the door, because it opened inward. The only possible thing was to have it at the top of the stairs.

"Come down, Nat, what are you doing?" called his wife.

"I won't be long," he shouted. "Just making everything ship-shape up here."

He did not want her to come; he did not want her to hear the pattering of the feet in the children's bedroom, the brushing of those wings against the door.

At five-thirty he suggested breakfast, bacon and fried bread, if only to stop the growing look of panic in his wife's eyes and to calm the fretful children. She did not know about the birds upstairs. The bedroom, luckily, was not over the kitchen. Had it been so she could not have failed to hear the sound of them, up there, tapping the boards. And the silly, senseless thud of the suicide birds, the death-and-glory boys, who flew into the bedroom, smashing their heads against the walls. He knew them of old, the herring gulls. They had no brains. The black-backs were different, they knew what they were doing. So did the buzzards, the hawks...

He found himself watching the clock, gazing at the hands that went so slowly round the dial. If his theory was not correct, if the attack did not cease with the turn of the tide, he knew they were beaten. They could not continue through the long day without air, without rest, without more fuel, without...his mind raced. He knew there were so many things they needed to withstand siege. They were not fully prepared. They were not ready. It might be that it would be safer in the towns after all. If he could get a message through, on the farm telephone, to his cousin, only a short journey by train up country they might be able to hire a car. That would be quicker— hire a car between tides...

His wife's voice, calling his name, drove away the sudden, desperate desire for sleep.

"What is it? What now?" he said sharply.

"The wireless," said his wife. "I've been watching the clock. It's nearly seven."

"Don't twist the knob," he said, impatient for the first time, "it's on the Home where it is. They'll speak from the Home."

They waited. The kitchen clock struck seven. There was no sound. No chimes, no music. They waited until a quarter past, switching to the Light. The result was the same. No news bulletin came through.

"We've heard wrong," he said, "they won't be broadcasting until eight o'clock."

They left it switched on, and Nat thought of the battery, wondered how much power was left in it. It was generally recharged when his wife went shopping in the town. If the battery failed they would not hear the instructions.

"It's getting light," whispered his wife, "I can't see it, but I can feel it. And the birds aren't hammering so loud."

She was right. The rasping, tearing sound grew fainter every moment. So did the shuffling, the jostling for place upon the step, upon the sills. The tide was on the turn. By eight there was no sound at all. Only the wind. The children, lulled at last by the stillness, fell asleep. At half past eight Nat switched the wireless off.

"What are you doing? We'll miss the news," said his wife.

"There isn't going to be any news," said Nat. "We've got to depend upon ourselves."

He went to the door and slowly pulled away the barricades. He drew the bolts, and kicking the bodies from the step outside the door breathed the cold air. He had six working hours before him, and he knew he must reserve his strength for the right things, not waste it in any way. Food, and light, and fuel; these were the necessary things. If he could get them in sufficiency, they could endure another night.

He stepped into the garden, and as he did so he saw the living birds. The gulls had gone to ride the sea, as they had done before; they sought sea food, and the buoyancy of the tide, before they returned to the attack. Not so the land birds. They waited and watched. Nat saw them, on the hedgerows, on the soil, crowded in the trees, outside in the field, line upon line of birds, all still, doing nothing.

He went to the end of his small garden. The birds did not move. They went on watching him.

"I've got to get food," said Nat to himself, "I've got to go to the farm to find food."

He went back to the cottage. He saw to the windows and

the doors. He went upstairs and opened the children's bedroom. It was empty, except for the dead birds on the floor. The living were out there, in the garden, in the fields. He went downstairs.

"I'm going to the farm," he said.

His wife clung to him. She had seen the living birds from the open door.

"Take us with you," she begged, "we can't stay here alone. I'd rather die than stay here alone."

He considered the matter. He nodded.

"Come on, then," he said, "bring baskets, and Johnny's pram. We can load up the pram."

They dressed against the biting wind, wore gloves and scarves. His wife put Johnny in the pram. Nat took Jill's hand.

"The birds," she whimpered, "they're all out there, in the fields."

"They won't hurt us," he said, "not in the light."

They started walking across the field towards the stile, and the birds did not move. They waited, their heads turned to the wind.

When they reached the turning to the farm, Nat stopped and told his wife to wait in the shelter of the hedge with the two children.

"But I want to see Mrs. Trigg," she protested. "There are lots of things we can borrow, if they went to market yesterday; not only bread, and . . ."

"Wait here," Nat interrupted. "I'll be back in a moment."

The cows were lowing, moving restlessly in the yard, and he could see a gap in the fence where the sheep had knocked their way through, to roam unchecked in the front garden before the farm-house. No smoke came from the chimneys. He was filled with misgivings. He did not want his wife or the children to go down to the farm.

"Don't jib now," said Nat, harshly, "do what I say."

She withdrew with the pram into the hedge, screening herself and the children from the wind.

He went down alone to the farm. He pushed his way through the herd of bellowing cows, which turned this way and that, distressed, their udders full. He saw the car standing by the gate, not put away in the garage. The windows of the farmhouse were smashed. There were many dead gulls lying in the yard and around the house. The living birds perched on the group of trees behind the farm and on the roof of the house. They were quite still. They watched him.

Jim's body lay in the yard... what was left of it. When the birds had finished, the cows had trampled him. His gun was beside him. The door of the house was shut and bolted, but as the windows were smashed it was easy to lift them and climb through. Trigg's body was close to the telephone. He must have been trying to get through to the exchange when the birds came for him. The receiver was hanging loose, the instrument torn from the wall. No sign of Mrs. Trigg. She would be upstairs. Was it any use going up? Sickened, Nat knew what he would find.

"Thank God," he said to himself, "there were no children."

He forced himself to climb the stairs, but half-way he turned and descended again. He could see her legs, protruding from the open bedroom door. Beside her were the bodies of the black-backed gulls, and an umbrella, broken.

"It's no use," thought Nat, "doing anything. I've only got five hours, less than that. The Triggs would understand. I must load up with what I can find."

He tramped back to his wife and children.

"I'm going to fill up the car with stuff," he said. "I'll put coal in it, and paraffin for the primus. We'll take it home and return for a fresh load."

"What about the Triggs?" asked his wife.

"They must have gone to friends," he said.

"Shall I come and help you, then?"

"No; there's a mess down there. Cows and sheep all over the place. Wait, I'll get the car. You can sit in it."

Clumsily he backed the car out of the yard and into the lane. His wife and the children could not see Jim's body from there.

"Stay here," he said, "never mind the pram. The pram can be fetched later. I'm going to load the car."

Her eyes watched his all the time. He believed she understood, otherwise she would have suggested helping him to find the bread and groceries.

They made three journeys altogether, backwards and forwards between their cottage and the farm, before he was satisfied they had everything they needed. It was surprising, once he started thinking, how many things were necessary. Almost the most important of all was planking for the windows. He had to go round searching for timber. He wanted to renew the boards on all the windows at the cottage. Candles, paraffin, nails, tinned stuff; the list was endless. Besides all that, he milked three of the cows. The rest, poor brutes, would have to go on bellowing.

On the final journey he drove the car to the bus-stop, got out, and went to the telephone box. He waited a few minutes, jangling the receiver. No good, though. The line was dead. He climbed on to a bank and looked over the countryside, but there was no sign of life at all, nothing in the fields but the waiting, watching birds. Some of them slept—he could see the beaks tucked into the feathers.

"You'd think they'd be feeding," he said to himself, "not just standing in that way."

Then he remembered. They were gorged with food. They had eaten their fill during the night. That was why they did not move this morning...

No smoke came from the chimneys of the council houses. He thought of the children who had run across the fields the night before.

"I should have known," he thought, "I ought to have taken them home with me."

He lifted his face to the sky. It was colourless and grey. The bare trees on the landscape looked bent and blackened by the east wind. The cold did not affect the living birds, waiting out there in the fields.

"This is the time they ought to get them," said Nat, "they're a sitting target now. They must be doing this all over the country. Why don't our aircraft take off now and spray them with mustard gas? What are all our chaps doing? They must know, they must see for themselves."

He went back to the car and got into the driver's seat.

"Go quickly past that second gate," whispered his wife. "The postman's lying there. I don't want Jill to see."

He accelerated. The little Morris bumped and rattled along the lane. The children shrieked with laughter.

"Up-a-down, up-a-down," shouted young Johnny.

It was a quarter to one by the time they reached the cottage. Only an hour to go.

"Better have cold dinner," said Nat. "Hot up something for yourself and the children, some of that soup. I've no time to eat now. I've got to unload all this stuff."

He got everything inside the cottage. It could be sorted later. Give them all something to do during the long hours ahead. First he must see to the windows and the doors.

He went round the cottage methodically, testing every window, every door. He climbed on to the roof also, and fixed boards across every chimney, except the kitchen. The cold was so intense he could hardly bear it, but the job had to be done. Now and again he would look up, searching the sky for aircraft. None came. As he worked he cursed the inefficiency of the authorities.

"It's always the same," he muttered, "they always let us down. Muddle, muddle, from the start. No plan, no real organization.

And we don't matter, down here. That's what it is. The people up country have priority. They're using gas up there, no doubt, and all the aircraft. We've got to wait and take what comes."

He paused, his work on the bedroom chimney finished, and looked out to sea. Something was moving out there. Something grey and white amongst the breakers.

"Good old Navy," he said, "they never let us down. They're coming down channel, they're turning in the bay."

He waited, straining his eyes, watering in the wind, towards the sea. He was wrong, though. It was not ships. The Navy was not there. The gulls were rising from the sea. The massed flocks in the fields, with ruffled feathers, rose in formation from the ground, and wing to wing soared upwards to the sky.

The tide had turned again.

Nat climbed down the ladder and went inside the kitchen. The family were at dinner. It was a little after two. He bolted the door, put up the barricade, and lit the lamp.

"It's night-time," said young Johnny.

His wife had switched on the wireless once again, but no sound came from it.

"I've been all round the dial," she said, "foreign stations, and that lot. I can't get anything."

"Maybe they have the same trouble," he said, "maybe it's the same right through Europe."

She poured out a plateful of the Triggs' soup, cut him a large slice of the Triggs' bread, and spread their dripping upon it.

They ate in silence. A piece of the dripping ran down young Johnny's chin and fell on to the table.

"Manners, Johnny," said Jill, "you should learn to wipe your mouth."

The tapping began at the windows, at the door. The rustling, the jostling, the pushing for position on the sills. The first thud of the suicide gulls upon the step.

"Won't America do something?" said his wife. "They've

always been our allies, haven't they? Surely America will do something?"

Nat did not answer. The boards were strong against the windows, and on the chimneys too. The cottage was filled with stores, with fuel, with all they needed for the next few days. When he had finished dinner he would put the stuff away, stack it neatly, get everything shipshape, handy-like. His wife could help him, and the children too. They'd tire themselves out, between now and a quarter to nine, when the tide would ebb; then he'd tuck them down on their mattresses, see that they slept good and sound until three in the morning.

He had a new scheme for the windows, which was to fix barbed wire in front of the boards. He had brought a great roll of it from the farm. The nuisance was, he'd have to work at this in the dark, when the lull came between nine and three. Pity he had not thought of it before. Still, as long as the wife slept, and the kids, that was the main thing.

The smaller birds were at the window now. He recognized the light tap-tapping of their beaks, and the soft brush of their wings. The hawks ignored the windows. They concentrated their attack upon the door. Nat listened to the tearing sound of splintering wood, and wondered how many million years of memory were stored in those little brains, behind the stabbing beaks, the piercing eyes, now giving them this instinct to destroy mankind with all the deft precision of machines.

"I'll smoke that last fag," he said to his wife. "Stupid of me, it was the one thing I forgot to bring back from the farm."

He reached for it, switched on the silent wireless. He threw the empty packet on the fire, and watched it burn.

# ESCORT

THERE is nothing remarkable about the *Ravenswing*, I can promise you that. She is between six and seven thousand tons, was built in 1926, and belongs to the Condor Line, port of register Hull. You can look her up in Lloyd's, if you have a mind. There is little to distinguish her from hundreds of other tramp steamers of her particular tonnage. She had sailed that same route and travelled those same waters for the three years I had served in her, and she was on the job some time before that. No doubt she will continue to do so for many years more, and will eventually end her days peacefully on the mud as her predecessor, the old *Gullswing*, did before her; unless the U-boats get her first.

She has escaped them once, but next time we may not have our escort. Perhaps I had better make it clear, too, that I myself am not a fanciful man. My name is William Blunt, and I have the reputation of living up to it. I never have stood for nonsense of any sort, and have no time for superstition. My father was a Non-conformist minister, and maybe that had something to do with it. I tell you this to prove my reliability, but, for that matter, you can ask anyone in Hull. And now, having introduced myself and the ship, I can get on with my story.

We were homeward bound from a Scandinavian port in the early part of the autumn. I won't give you the name of the port—the censor might stop me—but we had already made the trip there and back three times since the outbreak of war. The convoy system had not started in those first days, and the strain on the captain and myself was severe. I don't want you to infer that we were windy, or the crew either, but the North Sea in wartime is not a bed of roses, and I'll leave it at that.

When we left port, that October afternoon, I couldn't help thinking that it seemed a hell of a long way home, and it didn't put me in what you would call a rollicking humour when our little Scandinavian pilot told us with a grin that a Grimsby ship, six hours ahead of us, had been sunk without warning. The Nazi government had been giving out on the wireless, he said, that the North Sea could be called the German Ocean, and the British Fleet couldn't do anything about it. It was all right for the pilot: he wasn't coming with us. He waved a cheerful farewell as he climbed over the side, and soon his boat was a black speck bobbing astern of us at the harbour entrance, and we were heading for the open sea, our course laid for home.

It was about three o'clock in the afternoon, the sea was very still and grey, and I remember thinking to myself that a periscope wouldn't be easy to miss; at least we would have fair warning, unless the glass fell and it began to blow. However, it did the nerves no good to envisage something that was not going to happen, and I was pretty short with the first engineer when he started talking about the submarine danger, and why the hell didn't the Admiralty do something about it?

"Your job is to keep the old *Ravenswing* full steam ahead for home and beauty, isn't it?" I said. "If Winston Churchill wants your advice, no doubt he'll send for you." He had no answer to that, and I lit my pipe and went on to the bridge to take over from the captain.

I suppose I'm not out-of-the-way observant about my fellow-men, and I certainly didn't notice then that there was anything wrong with the captain. He was never much of a talker at any time. The fact that he went to his cabin at once meant little or nothing. I knew he was close at hand, if anything unusual should happen.

It turned very cold after nightfall, and later a thin rain began to fall. The ship rolled slightly as she met the longer seas. The sky was overcast with the rain, and there were no stars. The autumn nights were always black, of course, in northern waters, but this night the darkness seemed intensified. There would be small chance of sighting a periscope, I thought, under these conditions, and it might well be that we should receive no other intimation than the shock of the explosion. Someone said the other day that the U-boats carried a new type of torpedo, super-charged, and that explained why the ships attacked sank so swiftly.

The *Ravenswing* would founder in three or four minutes, if she was hit right amidships, and it might be that we should never even sight the craft that sank us. The submarine would vanish in the darkness; they would not bother to pick up survivors. They couldn't see them if they wanted to, not in this darkness. I glanced at the chap at the wheel; he was a little Welshman from Cardiff, and he had a trick of sucking his false teeth and clicking them back again every few minutes. We stood a pretty equal chance, he and I, standing side by side together on the bridge. It was then I turned suddenly and saw the captain standing in the entrance to his cabin. He was holding on for support, his face was very flushed, and he was breathing heavily.

"Is anything wrong, sir?" I said.

"This damn pain in my side," he gasped. "Started it yesterday, and thought I'd strained myself. Now I'm doubled up with the bloody thing. Got any aspirin?" Aspirin my foot, I thought. If he hasn't got acute appendicitis, I'll eat my hat. I'd seen a man attacked like that before; he'd been rushed to hospital and operated on in less than two hours. They'd taken an appendix out of him swollen as big as a fist.

"Have you a thermometer there?" I asked the captain.

"Yes," he said. "What the hell's the use of that? I haven't got a temperature. I've strained myself, I tell you. I want some aspirin."

I took his temperature. It was a hundred and four. The sweat was pouring down his forehead. I put my hand on his stomach and it was rigid, like a brick wall. I helped him to his berth and covered him up with blankets. Then I made him drink half a glass of brandy neat. It may be the worst thing you can do for appendicitis, but when you're hundreds of miles from a surgeon and in the middle of the North Sea in wartime you're apt to take chances.

The brandy helped to dull the pain a little, and that was the only thing that mattered. Whatever the result to the captain, it had but one result for me. I was in command of the *Ravenswing* from now on, and mine was the responsibility of bringing her home through those submarine-infested waters. I, William Blunt, had got to see this through.

It was bitter cold. All feeling had long since left my hands and feet. I was conscious of a dull pain in those parts of my body where my hands and feet should have been. But the effect was curiously impersonal. The pain might have belonged to someone else, the sick captain himself even, back there in his cabin, lying moaning and helpless as I had left him last, some forty-eight hours before. He was not my charge; I could do nothing for him. The steward nursed him with brandy and aspirin, and I remember feeling surprised, in a detached sort of way, that he didn't die.

"You ought to get some sleep. You can't carry on like this. Why don't you get some sleep?"

Sleep. That was the trouble. What was I doing at that moment but rocking on my two feet on the borderline of oblivion, with the ship in my charge, and this voice in my left ear the sound that brought me to my senses? It was Carter, the second mate. His face looked pinched and anxious.

"Supposing you get knocked up?" he was saying. "What am I going to do? Why don't you think of me?"

I told him to go to hell, and stamped down the bridge to bring the life back to my numbed feet, and to disguise the fact from Carter that sleep had nearly been victorious.

"What else do you think has kept me on the bridge for forty-eight hours but the thought of you," I said, "and the neat way you let the stern hawser drop adrift, with the second tug alongside, last time we were in Hull? Get me a cup of tea and a sandwich, and shut your bloody mouth."

My words must have relieved him, for he grinned back at me and shot down the ladder like a Jack-in-the-Box. I held on to the bridge and stared ahead, sweeping the horizon for what seemed like the hundred thousandth time, and seeing always the same blank face of the sea, slate grey and still. There were low-banked clouds to the westward, whether mist or rain I could not tell, but they gathered slowly without wind and the glass held steady, while there was a certain smell about the air, warning of fog. I swallowed my cup of tea and made short work of a sandwich, and I was feeling in my pocket for my pipe and a box of matches when the thing happened for which, I suppose, I had consciously been training myself since the captain went sick some forty-eight hours before.

"Object to port. Three-quarters of a mile to a mile distant. Looks like a periscope."

The words came from the lookout on the fo'c'sle head, and so flashed back to the watch on deck. As I snatched my glasses I caught a glimpse of the faces of the men lining the ship's side, curiously uniform they were, half-eager, half-defiant.

Yes. There she was. No doubt now. A thin grey line, like a needle, away there on our port bow, leaving a narrow wake behind her like a jagged ripple. Once again I was aware of Carter beside me, tense, expectant, and I noticed that his hands trembled slightly as he lifted the glasses in his turn. I gave the necessary alteration in our course and took up my glasses once more. Now the periscope was right ahead, and for a few minutes or so the thin line continued on its way as though indifferent to our manoeuvre: then, as I had feared, the submarine altered course, even as we had done, and the periscope bore down upon us, this time to starboard.

"She's seen us," said Carter.

"Yes," I said. He looked up at me, his brown eyes troubled like a spaniel puppy's. We altered course again and increased our speed, this time bringing our stern to the thin grey needle, so that for a moment it seemed as though the gap between us would be widened and she would pass away behind us, but, swift and relentless, she bore up again on our quarter, and little Carter began to swear, fluently and passionately, the futility of words a sop to his fear. I sympathised, seeing in a flash, as the proverbial drowning man is said to do, an episode in my own childhood when my father lectured me for lying; and even as I remembered this picture of a long-forgotten past I spoke down the mouth-tube to the engine room once more and ordered yet another alteration in our speed.

The watch below had now all hurriedly joined those on deck. They lined the side of the ship, as though hypnotised by the unwavering grey line that crept closer, ever closer.

"She's breaking surface," said Carter. "Watch that line of foam."

The periscope had come abeam of us and drawn ahead. It was now a little over a mile distant, on our port bow. Carter was right. She was breaking surface, even as he said. We could see the still water become troubled, and then slowly, inevitably, the squat conning tower appeared and the long lean form rose from the depths like a black slug, the water streaming from its decks.

"The bastards," whispered Carter to himself, "the filthy, stinking bastards."

The men clustered together below me on the deck watched the submarine with a strange indifference, like spectators at some show with which they had no concern. I saw one fellow point out some technical detail of the submarine to the man by his side, and then light a cigarette. His companion laughed and spat over the side of the ship into the water. I wondered how many of them could swim.

I gave the final order to the engine-room, then ordered all hands on deck to boat stations. My next order would depend on the commander of the submarine.

"They'll shell the boats," said Carter. "They won't let us get away, they'll shell the boats."

"Oh, for God's sake," I began, the pallor of his face begetting in me a furious senseless anger, when suddenly I caught sight of the wall of fog that was rolling down upon us from astern. I swung Carter round by the shoulders to meet it. "Look there," I said, "look there," and his jaw dropped and he grinned stupidly. Already the visibility around us was no more than a cable's length on either side, and the first drifting vapour stung us with its cold, sour smell. Above us the air was thick and clammy. In a moment our after-shrouds were lost to sight. I heard one fellow strike up the opening chorus of a comic song in a high falsetto voice, and he was immediately cursed to silence by his companions. Ahead of us lay the submarine, dark and immobile, the decks as yet unmanned and her long snout caught unexpectedly in a sudden shaft of light. Then the white fog that enveloped us crept forward and beyond, the sky descended, and our world was blotted out.

It wanted two minutes to midnight. I crouched low under cover of the bridge and flashed a torch on to my watch. No bell had been sounded since the submarine had first been sighted, some eight hours earlier. We waited. Darkness had travelled with the fog, and night had fallen early. There was silence everywhere, but for the creaking of the ship as she rolled in the swell and the thud of water slapping her sides as she lay over, first on one side, then the other. Still we waited. The cold was no longer so intense as it had been. There was a moist, clammy feeling in the air. The men talked in hushed whispers beneath the bridge. We went on waiting. Once I entered the cabin where the captain lay sick, and flashed my torch on to him. His face was flushed and puffy. His breathing was heavy and slow. He was sleeping fitfully, moaning now and again, and once he opened his eyes, but he did not recognise me. I went back to the bridge. The fog had lifted slightly, and I could see our forward-shrouds and the fo'c'sle head. I went down on to the deck and leant over the ship's side. The tide was running strongly to the south. It had turned three hours before, and for the fourth time that evening I began to calculate our drift. I was turning to the ladder to climb to the bridge once more when I heard footsteps running along the deck, and a man cannoned into me.

"Fog's lifting astern," he said breathlessly, "and there's something coming up on our starboard quarter."

I ran back along the deck with him. A group of men were clustered at the ship's side, talking eagerly. "It's a ship all right, sir," said one. "Looks like a Finnish barque. I can see her canvas."

I peered into the darkness with them. Yes, there she was, about a hundred yards distant, and bearing down upon us. A great three-masted vessel, with a cloud of canvas aloft. It was too late in the year for grain-ships. What the hell was she doing in these waters in wartime? Unless she was carrying timber. Had she seen us, though? That was the point. Here we were, without lights, skulking in the trough of the sea because of that damned submarine, and now risking almost certain collision with some old timber-ship.

If only I could be certain that the tide and the fog had put up a number of miles between us and the enemy. She was coming up fast, the old-timer, God knows where she found her wind—there was none on my left cheek that would blow out a candle. If she passed us at this rate there would be fifty yards to spare, no more, and with that hell-ship waiting yonder in the darkness somewhere the Finn would go straight to kingdom come.

"All right," I said, "she's seen us; she's bearing away." I could only make out her outline in the darkness as she travelled past abeam. A great high-sided vessel she was, in ballast probably, or there would never have been so much of her out of the water. I'd forgotten they had such bulky afterdecks. Her spars were not the clean things I remembered either; these were a mass of rigging, and the yards an extraordinary length, necessary, no doubt, for all that bunch of canvas.

"She's not going to pass us," said somebody, and I heard the blocks rattle and jump, and the rigging slat, as the great yards swung over. And was that faint high note, curious and immeasurably distant, the pipe of a boatswain's whistle? But the fog vapour was drifting down on us again, and the ship was hidden. We strained our eyes in the darkness, seeing nothing, and I was about to turn back to the bridge again when a thin call came to us across the water.

"Are you in distress?" came the hail. Whether her nationality was Finnish or not, at least her officer spoke good English, even if his phrasing was a little unusual. I was wary, though, and I did not answer. There was a pause, and then the voice travelled across to us once more. "What ship are you, and where are you bound?"

And then, before I could stop him, one of our fellows bellowed out: "There's an enemy submarine come to the surface about half-a-mile ahead of us." Someone smothered the idiot a minute too late and, for better or worse, our flag had been admitted.

We waited. None of us moved a finger. All was silent. Presently we heard a splash of oars and the low murmur of voices.

They were sending a boat across to us from the barque. There was something furtive and strange about the whole business. I was suspicious. I did not like it. I felt for the hard butt of my revolver, and was reassured. The sound of oars drew nearer. A long, low boat like a West Country gig drew out of the shadows, manned by half-a-dozen men. There was a fellow with a lantern in the bows. Someone, an officer I presumed, stood up in the stern. It was too dark to see his face. The boat pulled up beneath us and the men rested on their oars.

"Captain's compliments, gentlemen, and do you desire an escort?" inquired the officer.

"What the hell!" began one of our men, but I cursed him to quiet. I leaned over the side, shading my eyes from the light of the boat's lantern.

"Who are you?" I said.

"Lieutenant Arthur Mildmay, at your service, sir," replied the voice.

There was nothing foreign in his intonation, I could swear to that, but again I was struck by his phraseology. No snottie in the Navy ever talked like this. The Admiralty might have bought up a Finnish barque, of course, and armed her, as Von Luckner did in the last war, but the idea seemed unlikely.

"Are you camouflaged?" I asked.

"I beg your pardon?" he replied in some surprise. Then his English was not so fluent as I thought. Once again I felt for my revolver. "You're not trying to make a fool of me by any chance, are you?" I said sarcastically.

"Not in the least," replied the voice. "I repeat, the captain sends his compliments, and as you gave him to understand we are in the immediate vicinity of the enemy, he desires me to offer you his protection. Our orders are to escort any merchant ships we find to a port of safety."

"And who issued those orders?" I said.

"His Majesty King George, of course," replied the voice.

It was then, I think, that I felt for the first time a curious chill of fear. I remember swallowing hard. My throat felt dry, and I could not answer at once. I looked at the men around me, and they wore, one and all, a silly, dumb, unbelieving expression.

"He says the King sent him," said the fellow beside me, and then his voice trailed away uncertainly, and he fell silent.

I heard Carter tap me on the shoulder. "Send them away," he whispered. "There's something wrong; it's a trap."

The man kneeling in the bows of the gig flashed his lantern in my face, blinding me. The young lieutenant stepped across the thwarts and took the lantern from him. "Why not come aboard and speak to the captain yourself, if you are in doubt?" he said.

Still I could not see his face, but he wore some sort of cloak round his shoulders, and the hand that held the lantern was long and slim. The light that dazzled me brought a pain across my eyes so severe that for a few moments I could neither speak nor think, and then, to my surprise, I heard myself answer: "Very well, make room for me, then, in your boat."

Carter laid his hand on my arm. "You're crazy," he said. "You can't leave the ship."

I shook him off, obstinate for no reason, determined on my venture. "You're in charge, Carter," I said. "I shan't be long away. Let me go, you damn fool."

I ordered the ladder over the side, and wondered, with a certain irritation, why the stupid fellows gaped at me as they obeyed. I had that funny reckless feeling which comes upon you when you're half-drunk, and I wondered if the reason for it was my lack of sleep for over forty-eight hours.

I landed with a thud in the gig and stumbled to the stern beside the officer. The men bent to their oars, and the boat began to creep across the water to the barque. It was bitter cold. The clammy mugginess was gone. I turned up the collar of my coat and tried to catch a closer glimpse of my companion, but it was black as pitch in the boat and his features were completely hidden from me.

I felt the seat under me with my hand. It was like ice, freezing to the touch, and I plunged my hands deep in my pockets. The cold seemed to penetrate my greatcoat and find my flesh. My teeth chattered and I could not stop them. The chap in front of me, bending to his oar, was a great burly brute, with shoulders like an ox. His sleeves were rolled up above his elbows, his arms were bare. He was whistling softly between his teeth.

"You don't feel the cold, then?" I asked.

He did not answer, and I leant forward and looked into his face. He stared at me as though I did not exist, and went on whistling between his teeth. His eyes were deep set, sunken in his head. His cheekbones were very prominent and high. He wore a queer stovepipe of a hat, shiny and black.

"Look here," I said, tapping him on the knee, "I'm not here to be fooled, I can tell you that."

And then the lieutenant, as he styled himself, stood up beside me in the stern. "Ship ahoy," he called, his two hands to his mouth, and, looking up, I saw we were already beneath the barque, her great sides towering above us. A lantern appeared on the bulwark by the ladder, and again my eyes were dazzled by the sickly yellow light.

The lieutenant swung on to the ladder and I followed him, hand over fist, breathing hard, for the bitter cold caught at me and seemed to strike right down into my throat. I paused when I reached the deck, with a stitch in my side like a kicking horse, and in the queer half-light that came from the flickering lanterns I saw that this was no Finnish barque with a load of timber, no grain-ship in ballast, but a raider bristling with guns. Her decks were cleared for action, and the men were there ready at their stations. There was much activity and shouting, and a voice from for'ard calling out orders in a thin, high voice. There seemed to be a haze of smoke thick in the air, and a heavy sour stench, and with it all the cold dank chill I could not explain.

"What is it?" I called. "What's the game?" No one answered. Figures brushed past me, shouting and laughing at one another. A lad of about thirteen ran by, with a short blue jacket and long white trousers, while close beside me, crouching by his gun, was a great bearded fellow like my oarsman of the gig, with a striped stocking cap upon his head. Once again, above the hum and confusion, I heard the thin, shrill piping of the boatswain's whistle and, turning, I saw a crowd of jostling men running barefooted to the afterdeck, and I caught the gleam of steel in their hands.

"The captain will see you, if you come aft," said the lieutenant.

I followed him, angry and bewildered. Carter was right, I had been fooled; and yet, as I stumbled in the wake of the lieutenant, I heard English voices shouting on the deck, and funny unfamiliar English oaths.

We pushed through the door of the afterdeck, and the musty rank smell became sourer and more intense. It was darker still. Blinking, I found myself at the entrance of a large cabin, lit only by flickering lantern light, and in the centre of the cabin was a long table, and a man was sitting there in a funny high-backed chair. Three or four other men stood behind him, but the lantern light shone on his face alone. He was very thin, very pale, and his hair was ashen grey. I saw by the patch he wore that he had lost the sight of one eye, but the other eye looked through me in the cold abstracted way of someone who would get his business done and has little time to spare.

"Your name, my man?" he said, tapping with his hand upon the table before him.

"William Blunt, sir," I said, and I found myself standing to attention with my cap in my hands, my throat as dry as a bone, and that same funny chill of fear in my heart.

"You report there is an enemy vessel close at hand, I understand?"

"Yes, sir," I said. "A submarine came to the surface about a mile distant from us, some hours ago. She had been following us for half-an-hour before she broke surface. Luckily the fog came down and hid us. That was at about half-past four in the afternoon. Since then we have not attempted to steam, but have drifted without lights."

He listened to me in silence. The figures behind him did not move. There was something sinister in their immobility and his, as though my words meant nothing to them, as though they did not believe me or did not understand.

"I shall be glad to offer you my assistance, Mr. Blunt," he said at last. I stood awkwardly, still turning my cap in my hands. He did not mean to make game of me, I realized that, but what use was his ship to me?

"I don't quite see," I began, but he held up his hand. "The enemy will not attack you while you are under my protection," he said. "If you care to accept my escort, I shall be very pleased to give you safe conduct to England. The fog has lifted, and luckily the wind is with us."

I swallowed hard. I did not know what to say.

"We steam at eleven knots," I said awkwardly, and when he did not reply I stepped forward to his table, thinking he had not heard. "Supposing the blighter is still there?" I said. "He'll get the pair of us. She'll blow up like matchwood, this ship of yours. You stand even less chance than us."

The man seated by the table leant back in his chair. I saw him smile. "I've never run from a Frenchman yet," he said.

Once again I heard the boatswain's whistle, and the patter of bare feet overhead upon the deck. The lanterns swayed in a current of air from the swinging door. The cabin seemed very musty, very dark. I felt faint and queer, and something like a sob rose in my throat which I could not control.

"I'd like your escort," I stammered, and even as I spoke he rose in his chair and leant towards me. I saw the faded blue of his coat, and the ribbon across it. I saw his pale face very close, and the one blue eye. I saw him smile, and I felt the strength of the hand that held mine and saved me from falling.

They must have carried me to the boat and down the ladder, for when I opened my eyes again, with a queer dull ache at the back of my head, I was at the foot of my own gangway, and my own chaps were hauling me aboard. I could just hear the splash of oars as the gig pulled away back to the barque.

"Thank God you're back!" said Carter. "What the devil did they do to you? You're as white as chalk. Were they Finns or Boche?"

"Neither," I said curtly. "They're English, like ourselves. I saw the captain. I've accepted his escort home."

"Have you gone raving mad?" said Carter.

I did not answer, I went up to the bridge and gave orders for steaming. Yes, the fog was lifting, and above my head I could see the first pale glimmer of a star. I listened, well content, to the familiar noises of the ship as we got under way again. The throb of the screw, the thrash of the propeller. The relief was tremendous. No more silence, no more inactivity. The strain was broken and the men were themselves again, cheerful, cracking jokes at one another. The cold had vanished, and the curious dead fatigue that had been part of my mind and body for so long. The warmth was coming back to my hands and feet.

Slowly we began to draw ahead once more, ploughing our way in the swell, while to starboard of us, some hundred yards distant, came our escort, the white foam hissing from her bows, her cloud of canvas billowing to a wind that none of us could feel. I saw the helmsman beside me glance at her out of the tail of his eye, and when he thought I was not looking he wet his finger and held it in the air. Then his eye met mine, and fell again, and he whistled a song to show he did not care. I wondered if he thought me as mad as Carter did. Once I went in to see the captain. The steward was with him, and when I entered he switched on the lamp above the captain's berth.

"His fever's down," he said. "He's sleeping naturally at last. I don't think we're going to lose him, after all."

"No, I guess he'll be all right," I said.

I went back to the bridge, whistling the song I had heard from the sailor in the gig. It was a jaunty, lilting tune, familiar in a rum sort of way, but I could not put a name to it. The fog had cleared entirely, and the sky was ablaze with stars. We were steaming now at our full rate of knots, but still our escort kept abeam, and sometimes, if anything, she drew just a fraction ahead.

Whether the submarine was on the surface still, or whether she had dived, I neither knew nor cared, for I was full of the confidence which I had lacked before and which, after a while, seemed to possess the helmsman in his turn, so that he grinned at me, jerking his head at our escort, and said, "There don't seem to be no flies on Nancy, do there?" and fell, as I did, to whistling that nameless jaunty tune. Only Carter remained aloof. His fear had given way to sulky silence, and at last, sick of the sight of his moody face staring through the chartroom window, I ordered him below, and was aware of a new sense of freedom and relief when he had gone.

So the night wore on, and we, plunging and rolling in the wake of our escort, saw never a sight of periscope or lean grey hull again. At last the sky lightened to the eastward, and low down on the horizon appeared the streaky pallid dawn. Five bells struck, and away ahead of us, faint as a whisper, came the answering pipe of a boatswain's whistle. I think I was the only one that heard it. Then I heard the weak, tired voice of the captain calling me from his cabin. I went to him at once. He was propped up against his pillows, and I could tell from his face he was as weak as a rat, but his temperature was normal, even as the steward had said.

"Where are we, Blunt?" he said. "What's happened?"

"We'll be safely berthed before the people ashore have rung for breakfast," I said. "The coast's ahead of us now."

"What's the date, man?" he asked. I told him.

"We've made good time," he said. I agreed.

"I shan't forget what you've done, Blunt," he said. "I'll speak to the owners about you. You'll be getting promotion for this."

"Promotion my backside," I said. "It's not me that needs thanking, but our escort away on the starboard bow."

"Escort?" he said, staring at me. "What escort? Are we travelling with a bloody convoy?"

Then I told him the story, starting with the submarine, and the fog, and so on to the coming of the barque herself, and my own visit aboard her, not missing out an account of my own nerves and jumpiness, either. He listened to me, dazed and bewildered on his pillow.

"What's the name of your barque?" he said slowly, when I had finished.

I smote my hand on my knee. "It may be Old Harry for all I know; I never asked them," I said, and I began whistling the tune that the fellow had sung as he bent to his oars in the gig.

"I can't make it out," said the captain. "You know as well as I do there aren't any sailing ships left on the British register."

I shrugged my shoulders. Why the hell couldn't he accept the escort as naturally as the men and I had done?

"Get me a drink and stop whistling that confounded jig," said the captain. I laughed, and gave him his glass.

"What's wrong with it?" I said.

"It's *Lilliburlero*, centuries old. What makes you whistle that?"

I stared back at him, and I was not laughing any longer. "I don't know," I said, "I don't know."

He drank thirstily, watching me over the rim of his glass. "Where's your precious escort now?" he said.

"On the starboard bow," I repeated, and I went forward to the bridge again and gazed seaward, where I knew her to be.

The sun, like a great red globe, was topping the horizon, and the night clouds were scudding to the west. Far ahead lay the coast of England. But our escort had gone.

I turned to the fellow steering. "When did she go?" I asked.

"Beg pardon, sir?" he said.

"The sailing ship. What's happened to her?" I repeated.

The man looked puzzled, and cocked his eye at me curiously. "I've seen no sailing ship," he said. "There's a destroyer been abeam of us some time. She must have come up with us under cover of darkness. I've only noticed her since the sun rose."

I snatched up my glasses and looked to the west. The fellow was not dreaming. There was a destroyer with us, as he said. She plunged into the long seas, churning up the water and chucking it from her like a great white wall of foam. I watched her for a few minutes in silence, and then I lowered my glasses. The fellow steering gazed straight in front of him. Now daylight had come he seemed changed in a queer indefinable way. He no longer whistled jauntily. He was his usual stolid seaman self.

"We shall be docked by nine-thirty. We've made good time," I said.

"Yes, sir," he said.

Already I could see a black dot far ahead, and a wisp of smoke. The tugs were lying off for us. Carter was in my old place on the fo'c'sle head. The men were at their stations. I, on the captain's bridge, would bring his ship to port. He called me to him, five minutes before the tugs took us in tow, when the first gulls were wheeling overhead.

"Blunt," he said, "I've been thinking. That captain fellow you spoke to in the night, on board that sailing craft. You say he wore a black patch over one eye. Did he by any chance have an empty sleeve pinned to his breast as well?"

I did not answer. We looked at one another in silence. Then a shrill whistle warned me that the pilot's boat was alongside. Somewhere, faint and far, the echo sounded like a boatswain's pipe.

# SPLIT SECOND

MRS. ELLIS was methodical and tidy. Unanswered letters, unpaid bills, the litter and rummage of a slovenly writing-desk were things that she abhorred. Today, more than usual, she was in what her late husband used to call her "clearing" mood. She had wakened to this mood; it remained with her throughout breakfast and lasted the whole morning. Besides, it was the first of the month, and as she ripped off the page of her daily calendar and saw the bright clean 1 staring at her, it seemed to symbolise a new start to her day.

The hours ahead of her must somehow seem untarnished like the date; she must let nothing slide.

First she checked the linen. The smooth white sheets lying in rows upon their shelves, pillow slips beside, and one set still in its pristine newness from the shop, tied with blue ribbon, waiting for a guest who never came.

Next, the store cupboard. The stock of homemade jam pleased her, the labels, and the date in her own handwriting. There were also bottled fruit, and tomatoes, and chutney to her own recipe. She was sparing of these, keeping them in reserve for the holidays when Susan should be home, and even then, when she brought them down and put them proudly on the table, the luxury of the treat was spoilt by a little stab of disappointment; it would mean a gap upon the store cupboard shelf.

When she had closed the store cupboard and hidden the key (she could never be quite certain of Grace, her cook), Mrs. Ellis went into the drawing-room and settled herself at her desk. She was determined to be ruthless. The pigeon-holes were searched, and those old envelopes that she had kept because they were not torn and could be used again (to tradesmen, not to friends) were thrown away. She would buy fresh buff envelopes of a cheap quality instead.

Here were some receipts of two years back. Unnecessary to keep them now. Those of a year ago were filed, and tied with tape. A little drawer, stiff to open, she found crammed with old counterfoils from her chequebook. This was wasting space. Instead, she wrote in her clear handwriting, "Letters to Keep." In the future, the drawer would be used for this purpose.

She permitted herself the luxury of filling her blotter with new sheets of paper. The pen tray was dusted. A new pencil sharpened. And, steeling her heart, she threw the stub of the little old one, with worn rubber at the base, into the waste-paper basket.

She straightened the magazines on the side table, pulled the books to the front on the shelf beside the fire—Grace had an infuriating habit of pushing them all to the back—and filled the flower vases with clean water. Then with a bare ten minutes before Grace popped her head round the door and said, "Lunch is in," Mrs. Ellis sat down, a little breathless, before the fire, and smiled in satisfaction. Her morning had been very full indeed. Happy, well spent.

She looked about her drawing-room (Grace insisted on calling it the lounge and Mrs. Ellis was forever correcting her) and thought how comfortable it was, and bright, and how wise they had been not to move when poor Wilfred suggested it a few months before he died. They had so nearly taken that house in the country, because of his health, and his fad that vegetables should be picked fresh every morning, and then luckily—well, hardly luckily, it was most terribly sad and a fearful shock to her—but before they had signed the lease Wilfred had a heart attack and died. Mrs. Ellis was able to stay on in the home she knew and loved, and where she had first come as a bride ten years before.

People were inclined to say the locality was going downhill, that it had become worse than suburban. Nonsense. The blocks of flats that were going up at the top of the road could not be seen from her windows, and the houses, solid like her own, standing in a little circle of front garden, were quite unspoilt.

Besides, she liked the life. Her mornings, shopping in the town, her basket over her arm. The tradesmen knew her, treated her well. Morning coffee at eleven, at the Cosy Café opposite the bookshop, was a small pleasure she allowed herself on cold mornings—she could not get Grace to make good coffee—and in the summer the Cosy Café sold ice cream. Childishly, she would hurry back with this in a paper bag and eat it for lunch; it saved thinking of a sweet.

She believed in a brisk walk in the afternoons, and the heath was so close to hand it was just as good as the country; and in the evenings she read, or sewed, or wrote to Susan.

Life, if she thought deeply about it, which she did not, because to think deeply made her uncomfortable, was really built round Susan. Susan was nine years old, and her only child.

Because of Wilfred's ill-health and, it must be confessed, his irritability, Susan had been sent to boarding school at an early age. Mrs. Ellis had passed many sleepless nights before making this decision, but in the end she knew it would be for Susan's good. The child was healthy and high-spirited, and it was impossible to keep her quiet and subdued in one room with Wilfred fractious in another. It meant sending her down to the kitchen with Grace, and that, Mrs. Ellis decided, did not do.

Reluctantly, the school was chosen, some thirty miles away. It was easily reached within an hour-and-a-half by Green Line bus, the children seemed happy and well cared for, the principal was grey-haired and sympathetic, and as the prospectus described it, the place was a "home from home."

Mrs. Ellis left Susan, on the opening day of her first term, in agony of mind, but constant telephone calls between herself and the headmistress during the first week reassured her that Susan had settled placidly to her new existence.

When her husband died, Mrs. Ellis thought Susan would want to return home and go to a day school, but to her surprise and disappointment the suggestion was received with dismay, and even tears.

"But I love my school," said the child. "We have such fun, and I have lots of friends."

"You would make other friends at a day school," said her mother, "and think, we would be together in the evenings."

"Yes," answered Susan doubtfully, "but what would we do?"

Mrs. Ellis was hurt, but she did not permit Susan to see this. "Perhaps you are right," she said. "You are contented and happy where you are. Anyway, we shall always have the holidays."

The holidays were like brightly coloured beads on a frame, and stood out with significance in Mrs. Ellis's engagement diary, throwing the weeks between into obscurity.

How leaden was February, in spite of its twenty-eight days; how blue and interminable was March, for all that morning coffee at the Cosy Café, the choosing of library books, the visits with friends to the local cinema, or sometimes, more dashing, a matinée "in town."

Then April came, and danced its flowery way across the calendar. Easter, and daffodils, and Susan with glowing cheeks whipped by a spring wind, hugging her once again; honey for tea, scones baked by Grace ("You've been and grown again"), those afternoon walks across the heath, sunny and gay because of the figure running on ahead. May was quiet, and June pleasant because of wide-flung windows, and the snapdragons in the front garden; June was leisurely. Besides, there was the school play on Parents' Day, and Susan, with bright eyes, surely much the best of the pixies, and although she did not speak her actions were so good.

July dragged until the twenty-fourth, and then the weeks spun themselves into a sequence of glory until the last week in September. Susan at the sea...Susan on a farm...Susan on Dartmoor...Susan just at home, licking an ice cream, leaning out of a window.

"She swims quite well for her age," thus, casually, to a neighbour on the beach. "She insists on going in, even when it's cold."

"I don't mind saying," this to Grace, "that I hated going through that field of bullocks, but Susan didn't mind a scrap. She has a way with animals."

Bare scratched legs in sandals, summer frocks outgrown, a sunhat, faded, lying on the floor. October did not bear thinking about...But, after all, there was always plenty to do in the house. Forget November, and the rain, and the fogs that turned white upon the heath. Draw the curtains, poke the fire, settle to something, the *Weekly Home Companion*, Fashions for Young Folk. Not that pink, but the green with the smocked top and a wide sash would be just the thing for Susan at parties in the Christmas holidays. December...Christmas...

This was the best, this was the height of home enjoyment. As soon as Mrs. Ellis saw the first small trees standing outside the florist's and those orange boxes of dates in the grocer's window, her heart would give a little leap of excitement. Susan would be home in three weeks now. Then the laughter and the chatter. The nods between herself and Grace. The smiles of mystery. The furtiveness of wrappings.

All over in one day like the bursting of a swollen balloon; paper ribbon, cracker novelties, even presents, chosen with care, thrown aside. But no matter. It was worth it. Mrs. Ellis, looking down upon a sleeping Susan tucked in with a doll in her arms, turned down the light and crept off to her own bed, sapped, exhausted. The egg cosy, Susan's handiwork at school, hastily stitched, stood on her bedside table. Mrs. Ellis never ate boiled eggs, but, as she said to Grace, there is such a gleam in the hen's eye; it's very cleverly done.

The fever, the pace of the New Year. The Circus, the pantomime. Mrs. Ellis watched Susan, never the performers. "You should have seen her laugh when the seal blew the trumpet; I've never known a child with such a gift for enjoyment."

And how she stood out at parties, in the green frock, with her fair hair and blue eyes. Other children were so stumpy. Ill-made little bodies or big shapeless mouths. "She said, 'Thank you for a lovely time,' when we left, which was more than most of them did. And she won at musical chairs."

There were bad moments too, of course. The restless night, the high spot of colour, the sore throat, the temperature of 102. Shaking hands on the telephone. The doctor's reassuring voice. And his footsteps on the stairs, a steady, reliable man. "We had better take a swab, in case." A swab? That meant diphtheria, scarlet fever? A little figure being carried down in blankets, an ambulance, hospital. . . ?

Thank God, it proved to be a relaxed throat. Lots of them about. Too many parties, keep her quiet for a few days. Yes, Doctor, yes. The relief from dread anxiety, and on and on without a stop, the reading to Susan from her *Playbook Annual,* story after story, terrible and trite, "and so Nicky Nod *did* lose his treasure after all, which just served him right, didn't it, children?"

"All things pass," thought Mrs. Ellis, "pleasure and pain, and happiness and suffering, and I suppose my friends would say my life is a dull one, rather uneventful, but I am grateful for it, and contented, and although sometimes I feel I did not do my utmost for poor Wilfred—his was a difficult nature, luckily Susan has not inherited it—at least I believe I have succeeded in making a happy home for Susan." She looked about her, that first day of the month, and noticed with affection and appreciation those bits and pieces of furniture, the pictures on the walls, the ornaments on the mantelpiece, all the things she had gathered about her during ten years of marriage, which meant herself, her home.

The sofa and two chairs, part of an original suite, were worn but comfortable. The pouf by the fire, she had covered it herself. The fire irons, not quite so polished as they should be, she must speak to Grace. The rather melancholy portrait of Wilfred in that dark corner behind the bookshelf, at least he looked distinguished. And was, thought Mrs. Ellis to herself, hastily. The flower picture showed more to advantage over the mantelpiece; the green foliage harmonised so well with the green coat of the Staffordshire figure who stood with his lady beside the clock.

"I could do with new covers," thought Mrs. Ellis, "and curtains too, but they must wait. Susan has grown so enormously the last few months. Her clothes are more important. The child is tall for her age."

Grace looked round the door. "Lunch is in," she said.

"If she would open the door outright," thought Mrs. Ellis, "and come right into the room, I have mentioned it a hundred times. It's the sudden thrust of the head that is so disconcerting, and if I have anyone to lunch . . ."

She sat down to guinea-fowl and apple charlotte, and wondered if they were remembering to give Susan extra milk at school this term, and the Minidex tonic; the matron was inclined to be forgetful.

Suddenly, for no reason, she laid her spoon down on the plate, swept with a wave of such intense melancholy as to be almost unbearable. Her heart was heavy. Her throat tightened. She could not continue her lunch.

"Something is wrong with Susan," she thought. "This is a warning that she wants me."

She rang for coffee and went into the drawing-room. She crossed to the window and stood looking at the back of the house opposite. From an open window sagged an ugly red curtain, and a lavatory brush hung from a nail.

"The district *is* losing class," thought Mrs. Ellis. "I shall have lodging-houses for neighbours soon."

She drank her coffee, but the feeling of uneasiness, of apprehension, did not leave her. At last she went to the telephone and rang up the school.

The secretary answered. Surprised, and a little impatient, surely. Susan was perfectly all right. She had just eaten a good lunch. No, she had no sign of a cold. No one was ill in the school. Did Mrs. Ellis want to speak to Susan? The child was outside with the others, playing, but could be called in if necessary.

"No," said Mrs. Ellis, "it was just a foolish notion on my part that Susan might not be well. I am so sorry to have bothered you."

She hung up the receiver, and went to her bedroom to put on her outdoor clothes. A good walk would do her good. She gazed in satisfaction upon the photograph of Susan on the dressing table. The photographer had caught the expression in her eyes to perfection. Such a lovely light on the hair too.

Mrs. Ellis hesitated. Was it really a walk she needed? Or was this vague feeling of distress a sign that she was over-tired, that she had better rest? She looked with inclination at the downy quilt upon her bed. Her hot-water bottle, hanging by the washstand, would take only a moment to fill. She could loosen her girdle, throw off her shoes, and lie down for an hour on the bed, warm with the bottle under the downy quilt. No. She decided to be firm with herself. She went to the wardrobe and got out her camel coat, wound a scarf round her head, pulled on a pair of gauntlet gloves, and walked downstairs.

She went into the drawing-room, made up the fire, and put

the guard in front of it. Grace was apt to be forgetful of the fire. She opened the window at the top so that the room should not strike stuffy when she came back. She folded the daily papers ready to read when she returned, and replaced the marker in her library book.

"I'm going out for a little while. I shan't be long," she called down to the basement to Grace.

"All right, ma'am," came the answer.

Mrs. Ellis caught the whiff of cigarette, and frowned. Grace could do as she liked in the basement, but there was something not quite right about a maidservant smoking.

She shut the front door behind her, went down the steps and into the road, and turned left towards the heath. It was a dull, grey day. Mild for the time of year, almost to oppression. Later, there would be fog, perhaps, rolling up from London the way it did, in a great wall, stifling the clean air.

Mrs. Ellis made her "short round," as she always called it. Eastward, to the Viaduct ponds, and then back, circling, to the Vale of Health.

It was not an inviting afternoon, and she did not enjoy her walk. She kept wishing she was home again, in bed with a hot-water bottle, or sitting in the drawing-room beside the fire, soon to shut out the muggy, murky sky, and draw the curtains. She walked swiftly past nurses pushing prams, two or three of them in groups chatting together, their charges running ahead. Dogs barked beside the ponds. Solitary men in mackintoshes stared into vacancy. An old woman on a seat threw crumbs to chirping sparrows. The sky took on a darker, olive tone. Mrs. Ellis quickened her steps. The fairground by the Vale of Health looked sombre, the merry-go-round shrouded in its winter wrappings of canvas, and two lean cats stalked each other in and out of the palings. A milkman, whistling, clanked his tray of bottles and, lifting them to his cart, urged the pony to a trot.

"I must," thought Mrs. Ellis inconsequently, "get Susan a bicycle for her birthday. Nine is a good age for a first bicycle."

She saw herself choosing one, asking advice, feeling the handle-bars. The colour red, perhaps. Or a good blue. A little basket on the front and a leather bag, for tools, strapped to the back of the seat. The brakes must be sound but not too gripping, otherwise Susan would topple headfirst over the handle-bars and graze her face.

Hoops were out of fashion, which was a pity. When she had been a child there had been no fun like a good springy hoop, struck smartly with a little stick, bowling its way ahead of you. Quite an art to it, too. Susan would have been good with a hoop.

Mrs. Ellis came to the junction of two roads and crossed to the opposite side; the second road was her own, and her house the last one on the corner.

As she did so she saw the laundry van swinging down towards her, much too fast. She saw it swerve, heard the screech of its brakes. She saw the look of surprise on the face of the laundry boy. "I shall speak to the driver next time he calls," she said to herself. "One of these days there will be an accident." She thought of Susan on the bicycle, and shuddered. Perhaps a note to the manager of the laundry would do more good. "If you could possibly give a word of warning to your driver, I should be grateful. He takes his corners much too fast." And she would ask to remain anonymous. Otherwise the man might complain about carrying the heavy basket down the steps each time.

She had arrived at her own gate. She pushed it open, and noticed with annoyance that it was nearly off its hinges. The men calling for the laundry must have wrenched at it in some way and done the damage. The note to the manager would be stronger still. She would write immediately after tea. While it was on her mind.

She took out her key and put it in the Yale lock of the front door. It stuck. She could not turn it. How very irritating. She rang the bell. This would mean bringing Grace up from the basement, which she did not like. Better to call down, perhaps, and explain the situation. She leant over the steps and called down to the kitchen. "Grace, it's only me," she said, "my key has jammed in the door; could you come up and let me in?"

She paused. There was no sound from below. Grace must have gone out. This was sheer deceit. It was an agreed bargain between them that when Mrs. Ellis was out Grace must stay in. The house must not be left. But sometimes Mrs. Ellis suspected that Grace did not keep to the bargain. Here was proof.

She called once again, rather more sharply this time. "Grace?"

There was a sound of a window opening below, and a man thrust his head out of the kitchen. He was in his shirt sleeves. And he had not shaved.

"What are you bawling your head off about?" he said.

Mrs. Ellis was too stunned to answer. So this was what happened when her back was turned. Grace, respectable, well over thirty, had a man in the house. Mrs. Ellis swallowed, but kept her temper.

"Perhaps you will have the goodness to ask Grace to come upstairs and let me in," she said.

The sarcasm was wasted, of course. The man blinked at her, bewildered. "Who's Grace?" he said.

This was too much. So Grace had the nerve to pass under another name. Something fanciful, no doubt. Shirley, or Marlene. She was pretty sure now what must have happened. Grace had slipped out to the public house down the road to buy this man beer. The man was left to loll in the kitchen. He might even have been poking his fingers in the larder. Now she knew why there was so little left on the joint two days ago.

"If Grace is out," said Mrs. Ellis, and her voice was icy, "kindly let me in yourself. I prefer not to use the back entrance."

That would put him in his place. Mrs. Ellis trembled with rage. She was seldom angry; she was a mild, even-tempered woman. But this reception, from a lout in shirt sleeves at her own kitchen window, was rather more than she could bear. It was going to be unpleasant, the interview with Grace. Grace would give notice, in all probability. But some things could not be allowed to slide, and this was one of them.

She heard shuffling footsteps coming along the hall. The man had mounted from the basement. He opened the front door and stood there, staring at her.

"Who is it you want?" he said.

Mrs. Ellis heard the furious yapping of a little dog from the drawing-room. Callers... This was the end. How perfectly frightful, how really overwhelmingly embarrassing. Someone had called and Grace had let them in, or, worse still, this man in his shirt sleeves had done so. What would people think?

"Who is in the drawing-room, do you know?" she murmured swiftly.

"I think Mr. and Mrs. Bolton are in, but I'm not sure," he said. "I can hear the dog yapping. Was it them you wanted to see?"

Mrs. Ellis did not know a Mr. and Mrs. Bolton. She turned impatiently towards the drawing-room, first whipping off her coat and putting her gloves in her pocket.

"You had better go down to the basement again," she said to the man, who was still staring at her. "Tell Grace not to bring tea until I ring. These people may not stay."

The man appeared bewildered. "All right," he said, "I'm going down. But if you want Mr. and Mrs. Bolton again, ring twice."

He shuffled off down the basement stairs. He was drunk, no doubt. He meant to be insulting. If he proved difficult, later in the evening, after dark, it would mean ringing for the police.

Mrs. Ellis slipped into the lobby to hang up her coat. No

time to go upstairs if callers were in the drawing-room. She fumbled for the switch but the bulb had gone. Another pin-prick. Now she could not see herself in the mirror.

She stumbled over something, and bent to see what it was. It was a man's boot. And here was another, and a pair of shoes, and beside them a suitcase and an old rug. If Grace had allowed that man to put his things in her lobby, then Grace would go tonight. Crisis had come. High crisis.

Mrs. Ellis opened the drawing-room door, forcing a smile of welcome, not too warm, upon her lips. A little dog rushed towards her, barking furiously.

"Quiet, Judy," said a man, grey-haired, with horn spectacles, sitting before the fire. He was clicking a typewriter.

Something had happened to the room. It was covered with books and papers. Odds and ends of junk littered the floor. A parrot, in a cage, hopped on its perch and screeched a welcome. Mrs. Ellis tried to speak, but her voice would not come. Grace had gone raving mad. She had let that man into the house, and this one too, and they had brought the most terrible disorder; they had turned the room upside down; they had deliberately, maliciously, set themselves to destroy her things.

No. Worse. It was part of a great thieving plot. She had heard of such things. Gangs went about breaking into houses. Grace, perhaps, was not at fault. She was lying in the basement, gagged and bound. Mrs. Ellis felt her heart beating much too fast. She also felt a little faint.

"I must keep calm," she said to herself, "whatever happens, I must keep calm. If I can get to the telephone, to the police, it is the only hope. This man must not see that I am planning what to do."

The little dog kept sniffing at her heels. "Excuse me," said the intruder, pushing his horn spectacles on to his forehead, "but do you want anything? My wife is upstairs."

The diabolic cunning of the plot. The cool bluff of his sitting there, the typewriter on his knees. They must have brought all this stuff in through the door to the back garden; the French window was ajar. Mrs. Ellis glanced swiftly at the mantelpiece. It was as she feared. The Staffordshire figures had been removed, and the flower picture too. There must be a car, a van, waiting down the road... Her mind worked quickly. It might be that the man had not guessed her identity. Two could play at bluff. Memories of amateur theatricals flashed through her mind. Somehow she must detain these people until the police arrived. How fast they had worked. Her desk was gone, the bookshelves too, nor could she see her armchair. But she kept her eyes steadily on the stranger. He must not notice her brief glance round the room.

"Your wife is upstairs?" said Mrs. Ellis, her voice strained, yet calm.

"Yes," said the man, "if you've come for an appointment, she always makes them. You'll find her in the studio. Room in the front."

Steadily, softly, Mrs. Ellis left the drawing-room, but the wretched little dog had followed her.

One thing was certain. The man had not realised who she was. They believed the householder out of the way for the afternoon, and that she, standing now in the hall, listening, her heart beating, was some caller to be fobbed off with a lie about appointments.

She stood silently by the drawing-room door. The man had resumed typing on his machine. She marvelled at the coolness of it, the drawn-out continuity of the bluff. There had been nothing in the papers very recently about large scale robberies. This was something new, something outstanding. It was extraordinary that they should pick on her house. But they must know she was a widow, on her own, with one maidservant. The telephone had already been removed from the stand in the hall. There was a loaf of bread on it instead, and something that looked like meat wrapped up in newspaper. So they had brought provisions... There was a chance that the telephone in her bedroom had not yet been taken away, nor the wires cut. The man had said his wife was upstairs. It may have been part of his bluff, or it might be that he worked with a woman accomplice. This woman, even now, was probably turning out Mrs. Ellis's wardrobe, seizing her fur coat, ramming the single string of cultured pearls into a pocket.

Mrs. Ellis thought she could hear footsteps in her bedroom. Her anger overcame her fear. She had not the strength to do battle with the man, but she could face the woman. And if the worst came to the worst, she would run to the window, put her head out, and scream. The people next door would hear. Or someone might be passing in the street.

Stealthily, Mrs. Ellis crept upstairs. The little dog led the way with confidence. She paused outside her bedroom door. There was certainly movement from within. The dog waited, his eyes fixed upon her with intelligence.

At that moment the door of Susan's small bedroom opened, and a fat elderly woman looked out, blowzy and red in the face. She had a tabby cat under her arm. As soon as the dog saw the cat it started a furious yapping.

"Now that's torn it," said the woman. "What do you want to bring the dog upstairs for? They always fight when they meet. Do you know if the post's been yet? Oh, sorry. I thought you were Mrs. Bolton." She brought an empty milk bottle from under her other arm and put it down on the landing. "I'm blowed if I can manage the stairs today," she said, "somebody else will have to take it down for me. Is it foggy out?"

"No," said Mrs. Ellis, shocked into a natural answer, and then, feeling the woman's eyes upon her, hesitated between entering her bedroom door and withdrawing down the stairs. This evil-looking old woman was part of the gang and might call the man from below.

"Got an appointment?" said the other. "She won't see you if you haven't booked an appointment."

A tremor of a smile appeared on Mrs. Ellis's lips. "Thank you," she said, "yes, I have an appointment."

She was amazed at her own steadiness, and that she could carry off the situation with such aplomb. An actress on the London stage could not have played her part better.

The elderly woman winked and, drawing nearer, plucked Mrs. Ellis by the sleeve. "Is she going to do you straight or fancy?" she whispered. "It's the fancy ones that get the men. You know what I mean!" She nudged Mrs. Ellis and winked again. "I see by your ring you're married," she said. "You'd be surprised—even the quietest husbands like their pictures fancy. Take a tip from an old pro. Get her to do you fancy."

She lurched back into Susan's room, the cat under her arm, and shut the door.

"It's possible," thought Mrs. Ellis, the faint feeling coming over her once again, "that a group of lunatics have escaped from an asylum, and in their terrible, insane fashion they have broken into my house not to thieve, not to destroy my belongings, but because in some crazed, deluded fashion they believe themselves to be at home."

The publicity would be frightful once it became known. Headlines in the papers. Her photograph taken. So bad for Susan. Susan . . . That horrible, disgusting old woman in Susan's bedroom.

Emboldened, fortified, Mrs. Ellis opened her own bedroom door. One glance revealed the worst. The room was bare, stripped. There were several lights at various points, and a camera on a tripod. A divan was pushed against the wall. A young woman, with a crop of thick fuzzy hair, was kneeling on the floor, sorting papers.

"Who is it?" she said. "I don't see anyone without an appointment. You've no right to come in here."

Mrs. Ellis, calm, resolute, did not answer. She had made certain that the telephone, though it had been moved like the rest of her things, was still in the room. She went to it and lifted the receiver.

"Leave my telephone alone," cried the shock-haired girl, and she began to struggle to her knees.

"I want the police," said Mrs. Ellis firmly to the exchange, "I want them to come at once to 17 Elmhurst Road. I am in great danger. Please report this message to the police at once."

The girl was beside her now, taking the receiver from her. "Who's sent you here?" said the girl, her face sallow, colourless, against the fuzzy hair. "If you think you can come in snooping, you're mistaken. You won't find anything. Nor the police, neither. I have a trade licence for the work I do."

Her voice had risen, and the dog, alarmed, joined her with high-pitched barks. The girl opened the door and called down the stairs. "Harry?" she shouted. "Come here and throw this woman out."

Mrs. Ellis remained quite calm. She stood with her back to the wall, her hands folded. The exchange had taken her message. It would not be long now before the police arrived.

She heard the drawing-room door open from below and the man's voice called up, petulant, irritated. "What's the matter?" he shouted. "You know I'm busy. Can't you deal with the woman? She probably wants a special pose."

The girl's eyes narrowed. She looked closely at Mrs. Ellis. "What did my husband say to you?" she said.

Ah, thought Mrs. Ellis triumphantly, they're getting frightened. It's not such an easy game as they think. "I had no conversation with your husband," she said quietly; "he merely told me I should find you upstairs. In this room. Don't try any bluff with me. It's too late. I can see what you have been doing." She gestured at the room.

The girl stared at her. "You can't put any phony business

over on me," she said. "This studio is decent, respectable, every-one knows that. I take camera studies of children. Plenty of clients can testify to that. You've got no proof of anything else. Show me a negative, and then I might believe you?"

Mrs. Ellis wondered how long it would be before the police came. She must continue to play for time. Later, she might even feel sorry, perhaps, for this wretched deluded girl who had wrought such havoc in the bedroom, believing herself to be a photographer; but this moment, now, she must be calm, calm.

"Well?" said the girl. "What are you going to say when the police come? What's your story?"

It did not do to antagonise lunatics. Mrs. Ellis knew that. They must be humoured. She must humour this girl until the police came. "I shall tell them that I live here," she said gently. "That is all they will need to know. Nothing further."

The girl looked at her, puzzled, and lit a cigarette. "Then it is a pose you want?" she said. "That call was just a bluff? Why don't you come clean and say why you're here?"

The sound of their voices had attracted the attention of the old woman in Susan's room. She tapped on the door, which was already open, and stood on the threshold.

"Anything wrong, dear?" she said slyly to the girl.

"Push on out of it," said the girl impatiently, "this is none of your business. I don't interfere with you, and you don't inter-fere with me."

"I'm not interfering, dear," said the woman, "I only wanted to know if I could help. Difficult client, eh? Wants something outsize?"

"Oh, shut your mouth," said the girl.

The girl's husband, Bolton or whatever his name was, the spectacled man from the drawing-room, came upstairs and into the bedroom.

"Just what's going on?" he said.

The girl shrugged her shoulders and glanced at Mrs. Ellis. "I don't know," she said, "but I think it's blackmail."

"Has she got any negatives?" said the man swiftly.

"Not that I know of. Never seen her before."

"She might have got them from another client," said the elderly woman, watching.

The three of them stared at Mrs. Ellis. She was not afraid. She had the situation well in hand.

"I think we've all become a little overwrought," she said, "and much the best thing to do would be to go downstairs, sit quietly by the fire, and have a little chat, and you can talk to me about your work. Tell me, are you all three photographers?"

As she spoke, half of her mind was wondering where they had managed to hide her things. They must have bundled her bed into Susan's room; the wardrobe was in two parts, of course, and could be taken to pieces very soon; but her clothes . . . her ornaments . . . these must have been concealed in a lorry. Somewhere, there was a lorry filled with all her things. It might be parked down another road, or might have been driven off already by yet another accomplice. The police were good at tracing stolen goods, she knew that, and everything was insured; but such a mess had been made of the house; insurance would never cover that, unless there was some clause, some proviso against damage by lunatics; surely the insurance people would not call that an act of God . . . Her mind ran on and on, taking in the mess, the disorder, these people had created, and how many days and weeks would it take for her and Grace to get everything straight again?

Poor Grace. She had forgotten Grace. Grace must be shut up somewhere in that basement with that dreadful man in shirt sleeves, another of the gang, not a follower at all.

"Well," said Mrs. Ellis with the other half of her mind, the half that was acting so famously, "shall we do as I suggest and go downstairs?" She turned and led the way, and to her surprise they followed her, the man and his wife, not the horrible old woman. She remained above, leaning over the banisters.

"Call me if you want me," she said.

Mrs. Ellis could not bear to think of her fingering Susan's things in the little bedroom. "Won't you join us?" she said, steeling herself to courtesy. "It's far more cheerful down below."

The old woman smirked. "That's for Mr. and Mrs. Bolton to say," she said, "I don't push myself."

"If I can get all three of them pinned into the drawing-room," thought Mrs. Ellis, "and somehow lock the door, and make a tremendous effort at conversation, I might possibly keep their attention until the police arrive. There is, of course, the door into the garden, but then they will have to climb the fence, fall over that potting shed next door. The old woman, at least, would never do it."

"Now," said Mrs. Ellis, her heart turning over inside at the havoc of the drawing-room, "shall we sit down and recover ourselves, and you shall tell me all about this photography."

But she had scarcely finished speaking before there was a ring at the front door and a knock, authoritative, loud. The relief sent her dizzy. She steadied herself against the door. It was the police. The man looked at the girl, a question in his eye.

"Better have 'em in," he said, "she's got no proof." He crossed the hall and opened the front door. "Come in, officer," he said. "There's two of you, I see."

"We had a telephone call," Mrs. Ellis heard the constable say, "some trouble going on, I understand."

"I think there must be some mistake," said Bolton. "The fact is, we've had a caller and I think she got hysterical."

Mrs. Ellis walked into the hall. She did not recognise the constable, nor the young policeman from the beat. It was unfortunate, but it did not really matter. Both were stout, well-built men.

"I am not hysterical," she said firmly, "I am perfectly all right. I put the telephone call through the exchange."

The constable took out a notebook and a pencil. "What's the trouble?" he said. "But give me first your name and address."

Mrs. Ellis smiled patiently. She hoped he was not going to be a stupid man. "It's hardly necessary," she said, "but my name is Mrs. Wilfred Ellis of this address."

"Lodge here?" asked the constable.

Mrs. Ellis frowned. "No," she said, "this is my house, I live here." And then, because she saw a look flash from Bolton to his wife, she knew the time had come to be explicit. "I must speak to you alone, Constable," she said, "the matter is terribly urgent; I don't think you quite understand."

"If you have any charge to bring, Mrs. Ellis," said the officer, "you can bring it at the police station at the proper time. We were informed that somebody lodging here at Number 17 was in danger. Are you, or are you not, the person who gave that information to the exchange?"

Mrs. Ellis began to lose control.

"Of course I am that person," she said. "I returned home to find that my house had been broken into by thieves, these people here, dangerous thieves, lunatics, I don't know what they are, and my things carried away, the whole of my house turned upside down, the most terrible disorder everywhere." She talked so rapidly, her words fell over themselves.

The man from the basement had now joined them in the hall. He stared at the two policemen, his eyes goggling. "I saw her come to the door," he said. "I thought she was balmy. Wouldn't have let her in if I had known."

The constable, a little nettled, turned to the interrupter. "Who are you?" he said.

"Name of Upshaw," said the man, "William Upshaw. Me and my missus has the basement flat here."

"That man is lying," said Mrs. Ellis, "he does not live here; he belongs to this gang of thieves. Nobody lives in the basement except my maid—perhaps I should say cook-general—Grace Jackson, and if you will search the premises you will probably find her gagged and bound somewhere, and by that ruffian." She had now lost all restraint. She could hear her voice, usually low and quiet, rising to a hysterical pitch.

"Balmy," said the man from the basement, "you can see the straw in her hair."

"Quiet, please," said the constable, and turned to the young policeman, who murmured something in his ear. "Yes, yes," he said, "I've got the directory here."

He consulted another book. Mrs. Ellis watched him feverishly. Never had she seen such a stupid man. Why had they sent out such a slow-witted fool from the police station?

The constable now turned to the man in the horn spectacles. "Are you Henry Bolton?" he asked.

"Yes, officer," replied the man eagerly, "and this is my wife. We have the ground floor here. She uses an upstairs room for a studio. Camera portraits, you know."

There was a shuffle down the stairs, and the evil old woman came to the foot of the banisters. "My name's Baxter," she said, "Billie Baxter they used to call me in my old stage days. Used to be in the profession, you know. I have the first-floor back here at Number 17. I can witness this woman came as a sort of Paul Pry, and up to no good. I saw her looking through the keyhole of Mrs. Bolton's studio."

"Then she doesn't lodge here?" asked the constable. "I didn't think she did; the name isn't in the directory."

"We have never seen her before, officer," said Bolton. "Mr. Upshaw let her into the house through some error; she walked into our living-room, and then forced her way into my wife's studio, threatened her, and in hysterical fashion rang for the police."

The constable looked at Mrs. Ellis. "Anything to say?" he said.

Mrs. Ellis swallowed. If only she could keep calm, if only her heart would not beat so dreadfully fast, and the terrible desire to cry would not rise in her throat.

"Constable," she said, "there has been some terrible mistake. You are new to the district, perhaps, and the young policeman too—I don't seem to recognise him—but if you would kindly get through to your headquarters, they must know all about me; I have lived here for years. My maid Grace has been with me a very long time; I am a widow; my husband, Wilfred Ellis, has been dead two years; I have a little girl of nine at school. I went out for a walk on the heath this afternoon, and during my absence these people have broken into my house, seized or destroyed my belongings—the whole place is upside down; if you would please get through immediately to your headquarters . . ."

"There, there," said the constable, putting his notebook away, "that's all right; we can go into all that quietly down at the station. Now do any of you want to charge Mrs. Ellis with trespassing?"

There was silence. Nobody said anything.

"We don't wish to be unkind," said Bolton diffidently. "I think my wife and I are quite willing to let the matter pass."

"I think it should be clearly understood," interposed the shock-haired girl, "that anything this woman says about us at the police station is completely untrue."

"Quite," said the officer. "You will both be called, if needed, but I very much doubt the necessity. Now, Mrs. Ellis"—he turned to her, not harshly in any way, but with authority—"we have a car outside, and we can run you down to the station, and you can tell your story there. Have you a coat?"

Mrs. Ellis turned blindly to the lobby. She knew the police station well; it was barely five minutes away. It was best to go there direct. See someone in authority, not this fool, this hopeless, useless fool. But in the meantime, these people were getting away with their criminal story. By the time she and an additional police force returned, they would have fled. She groped for her coat in the dark lobby, stumbling again over the boots, the suitcases. "Constable," she said softly, "here, one minute."

He moved towards her. "Yes?" he said.

"They've taken away the electric bulb," she said rapidly in a low whisper. "It was perfectly all right this afternoon, and these boots, and this pile of suitcases, all these have been brought in, and thrown here; the suitcases are probably filled with my ornaments. I must ask you most urgently to leave the policeman in charge here until we return, to see that these people don't escape."

"That's all right, Mrs. Ellis," said the officer. "Now, are you ready to come along?"

She saw a look pass between the constable and the young policeman. The young policeman was trying to hide his smile. Mrs. Ellis felt certain that the constable was *not* going to remain in the house. And a new suspicion flashed into her mind. Could this officer and his subordinate be genuine members of the police force? Or were they, after all, members of the gang? This would explain their strange faces, their obvious mishandling of the situation. In which case they were now going to take her away to some lair, drug her, kill her possibly.

"I'm not going with you," she said swiftly.

"Now, Mrs. Ellis," said the constable, "don't give any trouble. You shall have a cup of tea down at the station, and no one is going to hurt you."

He seized her arm. She tried to shake it off. The young policeman moved closer.

"Help," she shouted, "help...help..."

There must be someone. Those people from next door, she

barely knew them, but no matter, if she raised her voice loud enough...

"Poor thing," said the man in shirt sleeves, "seems sad, don't it? I wonder how she got like it."

Mrs. Ellis saw his bulbous eyes fixed on her with pity, and she nearly choked.

"You rogue," she said, "how dare you, how dare you!" But she was being bundled down the steps, through the front garden and into the car, and there was another policeman at the wheel of the car; and she was thrust at the back, the constable keeping a steady hold upon her arm. The car turned downhill, past the stretch of heath; she tried to see out of the windows where they were going, but the bulk of the constable prevented her. After twisting and turning the car stopped, to her great surprise, in front of the police station. Then these men were genuine, after all. They were not members of the gang. Stupefied for a moment, but relieved, thankful, Mrs. Ellis stumbled from the car. The constable, still holding her arm, led her inside.

The hall was not unfamiliar; she remembered coming once before, years ago, when the ginger cat was lost; there was somebody in charge always, sitting at a sort of desk, everything very official, very brisk. She supposed she would stop here in the hall, but the constable led her on to an inner room, and here was another officer seated at a large desk, a more superior type altogether, thank heaven, and he looked intelligent.

She was determined to get her word in before the constable spoke. "There has been great confusion," she began. "I am Mrs. Ellis, of 17 Elmhurst Road, and my house has been broken into, robbery is going on at this moment on a huge scale; I believe the thieves to be very desperate and extraordinarily cunning; they have completely taken in the constable here, and the other policeman..."

To her indignation this superior officer did not look at her.

He raised his eyebrows at the constable, and the constable, who had taken off his hat, coughed and approached the desk. A policewoman, appearing from nowhere, stood beside Mrs. Ellis and held her arm.

The constable and the superior officer were talking together in low tones. Mrs. Ellis could not hear what they were saying. Her legs trembled with emotion. She felt her head swim. Thankfully, she accepted the chair dragged forward by the policewoman, and in a few moments she was given a cup of tea. She did not want it, though. Precious time was being lost.

"I must insist that you hear what I have to say," she said, and the policewoman tightened her grip on Mrs. Ellis's arm. The officer behind the desk motioned her forward, and she was assisted to another chair, the policewoman remaining beside her all the while.

"Now," he said, "what is it you want to tell me?"

Mrs. Ellis gripped her hands together. She had a premonition that this man, in spite of his superior face, was going to prove as great a fool as the constable.

"My name is Ellis," she said, "Mrs. Wilfred Ellis, of 17 Elmhurst Road. I am in the telephone book. I am very well known in the district, and have lived at Elmhurst Road for ten years. I am a widow, and I have one little girl of nine years at present at school. I employ one maidservant, Grace Jackson, who cooks for me and does general work. This afternoon I went for a short walk on the heath, round by the Viaduct and the Vale of Health ponds, and when I returned home I found my house had been broken into; my maid had disappeared; the rooms were already stripped of my belongings and the thieves were in possession of my home, putting up a stupendous act of bluff that deceived even the constable here. I put the call through to the exchange, which frightened the thieves, and I endeavoured to keep them pinned in my drawing-room until help arrived."

Mrs. Ellis paused for breath. She saw that the officer was paying attention to her story, and kept his eyes fixed upon her.

"Thank you," he said, "that is very helpful, Mrs. Ellis. Now, have you anything you can show me to prove your identity?"

She stared at him. Prove her identity? Well, of course. But not here, not actually on her person. She had come away without her handbag, and her calling cards were in the writing desk, and her passport—she and Wilfred had been to Dieppe once—was, if she remembered rightly, in the left-hand pigeonhole of the small writing desk in her bedroom.

But she suddenly remembered the havoc of the house. Nothing would be found...

"It's very unfortunate," she said to the officer, "but I didn't take my handbag with me when I went out for my walk this afternoon. I left it in the chest-of-drawers in the bedroom. My calling-cards are in the desk in the drawing-room, and there is a passport—rather out of date; my husband and I did not travel much—in a pigeonhole in a small desk in my bedroom. But everything has been upset, taken by these thieves. The house is in utter chaos."

The officer made a note on the pad beside him. "You can't produce your identity card or your ration book?" he asked.

"I have explained," said Mrs. Ellis, governing her temper. "My calling-cards are in my writing-desk. I don't know what you mean by ration book."

The officer went on writing on his pad. He glanced at the policewoman, who began feeling Mrs. Ellis's pockets, touching her in a familiar way. Mrs. Ellis tried to think which of her friends could be telephoned to, who could vouch for her, who could come at once by car and make these idiots, these stone-witted fools, see sense. "I must keep calm," she told herself again, "I must keep calm." The Collins were abroad; they would have been the best, but Netta Draycott should be at home; she was usually at home about this time because of the children.

"I have asked you," said Mrs. Ellis, "to verify my name and address in the telephone book. If you refuse to do that, ask the postmaster, or the manager of my bank, a branch of which is in the High Street, where I cashed a cheque on Saturday. Finally, would you care to ring up Mrs. Draycott, a friend of mine, 21 Charlton Court, the block of flats in Charlton Avenue, who will vouch for me?"

She sat back in the chair, exhausted. No nightmare, she told herself, could ever have the horror, the frustrated hopelessness, of her present plight. Little incident piled on little incident. If she had only remembered to bring her handbag, there was a calling-card case in her handbag. And all the while those thieves, those devils, breaking up her home, getting away with her precious things, her belongings...

"Now, Mrs. Ellis," said the officer, "we have checked up on your statements, you know, and they won't do. You are not in the telephone book, nor in the local directory."

"I assure you I am," said Mrs. Ellis with indignation. "Give me the books and I'll show you."

The constable, still standing, placed the books before her. She ran her finger down the name of Ellis to the position on the left-hand page where she knew it would be. The name Ellis was repeated, but not hers. And none with her address or number. She looked in the directory and saw that beside 17 Elmhurst Road were the names of Bolton, of Upshaw, of Baxter... She pushed both books away from her. She stared at the officer.

"There is something wrong with these books," she said, "they are not up to date, they are false, they are not the books I have at home."

The officer did not answer. He closed the books. "Now, Mrs. Ellis," he said, "I can see you are tired, and a rest would do you good. We will try to find your friends for you. If you will go along now, we will get in touch with them as soon as possible. I will send a doctor to you, and he may chat with you a little and give you a sedative, and then, after some rest, you will feel better in the morning and we may have news for you."

The policewoman helped Mrs. Ellis to her feet. "Come along now," she said.

"But my house?" said Mrs. Ellis. "Those thieves, and my maid Grace, Grace may be lying in the basement. Surely you are going to do something about the house? You won't permit them to get away with this monstrous crime? Even now we have wasted a precious half-hour—"

"That's all right, Mrs. Ellis," said the officer, "you can leave everything in our hands."

The policewoman led her away, still talking, still protesting, and now she was being taken down a corridor, and the policewoman kept saying: "Now, don't fuss, take it calmly; no one's going to hurt you," and she was in a little room with a bed; heavens . . . it was a cell, a cell where they put the prisoners, and the policewoman was helping her off with her coat, unpinning the scarf that was still tied round her hair, and because Mrs. Ellis felt so faint the policewoman made her lie down on the bed, covered her with the coarse grey blanket, placed the little hard pillow under her head.

Mrs. Ellis seized the woman's hands. Her face, after all, was not unkind. "I beg of you," she said, "ring up Hampstead 4072, the number of my friend Mrs. Draycott, and ask her to come here. The officer won't listen to me. He won't hear my story."

"Yes, yes, that will be all right," said the policewoman.

Now somebody else was coming into the room, the cell. Cleanshaven, alert, he carried a case in his hands. He said good evening to the policewoman, and opened his case. He took out a stethoscope and a thermometer. He smiled at Mrs. Ellis. "Feeling a little upset, I hear," he said. "Well, we'll soon put that to rights. Now, will you give me your wrist?"

Mrs. Ellis sat up on the hard narrow bed, pulling the blanket close. "Doctor," she said, "there is nothing whatever the matter with me. I admit I have been through a terrible experience, quite enough to unnerve anyone; my house has been broken into; no one here will listen to my story, but I am Mrs. Ellis, Mrs. Wilfred Ellis, if you can possibly persuade the authorities here..."

He was not listening to her. With the assistance of the policewoman he was taking her temperature, under her arm, not in the mouth, treating her like a child; and now he was feeling her pulse, dragging down her eyelids, listening to her chest... Mrs. Ellis went on talking.

"I realise this is a matter of routine. You are obliged to do this. But I want to warn you that my whole treatment, since I have been brought here, since the police came to my house before that, has been infamous, scandalous. I don't personally know our M.P., but I sincerely believe that when he hears my story he will take the matter up, and someone is going to answer for the consequences. Unfortunately I am a widow, no immediate relatives, my little daughter is away at school; my closest friends, a Mr. and Mrs. Collins, are abroad, but my bank manager..."

He was dabbing her arm with spirit; he was inserting a needle, and with a whimper of pain Mrs. Ellis fell back on to the hard pillow. The doctor went on holding her arm, and Mrs. Ellis, her head going round and round, felt a strange numb sensation as the injection worked into her bloodstream. Tears ran down her cheeks. She could not fight. She was too weak.

"How is that?" said the doctor. "Better, eh?"

Her throat was parched, her mouth without saliva. It was one of those drugs that paralysed you, made you helpless. But the emotion bubbling within her was eased, was still. The anger, the fear and frustration that had keyed her nerves to a point of contraction seemed to die away. She had explained things badly. The folly of coming out without her handbag had caused half the trouble. And the terrible, wicked cunning of those thieves. "Be still," she said to her mind, "be still. Rest now."

"Now," said the doctor, letting go her wrist, "supposing you tell me your story again. You say your name is Mrs. Ellis?"

Mrs. Ellis sighed and closed her eyes. Must she go into it all again? Had they not got the whole thing written down in their notebooks? What was the use, when the inefficiency of the whole establishment was so obvious? Those telephone books, directories, with wrong names, wrong addresses. Small wonder there were burglaries, murders, every sort of crime, with a police force that was obviously rotten to the core. What was the name of the Member? It was on the tip of her tongue. A nice man, sandy-haired, always looked so trustworthy on a poster. Hampstead was a safe seat, of course. He would take up her case ...

"Mrs. Ellis," said the doctor, "do you think you can remember now your real address?"

Mrs. Ellis opened her eyes. Wearily, patiently, she fixed them upon the doctor. "I live at 17 Elmhurst Road," she said mechanically. "I am a widow, my husband has been dead for two years. I have a little girl of nine at school. I went for a short walk on the heath this afternoon after lunch, and when I returned—"

He interrupted her. "Yes," he said, "we know that. We know what happened after your walk. What we want you to tell us is what happened before."

"I had lunch," said Mrs. Ellis. "I remember perfectly well what I ate. Guinea fowl and apple charlotte, followed by coffee. Then I nearly decided to take a nap upstairs on my bed, because I was not feeling very well, but decided the air would do me good."

As soon as she said this, she regretted it. The doctor looked at her keenly. "Ah!" he said. "You weren't feeling very well. Can you tell me what the trouble was?"

Mrs. Ellis knew what he was after. He and the rest of the

police force at the station wanted to certify her as insane. They would make out that she had suffered from some brainstorm, that her whole story was fabrication.

"There was nothing much the matter," she said quickly. "I was rather tired from sorting things during the morning. I tidied the linen, cleared out my desk in the drawing-room—all that took time."

"Can you describe your house, Mrs. Ellis?" he said. "The furniture, for instance, of your bedroom, your drawing-room?"

"Very easily," she answered, "but you must remember that the thieves who broke into the house this afternoon have done what I begin to fear is irreparable damage. Everything had been seized, hidden away. The rooms were strewn with rubbish, and there was a young woman upstairs in my bedroom pretending to be a photographer."

"Yes," he said, "don't worry about that. Just tell me about your furniture, how the various things were placed, and so on."

He was more sympathetic than she had thought. Mrs. Ellis launched into a description of every room in her house. She named the ornaments, the pictures, the position of the chairs and tables.

"And you say your cook is called Grace Jackson?"

"Yes, Doctor, she has been with me several years. She was in the kitchen when I left this afternoon; I remember most distinctly calling down to the basement and saying that I was going for a short walk and would not be long. I am extremely worried about her, Doctor. Those thieves will have got hold of her, perhaps kidnapped her."

"We'll see to that," said the doctor. "Now, Mrs. Ellis, you have been very helpful, and you have given such a clear account of your home that I think we shan't be long in tracing it, and your relations. You must stay here tonight, and I hope in the morning we shall have news for you. Now, you say your small daughter is at school? Can you remember the address?"

"Of course," said Mrs. Ellis, "and the telephone number too. The school is High Close, Bishops' Lane, Hatchworth, and the telephone number is Hatchworth 202. But I don't understand what you mean about tracing my home."

"There is nothing to worry about," said the doctor. "You are not ill, and you are not lying, I quite realise that. You are suffering from a temporary loss of memory that often happens to all sorts of people, and it quickly passes. We've had many cases before." He smiled. He stood up, his case in his hand.

"But it isn't true," said Mrs. Ellis, trying to raise herself from the pillow. "My memory is perfectly all right. I have given you every detail I can think of; I have told you my name, where I live, a description of my home, the address of my daughter at school..."

"All right," he said. "Now, don't worry. Just try to relax and have a little sleep. We shall find your friends for you."

He murmured something to the policewoman and left the cell. The policewoman came over to the bed and tucked in the blanket.

"Now, cheer up," she said, "do as the doctor said. Get a little rest. Everything will be all right, you'll see."

Rest... but how? Relax... But to what purpose? Even now her house was being looted, sacked, every room stripped. The thieves getting clear away with their booty, leaving no trace behind them. They would take Grace with them; poor Grace could not come down to the police station to give witness to her identity. But the people next door, the Furbers, surely they would be good enough; it would not be too much trouble... Mrs. Ellis supposed she should have called, been more friendly, had them to tea, but after all, people did not expect that unless they lived in the country, it was out of date. If the police officer had not got hold of Netta Draycott then the Furbers must be got in touch with at once...

Mrs. Ellis plucked at the policewoman's sleeve. "The Furbers," she said, "next door, at number 19, they will vouch for me. They are not friends of mine, but they know me well by sight. We have been neighbours for quite six years. The Furbers."

"Yes," said the policewoman, "try to get some sleep."

Oh, Susan, my Susan, if this had happened in the holidays, how much more fearful; what would we have done? Coming back from an afternoon walk to find those devils in the house, and then, who knows, that dreadful photographer woman and her husband taking a fancy to Susan, so pretty, so fair, and wanting to kidnap her...At least the child was safe, knew nothing of what was happening, and if only the story could be kept out of the newspapers, she need never know. So shameful, so degrading, a night spent in a prison cell through such crass stupidity, such appalling blunders...

"You've had a good sleep, then," said the policewoman, handing her a cup of tea.

"I don't know what you mean," said Mrs. Ellis. "I haven't slept at all."

"Oh, yes, you have." The woman smiled. "They all say that."

Mrs. Ellis blinked, sat up on the narrow bed. She had been speaking to the policewoman only a moment before. Her head ached abominably. She sipped at the tea, tasteless, unrefreshing. She yearned for her bed at home, for Grace coming in noiselessly, drawing the curtains.

"You're to have a wash," said the policewoman, "and I'll give you a comb through, and then you are to see the doctor again."

Mrs. Ellis suffered the indignity of washing under supervision, of having her hair combed; then her scarf and coat and gloves were given to her again and she was taken out of the cell, along the corridor, back through the hall to the room where they had questioned her the night before. This time a different officer sat at the desk, but she recognised the police constable, and the doctor too.

The last came towards her with that same bland smile on his

face. "How are you feeling today?" he said. "A little more like your true self?"

"On the contrary," said Mrs. Ellis, "I am feeling very unwell indeed, and shall continue to do so until I know what has happened at home. Is anyone here prepared to tell me what has happened since last night? Has anything at all been done to safeguard my property?"

The doctor did not answer, but guided her towards the chair at the desk. "Now," he said, "the officer here wants to show you a picture in a newspaper."

Mrs. Ellis sat down in the chair. The officer handed her a copy of the *News of the World*—a paper Grace took on Sundays; Mrs. Ellis never looked at it—and there was a photograph of a woman with a scarf round her head and chubby cheeks, wearing some sort of light-coloured coat. The photograph had a red circle round it, and underneath was written: "Missing from Home, Ada Lewis, aged 36, widow, of 105 Albert Buildings, Kentish Town." She handed the paper back across the desk. "I'm afraid I can't help you," she said. "I don't know this woman."

"The name Ada Lewis conveys nothing to you?" said the officer. "Nor Albert Buildings?"

"No," said Mrs. Ellis, "certainly not."

Suddenly she knew the purpose of the interrogation. The police thought that she was this missing woman, this Ada Lewis from Albert Buildings. Simply because she wore a light-coloured coat and had a scarf round her hair. She rose from the chair.

"This is absolutely preposterous," she said. "I have told you my name and my address, and you persist in disbelieving me. My detention here is an outrage; I demand to see a lawyer, my own lawyer..." But wait, she hadn't needed the services of a lawyer since Wilfred died, and the firm had moved or been taken over by somebody else; better not give the name; they would think she was lying once again; it was safer to give the name of the bank manager. . .

"One moment," said the officer, and she was interrupted once again, because somebody else came into the room, a seedy, common-looking man in a checked shabby suit, holding his trilby hat in his hand. "Can you identify this woman as your sister, Ada Lewis?" asked the officer.

A flush of fury swept Mrs. Ellis as the man stepped forward and peered into her face. "No, sir," he said, "this isn't Ada. Ada isn't so stout, and this woman's teeth seem to be her own. Ada wore dentures. Never seen this woman before."

"Thank you," said the officer, "that's all. You can go. We will let you know if we find your sister."

The seedy-looking man left the room. Mrs. Ellis turned in triumph to the officer behind the desk. "Now," she said, "perhaps you will believe me?"

The officer considered her for a moment, and then, glancing at the doctor, looked down at some notes on his desk. "Much as I would like to believe you," he said, "for it would save us all a great deal of trouble if I could, unfortunately I can't. Your facts have been proved wrong in every particular. So far."

"What do you mean?" said Mrs. Ellis.

"First, your address. You do not live at 17 Elmhurst Road because the house is occupied by various tenants who have lived there for some time and who are known to us. Number 17 is an apartment house and the floors are let separately. You are not one of the tenants."

Mrs. Ellis gripped the sides of her chair. The obstinate, proud, and completely unmoved face of the officer stared back at her. "You are mistaken," she said quietly. "Number 17 is not a lodging-house. It is a private house. My own."

The officer glanced down again at his notes. "There are no people called Furber living at number 19," he went on. "Number 19 is also a lodging-house. You are not in the directory under the name of Ellis, nor in the telephone book. There is no Ellis on the register of the branch of the bank you mentioned to us last night. Nor can we trace anyone of the name of Grace Jackson in the district."

Mrs. Ellis looked up at the doctor, at the police constable, at the policewoman, who was still standing by her side. "Is there some conspiracy?" she said. "Why are you all against me? I don't understand what I have done..." Her voice faltered. She must not break down. She must be firm with them, be brave, for Susan's sake. "You rang up my friend at Charlton Court?" she she asked. "Mrs. Draycott, that big block of flats?"

"Mrs. Draycott is not living at Charlton Court, Mrs. Ellis," said the police officer, "for the simple reason that Charlton Court no longer exists. It was destroyed by a fire bomb."

Mrs. Ellis stared at him in horror. A fire bomb? But how perfectly terrible! When? How? In the night? Disaster upon disaster... Who could have done it, anarchists, strikers, unemployed, gangs of people, possibly those who had broken into her house? Poor Netta and her husband and children; Mrs. Ellis felt her head reeling...

"Forgive me," she said, summoning her strength, her dignity, "I had no idea there had been such a fearful outrage. No doubt part of the same plot, those people in my house..."

Then she stopped, because she realised they were lying to her; everything was lies; they were not policemen; they had seized the building; they were spies; the government was to be overthrown; but then why bother with her, with a simple harmless individual like herself; why were they not getting on with the civil war, bringing machine guns into the street, marching to Buckingham Palace; why sit here, pretending to her?

A policeman came into the room and clicked his heels and stood before the desk. "Checked up on all the nursing homes," he said, "and the mental homes, sir, in the district, and within a radius of five miles. Nobody missing."

"Thank you," said the officer. Ignoring Mrs. Ellis, he looked across at the doctor. "We can't keep her here," he said. "You'll have to persuade them to take her at Moreton Hill. The matron *must* find a room. Say it's a temporary measure. Case of amnesia."

"I'll do what I can," said the doctor.

Moreton Hill. Mrs. Ellis knew at once what they meant by Moreton Hill. It was a well-known mental home somewhere near Highgate, very badly run, she always heard, a dreadful place.

"Moreton Hill?" she said. "You can't possibly take me there. It has a shocking reputation. The nurses are always leaving. I refuse to go to Moreton Hill. I demand to see a lawyer—no, my doctor, Dr. Godber; he lives in Parkwell Gardens."

The officer stared at her thoughtfully. "She must be a local woman," he said; "she gets the names right every time. But Godber went to Portsmouth, didn't he? I remember Godber."

"If he's at Portsmouth," said Mrs. Ellis, "he would only have gone for a few days. He's most conscientious. But his secretary knows me. I took Susan there last holidays."

Nobody listened to her, though, and the officer was consulting his notes again. "By the way," he said, "you gave me the name of that school correctly. Wrong telephone number, but right school. Co-educational. We got through to them last night."

"I'm afraid then," said Mrs. Ellis, "that you got the wrong school. High Close is most certainly not co-educational, and I should never have sent Susan there if it had been."

"High Close," repeated the officer, reading from his notes, "is a co-educational school, run by a Mr. Foster and his wife."

"It is run by a Miss Slater," said Mrs. Ellis, "a Miss Hilda Slater."

"You mean it *was* run by a Miss Slater," said the officer. "A Miss Slater had the school and then retired, and it was taken over by Mr. and Mrs. Foster. They have no pupil there of the name of Susan Ellis."

Mrs. Ellis sat very still in her chair. She looked at each face in turn. None was harsh. None was unfriendly. And the policewoman smiled encouragement. They all watched her steadily. At last she said: "You are not deliberately trying to mislead me? You do realise that I am anxious, most desperately anxious, to know what has happened? If all that you are saying is some kind of a game, some kind of torture, would you tell me so that I know, so that I can understand?"

The doctor took her hand, and the officer leant forward in his chair. "We are trying to help you," he said. "We are doing everything we can to find your friends."

Mrs. Ellis held tight to the doctor's hand. It had suddenly become a refuge. "I don't understand," she said, "what has happened. If I am suffering from loss of memory, why do I remember everything so clearly? My address, my name, people, the school... Where is Susan; where is my little girl?" She looked round her in blind panic. She tried to rise from the chair. "If Susan is not at High Close, where is she?"

Someone was patting her on the shoulder. Someone was giving her a glass of water.

"If Miss Slater had retired to give place to a Mr. and Mrs. Foster, I should have heard, they would have told me," she kept repeating. "I telephoned the school only yesterday. Susan was quite well, and playing in the grounds."

"Are you suggesting that Miss Slater answered you herself?" enquired the officer.

"No, the secretary answered. I telephoned because I had... what seemed to me a premonition that Susan might not be well. The secretary assured me that the child had eaten a good lunch and was playing. I am not making this up. It happened yesterday. I tell you, the secretary would have told me if Miss Slater was making changes in the school."

Mrs. Ellis searched the doubtful faces fixed upon her. And momentarily her attention was caught by the large 2 on the calendar standing on the desk.

"I *know* it was yesterday," she said, "because today is the second of the month, isn't it? And I distinctly remember tearing off the page in my calendar, and because it was the first of the month I decided to tidy my desk, sort out my papers, during the morning."

The police officer relaxed and smiled. "You are certainly very convincing," he said, "and we can all tell from your appearance, the fact that you have no money on you, that your shoes are polished, and other little signs, that you do definitely belong somewhere in this district; you have not wandered from any great distance. But you do not come from 17 Elmhurst Road, Mrs. Ellis, that is quite certain. For some reason, which we hope to discover, that address has become fixed in your mind, and other addresses too. I promise you everything will be done to clear your mind and to get you well again; and you need have no fear about going to Moreton Hill; I know it well, and they will look after you there."

Mrs. Ellis saw herself shut up behind those grey forbidding walls, grimly situated, frowning down upon the further ponds the far side of the heath. She had skirted those walls many times, pitying the inmates within. The man who came with the groceries had a wife who became insane. Mrs. Ellis remembered Grace coming to her one morning full of the story, "and he says they've taken her to Moreton Hill." Once inside, she would never get out. These men at the police station would not bother with her any more. And now there was this new, hideous misunderstanding about Susan, and the talk of a Mr. and Mrs. Foster taking over the school.

Mrs. Ellis leant forward, clasping her hands together. "I do assure you," she said, "that I don't want to make trouble. I have always been a very quiet, peaceable sort of person, not easily excited, never quarrelsome, and if I have really lost my memory I will do what the doctor tells me, take any drugs or medicines that will help. But I am worried, desperately worried, about my little girl and what you have told me about the school and Miss Slater's having retired. Would you do just one thing for me? telephone the school and ask them where you can get in touch with Miss Slater. It is just possible that she has taken the house down the road and removed there with some of the children, Susan amongst them; and whoever answered the telephone was new to the work and gave you vague information."

She spoke clearly, without any sort of hysteria or emotion; they must see that she was in deadly earnest, and this request of hers was not wild fancy.

The police officer glanced at the doctor, then he seemed to make up his mind. "Very well," he said, "we will do that. We will try to contact this Miss Slater, but it may take time. Meanwhile, I think it is best if you wait in another room while we put through the enquiry."

Mrs. Ellis stood up, this time without the help of the policewoman. She was determined to show that she was well, mentally and bodily, and quite capable of managing her affairs without the assistance of anybody, if it could be permitted. She wished she had a hat instead of the scarf, which she knew instinctively was unbecoming, and her hands were lost without her handbag. At least she had gloves. But gloves were not enough. She nodded briskly to the police officer and the doctor—at all costs she must show civility—and followed the policewoman to a waiting room. This time she was spared the indignity of a cell. Another cup of tea was brought to her.

"It's all they think about," she said to herself, "cups of tea, instead of getting on with their job."

Suddenly she remembered poor Netta Draycott and the

terrible tragedy of the fire bomb. Possibly she and her family had escaped and were now with friends, but there was no immediate means of finding out. "Is it all in the morning papers about the disaster?" she asked the policewoman.

"What disaster?" said the woman.

"The fire at Charlton Court the officer spoke to me about."

The policewoman stared at her with a puzzled expression. "I don't remember him saying anything about a fire," she said.

"Oh, yes, he did," said Mrs. Ellis. "He told me that Charlton Court had been destroyed by fire, by some bomb. I was aghast to hear it because I have friends living there. It must surely be in all the morning papers."

The woman's face cleared. "Oh, that," she said. "I think the officer was referring to some fire bomb during the war."

"No, no," said Mrs. Ellis impatiently. "Charlton Court was built a long time after the war. I remember the block being built when my husband and I first came to Hampstead. No, this accident apparently happened last night, the most dreadful thing."

The policewoman shrugged her shoulders. "I think you're mistaken," she said; "there's been no talk of any accident or disaster here."

An ignorant, silly sort of girl, thought Mrs. Ellis. It was a wonder she had passed her test into the force. She thought they only employed very intelligent women. She sipped her tea in silence. No use carrying on any sort of conversation with her. It seemed a long while before the door opened, but when it did it was to reveal the doctor, who stood on the threshold with a smile on his face.

"Well," he said, "I think we're a little nearer home. We were able to contact Miss Slater."

Mrs. Ellis rose to her feet, her eyes shining. "Oh, Doctor, thank heaven . . . Have you news of my daughter?"

"Steady a moment now. You mustn't get excited or we shall

have all last night's trouble over again, and that would never do. I take it, when you refer to your daughter, you mean someone who is called, or was called, Susan Ellis?"

"Yes, yes, of course," said Mrs. Ellis swiftly. "Is she all right, is she with Miss Slater?"

"No, she is not with Miss Slater, but she is perfectly well. I have spoken to her on the telephone myself, and I have her present address here in my notebook." The doctor patted his breast pocket and smiled again.

"Not with Miss Slater?" Mrs. Ellis stared in bewilderment. "Then the school *has* been handed over; you spoke to these people called Foster. Is it next door? Have they moved far? What has happened?"

The doctor took her hand and led her to the seat once more. "Now," he said, "I want you to think quite calmly and quite clearly and not be agitated in any way, and your trouble will be cleared up, your mind will be free again. You remember last night you gave us the name of your maid, Grace Jackson?"

"Yes, Doctor."

"Now, take your time. Tell us a little about Grace Jackson."

"Have you found her? Is she at home? Is she all right?"

"Never mind for the moment. Describe Grace Jackson."

Mrs. Ellis was horribly afraid poor Grace had been found murdered, and they were going to ask her to identify the body. "She is a big girl," she said, "at least not really a girl, about my own age, but you know how one is inclined to talk of a servant as a girl; she has a large bust, rather thick ankles, brownish hair, grey eyes, and she would be wearing, let me see, I think she may not have changed into her cap and apron when those thieves arrived; she was still probably in her overalls. She is inclined to change rather late in the afternoon; I have often spoken about it; it looks so bad to open the front door in overalls, slovenly, like a boarding-house. Grace has good teeth and a pleasant expression, though of course if anything has happened to her she would hardly—" Mrs. Ellis broke off. Murdered, battered. Grace would not be smiling.

The doctor did not seem to notice this. He was looking closely at Mrs. Ellis. "You know," he said, "you have given a very accurate description of yourself."

"Myself?" said Mrs. Ellis.

"Yes. Figure, colouring, and so on. We think, you know, it is just possible that your amnesia has taken the form of mistaken identity and that you are really Grace Jackson, believing yourself to be a Mrs. Ellis, and now we are doing our best to trace the relatives of Grace Jackson."

This was too much. Mrs. Ellis swallowed. Outraged pride rose in her. "Doctor," she said rapidly, "you have gone a little too far. I bear no sort of resemblance to my maid, Grace Jackson, and if and when you ever find trace of the unfortunate girl, she would be the first to agree with me. Grace has been in my employment seven years; she came originally from Scotland; her parents were Scottish, I believe—in fact, I know it, because she used to go for her holiday to Aberdeen. Grace is a good, hard-working, and I like to think honest girl; we have had our little ups and downs, but nothing serious; she is inclined to be obstinate; I am obstinate myself—who is not?—but..."

If only the doctor would not look at her in that smiling, patronising way. "You see," he said, "you do know a very great deal about Grace Jackson."

Mrs. Ellis could have hit him. He was so self-assured, so confident. "I must keep my temper," she told herself. "I must, I must..." Aloud she said: "Doctor, I know about Grace Jackson because, as I have told you, she has been in my employment for seven years. If she is found ill or in any way hurt, I shall hold the police force here responsible, because, in spite of my entreaties, I do not believe they kept a watch on my house last night. Now perhaps you will be good enough to tell me where I can find my child. She, at least, will recognise me."

Mrs. Ellis considered she had been very restrained, very calm. In spite of terrible provocation she had not lost control of herself.

"You insist that your age is thirty-five?" said the doctor, switching the subject. "And that Grace Jackson was approximately the same?"

"I was thirty-five in August last," said Mrs. Ellis. "I believe Grace to be a year younger, I am not sure."

"You certainly don't look more," said the doctor, smiling.

Surely, at such a moment, he was not going to attempt to appease her by gallantry?

"But," he continued, "following upon the telephone conversation I have just had, Grace Jackson would be, today, at least fifty-five or fifty-six."

"There are probably," said Mrs. Ellis icily, "several persons of the name of Grace Jackson employed as domestic servants. If you propose tracing every one of them, it will take you and the police force a considerable time. I am sorry to insist, but I must know the whereabouts of my daughter Susan before anything else."

He was relenting; she could see it in his eye. "As a matter of fact," he said, "it happens, very conveniently, that Miss Slater was able to put us in touch with her; we have spoken to her on the telephone, and she is only a short distance away, in St. John's Wood. She is not sure, but she thinks she would remember Grace Jackson if she saw her."

For a moment Mrs. Ellis was speechless. What in the world was Susan doing in St. John's Wood? And how monstrous to drag the child to the telephone and question her about Grace. Of course she would be bewildered and say she "thought" she would remember Grace, though goodness only knows it was only two months since Grace was waving her goodbye from the doorstep when she left for school.

Then she suddenly remembered the Zoo. Perhaps, if these

changes at school were all being decided upon in a great hurry, one of the junior mistresses had taken a party of children up to London to the Zoo, to be out of the way. The Zoo or Madame Tussaud's.

"Do you know where she spoke from?" asked Mrs. Ellis sharply. "I mean, somebody was in charge, somebody was looking after her?"

"She spoke from 2a Halifax Avenue," said the doctor, "and I don't think you will find she needs any looking after. She sounded very capable, and I heard her turn from the telephone and call to a little boy named Keith to keep quiet and not make so much noise, because she couldn't hear herself speak."

A tremor of a smile appeared on Mrs. Ellis's lips. How clever of Susan to have shown herself so quick and lively. It was just like her, though. She was so advanced for her age. Such a little companion. But Keith . . . It sounded very much as though the school *had* suddenly become co-educational; this was a mixed party being taken to the Zoo or Madame Tussaud's. They were all having lunch, perhaps, at Halifax Avenue, relations of Miss Slater's, or these Fosters, but really the whole thing was most inexcusable, that changes should come about like this, and the children be taken backwards and forwards from High Close to London without any attempt to notify the parents. Mrs. Ellis would write very strongly to Miss Slater about it, and if the school had changed hands and was to be co-educational, she would remove Susan at the end of the term.

"Doctor," she said, "I am ready to go to Halifax Avenue at once, if the authorities here will only permit me to do so."

"Very well," said the doctor. "I am afraid I can't accompany you, but we have arranged for that, and Sister Henderson, who knows all about the matter, will go with you."

He nodded to the policewoman, who opened the door of the waiting room and admitted a severe middle-aged woman in nurse's uniform. Mrs. Ellis said nothing, but her mouth tightened. She was very sure that Sister Henderson had been summoned from Moreton Hill.

"Now, Sister," said the doctor cheerfully, "this is the lady, and you know where to take her and what to do; and I think you will only be a few minutes at Halifax Avenue, and then we hope things will be straightened out."

"Yes, Doctor," said the nurse. She looked across at Mrs. Ellis with a quick professional eye.

"If only I had a hat," thought Mrs. Ellis, "if only I had not come out with nothing but this wretched scarf, and I can feel bits and pieces of hair straggling at the back of my neck. No powder compact on me, no comb, nothing. Of course I must look terrible to them, ungroomed, common..."

She straightened her shoulders, resisted an impulse to put her hands in her pockets. She walked stiffly towards the open door. The doctor, the Sister, and the policewoman conducted her down the steps of the police station to a waiting car. A uniformed chauffeur was to drive, she was thankful to see, and she climbed into the car, followed by the Sister.

The awful thought flashed through her mind that there might be some charge for the night's lodging in the cell and for the cups of tea; also, should she have tipped the policewoman? But anyway, she had no money. It was impossible. She nodded brightly to the policewoman as a sort of sop, to show she had no ill feeling. She felt rather different towards the doctor. She bowed rather formally, coldly. The car drove away.

Mrs. Ellis wondered if she was expected to make conversation with the Sister, who sat stalwart and forbidding at her side. Better not, perhaps. Anything she said might be taken as evidence of mental disturbance. She stared straight in front of her, her gloved hands primly folded on her lap. The traffic jams were very bad, worse than she had ever known. There must be a motor exhibition on. So many American cars on the road. A rally, perhaps...

She did not think much of Halifax Avenue when they came to it. Houses very shabby, and quite a number with windows broken. The car drew up at a small house that had 2a written on the pillar outside. Curious place to take a party of children for lunch. A good Lyons café would have been so much better.

The Sister got out of the car and waited to help Mrs. Ellis. "We shan't be long," she said to the chauffeur.

"That's what you think," said Mrs. Ellis to herself, "but I shall certainly stay with Susan as long as I please."

They walked through the piece of front garden to the front door. The Sister rang the bell. Mrs. Ellis saw a face looking at them from the front window and then quickly dart behind a curtain. Good heavens... It was Dorothy, Wilfred's younger sister, who was a schoolteacher in Birmingham; of course it was, it must be... Everything became clearer; the Fosters must know Dorothy; people to do with education always knew each other, but how awkward, what a bore. Mrs. Ellis had never cared for Dorothy, had stopped writing to her in fact; Dorothy had been so unpleasant when poor Wilfred died, and had insisted that the writing bureau was hers, and rather a nice piece of jewellery that Mrs. Ellis had always understood Wilfred's mother had given to her, Mrs. Ellis; and in fact the whole afternoon after the funeral had been spent in such unpleasant argument and discussion that Mrs. Ellis had been only too glad to send Dorothy away with the jewellery, and the bureau, and a very nice rug to which she had no right at all. Dorothy was the last person Mrs. Ellis wanted to see, and especially in these very trying circumstances, with this Sister at her side, and herself looking so untidy, without a hat or a bag.

There was no time to compose herself because the door opened. No... no, it was not Dorothy after all, but... how strange, so very like her. That same thin nose and rather peeved expression. A little taller, perhaps, and the hair was lighter. The resemblance, though, was really quite extraordinary.

"Are you Mrs. Drew?" asked the Sister.

"Yes," answered the young woman, and then because a child was calling from an inner room she called back over her shoulder impatiently, "Oh, be quiet, Keith, do, for heaven's sake."

A little boy of about five appeared along the hall dragging a toy on wheels. "Dear little fellow," thought Mrs. Ellis, "what a tiresome nagging mother. But where are all the children; where is Susan?"

"This is the person I have brought along for you to identify," said the Sister.

"You had better come inside," said Mrs. Drew rather grudgingly. "I'm afraid everything's in a fearful mess. I've got no help, and you know how it is."

Mrs. Ellis, whose temper was beginning to rise again, stepped neatly over a broken toy on the door mat and, followed by the Sister, went into what she supposed was this Mrs. Drew's living-room. It was certainly a mess. Remains of breakfast not cleared away—or was it lunch?—and toys everywhere, and some material for cutting out spread on a table by the window.

Mrs. Drew laughed apologetically. "What with Keith's toys and my material—I'm a dressmaker in my spare time—and trying to get a decent meal for my husband when he comes home in the evening, life isn't a bed of roses," she said. Her voice was *so* like Dorothy's. Mrs. Ellis could hardly take her eyes off her. The same note of complaint.

"We don't want to take up your time," said the Sister civilly, "if you will just say whether this person is Grace Jackson or not."

The young woman, Mrs. Drew, stared at Mrs. Ellis thoughtfully. "No," she said at length, "I'm sure she is not. I haven't seen Grace for years, not since I married; I used to look her up in Hampstead occasionally before then; but she had quite a different appearance from this person. She was stouter, darker, older too."

"Thank you," said the Sister, "then you are sure you have never seen this lady before?"

"No, never," said Mrs. Drew.

"Very well then," said the Sister, "we needn't detain you any longer."

She turned, as though to go, but Mrs. Ellis was not to be fobbed off with the nonsense that had just passed.

"Excuse me," she said to Mrs. Drew, "there has been a most unfortunate misunderstanding all round, but I understand you spoke to the doctor at the police station at Hampstead this morning, or someone did from this house, and that you have a party of school children here from High Close, my child amongst them. Can you tell me if she is still here; is anyone from the school in charge?"

The Sister was about to intervene, but Mrs. Drew did not notice this, because the little boy had come into the room, dragging his toy. "Keith, I *told* you to stay outside," she nagged.

Mrs. Ellis smiled at the boy. She loved all children. "What a pretty boy," she said, and she held out her hand to him. He took it, holding it tight.

"He doesn't usually take to strangers," said Mrs. Drew, "he's very shy. It makes me wild at times when he won't speak and hangs his head."

"I was shy myself as a child, I understand it," said Mrs. Ellis.

Keith looked up at her with confidence and trust. Her heart warmed to him. But she was forgetting Susan... "We were talking about the party from High Close," she said.

"Yes," said Mrs. Drew, "but that police officer was rather an idiot, I'm afraid, and got everything wrong. My name was Susan Ellis before I married, and I used to go to school at High Close, and that's where the mistake came in. There are no children from the school here."

"What a remarkable coincidence," said Mrs. Ellis, smiling, "because my name is Ellis, and my daughter is called Susan, and an even stranger coincidence is that you are so like a sister of my late husband's."

"Oh?" said Mrs. Drew. "Well, the name is common enough, isn't it? The butcher is Ellis, down the road."

Mrs. Ellis flushed. Not a very tactful remark. And she felt suddenly nervous, too, because the Sister was advancing and was leaning forward as though to take her by the arm and walk to the front door. Mrs. Ellis was determined not to leave the house. Or, at any rate, not to leave it with the Sister.

"I've always found High Close such a homey sort of school," she said rapidly, "but I am rather distressed about the changes they are making there, and I am afraid it is going to be on rather a different tone in the future."

"I don't think they've changed it much," said Mrs. Drew. "Most small children are horrible little beasts, anyway, and it does them good not to see too much of their parents and to be thoroughly well mixed up with every sort of type."

"I'm afraid I don't agree with you on that," said Mrs. Ellis. So peculiar. The tone, the expression might have been Dorothy's.

"Of course," said Mrs. Drew, "I can't help being grateful to old Slaty. She's a funny old stick, but a heart of gold, and she did her best for me, I'll say that, and kept me in the holidays after my mother was killed in a street accident."

"How good of her," said Mrs. Ellis, "and what a dreadful thing for you."

Mrs. Drew laughed. "I was pretty tough, I think," she said. "I don't remember much about it. But I do remember my mother was a very kind person, and pretty too. I think Keith takes after her."

The little boy had not relinquished Mrs. Ellis's hand.

"It's time we were getting along," said the Sister. "Come now, Mrs. Drew has told us all we need to know."

"I don't want to go," said Mrs. Ellis calmly, "and you have no right to make me go."

The Sister exchanged a glance with Mrs. Drew. "I'm sorry," she said in a low tone, "I shall have to get the chauffeur. I wanted them to send another nurse with me, but they said it wouldn't be necessary."

"That's all right," said Mrs. Drew. "So many people are bats these days, one extra doesn't make much difference. But perhaps I had better remove Keith to the kitchen, or she may kidnap him."

Keith, protesting, was carried from the room.

Once again the Sister looked at Mrs. Ellis. "Come along now," she said, "be reasonable."

"No," said Mrs. Ellis, and with a quickness that surprised herself she reached out to the table where Mrs. Drew had been cutting out material, and seized the pair of scissors. "If you come near me, I shall stab you," she said.

The Sister turned and went quickly out of the room and down the steps, calling for the chauffeur. The next few moments passed quickly, but for all this Mrs. Ellis had time to realise that her tactics were brilliant, rivalling the heroes of detective fiction. She crossed the room, opened the long French windows that gave on to a back yard. The window of the bedroom was open; she could hear the chauffeur calling.

"Tradesmen's entrance is ajar," he shouted. "She must have gone this way."

"Let them go on with their confusion," thought Mrs. Ellis, leaning against the bed. "Let them. Good luck to them in their running about. This will take down some of the Sister's weight. Not much running about for her at Moreton Hill. Cups of tea at all hours, and sweet biscuits, while the patients are given bread and water."

The movement went on for some time. Somebody used the telephone. There was more talk. And then, when Mrs. Ellis was nearly dozing off against the bed valance, she heard the car drive away. Everything was silent. Mrs. Ellis listened. The only sound was the little boy playing in the hall below. She crept to the door and listened once again. The wheeled toy was being dragged backwards and forwards, up and down the hall. And there was a new sound coming from the living-room. The sound of a sewing-machine going at great speed. Mrs. Drew was at work.

The Sister and the chauffeur had gone. An hour, two hours must have passed since they had left. Mrs. Ellis glanced at the clock on the mantelpiece. It was two o'clock. What an untidy, scattered sort of room, everything all over the place. Shoes in the middle of the floor, a coat flung down on a chair, and Keith's cot had not been made up; the blankets were rumpled anyhow.

"Badly brought up," thought Mrs. Ellis, "and such rough, casual manners. But poor girl, if she had no mother..."

She took a last glance round the room, and she saw with a shrug of her shoulder that even Mrs. Drew's calendar had a printing error. It said 1952 instead of 1932. How careless...

She tiptoed to the head of the stairs. The door of the living-room was shut. The sound of the sewing-machine came at breathless speed. "They must be hard up," thought Mrs. Ellis, "if she has to do dressmaking. I wonder what her husband does for a living." Softly she crept downstairs. She made no sound. And if she had, the sound of the sewing-machine would have covered it. As she passed the living-room door it opened. The boy stood there, staring at her. He said nothing. He smiled. Mrs. Ellis smiled back at him. She could not help herself. She had a feeling that he would not give her away.

"Shut the door, Keith, *do*," nagged his mother from within. The door slammed. The sound of the sewing-machine became more distant, muffled. Mrs. Ellis let herself out of the house and slipped away... She turned northward, like an animal scenting direction, because northward was her home.

She was soon swallowed up in traffic, the buses swinging

past her in the Finchley Road. Her feet began to ache and she was tired, but she could not take a bus or summon a taxi because she had no money. No one looked at her; no one bothered with her; they were all intent upon their business, either going from home or returning, and it seemed to Mrs. Ellis, as she toiled up the hill towards Hampstead, that for the first time in her life she was friendless and alone. She wanted her house, her home, the consolation of her own surroundings; she wanted to take up her normal, everyday life that had been interrupted in so brutal a fashion. There was so much to straighten out, so much to do, and Mrs. Ellis did not know where to begin or whom to ask for help.

"I want everything to be as it was before that walk yesterday," thought Mrs. Ellis, her back aching, her feet throbbing. "I want my home. I want my little girl."

And here was the heath once again. This was where she had stood before crossing the road. She even remembered what she had been thinking about. She had been planning to buy a red bicycle for Susan. Something light—but strong, a good make.

The memory of the bicycle made her forget her troubles, her fatigue. As soon as all this muddle and confusion were over, she would buy a red bicycle for Susan.

Why, though, for the second time, that screech of brakes when she crossed the road, and the vacant face of the laundry boy looking down at her?

# KISS ME AGAIN, STRANGER

I LOOKED around for a bit, after leaving the army and before settling down, and then I found myself a job up Hampstead way, in a garage it was, at the bottom of Haverstock Hill near Chalk Farm, and it suited me fine. I'd always been one for tinkering with engines, and in REME that was my work and I was trained to it—it had always come easy to me, anything mechanical.

My idea of having a good time was to lie on my back in my greasy overalls under a car's belly, or a lorry's, with a spanner in my hand, working on some old bolt or screw, with the smell of oil about me, and someone starting up an engine, and the other chaps around clattering their tools and whistling. I never minded the smell or the dirt. As my old Mum used to say when I'd be that way as a kid, mucking about with a grease can, "It won't hurt him, it's clean dirt," and so it is, with engines.

The boss at the garage was a good fellow, easy-going, cheerful, and he saw I was keen on my work. He wasn't much of a mechanic himself, so he gave me the repair jobs, which was what I liked.

I didn't live with my old Mum—she was too far off, over Shepperton way, and I saw no point in spending half the day getting to and from my work. I like to be handy, have it on the spot, as it were. So I had a bedroom with a couple called Thompson, only about ten minutes' walk away from the garage. Nice people, they were. He was in the shoe business, cobbler I suppose he'd be called, and Mrs. Thompson cooked the meals and kept the house for him over the shop. I used to eat with them, breakfast and supper—we always had a cooked supper—and being the only lodger I was treated as family.

I'm one for routine. I like to get on with my job, and then when the day's work's over settle down to a paper and a smoke and a bit of music on the wireless, variety or something of the sort, and then turn in early. I never had much use for girls, not even when I was doing my time in the army. I was out in the Middle East, too, Port Said and that.

No, I was happy enough living with the Thompsons, carrying on much the same day after day, until that one night, when it happened. Nothing's been the same since. Nor ever will be. I don't know...

The Thompsons had gone to see their married daughter up at Highgate. They asked me if I'd like to go along, but somehow I didn't fancy barging in, so instead of staying home alone after leaving the garage I went down to the picture palace, and taking a look at the poster saw it was cowboy and Indian stuff—there was a picture of a cowboy sticking a knife into the Indian's guts. I like that—proper baby I am for westerns—so I paid my one and twopence and went inside. I handed my slip of paper to the usherette and said, "Back row, please," because I like sitting far back and leaning my head against the board.

Well, then I saw her. They dress the girls up no end in some of these places, velvet tams and all, making them proper guys. They hadn't made a guy out of this one, though. She had copper hair, page-boy style I think they call it, and blue eyes, the kind that look short-sighted but see further than you think, and go dark by night, nearly black, and her mouth was sulky-looking, as if she was fed up, and it would take someone giving her the world to make her smile. She hadn't freckles, nor a milky skin, but warmer than that, more like a peach, and natural too. She was small and slim, and her velvet coat—blue it was—fitted her close, and the cap on the back of her head showed up her copper hair.

I bought a programme—not that I wanted one, but to delay going in through the curtain—and I said to her, "What's the picture like?"

She didn't look at me. She just went on staring into nothing, at the opposite wall. "The knifing's amateur," she said, "but you can always sleep."

I couldn't help laughing. I could see she was serious though. She wasn't trying to have me on or anything.

"That's no advertisement," I said. "What if the manager heard you?"

Then she looked at me. She turned those blue eyes in my direction, still fed-up they were, not interested, but there was something in them I'd not seen before, and I've never seen it since, a kind of laziness like someone waking from a long dream and glad to find you there. Cats' eyes have that gleam sometimes, when you stroke them, and they purr and curl themselves into a ball and let you do anything you want. She looked at me this way a moment, and there was a smile lurking somewhere behind her mouth if you gave it a chance, and tearing my slip of paper in half she said, "I'm not paid to advertise. I'm paid to look like this and lure you inside."

She drew aside the curtains and flashed her torch in the darkness. I couldn't see a thing. It was pitch black, like it always is at first until you get used to it and begin to make out the shapes of the other people sitting there, but there were two great heads on the screen and some chap saying to the other, "If you don't come clean I'll put a bullet through you," and somebody broke a pane of glass and a woman screamed.

"Looks all right to me," I said, and began groping for somewhere to sit.

She said, "This isn't the picture, it's the trailer for next week," and she flicked on her torch and showed me a seat in the back row, one away from the gangway.

I sat through the advertisements and the news reel, and then some chap came and played the organ, and the colours of the curtains over the screen went purple and gold and green— funny, I suppose they think they have to give you your money's worth—and looking around I saw the house was half empty— and I guessed the girl had been right, the big picture wasn't going to be much, and that's why nobody much was there.

Just before the hall went dark again she came sauntering down the aisle. She had a tray of ice-creams, but she didn't even bother to call them out and try and sell them. She could have been walking in her sleep, so when she went up the other aisle I beckoned to her.

"Got a sixpenny one?" I said.

She looked across at me. I might have been something dead under her feet, and then she must have recognized me, because that half-smile came back again, and the lazy look in the eye, and she walked round the back of the seats to me.

"Wafer or cornet?" she said.

I didn't want either, to tell the truth. I just wanted to buy something from her and keep her talking.

"Which do you recommend?" I asked.

She shrugged her shoulders. "Cornets last longer," she said, and put one in my hand before I had time to give her my choice.

"How about one for you too?" I said.

"No thanks," she said, "I saw them made."

And she walked off, and the place went dark, and there I was sitting with a great sixpenny cornet in my hand looking a fool. The damn thing slopped all over the edge of the holder, spilling on to my shirt, and I had to ram the frozen stuff into my mouth as quick as I could for fear it would all go on my knees, and I turned sideways, because someone came and sat in the empty seat beside the gangway.

I finished it at last, and cleaned myself up with my pocket handkerchief, and then concentrated on the story flashing across the screen. It was a western all right, carts lumbering over prairies, and a train full of bullion being held to ransom, and the heroine in breeches one moment and full evening dress the next. That's the way pictures should be, not a bit like real life at all; but as I watched the story I began to notice the whiff of scent in the air, and I didn't know what it was or where it came from, but it was there just the same. There was a man to the right of me, and on my left were two empty seats, and it certainly wasn't the people in front, and I couldn't keep turning round and sniffing.

I'm not a great one for liking scent. It's too often cheap and nasty, but this was different. There was nothing stale about it, or stuffy, or strong; it was like the flowers they sell up in the West End in the big flower shops before you get them on the barrows—three bob a bloom sort of touch, rich chaps buy them for actresses and such—and it was so darn good, the smell of it there, in that murky old picture palace full of cigarette smoke, that it nearly drove me mad.

At last I turned right round in my seat, and I spotted where it came from. It came from the girl, the usherette; she was leaning on the back board behind me, her arms folded across it.

"Don't fidget," she said. "You're wasting one and twopence. Watch the screen."

But not out loud, so that anyone could hear. In a whisper, for me alone. I couldn't help laughing to myself. The cheek of it! I knew where the scent came from now, and somehow it made me enjoy the picture more. It was as though she was beside me in one of the empty seats and we were looking at the story together.

When it was over, and the lights went on, I saw I'd sat

through the last showing and it was nearly ten. Everyone was clearing off for the night. So I waited a bit, and then she came down with her torch and started squinting under the seats to see if anybody had dropped a glove or a purse, the way they do and only remember about afterwards when they get home, and she took no more notice of me than if I'd been a rag which no one would bother to pick up.

I stood up in the back row, alone—the house was clear now—and when she came to me she said, "Move over, you're blocking the gangway," and flashed about with her torch, but there was nothing there, only an empty packet of Player's which the cleaners would throw away in the morning. Then she straightened herself and looked me up and down, and taking off the ridiculous cap from the back of her head that suited her so well she fanned herself with it and said, "Sleeping here tonight?" and then went off, whistling under her breath, and disappeared through the curtains.

It was proper maddening. I'd never been taken so much with a girl in my life. I went into the vestibule after her, but she had gone through a door to the back, behind the box-office place, and the commissionaire chap was already getting the doors to and fixing them for the night. I went out and stood in the street and waited. I felt a bit of a fool, because the odds were that she would come out with a bunch of others, the way girls do. There was the one who had sold me my ticket, and I dare say there were other usherettes up in the balcony, and perhaps a cloak-room attendant too, and they'd all be giggling together, and I wouldn't have the nerve to go up to her.

In a few minutes, though, she came swinging out of the place alone. She had a mac on, belted, and her hands in her pockets, and she had no hat. She walked straight up the street, and she didn't look to right or left of her. I followed, scared that she would turn round and see me off, but she went on walking, fast and direct, staring straight in front of her, and as she moved her copper page-boy hair swung with her shoulders.

Presently she hesitated, then crossed over and stood waiting for a bus. There was a queue of four or five people, so she didn't see me join the queue, and when the bus came she climbed on to it, ahead of the others, and I climbed too, without the slightest notion where it was going, and I couldn't have cared less. Up the stairs she went with me after her, and settled herself in the back seat, yawning, and closed her eyes.

I sat myself down beside her, nervous as a kitten, the point being that I never did that sort of thing as a rule and expected a rocket, and when the conductor stumped up and asked for fares I said, "Two sixpennies, please," because I reckoned she would never be going the whole distance and this would be bound to cover her fare and mine too.

He raised his eyebrows—they like to think themselves smart, some of these fellows—and he said, "Look out for the bumps when the driver changes gear. He's only just passed his test." And he went down the stairs chuckling, telling himself he was no end of a wag, no doubt.

The sound of his voice woke the girl, and she looked at me out of her sleepy eyes, and looked too at the tickets in my hand—she must have seen by the colour they were sixpennies—and she smiled, the first real smile I had got out of her that evening, and said without any sort of surprise, "Hullo, stranger."

I took out a cigarette, to put myself at ease, and offered her one, but she wouldn't take it. She just closed her eyes again, to settle herself to sleep. Then, seeing there was no one else to notice up on the top deck, only an Air Force chap in the front slopped over a newspaper, I put out my hand and pulled her head down on my shoulder, and got my arm round her, snug and comfortable, thinking of course she'd throw it off and blast me to hell. She didn't though. She gave a sort of laugh to herself, and settled down like as if she might have been in an armchair, and she said, "It's not every night I get a free ride and a free pillow. Wake me at the bottom of the hill, before we get to the cemetery."

I didn't know what hill she meant, or what cemetery, but I wasn't going to wake her, not me. I had paid for two sixpennies, and I was darn well going to get value for my money.

So we sat there together, jogging along in the bus, very close and very pleasant, and I thought to myself that it was a lot more fun than sitting at home in the bed-sit reading the football news, or spending an evening up Highgate at Mr. and Mrs. Thompson's daughter's place.

Presently I got more daring, and let my head lean against hers, and tightened up my arm a bit, not too obvious-like, but nicely. Anyone coming up the stairs to the top deck would have taken us for a courting couple.

Then, after we had had about fourpenny-worth, I got anxious. The old bus wouldn't be turning round and going back again, when we reached the sixpenny limit; it would pack up for the night, we'd have come to the terminus. And there we'd be, the girl and I, stuck out somewhere at the back of beyond, with no return bus, and I'd got about six bob in my pocket and no more. Six bob would never pay for a taxi, not with a tip and all. Besides, there probably wouldn't be any taxis going.

What a fool I'd been not to come out with more money. It was silly, perhaps, to let it worry me, but I'd acted on impulse right from the start, and if only I'd known how the evening was going to turn out I'd have had my wallet filled. It wasn't often I went out with a girl, and I hate a fellow who can't do the thing in style. Proper slap-up do at a Corner House—they're good these days with that help-yourself service—and if she had a fancy for something stronger than coffee or orangeade, well, of course as late as this it wasn't much use, but nearer home I knew where to go. There was a pub where my boss went, and you paid for your gin and kept it there, and could go in and have a drink from your bottle when you felt like it. They have the same sort of racket at the posh night clubs up West, I'm told, but they make you pay through the nose for it.

Anyway, here I was riding a bus to the Lord knows where, with my girl beside me—I called her "my girl" just as if she really was and we were courting—and bless me if I had the money to take her home. I began to fidget about, from sheer nerves, and I fumbled in one pocket after another, in case by a piece of luck I should come across a half-crown, or even a ten-bob note I had forgotten all about, and I suppose I disturbed her with all this, because she suddenly pulled my ear and said, "Stop rocking the boat."

Well, I mean to say... It just got me. I can't explain why. She held my ear a moment before she pulled it, like as though she were feeling the skin and liked it, and then she just gave it a lazy tug. It's the kind of thing anyone would do to a child, and the way she said it, as if she had known me for years and we were out picnicking together, "Stop rocking the boat." Chummy, matey, yet better than either.

"Look here," I said, "I'm awfully sorry, I've been and done a darn silly thing. I took tickets to the terminus because I wanted to sit beside you, and when we get there we'll be turned out of the bus, and it will be miles from anywhere, and I've only got six bob in my pocket."

"You've got legs, haven't you?" she said.

"What d'you mean, I've got legs?"

"They're meant to walk on. Mine were," she answered.

Then I knew it didn't matter, and she wasn't angry either, and the evening was going to be all right. I cheered up in a second, and gave her a squeeze, just to show I appreciated her being such a sport—most girls would have torn me to shreds—and I said, "We haven't passed a cemetery, as far as I know. Does it matter very much?"

"Oh, there'll be others," she said. "I'm not particular."

I didn't know what to make of that. I thought she wanted to get out at the cemetery stopping point because it was her nearest stop for home, like the way you say, "Put me down at Woolworth's" if you live handy. I puzzled over it for a bit, and then I said, "How do you mean, there'll be others? It's not a thing you see often along a bus route."

"I was speaking in general terms," she answered. "Don't bother to talk, I like you silent best."

It wasn't a slap on the face, the way she said it. Fact was, I knew what she meant. Talking's all very pleasant with people like Mr. and Mrs. Thompson, over supper, and you say how the day has gone, and one of you reads a bit out of the paper, and the other says, "Fancy, there now," and so it goes on, in bits and pieces until one of you yawns, and somebody says, "Who's for bed?" Or it's nice enough with a chap like the boss, having a cuppa mid-morning, or about three when there's nothing doing, "I'll tell you what I think, those blokes in the government are making a mess of things, no better than the last lot," and then we'll be interrupted with someone coming to fill up with petrol. And I like talking to my old Mum when I go and see her, which I don't do often enough, and she tells me how she spanked my bottom when I was a kid, and I sit on the kitchen table like I did then, and she bakes rock cakes and gives me peel, saying, "You always were one for peel." That's talk, that's conversation.

But I didn't want to talk to my girl. I just wanted to keep my arm round her the way I was doing, and rest my chin against her head, and that's what she meant when she said she liked me silent. I liked it too.

One last thing bothered me a bit, and that was whether I could kiss her before the bus stopped and we were turned out at the terminus. I mean, putting an arm round a girl is one thing, and kissing her is another. It takes a little time as a rule to warm up. You start off with a long evening ahead of you, and by the time you've been to a picture or a concert, and then had something to eat and to drink, well, you've got yourselves acquainted, and it's the usual thing to end up with a bit of kissing and a cuddle, the girls expect it. Truth to tell, I was never much of a one for kissing. There was a girl I walked out with back home, before I went into the army, and she was quite a good sort, I liked her. But her teeth were a bit prominent, and even if you shut your eyes and tried to forget who it was you were kissing, well, you knew it was her, and there was nothing to it. Good old Doris from next door. But the opposite kind are even worse, the ones that grab you and nearly eat you. You come across plenty of them, when you're in uniform. They're much too eager, and they muss you about, and you get the feeling they can't wait for a chap to get busy about them. I don't mind saying it used to make me sick. Put me dead off, and that's a fact. I suppose I was born fussy. I don't know.

But now, this evening in the bus, it was all quite different. I don't know what it was about the girl—the sleepy eyes, and the copper hair, and somehow not seeming to care if I was there yet liking me at the same time; I hadn't found anything like this before. So I said to myself, "Now, shall I risk it, or shall I wait?" and I knew, from the way the driver was going and the conductor was whistling below and saying "goodnight" to the people getting off, that the final stop couldn't be far away; and my heart began to thump under my coat, and my neck grew hot below the collar—darn silly, only a kiss you know, she couldn't kill me—and then . . . It was like diving off a spring-board. I thought, "Here goes," and I bent down, and turned her face to me, and lifted her chin with my hand, and kissed her good and proper.

Well, if I was poetical, I'd say what happened then was a revelation. But I'm not poetical, and I can only say that she kissed me back, and it lasted a long time, and it wasn't a bit like Doris.

Then the bus stopped with a jerk, and the conductor called out in a sing-song voice, "All out, please." Frankly, I could have wrung his neck.

She gave me a kick on the ankle. "Come on, move," she said, and I stumbled from my seat and racketed down the stairs, she following behind, and there we were, standing in a street. It was beginning to rain too, not badly but just enough to make you notice and want to turn up the collar of your coat, and we were right at the end of a great wide street, with deserted unlighted shops on either side, the end of the world it looked to me, and sure enough there was a hill over to the left, and at the bottom of the hill a cemetery. I could see the railings and the white tombstones behind, and it stretched a long way, nearly half-way up the hill. There were acres of it.

"God darn it," I said, "is this the place you meant?"

"Could be," she said, looking over her shoulder vaguely, and then she took my arm. "What about a cup of coffee first?" she said.

First. . .? I wondered if she meant before the long trudge home, or was this home? It didn't really matter. It wasn't much after eleven. And I could do with a cup of coffee, and a sandwich too. There was a stall across the road, and they hadn't shut up shop.

We walked over to it, and the driver was there too, and the conductor, and the Air Force fellow who had been up in front on the top deck. They were ordering cups of tea and sandwiches, and we had the same, only coffee. They cut them tasty at the stalls, the sandwiches, I've noticed it before, nothing stingy about it, good slices of ham between thick white bread, and the coffee is piping hot, full cups too, good value, and I thought to myself "Six bob will see this lot all right."

I noticed my girl looking at the Air Force chap, sort of thoughtful-like, as though she might have seen him before, and he looked at her too. I couldn't blame him for that. I didn't mind either; when you're out with a girl it gives you a kind of pride if other chaps notice her. And you couldn't miss this one. Not my girl.

Then she turned her back on him, deliberate, and leant with her elbows on the stall, sipping her hot coffee, and I stood beside her doing the same. We weren't stuck up or anything, we were pleasant and polite enough, saying good evening all round, but anyone could tell that we were together, the girl and I, we were on our own. I liked that. Funny, it did something to me inside, gave me a protective feeling. For all they knew we might have been a married couple on our way home.

They were chaffing a bit, the other three and the chap serving the sandwiches and tea, but we didn't join in.

"You want to watch out, in that uniform," said the conductor to the Air Force fellow, "or you'll end up like those others. It's late too, to be out on your own."

They all started laughing. I didn't quite see the point, but I supposed it was a joke.

"I've been awake a long time," said the Air Force fellow. "I know a bad lot when I see one."

"That's what the others said, I shouldn't wonder," remarked the driver, "and we know what happened to them. Makes you shudder. But why pick on the Air Force, that's what I want to know?"

"It's the colour of our uniform," said the fellow. "You can spot it in the dark."

They went on laughing in that way. I lighted up a cigarette, but my girl wouldn't have one.

"I blame the war for all that's gone wrong with the women," said the coffee-stall bloke, wiping a cup and hanging it up behind. "Turned a lot of them barmy, in my opinion. They don't know the difference between right or wrong."

"'Tisn't that, it's sport that's the trouble," said the conductor. "Develops their muscles and that, what weren't never meant to be developed. Take my two youngsters, f'r instance. The girl can knock the boy down any time, she's a proper little bully. Makes you think."

"That's right," agreed the driver, "equality of the sexes, they call it, don't they? It's the vote that did it. We ought never to have given them the vote."

"Garn," said the Air Force chap, "giving them the vote didn't turn the women barmy. They've always been the same, under the skin. The people out East know how to treat 'em. They keep 'em shut up, out there. That's the answer. Then you don't get any trouble."

"I don't know what my old woman would say if I tried to shut her up," said the driver. And they all started laughing again.

My girl plucked at my sleeve and I saw she had finished her coffee. She motioned with her head towards the street.

"Want to go home?" I said.

Silly. I somehow wanted the others to believe we were going home. She didn't answer. She just went striding off, her hands in the pockets of her mac. I said goodnight, and followed her, but not before I noticed the Air Force fellow staring after her over his cup of tea.

She walked off along the street, and it was still raining, dreary somehow, made you want to be sitting over a fire somewhere snug, and when she had crossed the street, and had come to the railings outside the cemetery she stopped, and looked up at me, and smiled.

"What now?" I said.

"Tombstones are flat," she said, "sometimes."

"What if they are?" I asked, bewildered-like.

"You can lie down on them," she said.

She turned and strolled along, looking at the railings, and then she came to one that was bent wide, and the next beside it broken, and she glanced up at me and smiled again.

"It's always the same," she said. "You're bound to find a gap if you look long enough."

She was through that gap in the railings as quick as a knife through butter. You could have knocked me flat.

"Here, hold on," I said, "I'm not as small as you."

But she was off and away, wandering among the graves. I got through the gap, puffing and blowing a bit, and then I looked around, and bless me if she wasn't lying on a long flat gravestone, with her arms under her head and her eyes closed.

Well, I wasn't expecting anything. I mean, it had been in my mind to see her home and that. Date her up for the next evening. Of course, seeing as it was late, we could have stopped a bit when we came to the doorway of her place. She needn't have gone in right away. But lying there on the gravestone wasn't hardly natural.

I sat down, and took her hand.

"You'll get wet lying there," I said. Feeble, but I didn't know what else to say.

"I'm used to that," she said.

She opened her eyes and looked at me. There was a street light not far away, outside the railings, so it wasn't all that dark, and anyway in spite of the rain the night wasn't pitch black, more murky somehow. I wish I knew how to tell about her eyes, but I'm not one for fancy talk. You know how a luminous watch shines in the dark. I've got one myself. When you wake up in the night, there it is on your wrist, like a friend. Somehow my girl's eyes shone like that, but they were lovely too. And they weren't lazy cat's eyes any more. They were loving and gentle, and they were sad, too, all at the same time.

"Used to lying in the rain?" I said.

"Brought up to it," she answered. "They gave us a name in the shelters. The dead-end kids, they used to call us, in the war days."

"Weren't you never evacuated?" I asked.

"Not me," she said. "I never could stop any place. I always came back."

"Parents living?"

"No. Both of them killed by the bomb that smashed my home." She didn't speak tragic-like. Just ordinary.

"Bad luck," I said.

She didn't answer that one. And I sat there, holding her hand, wanting to take her home.

"You been on your job some time, at the picture-house?" I asked.

"About three weeks," she said. "I don't stop anywhere long. I'll be moving on again soon."

"Why's that?"

"Restless," she said.

She put up her hands suddenly and took my face and held it. It was gentle the way she did it, not as you'd think.

"You've got a good kind face. I like it," she said to me.

It was queer. The way she said it made me feel daft and soft, not sort of excited like I had been in the bus, and I thought to myself, well, maybe this is it, I've found a girl at last I really want. But not for an evening, casual. For going steady.

"Got a bloke?" I asked.

"No," she said.

"I mean, regular."

"No, never."

It was a funny line of talk to be having in a cemetery, and she lying there like some figure carved on the old tombstone.

"I haven't got a girl either," I said. "Never think about it, the way other chaps do. Faddy, I guess. And then I'm keen on my job. Work in a garage, mechanic you know, repairs, anything that's going. Good pay. I've saved a bit, besides what I send my old Mum. I live in digs. Nice people, Mr. and Mrs. Thompson, and my boss at the garage is a nice chap too. I've never been lonely, and I'm not lonely now. But since I've seen you, it's made me think. You know, it's not going to be the same any more."

She never interrupted once, and somehow it was like speaking my thoughts aloud.

"Going home to the Thompsons is all very pleasant and nice," I said, "and you couldn't wish for kinder people. Good grub too, and we chat a bit after supper, and listen to the wireless. But d'you know, what I want now is different. I want to come along and fetch you from the cinema, when the programme's over, and you'd be standing there by the curtains, seeing the people out, and you'd give me a bit of a wink to show me you'd be going through to change your clothes and I could wait for you. And then you'd come out into the street, like you did tonight, but you wouldn't go off on your own, you'd take my arm, and if you didn't want to wear your coat I'd carry it for you, or a parcel maybe, or whatever you had. Then we'd go off to the Corner House or some place for supper, handy. We'd have a table reserved—they'd know us, the waitresses and them; they'd keep back something special, just for us."

I could picture it too, clear as anything. The table with the ticket on "Reserved." The waitress nodding at us, "Got curried eggs tonight." And we going through to get our trays, and my girl acting like she didn't know me, and me laughing to myself.

"D'you see what I mean?" I said to her. "It's not just being friends, it's more than that."

I don't know if she heard. She lay there looking up at me, touching my ear and my chin in that funny, gentle way. You'd say she was sorry for me.

"I'd like to buy you things," I said, "flowers sometimes. It's nice to see a girl with a flower tucked in her dress, it looks clean and fresh. And for special occasions, birthdays, Christmas, and that, something you'd seen in a shop window, and wanted, but hadn't liked to go in and ask the price. A brooch perhaps, or a bracelet, something pretty. And I'd go in and get it when you weren't with me, and it'd cost much more than my week's pay, but I wouldn't mind."

I could see the expression on her face, opening the parcel. And she'd put it on, what I'd bought, and we'd go out together, and she'd be dressed up a bit for the purpose, nothing glaring I don't mean, but something that took the eye. You know, saucy.

"It's not fair to talk about getting married," I said, "not in these days, when everything's uncertain. A fellow doesn't mind the uncertainty, but it's hard on a girl. Cooped up in a couple of rooms maybe, and queueing and rations and all. They like their freedom, and being in a job, and not being tied down, the same as us. But it's nonsense the way they were talking back in the coffee stall just now. About girls not being the same as in old days, and the war to blame. As for the way they treat them out East—I've seen some of it. I suppose that fellow meant to be funny, they're all smart Alicks in the Air Force, but it was a silly line of talk, I thought."

She dropped her hands to her side and closed her eyes. It was getting quite wet there on the tombstone. I was worried for her, though she had her mac of course, but her legs and feet were damp in her thin stockings and shoes.

"You weren't ever in the Air Force, were you?" she said.

Queer. Her voice had gone quite hard. Sharp, and different. Like as if she was anxious about something, scared even.

"Not me," I said, "I served my time with REME. Proper lot they were. No swank, no nonsense. You know where you are with them."

"I'm glad," she said. "You're good and kind. I'm glad."

I wondered if she'd known some fellow in the RAF who had let her down. They're a wild crowd, the ones I've come across. And I remembered the way she'd looked at the boy drinking his tea at the stall. Reflective, somehow. As if she was thinking back. I couldn't expect her not to have been around a bit, with her looks, and then brought up to play about the shelters, with-

out parents, like she said. But I didn't want to think of her being hurt by anyone.

"Why, what's wrong with them?" I said. "What's the RAF
done to you?"

"They smashed my home," she said.

"That was the Germans, not our fellows."

"It's all the same, they're killers, aren't they?" she said.

I looked down at her, lying on the tombstone, and her voice
wasn't hard any more, like when she'd asked me if I'd been in
the Air Force, but it was tired, and sad, and oddly lonely, and it
did something queer to my stomach, right in the pit of it, so
that I wanted to do the darndest silliest thing and take her
home with me, back to where I lived with Mr. and Mrs.
Thompson, and say to Mrs. Thompson—she was a kind old
soul, she wouldn't mind—"Look, this is my girl. Look after
her." Then I'd know she'd be safe, she'd be all right, nobody
could do anything to hurt her. That was the thing I was afraid
of suddenly, that someone would come along and hurt my girl.

I bent down and put my arms round her and lifted her up
close.

"Listen," I said, "it's raining hard. I'm going to take you
home. You'll catch your death, lying here on the wet stone."

"No," she said, her hands on my shoulders, "nobody ever
sees me home. You're going back where you belong, alone."

"I won't leave you here," I said.

"Yes, that's what I want you to do. If you refuse I shall be angry. You wouldn't want that, would you?"

I stared at her, puzzled. And her face was queer in the murky
old light there, whiter than before, but it was beautiful, Jesus
Christ, it was beautiful. That's blasphemy. But I can't say it no
other way.

"What do you want me to do?" I asked.

"I want you to go and leave me here, and not look back,"
she said, "like someone dreaming, sleep-walking, they call it.

Go back walking through the rain. It will take you hours. It doesn't matter, you're young and strong and you've got long legs. Go back to your room, wherever it is, and get into bed, and go to sleep, and wake and have your breakfast in the morning, and go off to work, the same as you always do."

"What about you?"

"Never mind about me. Just go."

"Can I call for you at the cinema tomorrow night? Can it be like what I was telling you, you know...going steady?"

She didn't answer. She only smiled. She sat quite still, looking in my face, and then she closed her eyes and threw back her head and said, "Kiss me again, stranger."

I left her, like she said. I didn't look back. I climbed through the railings of the cemetery, out on to the road. No one seemed to be about, and the coffee stall by the bus stop had closed down, the boards were up.

I started walking the way the bus had brought us. The road was straight, going on for ever. A High Street it must have been. There were shops on either side, and it was right away north-east of London, nowhere I'd ever been before. I was proper lost, but it didn't seem to matter. I felt like a sleepwalker, just as she said.

I kept thinking of her all the time. There was nothing else, only her face in front of me as I walked. They had a word for it in the army, when a girl gets a fellow that way, so he can't see straight or hear right or know what he's doing; and I thought it a lot of cock, or it only happened to drunks, and now I knew it was true and it had happened to me. I wasn't going to worry any more about how she'd get home; she'd told me not to, and she must have lived handy, she'd never have ridden out so far else, though it was funny living such a way from her work. But maybe in time she'd tell me more, bit by bit. I wouldn't drag it from her. I had one thing fixed in my mind, and that was to pick her up the next evening from the picture palace. It was firm and set, and nothing would budge me from that. The hours in between would just be a blank for me until ten p.m. came round.

I went on walking in the rain, and presently a lorry came along and I thumbed a lift, and the driver took me a good part of the way before he had to turn left in the other direction, and so I got down and walked again, and it must have been close on three when I got home.

I would have felt bad, in an ordinary way, knocking up Mr. Thompson to let me in, and it had never happened before either, but I was all lit up inside from loving my girl, and I didn't seem to mind. He came down at last and opened the door. I had to ring several times before he heard, and there he was, grey with sleep, poor old chap, his pyjamas all crumpled from the bed.

"Whatever happened to you?" he said. "We've been worried, the wife and me. We thought you'd been knocked down, run over. We came back here and found the house empty and your supper not touched."

"I went to the pictures," I said.

"The pictures?" He stared up at me, in the passage-way. "The pictures stop at ten o'clock."

"I know," I said, "I went walking after that. Sorry. Good-night."

And I climbed up the stairs to my room, leaving the old chap muttering to himself and bolting the door, and I heard Mrs. Thompson calling from her bedroom, "What is it? Is it him? Is he come home?"

I'd put them to trouble and to worry, and I ought to have gone in there and then and apologized, but I couldn't some-how, it wouldn't have come right; so I shut my door and threw off my clothes and got into bed, and it was like as if she was with me still, my girl, in the darkness.

They were a bit quiet at breakfast the next morning, Mr.

and Mrs. Thompson. They didn't look at me. Mrs. Thompson gave me my kipper without a word, and he went on looking at his newspaper.

I ate my breakfast, and then I said, "I hope you had a nice evening up at Highgate?" and Mrs. Thompson, with her mouth a bit tight, she said, "Very pleasant, thank you, we were home by ten," and she gave a little sniff and poured Mr. Thompson out another cup of tea.

We went on being quiet, no one saying a word, and then Mrs. Thompson said, "Will you be in to supper this evening?" and I said, "No, I don't think so. I'm meeting a friend," and then I saw the old chap look at me over his spectacles.

"If you're going to be late," he said, "we'd best take the key for you."

Then he went on reading his paper. You could tell they were proper hurt that I didn't tell them anything, or say where I was going.

I went off to work, and we were busy at the garage that day, one job after the other came along, and any other time I wouldn't have minded. I liked a full day and often worked overtime, but today I wanted to get away before the shops closed; I hadn't thought about anything else since the idea came into my head.

It was getting on for half past four, and the boss came to me and said, "I promised the doctor he'd have his Austin this evening, I said you'd be through with it by seven-thirty. That's OK, isn't it?"

My heart sank. I'd counted on getting off early, because of what I wanted to do. Then I thought quickly that if the boss let me off now, and I went out to the shop before it closed, and came back again to do the job on the Austin, it would be all right, so I said, "I don't mind working a bit of overtime, but I'd like to slip out now, for half an hour, if you're going to be here. There's something I want to buy before the shops shut."

He told me that suited him, so I took off my overalls and washed and got my coat and I went off to the line of shops down at the bottom of Haverstock Hill. I knew the one I wanted. It was a jeweller's, where Mr. Thompson used to take his clock to be repaired, and it wasn't a place where they sold trash at all, but good stuff, solid silver frames and that, and cutlery.

There were rings, of course, and a few fancy bangles, but I didn't like the look of them. All the girls in the NAAFI used to wear bangles with charms on them, quite common it was, and I went on staring in at the window and then I spotted it, right at the back.

It was a brooch. Quite small, not much bigger than your thumbnail, but with a nice blue stone on it and a pin at the back, and it was shaped like a heart. That was what got me, the shape. I stared at it a bit, and there wasn't a ticket to it, which meant it would cost a bit, but I went in and asked to have a look at it. The jeweller got it out of the window for me, and he gave it a bit of a polish and turned it this way and that, and I saw it pinned on my girl, showing up nice on her frock or her jumper, and I knew this was it.

"I'll take it," I said, and then asked him the price.

I swallowed a bit when he told me, but I took out my wallet and counted the notes, and he put the heart in a box wrapped up careful with cotton wool, and made a neat package of it, tied with fancy string. I knew I'd have to get an advance from the boss before I went off work that evening, but he was a good chap and I was certain he'd give it to me.

I stood outside the jeweller's, with the packet for my girl safe in my breast pocket, and I heard the church clock strike a quarter to five. There was time to slip down to the cinema and make sure she understood about the date for the evening, and then I'd beat it fast up the road and get back to the garage, and I'd have the Austin done by the time the doctor wanted it.

When I got to the cinema my heart was beating like a sledge-hammer and I could hardly swallow. I kept picturing to myself how she'd look, standing there by the curtains going in, with the velvet jacket and the cap on the back of her head.

There was a bit of a queue outside, and I saw they'd changed the programme. The poster of the western had gone, with the cowboy throwing a knife in the Indian's guts, and they had instead a lot of girls dancing, and some chap prancing in front of them with a walking-stick. It was a musical.

I went in, and didn't go near the box office but looked straight to the curtains, where she'd be. There was an usherette there all right, but it wasn't her. This was a great tall girl, who looked silly in the clothes, and she was trying to do two things at once—tear off the slips of tickets as the people went past, and hang on to her torch at the same time.

I waited a moment. Perhaps they'd switched over positions and my girl had gone up to the circle. When the last lot had got in through the curtains and there was a pause and she was free, I went up to her and I said, "Excuse me, do you know where I could have a word with the other young lady?"

She looked at me. "What other young lady?"

"The one who was here last night, with copper hair," I said.

She looked at me closer then, suspicious-like.

"She hasn't shown up today," she said. "I'm taking her place."

"Not shown up?"

"No. And it's funny you should ask. You're not the only one. The police was here not long ago. They had a word with the manager, and the commissionaire too, and no one's said anything to me yet, but I think there's been trouble."

My heart beat different then. Not excited, bad. Like when someone's ill, took to hospital, sudden.

"The police?" I said. "What were they here for?"

"I told you, I don't know," she answered, "but it was something to do with her, and the manager went with them to the police station, and he hasn't come back yet. This way, please, circle on the left, stalls to the right."

I just stood there, not knowing what to do. It was like as if the floor had been knocked away from under me.

The tall girl tore another slip off a ticket and then she said to me, over her shoulder, "Was she a friend of yours?"

"Sort of," I said. I didn't know what to say.

"Well, if you ask me, she was queer in the head, and it wouldn't surprise me if she'd done away with herself and they'd found her dead. No, ice-creams served in the interval, after the news reel."

I went out and stood in the street. The queue was growing for the cheaper seats, and there were children too, talking, excited. I brushed past them and started walking up the street, and I felt sick inside, queer. Something had happened to my girl. I knew it now. That was why she had wanted to get rid of me last night, and for me not to see her home. She was going to do herself in, there in the cemetery. That's why she talked funny and looked so white, and now they'd found her, lying there on the grave-stone by the railings.

If I hadn't gone away and left her she'd have been all right. If I'd stayed with her just five minutes longer, coaxing her, I'd have got her round to my way of thinking and seen her home, standing no nonsense, and she'd be at the picture palace now, showing the people to their seats.

It might be it wasn't as bad as what I feared. It might be she was found wandering, lost her memory and got picked up by the police and taken off, and then they found out where she worked and that, and now the police wanted to check up with the manager at the cinema to see if it was so. If I went down to the police station and asked them there, maybe they'd tell me what had happened, and I could say she was my girl, we were walking out, and it wouldn't matter if she didn't recognize me even, I'd stick to the story. I couldn't let down my boss, I had to get that job done on the Austin, but afterwards, when I'd finished, I could go down to the police station.

All the heart had gone out of me, and I went back to the garage hardly knowing what I was doing, and for the first time ever the smell of the place turned my stomach, the oil and the grease, and there was a chap roaring up his engine, before backing out his car, and a great cloud of smoke coming from his exhaust, filling the workshop with stink.

I went and got my overalls, and put them on, and fetched the tools, and started on the Austin, and all the time I was wondering what it was that had happened to my girl, if she was down at the police station, lost and lonely, or if she was lying somewhere...dead. I kept seeing her face all the time like it was last night.

It took me an hour and a half, not more, to get the Austin ready for the road, filled up with petrol and all, and I had her facing outwards to the street for the owner to drive out, but I was all in by then, dead tired, and the sweat pouring down my face. I had a bit of a wash and put on my coat, and I felt the package in the breast pocket. I took it out and looked at it, done so neat with the fancy ribbon, and I put it back again, and I hadn't noticed the boss come in—I was standing with my back to the door.

"Did you get what you wanted?" he said, cheerful-like and smiling.

He was a good chap, never out of temper, and we got along well.

"Yes," I said.

But I didn't want to talk about it. I told him the job was done and the Austin was ready to drive away. I went to the office with him so that he could note down the work done, and the overtime, and he offered me a fag from the packet lying on his desk beside the evening paper.

"I see Lady Luck won the three-thirty," he said. "I'm a couple of quid up this week."

He was entering my work in his ledger, to keep the pay-roll right.

"Good for you," I said.

"Only backed it for a place, like a clot," he said. "She was twenty-five to one. Still, it's all in the game."

I didn't answer. I'm not one for drinking, but I needed one bad, just then. I mopped my forehead with my handkerchief. I wished he'd get on with the figures, and say goodnight, and let me go.

"Another poor devil's had it," he said. "That's the third now in three weeks, ripped right up the guts, same as the others. He died in hospital this morning. Looks like there's a hoodoo on the RAF."

"What was it, flying jets?" I asked.

"Jets?" he said. "No, damn it, murder. Sliced up the belly, poor sod. Don't you ever read the papers? It's the third one in three weeks, done identical, all Air Force fellows, and each time they've found 'em near a graveyard or a cemetery. I was saying just now, to that chap who came in for petrol, it's not only men who go off their rockers and turn sex maniacs, but women too. They'll get this one all right though, you see. It says in the paper they've a line on her, and expect an arrest shortly. About time too, before another poor blighter cops it."

He shut up his ledger and stuck his pencil behind his ear.

"Like a drink?" he said. "I've got a bottle of gin in the cupboard."

"No," I said, "no, thanks very much. I've . . . I've got a date."

"That's right," he said, smiling, "enjoy yourself."

I walked down the street and bought an evening paper. It was like what he said about the murder. They had it on the front page. They said it must have happened about two a.m. Young fellow in the Air Force, in north-east London. He had managed to stagger to a call-box and get through to the police, and they found him there on the floor of the box when they arrived.

He made a statement in the ambulance before he died. He said a girl called to him, and he followed her, and he thought it was just a bit of love-making—he'd seen her with another fellow drinking coffee at a stall a little while before—and he thought she'd thrown this other fellow over and had taken a fancy to him, and then she got him, he said, right in the guts.

It said in the paper that he had given the police a full description of her, and it said also that the police would be glad if the man who had been seen with the girl earlier in the evening would come forward to help in identification.

I didn't want the paper any more. I threw it away. I walked about the streets till I was tired, and when I guessed Mr. and Mrs. Thompson had gone to bed I went home, and groped for the key they'd left on a piece of string hanging inside the letter-box, and I let myself in and went upstairs to my room.

Mrs. Thompson had turned down the bed and put a thermos of tea for me, thoughtful-like, and the evening paper, the late edition.

They'd got her. About three o'clock in the afternoon. I didn't read the writing, nor the name nor anything. I sat down on my bed, and took up the paper, and there was my girl staring up at me from the front page.

Then I took the package from my coat and undid it, and threw away the wrapper and the fancy string, and sat there looking down at the little heart I held in my hand.

# THE BLUE LENSES

THIS WAS the day for the bandages to be removed and the blue lenses fitted. Marda West put her hand up to her eyes and felt the crêpe binder, and the layer upon layer of cotton-wool beneath. Patience would be rewarded at last. The days had passed into weeks since her operation, and she had lain there suffering no physical discomfort, but only the anonymity of darkness, a negative feeling that the world and the life around was passing her by. During the first few days there had been pain, mercifully allayed by drugs, and then the sharpness of this wore down, dissolved, and she was left with a sense of great fatigue, which they assured her was reaction after shock. As for the operation itself, it had been successful. Here was definite promise. A hundred per cent successful.

"You will see," the surgeon told her, "more clearly than ever before."

"But how can you tell?" she urged, desiring her slender thread of faith to be reinforced.

"Because we examined your eyes when you were under the anaesthetic," he replied, "and again since, when we put you under for a second time. We would not lie to you, Mrs. West."

This reassurance came from them two or three times a day, and she had to steel herself to patience as the weeks wore by, so that she referred to the matter perhaps only once every twenty-four hours, and then by way of a trap, to catch them unawares. "Don't throw the roses out. I should like to see them," she would say, and the day-nurse would be surprised into the admission, "They'll be over before you can do that." Which meant that she would not see this week.

Actual dates were never mentioned. Nobody said, "On the fourteenth of the month you will have your eyes." And the subterfuge continued, the pretence that she did not mind and was content to wait. Even Jim, her husband, was now classed in the category of "them," the staff of the hospital, and no longer treated as a confidante.

Once, long ago, every qualm and apprehension had been admitted and shared. This was before the operation. Then, fearful of pain and blindness, she had clung to him and said, "What if I never see again, what will happen to me?" picturing herself as helpless and maimed. And Jim, whose anxiety was no less harsh than hers, would answer, "Whatever comes, we'll go through it together."

Now, for no known reason except that darkness, perhaps, had made her more sensitive, she was shy to discuss her eyes with him. The touch of his hand was the same as it had ever been, and his kiss, and the warmth of his voice; but always, during these days of waiting, she had the seed of fear that he, like the staff at the hospital, was being too kind. The kindness of those who knew towards the one who must not be told. Therefore, when at last it happened, when at his evening visit the surgeon said, "Your lenses will be fitted tomorrow," surprise was greater than joy. She could not say anything, and he had left the room before she could thank him. It was really true. The long agony had ended. She permitted herself only a last feeler, before the day-nurse went off duty—"They'll take some getting used to, and hurt a bit at first?"—her statement of fact put as a careless question. But the voice of the woman who had tended her through so many weary days replied, "You won't know you've got them, Mrs. West."

Such a calm, comfortable voice, and the way she shifted the

pillows and held the glass to the patient's lips, the hand smelling faintly of the Morny French Fern soap with which she washed her, these things gave confidence and implied that she could not lie.

"Tomorrow I shall see you," said Marda West, and the nurse, with the cheerful laugh that could be heard sometimes down the corridor outside, answered, "Yes, I'll give you your first shock."

It was a strange thought how memories of coming into the nursing-home were now blunted. The staff who had received her were dim shadows, the room assigned to her, where she still lay, like a wooden box built only to entrap. Even the surgeon, brisk and efficient during those two rapid consultations when he had recommended an immediate operation, was a voice rather than a presence. He gave his orders and the orders were carried out, and it was difficult to reconcile this bird-of-passage with the person who, those several weeks ago, had asked her to surrender herself to him, who had in fact worked this miracle upon the membranes and the tissues which were her living eyes.

"Aren't you feeling excited?" This was the low, soft voice of her night-nurse, who, more than the rest of them, understood what she had endured. Nurse Brand, by day, exuded a daytime brightness; she was a person of sunlight, of bearing in fresh flowers, of admitting visitors. The weather she described in the world outside appeared to be her own creation. "A real scorcher," she would say, flinging open windows, and her patient would sense the cool uniform, the starched cap, which somehow toned down the penetrating heat. Or else she might hear the steady fall of rain and feel the slight chill accompanying it. "This is going to please the gardeners, but it'll put paid to Matron's day on the river."

Meals, too, even the dullest of lunches, were made to appear delicacies through her method of introduction. "A morsel of brill *au beurre*?" she would suggest happily, whetting reluctant appetite, and the boiled fish that followed must be eaten, for all its tastelessness, because otherwise it would seem to let down Nurse Brand, who had recommended it. "Apple fritters—you can manage two, I'm sure," and the tongue began to roll the imaginary fritter, crisp as a flake and sugared, which in reality had a languid, leathery substance. And so her cheerful optimism brooked no discontent—it would be offensive to complain, lacking in backbone to admit, "Let me just lie. I don't want anything."

The night brought consolation and Nurse Ansel. She did not expect courage. At first, during pain, it had been Nurse Ansel who had administered the drugs. It was she who had smoothed the pillows and held the glass to the parched lips. Then, with the passing weeks, there had been the gentle voice and the quiet encouragement. "It will soon pass. This waiting is the worst." At night the patient had only to touch the bell, and in a moment Nurse Ansel was by the bed. "Can't sleep? I know, it's wretched for you. I'll give you just two and a half grains, and the night won't seem so long."

How compassionate, that smooth and silken voice. The imagination, making fantasies through enforced rest and idleness, pictured some reality with Nurse Ansel that was not hospital—a holiday abroad, perhaps, for the three of them, and Jim playing golf with an unspecified male companion, leaving her, Marda, to wander with Nurse Ansel. All she did was faultless. She never annoyed. The small shared intimacies of night-time brought a bond between nurse and patient that vanished with the day, and when she went off duty, at five minutes to eight in the morning, she would whisper, "Until this evening," the very whisper stimulating anticipation, as though eight o'clock that night would not be clocking-in but an assignation.

Nurse Ansel understood complaint. When Marda West said wearily, "It's been such a long day," her answering "Has it?" implied that for her too the day had dragged, that in some hostel she had tried to sleep and failed, that now only did she hope to come alive.

It was with a special secret sympathy that she would announce the evening visitor. "Here is someone you want to see, a little earlier than usual," the tone suggesting that Jim was not the husband of ten years but a troubadour, a lover, someone whose bouquet of flowers had been plucked in an enchanted garden and now brought to a balcony. "What gorgeous lilies!" the exclamation half a breath and half a sigh, so that Marda West imagined exotic dragon-petalled beauties growing to heaven, and Nurse Ansel, a little priestess, kneeling. Then, shyly, the voice would murmur, "Good evening, Mr. West. Mrs. West is waiting for you." She would hear the gentle closing of the door, the tip-toeing out with the lilies, and the almost soundless return, the scent of the flowers filling the room.

It must have been during the fifth week that Marda West had tentatively suggested, first to Nurse Ansel and then to her husband, that perhaps when she returned home the night-nurse might go with them for the first week. It would chime with Nurse Ansel's own holiday. Just a week. Just so that Marda West could settle to home again.

"Would you like me to?" Reserve lay in the voice, yet promise too.

"I would. It's going to be so difficult at first." The patient, not knowing what she meant by difficult, saw herself as helpless still, in spite of the new lenses, and needing the protection and the reassurance that up to the present only Nurse Ansel had given her. "Jim, what about it?"

His comment was something between surprise and indulgence. Surprise that his wife considered a nurse a person in her own right, and indulgence because it was the whim of a sick woman. At least, that was how it seemed to Marda West, and later, when the evening visit was over and he had gone home, she said to the night-nurse, "I can't make out whether my husband thought it a good idea or not."

The answer was quiet yet reassuring. "Don't worry. Mr. West is reconciled."

But reconciled to what? The change in routine? Three people round the table, conversation, the unusual status of a guest who, devoting herself to her hostess, must be paid? (Though the last would not be mentioned, but glossed over at the end of a week in an envelope.)

"Aren't you feeling excited?" Nurse Ansel, by the pillow, touched the bandages, and it was the warmth in the voice, the certainty that only a few hours now would bring revelation, which stifled at last all lingering doubt of success. The operation had not failed. Tomorrow she would see once more.

"In a way," said Marda West, "it's like being born again. I've forgotten how the world looks."

"Such a wonderful world," murmured Nurse Ansel, "and you've been patient for so long."

The sympathetic hand expressed condemnation of all those who had insisted upon bandages through the waiting weeks. Greater indulgence might have been granted had Nurse Ansel herself been in command and waved a wand.

"It's queer," said Marda West, "tomorrow you won't be a voice to me any more. You'll be a person."

"Aren't I a person now?"

A note of gentle teasing, of pretended reproach, which was all part of the communication between them, so soothing to the patient. This must surely, when sight came back, be foregone.

"Yes, of course, but it's bound to be different."

"I don't see why."

Even knowing she was dark and small—for so Nurse Ansel had described herself—Marda West must be prepared for surprise at the first encounter, the tilt of the head, the slant of the eyes, or perhaps some unexpected facial form like too large a mouth, too many teeth.

"Look, feel..." and not for the first time Nurse Ansel took her patient's hand and passed it over her own face, a little embarrassing, perhaps, because it implied surrender, the patient's hand a captive. Marda West, withdrawing it, said with a laugh, "It doesn't tell me a thing."

"Sleep, then. Tomorrow will come too soon." There came the familiar routine of the bell put within reach, the last-minute drink, the pill, and then the soft, "Good night, Mrs. West. Ring if you want me."

"Thank you. Good night."

There was always a slight sense of loss, of loneliness, as the door closed and she went away, and a feeling of jealousy, too, because there were other patients who received these same mercies, and who, in pain, would also ring their bells. When she awoke—and this often happened in the small hours—Marda West would no longer picture Jim at home, lonely on his pillow, but would have an image of Nurse Ansel, seated perhaps by someone's bed, bending to give comfort, and this alone would make her reach for the bell, and press her thumb upon it, and say, when the door opened, "Were you having a nap?"

"I never sleep on duty."

She would be seated, then, in the cubby-hole midway along the passage, perhaps drinking tea or entering particulars of charts into a ledger. Or standing beside a patient, as she now stood beside Marda West.

"I can't find my handkerchief."

"Here it is. Under your pillow all the time."

A pat on the shoulder (and this in itself was a sort of delicacy), a few moments of talk to prolong companionship, and then she would be gone, to answer other bells and other requests.

"Well, we can't complain of the weather!" Now it was the day itself, and Nurse Brand coming in like the first breeze of morning, a hand on a barometer set fair. "All ready for the great event?" she asked. "We must get a move on, and keep your prettiest nightie to greet your husband."

It was her operation in reverse. This time in the same room, though, and not a stretcher, but only the deft hands of the surgeon with Nurse Brand to help him. First came the disappearance of the crêpe, the lifting of the bandages and lint, the very slight prick of an injection to dull feeling. Then he did something to her eyelids. There was no pain. Whatever he did was cold, like the slipping of ice where the bandages had been, yet soothing too.

"Now, don't be disappointed," he said. "You won't know any difference for about half an hour. Everything will seem shadowed. Then it will gradually clear. I want you to lie quietly during that time."

"I understand. I won't move."

The longed-for moment must not be too sudden. This made sense. The dark lenses, fitted inside her lids, were temporary for the first few days. Then they would be removed and others fitted.

"How much shall I see?" The question dared at last.

"Everything. But not immediately in colour. Just like wearing sunglasses on a bright day. Rather pleasant."

His cheerful laugh gave confidence, and when he and Nurse Brand had left the room she lay back again, waiting for the fog to clear and for that summer day to break in upon her vision, however subdued, however softened by the lenses.

Little by little the mist dissolved. The first object was angular, a wardrobe. Then a chair. Then, moving her head, the gradual forming of the window's shape, the vases on the sill, the flowers Jim had brought her. Sounds from the street outside merged with the shapes, and what had seemed sharp before was now in harmony. She thought to herself, "I wonder if I can cry? I wonder if the lenses will keep back tears," but, feeling the blessing of sight restored, she felt the tears as well, nothing to be ashamed of—one or two which were easily brushed away.

All was in focus now. Flowers, the wash-basin, the glass with the thermometer in it, her dressing-gown. Wonder and relief were so great that they excluded thought.

"They weren't lying to me," she thought. "It's happened. It's true."

The texture of the blanket covering her, so often felt, could now be seen as well. Colour was not important. The dim light caused by the blue lenses enhanced the charm, the softness of all she saw. It seemed to her, rejoicing in form and shape, that colour would never matter. There was time enough for colour. The blue symmetry of vision itself was all-important. To see, to feel, to blend the two together. It was indeed rebirth, the discovery of a world long lost to her.

There seemed to be no hurry now. Gazing about the small room and dwelling upon every aspect of it was richness, something to savour. Hours could be spent just looking at the room and feeling it, travelling through the window and to the windows of the houses opposite.

"Even a prisoner," she decided, "could find comfort in his cell if he had been blinded first, and had recovered his sight."

She heard Nurse Brand's voice outside, and turned her head to watch the opening door.

"Well . . . are we happy once more?"

Smiling, she saw the figure dressed in uniform come into the room, bearing a tray, her glass of milk upon it. Yet, incongruous, absurd, the head with the uniformed cap was not a woman's head at all. The thing bearing down upon her was a cow . . . a cow on a woman's body. The frilled cap was perched upon wide horns. The eyes were large and gentle, but cow's eyes, the nostrils broad and humid, and the way she stood there, breathing, was the way a cow stood placidly in pasture, taking the day as it came, content, unmoved.

"Feeling a bit strange?"

The laugh was a woman's laugh, a nurse's laugh, Nurse Brand's laugh, and she put the tray down on the cupboard beside the bed. The patient said nothing. She shut her eyes, then opened them again. The cow in the nurse's uniform was with her still.

"Confess now," said Nurse Brand, "you wouldn't know you had the lenses in, except for the colour."

It was important to gain time. The patient stretched out her hand carefully for the glass of milk. She sipped the milk slowly. The mask must be worn on purpose. Perhaps it was some kind of experiment connected with the fitting of the lenses—though how it was supposed to work she could not imagine. And it was surely taking rather a risk to spring such a surprise, and, to people weaker than herself who might have undergone the same operation, downright cruel?

"I see very plainly," she said at last. "At least, I think I do."

Nurse Brand stood watching her, with folded arms. The broad uniformed figure was much as Marda West had imagined it, but that cow's head tilted, the ridiculous frill of the cap perched on the horns...where did the head join the body, if mask it in fact was?

"You don't sound too sure of yourself," said Nurse Brand. "Don't say you're disappointed, after all we've done for you."

The laugh was cheerful, as usual, but she should be chewing grass, the slow jaws moving from side to side.

"I'm sure of myself," answered her patient, "but I'm not so sure of you. Is it a trick?"

"Is what a trick?"

"The way you look...your...face?"

Vision was not so dimmed by the blue lenses that she could not distinguish a change of expression. The cow's jaw distinctly dropped.

"Really, Mrs. West!" This time the laugh was not so cordial. Surprise was very evident. "I'm as the good God made me. I dare say he might have made a better job of it."

The nurse, the cow, moved from the bedside towards the window and drew the curtains more sharply back, so that the full light filled the room. There was no visible join to the mask: the head blended to the body. Marda West saw how the cow, if she stood at bay, would lower her horns.

"I didn't mean to offend you," she said, "but it *is* just a little strange. You see..."

She was spared explanation because the door opened and the surgeon came into the room. At least, the surgeon's voice was recognizable as he called, "Hullo! How goes it?" and his figure in the dark coat and the sponge-bag trousers was all that an eminent surgeon's should be, but...that terrier's head, ears pricked, the inquisitive, searching glance? In a moment surely he would yap, and a tail wag swiftly?

This time the patient laughed. The effect was ludicrous. It must be a joke. It was, it had to be; but why go to such expense and trouble, and what in the end was gained by the deception? She checked her laugh abruptly as she saw the terrier turn to the cow, the two communicate with each other soundlessly. Then the cow shrugged its too ample shoulders.

"Mrs. West thinks us a bit of a joke," she said. But the nurse's voice was not over-pleased.

"I'm all for that," said the surgeon. "It would never do if she took a dislike to us, would it?"

Then he came and put his hand out to his patient, and bent close to observe her eyes. She lay very still. He wore no mask either. None, at least, that she could distinguish. The ears were pricked, the sharp nose questing. He was even marked, one ear black, the other white. She could picture him at the entrance to a fox's lair, sniffing, then quick on the scent scuffing down the tunnel, intent upon the job for which he was trained.

"Your name ought to be Jack Russell," she said aloud.

"I beg your pardon?"

He straightened himself but still stood beside the bed, and the bright eye had a penetrating quality, one ear cocked.

"I mean," Marda West searched for words, "the name seems to suit you better than your own."

She felt confused. Mr. Edmund Greaves, with all the letters after him on the plate in Harley Street, what must he think of her?

"I know a James Russell," he said to her, "but he's an orthopaedic surgeon and breaks your bones. Do you feel I've done that to you?"

His voice was brisk, but he sounded a little surprised, as Nurse Brand had done. The gratitude which was owed to their skill was not forthcoming.

"No, no, indeed," said the patient hastily, "nothing is broken at all, I'm in no pain. I see clearly. Almost too clearly, in fact."

"That's as it should be," he said, and the laugh that followed resembled a short sharp bark.

"Well, nurse," he went on, "the patient can do everything within reason except remove the lenses. You've warned her, I suppose?"

"I was about to, sir, when you came in."

Mr. Greaves turned his pointed terrier nose to Marda West.

"I'll be in on Thursday," he said, "to change the lenses. In the meantime, it's just a question of washing out the eyes with a solution three times a day. They'll do it for you. Don't touch them yourself. And above all don't fiddle with the lenses. A patient did that once and lost his sight. He never recovered it."

"If you tried that," the terrier seemed to say, "you would get what you deserved. Better not make the attempt. My teeth are sharp."

"I understand," said the patient slowly. But her chance had gone. She could not now demand an explanation. Instinct warned her that he would not understand. The terrier was saying something to the cow, giving instructions. Such a sharp staccato sentence, and the foolish head nodded in answer. Surely on a hot day the flies would bother her—or would the frilled cap keep insects away?

As they moved to the door the patient made a last attempt.

"Will the permanent lenses," she asked, "be the same as these?"

"Exactly the same," yapped the surgeon, "except that they won't be tinted. You'll see the natural colour. Until Thursday, then."

He was gone, and the nurse with him. She could hear the murmur of voices outside the door. What happened now? If it was really some kind of test, did they remove their masks instantly? It seemed to Marda West of immense importance that she should find this out. The trick was not truly fair: it was a misuse of confidence. She slipped out of bed and went to the door. She could hear the surgeon say, "One and a half grains. She's a little overwrought. It's the reaction, of course."

Bravely, she flung open the door. They were standing there in the passage, wearing the masks still. They turned to look at her, and the sharp bright eyes of the terrier, the deep eyes of the cow, both held reproach, as though the patient, by confronting them, had committed a breach of etiquette.

"Do you want anything, Mrs. West?" asked Nurse Brand.

Marda West stared beyond them down the corridor. The whole floor was in the deception. A maid, carrying dust-pan and brush, coming from the room next door, had a weasel's head upon her small body, and the nurse advancing from the other side was a little prancing kitten, her cap coquettish on her furry curls, the doctor beside her a proud lion. Even the porter, arriving at that moment in the lift opposite, carried a boar's head between his shoulders. He lifted out luggage, uttering a boar's heavy grunt.

The first sharp prick of fear came to Marda West. How could they have known she would open the door at that minute? How could they have arranged to walk down the corridor wearing masks, the other nurses and the other doctor, and the maid appear out of the room next door, and the porter come up in the lift? Something of her fear must have shown in her face, for Nurse Brand, the cow, took hold of her and led her back into her room.

"Are you feeling all right, Mrs. West?" she asked anxiously.

Marda West climbed slowly into bed. If it was a conspiracy what was it all for? Were the other patients to be deceived as well?

"I'm rather tired," she said. "I'd like to sleep."

"That's right," said Nurse Brand, "you got a wee bit excited."

She was mixing something in the medicine glass, and this time, as Marda West took the glass, her hand trembled. Could a cow see clearly how to mix medicine? Supposing she made a mistake?

"What are you giving me?" she asked.

"A sedative," answered the cow.

Buttercups and daisies. Lush green grass. Imagination was strong enough to taste all three in the mixture. The patient shuddered. She lay down on her pillow and Nurse Brand drew the curtains close.

"Now just relax," she said, "and when you wake up you'll feel so much better." The heavy head stretched forward—in a moment it would surely open its jaws and moo.

The sedative acted swiftly. Already a drowsy sensation filled the patient's limbs.

Soon peaceful darkness came, but she awoke, not to the sanity she had hoped for, but to lunch brought in by the kitten. Nurse Brand was off duty.

"How long must it go on for?" asked Marda West. She had resigned herself to the trick. A dreamless sleep had restored energy and some measure of confidence. If it was somehow necessary to the recovery of her eyes, or even if they did it for some unfathomable reason of their own, it was their business.

"How do you mean, Mrs. West?" asked the kitten, smiling. Such a flighty little thing, with its pursed-up mouth, and even as it spoke it put a hand to its cap.

"This test on my eyes," said the patient, uncovering the boiled chicken on her plate. "I don't see the point of it. Making yourselves such guys. What is the object?"

The kitten, serious, if a kitten could be serious, continued to stare at her. "I'm sorry, Mrs. West," she said, "I don't follow you. Did you tell Nurse Brand you couldn't see properly yet?"

"It's not that I can't see," replied Marda West. "I see perfectly well. The chair is a chair. The table is a table. I'm about to eat boiled chicken. But why do you look like a kitten, and a tabby kitten at that?"

Perhaps she sounded ungracious. It was hard to keep her voice steady. The nurse—Marda West remembered the voice, it was Nurse Sweeting, and the name suited her—drew back from the trolley-table.

"I'm sorry," she said, "if I don't come up to scratch. I've never been called a cat before."

Scratch was good. The claws were out already. She might purr to the lion in the corridor, but she was not going to purr to Marda West.

"I'm not making it up," said the patient. "I see what I see. You are a cat, if you like, and Nurse Brand's a cow."

This time the insult must sound deliberate. Nurse Sweeting had fine whiskers to her mouth. The whiskers bristled.

"If you please, Mrs. West," she said, "will you eat your chicken, and ring the bell when you are ready for the next course?"

She stalked from the room. If she had a tail, thought Marda West, it would not be wagging, like Mr. Greaves's, but twitching angrily.

No, they could not be wearing masks. The kitten's surprise and resentment had been too genuine. And the staff of the hospital could not possibly put on such an act for one patient, for Marda West alone—the expense would be too great. The fault must lie in the lenses, then. The lenses, by their very nature, by some quality beyond the layman's understanding, must transform the person who was perceived through them.

A sudden thought struck her, and pushing the trolley-table aside she climbed out of bed and went over to the dressing-table. Her own face stared back at her from the looking-glass. The dark lenses concealed the eyes, but the face was at least her own.

"Thank heaven for that," she said to herself, but it swung her back to thoughts of trickery. That her own face should seem unchanged through the lenses suggested a plot, and that her first idea of masks had been the right one. But why? What did they gain by it? Could there be a conspiracy amongst them to drive her mad? She dismissed the idea at once—it was too fanciful. This was a reputable London nursing-home, and the staff was well known. The surgeon had operated on royalty. Besides, if they wanted to send her mad, or kill her even, it would be simple enough with drugs. Or with anaesthetics. They could have given her too much anaesthetic during the operation, and just let her die. No one would take the round-about way of dressing up staff and doctors in animals' masks.

She would try one further proof. She stood by the window, the curtain concealing her, and watched for passers-by. For the moment there was no one in the street. It was the lunch-hour, and traffic was slack. Then, at the other end of the street, a taxi crossed, too far away for her to see the driver's head. She waited. The porter came out from the nursing-home and stood on the steps, looking up and down. His boar's head was clearly visible. He did not count, though. He could be part of the plot. A van drew near, but she could not see the driver...yes, he slowed as he went by the nursing-home and craned from his seat, and she saw the squat frog's head, the bulging eyes.

Sick at heart, she left the window and climbed back into bed. She had no further appetite and pushed away her plate, the rest of the chicken untasted. She did not ring her bell, and after a while the door opened. It was not the kitten. It was the little maid with the weasel's head.

"Will you have plum tart or ice cream, madam?" she asked.

Marda West, her eyes half-closed, shook her head. The weasel, shyly edging forward to take the tray, said, "Cheese, then, and coffee to follow?"

The head joined the neck without any fastening. It could not be a mask, unless some designer, some genius, had invented masks that merged with the body, blending fabric to skin.

"Coffee only," said Marda West.

The weasel vanished. Another knock on the door and the kitten was back again, her back arched, her fluff flying. She plonked the coffee down without a word, and Marda West, irritated—for surely, if anyone was to show annoyance, it should be herself?—said sharply, "Shall I pour you some milk in the saucer?"

The kitten turned. "A joke's a joke, Mrs. West," she said, "and I can take a laugh with anyone. But I can't stick rudeness."

"Miaow," said Marda West.

The kitten left the room. No one, not even the weasel, came to remove the coffee. The patient was in disgrace. She did not care. If the staff of the nursing-home thought they could win this battle, they were mistaken. She went to the window again.

An elderly cod, leaning on two sticks, was being helped into a waiting car by the boar-headed porter. It could not be a plot. They could not know she was watching them. Marda went to the telephone and asked the exchange to put her through to her husband's office. She remembered a moment afterwards that he would still be at lunch. Nevertheless, she got the number, and as luck had it he was there.

"Jim . . . Jim, darling."

"Yes?"

The relief to hear the loved familiar voice. She lay back on the bed, the receiver to her ear.

"Darling, when can you get here?"

"Not before this evening, I'm afraid. It's one hell of a day, one thing after another. Well, how did it go? Is everything O.K.?"

"Not exactly."

"What do you mean? Can't you see? Greaves hasn't bungled it, has he?"

How was she to explain what had happened to her? It sounded so foolish over the telephone.

"Yes, I can see. I can see perfectly. It's just that . . . that all the nurses look like animals. And Greaves, too. He's a fox terrier. One of those little Jack Russells they put down the foxes' holes."

"What on earth are you talking about?"

He was saying something to his secretary at the same time, something about another appointment, and she knew from the tone of his voice that he was very busy, very busy, and she had chosen the worst time to ring him up. "What do you mean about Jack Russell?" he repeated.

Marda West knew it was no use. She must wait till he came. Then she would try to explain everything, and he would be able to find out for himself what lay behind it.

"Oh, never mind," she said. "I'll tell you later."

"I'm sorry," he told her, "but I really am in a tearing hurry. If the lenses don't help you, tell somebody. Tell the nurses, the Matron."

"Yes," she said, "yes."

Then she rang off. She put down the telephone. She picked up a magazine, one left behind at some time or other by Jim himself, she supposed. She was glad to find that reading did not hurt her eyes. Nor did the blue lenses make any difference, for the photographs of men and women looked normal, as they had always done. Wedding groups, social occasions, débutantes, all were as usual. It was only here, in the nursing-home itself and in the street outside, that they were different.

It was much later in the afternoon that Matron called in to have a word with her. She knew it was Matron because of her clothes. But inevitably now, without surprise, she observed the sheep's head.

"I hope you're quite comfortable, Mrs. West?"

A note of gentle inquiry in the voice. A suspicion of a baa?

"Yes, thank you."

Marda West spoke guardedly. It would not do to ruffle the Matron. Even if the whole affair was some gigantic plot, it would be better not to aggravate her.

"The lenses fit well?"

"Very well."

"I'm so glad. It was a nasty operation, and you've stood the period of waiting so very well."

That's it, thought the patient. Butter me up. Part of the game, no doubt.

"Only a few days, Mr. Greaves said, and then you will have them altered and the permanent ones fitted."

"Yes, so he said."

"It's rather disappointing not to observe colour, isn't it?"

"As things are, it's a relief."

The retort slipped out before she could check herself. The

Matron smoothed her dress. And if you only knew, thought the patient, what you look like, with that tape under your sheep's chin, you would understand what I mean.

"Mrs. West..." The Matron seemed uncomfortable, and turned her sheep's head away from the woman in the bed. "Mrs. West, I hope you won't mind what I'm going to say, but our nurses do a fine job here and we are all very proud of them. They work long hours, as you know, and it is not really very kind to mock them, although I am sure you intended it in fun."

Baa...Baa...Bleat away. Marda West tightened her lips.

"Is it because I called Nurse Sweeting a kitten?"

"I don't know what you called her, Mrs. West, but she was quite distressed. She came to me in the office nearly crying."

Spitting, you mean. Spitting and scratching. Those capable little hands are really claws.

"It won't happen again."

She was determined not to say more. It was not her fault. She had not asked for lenses that deformed, for trickery, for make believe.

"It must come very expensive," she added, "to run a nursing-home like this."

"It is," said the Matron. Said the sheep. "It can only be done because of the excellence of the staff, and the cooperation of all our patients."

The remark was intended to strike home. Even a sheep can turn.

"Matron," said Marda West, "don't let's fence with each other. What is the object of it all?"

"The object of what, Mrs. West?"

"This tomfoolery, this dressing up." There, she had said it. To enforce her argument she pointed at the Matron's cap. "Why pick on that particular disguise? It's not even funny."

There was silence. The Matron, who had made as if to sit

down to continue her chat, changed her mind. She moved slowly to the door.

"We, who were trained at St. Hilda's, are proud of our badge," she said. "I hope, when you leave us in a few days, Mrs. West, that you will look back on us with greater tolerance than you appear to have now."

She left the room. Marda West picked up the magazine she had thrown down, but the matter was dull. She closed her eyes. She opened them again. She closed them once more. If the chair had become a mushroom and the table a haystack, then the blame could have been put on the lenses. Why was it only people had changed? What was so wrong with people? She kept her eyes shut when her tea was brought her, and when the voice said pleasantly, "Some flowers for you, Mrs. West," she did not even open them, but waited for the owner of the voice to leave the room. The flowers were carnations. The card was Jim's. And the message on it said, "Cheer up. We're not as bad as we seem."

She smiled, and buried her face in the flowers. Nothing false about them. Nothing strange about the scent. Carnations were carnations, fragrant, graceful. Even the nurse on duty who came to put them in water could not irritate her with her pony's head. After all, it was a trim little pony, with a white star on its forehead. It would do well in the ring. "Thank you," smiled Marda West.

The curious day dragged on, and she waited restlessly for eight o'clock. She washed and changed her nightgown, and did her hair. She drew her own curtains and switched on the bed-side lamp. A strange feeling of nervousness had come upon her. She realized, so strange had been the day, that she had not once thought about Nurse Ansel. Dear, comforting, bewitching Nurse Ansel. Nurse Ansel, who was due to come on duty at eight. Was she also in the conspiracy? If she was, then Marda West would have a showdown. Nurse Ansel would never lie.

She would go up to her, and put her hands on her shoulders, and take the mask in her two hands, and say to her, "There, now take it off. You won't deceive me." But if it was the lenses, if all the time it was the lenses that were at fault, how was she to explain it?

She was sitting at the dressing-table, putting some cream on her face, and the door must have opened without her being aware; but she heard the well-known voice, the soft beguiling voice, and it said to her, "I nearly came before. I didn't dare. You would have thought me foolish." It slid slowly into view, the long snake's head, the twisting neck, the pointed barbed tongue swiftly thrusting and swiftly withdrawn, it came into view over her shoulders, through the looking-glass.

Marda West did not move. Only her hand, mechanically, continued to cream her cheek. The snake was not motionless: it turned and twisted all the time, as though examining the pots of cream, the scent, the powder.

"How does it feel to see yourself again?"

Nurse Ansel's voice emerging from the head seemed all the more grotesque and horrible, and the very fact that as she spoke the darting tongue spoke too paralysed action. Marda West felt sickness rise in her stomach, choking her, and suddenly physical reaction proved too strong. She turned away, but as she did so the steady hands of the nurse gripped her, she suffered herself to be led to her bed, she was lying down, eyes closed, the nausea passing.

"Poor dear, what have they been giving you? Was it the sedative? I saw it on your chart," and the gentle voice, so soothing and so calm, could only belong to one who understood. The patient did not open her eyes. She did not dare. She lay there on the bed, waiting.

"It's been too much for you," said the voice. "They should have kept you quiet, the first day. Did you have visitors?"

"No."

"Nevertheless, you should have rested. You look really pale. We can't have Mr. West seeing you like this. I've half a mind to telephone him to stay away."

"No . . . please, I want to see him. I must see him."

Fear made her open her eyes, but directly she did so the sickness gripped her again, for the snake's head, longer than before, was twisting out of its nurse's collar, and for the first time she saw the hooded eye, a pin's head, hidden. She put her hand over her mouth to stifle her cry.

A sound came from Nurse Ansel, expressing disquiet.

"Something has turned you very sick," she said. "It can't be the sedative. You've often had it before. What was the dinner this evening?"

"Steamed fish. I wasn't hungry."

"I wonder if it was fresh. I'll see if anyone has complained. Meanwhile, lie still, dear, and don't upset yourself."

The door quietly opened and closed again, and Marda West, disobeying instructions, slipped from her bed and seized the first weapon that came to hand, her nail-scissors. Then she returned to her bed again, her heart beating fast, the scissors concealed beneath the sheet. Revulsion had been too great. She must defend herself, should the snake approach her. Now she was certain that what was happening was real, was true. Some evil force encompassed the nursing-home and its inhabitants, the Matron, the nurses, the visiting doctors, her surgeon—they were all caught up in it, they were all partners in some gigantic crime, the purpose of which could not be understood. Here, in Upper Watling Street, the malevolent plot was in process of being hatched, and she, Marda West, was one of the pawns; in some way they were to use her as an instrument.

One thing was very certain. She must not let them know that she suspected them. She must try and behave with Nurse Ansel as she had done hitherto. One slip, and she was lost. She must pretend to be better. If she let sickness overcome her,

Nurse Ansel might bend over her with that snake's head, that darting tongue.

The door opened and she was back. Marda West clenched her hands under the sheet. Then she forced a smile.

"What a nuisance I am," she said. "I felt giddy, but I'm better now."

The gliding snake held a bottle in her hand. She came over to the wash-basin and, taking the medicine-glass, poured out three drops.

"This should settle it, Mrs. West," she said, and fear gripped the patient once again, for surely the words themselves constituted a threat. "This should settle it"—settle what? Settle her finish? The liquid had no colour, but that meant nothing. She took the medicine-glass handed to her, and invented a subterfuge.

"Could you find me a clean handkerchief, in the drawer there?"

"Of course."

The snake turned its head, and as it did so Marda West poured the contents of the glass on to the floor. Then fascinated, repelled, she watched the twisting head peer into the contents of the dressing-table drawer, search for a handkerchief, and bring it back again. Marda West held her breath as it drew near the bed, and this time she noticed that the neck was not the smooth glow-worm neck that it had seemed on first encounter, but had scales upon it, zig-zagged. Oddly, the nurse's cap was not ill-fitting. It did not perch incongruously as had the caps of kitten, sheep, and cow. She took the handkerchief.

"You embarrass me," said the voice, "staring at me so hard. Are you trying to read my thoughts?"

Marda West did not answer. The question might be a trap.

"Tell me," the voice continued, "are you disappointed? Do I look as you expected me to look?"

Still a trap. She must be careful. "I think you do," she said slowly, "but it's difficult to tell with the cap. I can't see your hair."

Nurse Ansel laughed, the low, soft laugh that had been so alluring during the long weeks of blindness. She put up her hands, and in a moment the whole snake's head was revealed, the flat, broad top, the tell-tale adder's V. "Do you approve?" she asked.

Marda West shrank back against her pillow. Yet once again she forced herself to smile.

"Very pretty," she said, "very pretty indeed."

The cap was replaced, the long neck wriggled, and then, deceived, it took the medicine-glass from the patient's hand and put it back upon the wash-basin. It did not know everything.

"When I go home with you," said Nurse Ansel, "I needn't wear uniform—that is, if you don't want me to. You see, you'll be a private patient then, and I your personal nurse for the week I'm with you."

Marda West felt suddenly cold. In the turmoil of the day she had forgotten the plans. Nurse Ansel was to be with them for a week. It was all arranged. The vital thing was not to show fear. Nothing must seem changed. And then, when Jim arrived, she would tell him everything. If he could not see the snake's head as she did—and indeed, it was possible that he would not, if her hypervision was caused by the lenses—he must just understand that for reasons too deep to explain she no longer trusted Nurse Ansel, could not, in fact, bear her to come home. The plan must be altered. She wanted no one to look after her. She only wanted to be home again, with him.

The telephone rang on the bedside-table and Marda West seized it, as she might seize salvation. It was her husband.

"Sorry to be late," he said. "I'll jump into a taxi and be with you right away. The lawyer kept me."

"Lawyer?" she asked.

"Yes, Forbes & Millwall, you remember, about the trust fund."

She had forgotten. There had been so many financial discussions before the operation. Conflicting advice, as usual. And finally Jim had put the whole business into the hands of the Forbes & Millwall people.

"Oh, yes. Was it satisfactory?"

"I think so. Tell you directly."

He rang off, and looking up she saw the snake's head watching her. No doubt, thought Marda West, no doubt you would like to know what we were saying to one another.

"You must promise not to get too excited when Mr. West comes." Nurse Ansel stood with her hand upon the door.

"I'm not excited. I just long to see him, that's all."

"You're looking very flushed."

"It's warm in here."

The twisting neck craned upward, then turned to the window. For the first time Marda West had the impression that the snake was not entirely at its ease. It sensed tension. It knew, it could not help but know, that the atmosphere had changed between nurse and patient.

"I'll open the window just a trifle at the top."

If you were all snake, thought the patient, I could push you through. Or would you coil yourself round my neck and strangle me?

The window was opened, and pausing a moment, hoping perhaps for a word of thanks, the snake hovered at the end of the bed. Then the neck settled in the collar, the tongue darted rapidly in and out, and with a gliding motion Nurse Ansel left the room.

Marda West waited for the sound of the taxi in the street outside. She wondered if she could persuade Jim to stay the night in the nursing-home. If she explained her fear, her terror, surely he would understand. She would know in an instant if he had sensed anything wrong himself. She would ring the bell, make a pretext of asking Nurse Ansel some question, and then, by the expression on his face, by the tone of his voice, she would discover whether he saw what she saw herself.

The taxi came at last. She heard it slow down, and then the door slammed and, blessedly, Jim's voice rang out in the street below. The taxi went away. He would be coming up in the lift. Her heart began to beat fast, and she watched the door. She heard his footstep outside, and then his voice again—he must be saying something to the snake. She would know at once if he had seen the head. He would come into the room either startled, not believing his eyes, or laughing, declaring it a joke, a pantomime. Why did he not hurry? Why must they linger there, talking, their voices hushed?

The door opened, the familiar umbrella and bowler hat the first objects to appear round the corner, then the comforting burly figure, but—God ... no ... please God, not Jim too, not Jim, forced into a mask, forced into an organization of devils, of liars ... Jim had a vulture's head. She could not mistake it. The brooding eye, the blood-tipped beak, the flabby folds of flesh. As she lay in sick and speechless horror, he stood the umbrella in a corner and put down the bowler hat and the folded overcoat.

"I gather you're not too well," he said, turning his vulture's head and staring at her, "feeling a bit sick and out of sorts. I won't stay long. A good night's rest will put you right."

She was too numb to answer. She lay quite still as he approached the bed and bent to kiss her. The vulture's beak was sharp.

"It's reaction, Nurse Ansel says," he went on, "the sudden shock of being able to see again. It works differently with different people. She says it will be much better when we get you home."

We . . . Nurse Ansel and Jim. The plan still held, then.

"I don't know," she said faintly, "that I want Nurse Ansel to come home."

"Not want Nurse Ansel?" He sounded startled. "But it was you who suggested it. You can't suddenly chop and change."

There was no time to reply. She had not rung the bell, but Nurse Ansel herself came into the room. "Cup of coffee, Mr. West?" she said. It was the evening routine. Yet tonight it sounded strange, as though it had been arranged outside the door.

"Thanks, Nurse, I'd love some. What's this nonsense about not coming home with us?" The vulture turned to the snake, the snake's head wriggled, and Marda West knew, as she watched them, the snake with darting tongue, the vulture with his head hunched between his man's shoulders, that the plan for Nurse Ansel to come home had not been her own after all; she remembered now that the first suggestion had come from Nurse Ansel herself. It had been Nurse Ansel who had said that Marda West needed care during convalescence. The suggestion had come after Jim had spent the evening laughing and joking and his wife had listened, her eyes bandaged, happy to hear him. Now, watching the smooth snake whose adder's V was hidden beneath the nurse's cap, she knew why Nurse Ansel wanted to return with her, and she knew too why Jim had not opposed it, why in fact he had accepted the plan at once, had declared it a good one.

The vulture opened its blood-stained beak. "Don't say you two have fallen out?"

"Impossible." The snake twisted its neck, looked sideways at the vulture, and added, "Mrs. West is just a little bit tired tonight. She's had a trying day, haven't you, dear?"

How best to answer? Neither must know. Neither the vulture, nor the snake, nor any of the hooded beasts surrounding her and closing in, must ever guess, must ever know.

"I'm all right," she said. "A bit mixed-up. As Nurse Ansel says, I'll be better in the morning."

The two communicated in silence, sympathy between them. That, she realized now, was the most frightening thing of all. Animals, birds, and reptiles had no need to speak. They moved, they looked, they knew what they were about. They would not destroy her, though. She had, for all her bewildered terror, the will to live.

"I won't bother you," said the vulture, "with these documents tonight. There's no violent hurry anyway. You can sign them at home."

"What documents?"

If she kept her eyes averted she need not see the vulture's head. The voice was Jim's, steady and reassuring.

"The trust fund papers Forbes & Millwall gave me. They suggest I should become a co-director of the fund."

The words struck a chord, a thread of memory belonging to the weeks before her operation. Something to do with her eyes. If the operation was not successful she would have difficulty in signing her name.

"What for?" she asked, her voice unsteady. "After all, it is my money."

He laughed. And, turning to the sound, she saw the beak open. It gaped like a trap, and then closed again.

"Of course it is," he said. "That's not the point. The point is that I should be able to sign for you, if you should be ill or away."

Marda West looked at the snake, and the snake, aware, shrank into its collar and slid towards the door. "Don't stay too long, Mr. West," murmured Nurse Ansel. "Our patient must have a real rest tonight."

She glided from the room and Marda West was left alone with her husband. With the vulture.

"I don't propose to go away," she said, "or be ill."

"Probably not. That's neither here nor there. These fellows always want safeguards. Anyway, I won't bore you with it now."

Could it be that the voice was over-casual? That the hand, stuffing the document into the pocket of the greatcoat, was a claw? This was a possibility, a horror, perhaps, to come. The bodies changing too, hands and feet becoming wings, claws, hoofs, paws, with no touch of humanity left to the people about her. The last thing to go would be the human voice. When the human voice went, there would be no hope. The jungle would take over, multitudinous sounds and screams coming from a hundred throats.

"Did you really mean that," Jim asked, "about Nurse Ansel?"

Calmly she watched the vulture pare his nails. He carried a file in his pocket. She had never thought about it before—it was part of Jim, like his fountain pen and his pipe. Yet now there was reasoning behind it: a vulture needed sharp claws for tearing its victim.

"I don't know," she said. "It seemed to me rather silly to go home with a nurse, now that I can see again."

He did not answer at once. The head sank deeper between the shoulders. His dark city suit was like the humped feathers of a large brooding bird. "I think she's a treasure," he said. "And you're bound to feel groggy at first. I vote we stick to the plan. After all, if it doesn't work we can always send her away."

"Perhaps," said his wife.

She was trying to think if there was anyone left whom she could trust. Her family was scattered. A married brother in South Africa, friends in London, no one with whom she was intimate. Not to this extent. No one to whom she could say that her nurse had turned into a snake, her husband into a vulture. The utter hopelessness of her position was like damnation itself. This was her hell. She was quite alone, coldly conscious of the hatred and cruelty about her.

"What will you do this evening?" she asked quietly.

"Have dinner at the club, I suppose," he answered. "It's becoming rather monotonous. Only two more days of it, thank goodness. Then you'll be home again."

Yes, but once at home, once back there, with a vulture and a snake, would she not be more completely at their mercy than she was here?

"Did Greaves say Thursday for certain?" she asked.

"He told me so this morning, when he telephoned. You'll have the other lenses then, the ones that show colour."

The ones that would show the bodies too. That was the explanation. The blue lenses only showed the heads. They were the first test. Greaves, the surgeon, was in this too, very naturally. He had a high place in the conspiracy—perhaps he had been bribed. Who was it, she tried to remember, who had suggested the operation in the first place? Was it the family doctor, after a chat with Jim? Didn't they both come to her together and say that this was the only chance to save her eyes? The plot must lie deep in the past, extend right back through the months, perhaps the years. But, in heaven's name, for what purpose? She sought wildly in her memory to try to recall a look, or sign, or word which would give her some insight into this dreadful plot, this conspiracy against her person or her sanity.

"You look pretty peaky," he said suddenly. "Shall I call Nurse Ansel?"

"No . . ." It broke from her, almost a cry.

"I think I'd better go. She said not to stay long."

He got up from the chair, a heavy, hooded figure, and she closed her eyes as he came to kiss her good night. "Sleep well, my poor pet, and take it easy."

In spite of her fear she felt herself clutch at his hand.

"What is it?" he asked.

The well-remembered kiss would have restored her, but not the stab of the vulture's beak, the thrusting blood-stained beak.

When he had gone she began to moan, turning her head upon the pillow.

"What am I to do?" she said. "What am I to do?"

The door opened again and she put her hand to her mouth. They must not hear her cry. They must not see her cry. She pulled herself together with a tremendous effort.

"How are you feeling, Mrs. West?"

The snake stood at the bottom of the bed, and by her side the house physician. She had always liked him, a young pleasant man, and although like the others he had an animal's head it did not frighten her. It was a dog's head, an Aberdeen's, and the brown eyes seemed to quiz her. Long ago, as a child, she had owned an Aberdeen.

"Could I speak to you alone?" she asked.

"Of course. Do you mind, nurse?" He jerked his head at the door, and she had gone. Marda West sat up in bed and clasped her hands.

"You'll think me very foolish," she began, "but it's the lenses. I can't get used to them."

He came over, the trustworthy Aberdeen, head cocked in sympathy.

"I'm sorry about that," he said. "They don't hurt you, do they?"

"No," she said, "no, I can't feel them. It's just that they make everyone look strange."

"They're bound to do that, you know. They don't show colour." His voice was cheerful, friendly. "It comes as a bit of a shock when you've worn bandages so long," he said, "and you mustn't forget you were pulled about quite a bit. The nerves behind the eyes are still very tender."

"Yes," she said. His voice, even his head, gave her confidence. "Have you known people who've had this operation before?"

"Yes, scores of them. In a couple of days you'll be as right as rain." He patted her on the shoulder. Such a kindly dog. Such a sporting, cheerful dog, like the long-dead Angus. "I'll tell you another thing," he continued. "Your sight may be better after this than it's ever been before. You'll actually see more clearly in every way. One patient told me that it was as though she had been wearing spectacles all her life, and then, because of the operation, she realized she saw all her friends and her family as they really were."

"As they really were?" She repeated his words after him.

"Exactly. Her sight had always been poor, you see. She had thought her husband's hair was brown, but in reality it was red, bright red. A bit of a shock at first. But she was delighted."

The Aberdeen moved from the bed, patted the stethoscope on his jacket, and nodded his head. "Mr. Greaves did a wonderful job on you, I can promise you that," he said. "He was able to strengthen a nerve he thought had perished. You've never had the use of it before—it wasn't functioning. So who knows, Mrs. West, you may have made medical history. Anyway, sleep well and the best of luck. See you in the morning. Good night." He trotted from the room. She heard him call good night to Nurse Ansel as he went down the corridor.

The comforting words had turned to gall. In one sense they were a relief, because his explanation seemed to suggest there was no plot against her. Instead, like the woman patient before her with the deepened sense of colour, she had been given vision. She used the words he had used himself. Marda West could see people as they really were. And those whom she had loved and trusted most were in truth a vulture and a snake . . .

The door opened and Nurse Ansel, with the sedative, entered the room.

"Ready to settle down, Mrs. West?" she asked.

"Yes, thank you."

There might be no conspiracy, but even so all trust, all faith, were over.

"Leave it with a glass of water. I'll take it later."

She watched the snake put the glass on the bedside table. She watched her tuck in the sheet. Then the twisting neck peered closer and the hooded eyes saw the nail-scissors half-hidden beneath the pillow.

"What have you got there?"

The tongue darted and withdrew. The hand stretched out for the scissors. "You might have cut yourself. I'll put them away, shall I, for safety's sake?"

Her one weapon was pocketed, not replaced on the dressing-table. The very way Nurse Ansel slipped the scissors into her pocket suggested that she knew of Marda West's suspicions. She wanted to leave her defenceless.

"Now, remember to ring your bell if you want anything."

"I'll remember."

The voice that had once seemed tender was over-smooth and false. How deceptive are ears, thought Marda West, what traitors to truth. And for the first time she became aware of her own new latent power, the power to tell truth from falsehood, good from evil.

"Good night, Mrs. West."

"Good night."

Lying awake, her bedside clock ticking, the accustomed traffic sounds coming from the street outside, Marda West decided upon her plan. She waited until eleven o'clock, an hour past the time when she knew that all the patients were settled and asleep. Then she switched out her light. This would deceive the snake, should she come to peep at her through the window-slide in the door. The snake would believe that she slept. Marda West crept out of bed. She took her clothes from the wardrobe and began to dress. She put on her coat and shoes and tied a scarf over her head. When she was ready she went to the door and softly turned the handle. All was quiet in the corridor. She stood there motionless. Then she took one step across the threshold and looked to the left, where the nurse on duty sat. The snake was there. The snake was sitting crouched over a book. The light from the ceiling shone upon her head, and there could be no mistake. There were the trim uniform, the white starched front, the stiff collar, but rising from the collar the twisting neck of the snake, the long, flat, evil head.

Marda West waited. She was prepared to wait for hours. Presently the sound she hoped for came, the bell from a patient. The snake lifted its head from the book and checked the red light on the wall. Then, slipping on her cuffs, she glided down the corridor to the patient's room. She knocked and entered. Directly she had disappeared Marda West left her own room and went to the head of the staircase. There was no sound. She listened carefully, and then crept downstairs. There were four flights, four floors, but the stairway itself was not visible from the cubby-hole where the night nurses sat on duty. Luck was with her.

Down in the main hall the lights were not so bright. She waited at the bottom of the stairway until she was certain of not being observed. She could see the night-porter's back—his head was not visible, for he was bent over his desk—but when it straightened she noticed the broad fish face. She shrugged her shoulders. She had not dared all this way to be frightened by a fish. Boldly she walked through the hall. The fish was staring at her.

"Do you want anything, madam?" he said.

He was as stupid as she expected. She shook her head.

"I'm going out. Good night," she said, and she walked straight past him, out of the swing-door, and down the steps into the street. She turned swiftly to the left, and, seeing a taxi at the further end, called and raised her hand. The taxi slowed and waited. When she came to the door she saw that the driver had the squat black face of an ape. The ape grinned. Some instinct warned her not to take the taxi.

"I'm sorry," she said. "I made a mistake."

The grin vanished from the face of the ape. "Make up your mind, lady," he shouted, and let in his clutch and swerved away.

Marda West continued walking down the street. She turned right, and left, and right again, and in the distance she saw the lights of Oxford Street. She began to hurry. The friendly traffic drew her like a magnet, the distant lights, the distant men and women. When she came to Oxford Street she paused, wondering of a sudden where she should go, whom she could ask for refuge. And it came to her once again that there was no one, no one at all; because the couple passing her now, a toad's head on a short black body clutching a panther's arm, could give her no protection, and the policeman standing at the corner was a baboon, the woman talking to him a little prinked-up pig. No one was human, no one was safe, the man a pace or two behind her was like Jim, another vulture. There were vultures on the pavement opposite. Coming towards her, laughing, was a jackal.

She turned and ran. She ran, bumping into them, jackals, hyenas, vultures, dogs. The world was theirs, there was no human left. Seeing her run they turned and looked at her, they pointed, they screamed and yapped, they gave chase, their footsteps followed her. Down Oxford Street she ran, pursued by them, the night all darkness and shadow, the light no longer with her, alone in an animal world.

"Lie quite still, Mrs. West, just a small prick, I'm not going to hurt you."

She recognized the voice of Mr. Greaves, the surgeon, and dimly she told herself that they had got hold of her again. She was back at the nursing-home, and it did not matter now—she might as well be there as anywhere else. At least in the nursing-home the animal heads were known.

They had replaced the bandages over her eyes, and for this she was thankful. Such blessed darkness, the evil of the night hidden.

"Now, Mrs. West, I think your troubles are over. No pain and no confusion with these lenses. The world's in colour again."

The bandages were being lightened after all. Layer after layer removed. And suddenly everything was clear, was day, and the face of Mr. Greaves smiled down at her. At his side was a rounded, cheerful nurse.

"Where are your masks?" asked the patient.

"We didn't need masks for this little job," said the surgeon. "We were only taking out the temporary lenses. That's better, isn't it?"

She let her eyes drift round the room. She was back again all right. This was the shape, there was the wardrobe, the dressing-table, the vases of flowers. All in natural colour, no longer veiled. But they could not fob her off with stories of a dream. The scarf she had put round her head before slipping away in the night lay on the chair.

"Something happened to me, didn't it?" she said. "I tried to get away."

The nurse glanced at the surgeon. He nodded his head.

"Yes," he said, "you did. And, frankly, I don't blame you. I blame myself. Those lenses I inserted yesterday were pressing upon a tiny nerve, and the pressure threw out your balance. That's all over now."

His smile was reassuring. And the large warm eyes of Nurse Brand—it must surely be Nurse Brand—gazed down at her in sympathy.

"It was very terrible," said the patient. "I can never explain how terrible."

"Don't try," said Mr. Greaves. "I can promise you it won't happen again."

The door opened and the young physician entered. He too was smiling. "Patient fully restored?" he asked.

"I think so," said the surgeon. "What about it, Mrs. West?"

Marda West stared gravely at the three of them, Mr. Greaves, the house physician, and Nurse Brand, and she wondered what palpitating wounded tissue could so transform three individuals into prototypes of an animal kingdom, what cell linking muscle to imagination.

"I thought you were dogs," she said. "I thought you were a hunt terrier, Mr. Greaves, and that you were an Aberdeen."

The house physician touched his stethoscope and laughed.

"But I am," he said, "it's my native town. Your judgement was not wholly out, Mrs. West. I congratulate you."

Marda West did not join in the laugh.

"That's all right for you," she said. "Other people were not so pleasant." She turned to Nurse Brand. "I thought you were a cow," she said, "a kind cow. But you had sharp horns."

This time it was Mr. Greaves who took up the laugh. "There you are, nurse," he said, "just what I've often told you. Time they put you out to grass and to eat the daisies."

Nurse Brand took it in good part. She straightened the patient's pillows and her smile was benign. "We get called some funny things from time to time," she said. "That's all part of our job."

The doctors were moving towards the door, still laughing, and Marda West, sensing the normal atmosphere, the absence of all strain, said, "Who found me, then? What happened? Who brought me back?"

Mr. Greaves glanced back at her from the door. "You didn't get very far, Mrs. West, and a damn good job for you, or you mightn't be here now. The porter followed you."

"It's all finished with now," said the house physician, "and the episode lasted five minutes. You were safely in your bed before any harm was done, and I was here. So that was that. The person who really had the full shock was poor Nurse Ansel when she found you weren't in your bed."

Nurse Ansel . . . The revulsion of the night before was not so easily forgotten. "Don't say our little starlet was an animal too?" smiled the house doctor. Marda West felt herself colour. Lies would have to begin. "No," she said quickly, "no, of course not."

"Nurse Ansel is here now," said Nurse Brand. "She was so upset when she went off duty that she wouldn't go back to the hostel to sleep. Would you care to have a word with her?"

Apprehension seized the patient. What had she said to Nurse Ansel in the panic and fever of the night? Before she could answer the house doctor opened the door and called down the passage.

"Mrs. West wants to say good morning to you," he said. He was smiling all over his face. Mr. Greaves waved his hand and was gone, Nurse Brand went after him, and the house doctor, saluting with his stethoscope and making a mock bow, stepped back against the wall to admit Nurse Ansel. Marda West stared, then tremulously began to smile and held out her hand.

"I'm sorry," she said, "you must forgive me."

How could she have seen Nurse Ansel as a snake! The hazel eyes, the clear olive skin, the dark hair trim under the frilled cap. And that smile, that slow, understanding smile.

"Forgive you, Mrs. West?" said Nurse Ansel. "What have I to forgive you for? You've been through a terrible ordeal."

Patient and nurse held hands. They smiled at one another. And, oh heaven, thought Marda West, the relief, the thankfulness, the load of doubt and despair that was swept away with the new-found sight and knowledge.

"I still don't understand what happened," she said, clinging to the nurse. "Mr. Greaves tried to explain. Something about a nerve."

Nurse Ansel made a face towards the door. "He doesn't know himself," she whispered, "and he's not going to say either, or he'll find himself in trouble. He fixed those lenses too deep, that's all. Too near a nerve. I wonder it didn't kill you."

She looked down at her patient. She smiled with her eyes. She was so pretty, so gentle. "Don't think about it," she said. "You're going to be happy from now on. Promise me?"

"I promise," said Marda West.

The telephone rang, and Nurse Ansel let go her patient's hand and reached for the receiver. "You know who this is going to be," she said. "Your poor husband." She gave the receiver to Marda West.

"Jim . . . Jim, is that you?"

The loved voice sounding so anxious at the other end. "Are you all right?" he said. "I've been through to Matron twice, she said she would let me know. What the devil has been happening?"

Marda West smiled and handed the receiver to the nurse.

"You tell him," she said.

Nurse Ansel held the receiver to her ear. The skin of her hand was olive smooth, the nails gleaming with a soft pink polish.

"Is that you, Mr. West?" she said. "Our patient gave us a fright, didn't she?" She smiled and nodded at the woman in the bed. "Well, you don't have to worry any more. Mr. Greaves changed the lenses. They were pressing on a nerve, and everything is now all right. She can see perfectly. Yes, Mr. Greaves said we could come home tomorrow."

The endearing voice blended to the soft colouring, the hazel eyes. Marda West reached once more for the receiver.

"Jim, I had a hideous night," she said. "I'm only just beginning to understand it now. A nerve in the brain . . ."

"So I gather," he said. "How damnable. Thank God they traced it. That fellow Greaves can't have known his job."

"It can't happen again," she said. "Now the proper lenses are in, it can't happen again."

"It had better not," he said, "or I'll sue him. How are you feeling in yourself?"

"Wonderful," she said, "bewildered, but wonderful."

"Good girl," he said. "Don't excite yourself. I'll be along later."

His voice went. Marda West gave the receiver to Nurse Ansel, who replaced it on the stand.

"Did Mr. Greaves really say I could go home tomorrow?" she asked.

"Yes, if you're good." Nurse Ansel smiled and patted her patient's hand. "Are you sure you still want me to come with you?" she asked.

"Why, yes," said Marda West. "Why, it's all arranged."

She sat up in bed and the sun came streaming through the window, throwing light on the roses, the lilies, the tall-stemmed iris. The hum of traffic outside was close and friendly. She thought of her garden waiting for her at home, and her own bedroom, her own possessions, the day-by-day routine of home to be taken up again with sight restored, the anxiety and fear of the past months put away for ever.

"The most precious thing in the world," she said to Nurse Ansel, "is sight. I know now. I know what I might have lost."

Nurse Ansel, hands clasped in front of her, nodded her head in sympathy. "You've got your sight back," she said, "that's the miracle. You won't ever lose it now."

She moved to the door. "I'll slip back to the hostel and get some rest," she said. "Now I know everything is well with you I'll be able to sleep. Is there anything you want before I go?"

"Give me my face-cream and my powder," said the patient, "and the lipstick and the brush and comb."

Nurse Ansel fetched the things from the dressing-table and put them within reach upon the bed. She brought the hand-mirror, too, and the bottle of scent, and with a little smile of intimacy sniffed at the stopper. "Gorgeous," she murmured. "This is what Mr. West gave you, isn't it?"

Already, thought Marda West, Nurse Ansel fitted in. She saw herself putting flowers in the small guest-room, choosing the right books, fitting a portable wireless in case Nurse Ansel should be bored in the evenings.

"I'll be with you at eight o'clock."

The familiar words, said every morning now for so many days and weeks, sounded in her ear like a melody, loved through repetition. At last they were joined to the individual, the person who smiled, the one whose eyes promised friendship and loyalty.

"See you this evening."

The door closed. Nurse Ansel had gone. The routine of the nursing-home, broken by the fever of the night before, resumed its usual pattern. Instead of darkness, light. Instead of negation, life.

Marda West took the stopper from the scent-bottle and put it behind her ears. The fragrance filtered, becoming part of the warm, bright day. She lifted the hand-mirror and looked into it. Nothing changed in the room, the street noises penetrated from outside, and presently the little maid who had seemed a weasel yesterday came in to dust the room. She said, "Good morning," but the patient did not answer. Perhaps she was tired. The maid dusted, and went her way.

Then Marda West took up the mirror and looked into it once more. No, she had not been mistaken. The eyes that stared back at her were doe's eyes, wary before sacrifice, and the timid deer's head was meek, already bowed.

# LA SAINTE-VIERGE

IT WAS hot and sultry, that oppressive kind of heat where there is no air, no life. The trees were motionless and dull, their drooping leaves colourless with summer dust. The ditches smelt of dead ferns and long-dried mud, and the grasses of the fields were blistered and brown. The village seemed asleep. No one stirred among the few scattered cottages on the hill-side; strange, uneven cottages, huddled together for fear of loneliness, with white walls and no windows, and small gardens massed with orange flowers.

A greater silence still filled the fields, where the pale corn lay heaped in awkward stacks, left by some neglectful labourer. Not even a breeze stirred the heather on the hills, lonely treeless hills, whose only dwellers were a host of bees and a few lizards. Below them the wide sea stretched like a sheet of ice into eternity, a chart of silver crinkled by the sun.

Away from the hills, towards the scattered houses, was a narrow, muddy lane leading to nowhere. At first it seemed one of those shy, twisting lanes, tempting to explore, that finish in a distant village or an unknown beach, but this one dissolved into a straggling path that soon lost itself among tall weeds. In a sheltered corner of the lane Marie was washing her linen in a pool.

The water looked like a basin of spilt milk, white with soft soap, and the clothes lay limp upon the slippery stones. Marie scrubbed hard, scornful of the heat, her black hair screwed behind her head in a tight knot; now and again she brushed away with an impatient hand the streaks of perspiration that trickled from her forehead.

Her face was thin and childish, rather plain and pathetic, and though she was twenty-three she looked little more than seventeen. There were tired lines under her eyes, and her hands were rough and uncared for. She was a typical Breton peasant, hard-working and reserved, whose only beauty was her youth, which would quickly pass. When the Breton women sorrow they show no grief upon their faces, they would rather die than let their tears be seen; thus Marie bore no outward trace of the pain that was in her heart.

She was thinking of Jean, her husband. She lived for him; there was nothing else in her life. She was a woman who would love but once, and give everything. There was no part of her body and soul that did not belong to him; she had no thought and no wish beyond his happiness. He was her lover and her child. Yet she never told him this, she did not even understand it herself. She was ignorant and unintelligent; it was only her heart that knew.

"He is going away from me," she was thinking, "he is going in his boat on that terrible sea. Only a year ago now since my brother was drowned in the sudden gale that came after the hot weather. I am afraid, so terribly afraid. Jean is ashamed of me; he thinks I am not fit to be the wife of a fisherman. I cannot help it. The coast is dangerous, more dangerous than anywhere else in Brittany. And these storms—the mists—the odd currents. Jean is rash and he loves danger, he does not mind. If he could be safe and return to me unharmed, I would work my fingers to the bone."

Every few months Marie would go through this agony, when Jean and the other fishermen went to sea and stayed for ten days without sight of land. The weather was uncertain and storms were frequent; the frail boats stood very little chance against a heavy sea. "I must not let him see I am afraid," she said to herself. "He cannot understand it, and I irritate him."

She paused in her work and sank back upon her heels. Her throat was dry, and she had an aching, sick feeling below her heart. It would be terrible to be alone without him, worse than it had ever been before. Something was going to happen. If only she had not the feeling that something was going to happen. The sun shone down upon her uncovered head, and she was aware of her great weariness.

There was no one near her, and through the trees the village looked dusty and lifeless. The linen lay in an untidy heap by her side. What did it matter whether it was clean or dirty?

She closed her eyes, and was filled with a sense of unbelievable loneliness. "Jean," she whispered, "Jean."

From across the fields came the sound of the chapel bell striking the hour. Marie sat up and listened, and over her face came a strange smile, a smile in which hope and shame were mingled. She had suddenly remembered the Sainte-Vierge. In her mind she saw the figure in the chapel, Notre Dame des Bonnes Nouvelles, with the infant Jesus in her arms.

"I will go this evening," she thought. "When it is dark I will go to the Sainte-Vierge and tell her my trouble. I shall ask her to watch over Jean when he is at sea." She rose to her feet and began to lay her washing in the basket.

Her memory of the chapel had stopped the sick feeling in her heart, and as she walked through the fields and the village she was conscious only of her weariness. When she had left her basket in the cottage Marie went down the hill to the harbour, where she hoped to find Jean.

She walked towards a group of men who were standing on the edge of the quay, by a heap of old nets and discarded sails. Jean was among them, laughing and talking. Marie felt so proud as she looked at him. He was a good head taller than any of the others, with great broad shoulders and a mass of dark hair.

She ran forward, waving her hand. Jean's eyes narrowed as he saw her, and he muttered a curse under his breath. "Shut your mouths," he said to the other men, "here comes the child." They laughed awkwardly, and some of them began to move away.

"What are you doing down here?" asked Jean.

"It is settled, then, that you sail," said Marie breathlessly. "What time do you leave?"

"At midnight, so as to catch the tide," he replied. "But listen here, I must have supper early tonight, there are a lot of things I have to do. Jacques here wants me to help him with his boat."

He winked at the young fisherman next to him, who carefully avoided Marie's eye.

"Yes," said the lad, "that's right," and strolled away towards the beach. Marie did not notice anything, but the sick feeling had begun again in her heart.

"Come away," she said to Jean, "I have something to tell you." He followed her rather unwillingly up the hill.

They paused halfway, and turned back to look at the sea. The heat of the afternoon had passed, and in about four hours' time the sun would sink below the horizon. The sea shone like splintered silver, while westwards beyond the beacon streams of burnt clouds were massing in a purple haze. Down in the bay some children were bathing, and the sound of their voices and splashes floated up to the hill. The gulls wheeled and screamed around the harbour, searching for food.

Marie turned away, and climbed towards the village. She had a vivid mental picture of the sea, and was aware that it was the last time she would look at it with Jean. Subconsciously, in the depths of her being, she consecrated the spot. Jean spat out the fag end of his cigarette; he was not thinking of anything.

Theirs was the last cottage beyond the village shop—a funny little white place with a prim garden. Marie went straight to the living-room, and began to lay the supper things on the table.

She went about her work mechanically; she had no idea what she was doing. There was only one thought in her mind—in a few hours he would be gone.

Jean's shadow loomed in the doorway. "You were wanting to tell me something?" he asked. Marie did not answer for a moment. Her love for him was so great that she felt it would choke her if she spoke. She wanted to kneel at his feet, to bury her head against him, to implore him to stay with her. If only he would understand to what depths of degradation she would sink for his sake. Everything she had ever felt for him came back to her at this moment. Yet she said nothing, and no sign appeared on her stolid little face.

"What is it?" he asked again.

"It is nothing," she answered slowly, "nothing. The Curé was here today, and hoped you would see him before you go."

She turned to pick up a plate, conscious of the lie, conscious of her failure. He would never know now.

"I will see," said Jean, "but I don't think there will be any time. This boat of Jacques'—and the nets." He left the rest unfinished, and went out into the garden.

The next few hours passed rapidly. After supper Marie washed up the dishes and put away her clean linen. Then she had her mending to do, mostly things for Jean.

She worked until it became too dark to see, for she was very thrifty and would not use a lamp. At ten o'clock Jean came in to say good-bye. "May I come with you and help Jacques with his boat?" she asked.

"No, no, you will be in the way," he replied quickly. "We cannot work and talk as well."

"But I will not say a word."

"No, I won't have you come. You are tired, too; it is this heat. If I know that you are here in bed I shall be happy, and think about you."

He put his arms round her and kissed her gently. Marie

closed her eyes. It was the end of everything. "You will be careful, you will come back to me?" She clung to him like a child.

"Are you mad, you silly girl?" he said, and he laughed as he shut the door and left her. For a few minutes Marie stood motionless in the middle of the room. Then she went to the window and looked out, but he was already out of sight. It was a beautiful evening, very clear and bright, for there was a full moon.

Marie sat down by the window, her hands in her lap. She felt as if she were living in a dream. "I think I must be ill," she said to herself. "I've never felt like this before."

There were no tears on her cheeks, only deep shadows in her eyes. Slowly she rose to her feet, and after putting a shawl round her head and over her shoulders she opened the door and stepped outside. There was no one about, and everything was quite still. Marie slipped through the garden and crossed the lane. In a few minutes she was running across the field that led to the chapel.

The Chapel des Bonnes Nouvelles was very old, and was no longer used for services. The door remained open day and night, so that the peasants could go in and pray when they wanted, for they always felt a little in awe of the new church at the end of the village.

Marie pushed open the creaking door, then paused to listen. The chapel was quite deserted. Through the low window by the altar the moon shone now and again, lighting the nave. There had probably been no one inside for days. A few leaves lay on the rough stone floor, where they had blown in from the open door. The white-washed walls were grimy, and great cobwebs hung from the rafters in the roof.

Hanging by nails on the wall, on either side of the altar, were gifts presented by the peasants who had prayed there: roughly carved models of ships, pathetic little toy boats, brightly coloured balls, and strings of glass and wooden beads. They had lain there many years, perhaps, and were covered in dust. There were even a few wedding wreaths, now old and faded, given by the brides of long ago. All over the walls were inscriptions written in pencil, prayers and thanksgivings to Notre Dame des Bonnes Nouvelles, *"Mère, priez pour nous,"* *"Notre Dame des Bonnes Nouvelles, sauvez mon fils qui est sur mer."*

Marie went slowly to the rails and knelt down. The altar was bare of flowers, and alone in the centre stood the figure of the Sainte-Vierge. Her golden crown was crooked on her head, and covered in cobwebs. Her right arm had been lost, and in the other she held the little figure of the infant Jesus, who had no fingers on His hands. Her robe had once been blue, but the colour had come off long ago, and it was now a dirty brown. Her face was round and expressionless, the face of a cheap doll. She had large blue eyes that looked vacantly before her, while her scarlet cheeks clashed with her cracked painted lips. Her mouth was set in a silly smile, and the plaster was coming off at the corners. Round her neck she wore string upon string of glass beads, the offerings of the fishermen, and someone had even hung a wreath over her baby's head. It dangled sideways and hid his face.

Marie knelt by the rails and gazed at the Sainte-Vierge. The figure was the most beautiful and sacred thing in her life. She did not notice the dust and the broken plaster, the toppling crown and the silly painted smile—to Marie she was the fulfiller of all prayers, the divine mother of the fishermen. As she knelt she prayed, not in words but in the thoughts that wandered at will through her mind, and her prayers were all for Jean, for his safety and his return.

"Oh! Mother," she said, "if it is wrong for me to love him so much, then punish me as you will, but bring him safely back to me. He is young and brave, yet helpless as a child, he would not understand death. I care not if my heart breaks, nor if he should cease to love me and should ill-treat me, it is only his happiness I ask, and that he shall never know pain or hardship."

A fly settled on the nose of the Sainte-Vierge, and brushed a scrap of coloured plaster off her cheek.

"I have put all my trust in you," said Marie, "and I know that you will watch over him when he is at sea. Though waves rise up and threaten his boat, if you protect him I shall have no fear. I will bring fresh flowers every morning and lay them at the feet of the little Jesus. When I am working in the day I will sing songs and be gay, and these will be prayers to you for his safety. Oh! Mother, if you could only show me by a sign that all will be well!"

A drip of water from the roof fell down upon the Sainte-Vierge and left a dirty streak across her left eye.

It was very dark now. Away across the fields a woman was calling to a child. A faint breeze stirred in the trees, and far in the distance the waves broke dully on the shingle beach.

Marie gazed upon the figure until she drooped from weariness, and everything was blurred and strange before her eyes. The walls of the chapel lay in shadow; even the altar sank into nothingness. All that remained was the image of the Sainte-Vierge, her face lit up by a chance ray of moonlight. And as Marie watched the figure it seemed to her that the cracked, painted smile became a thing of beauty, and that the doll's eyes looked down upon her with tenderness and love. The tawdry crown shone in the darkness, and Marie was filled with awe and wonder.

She did not know that it shone only by the light of the moon. She lifted up her arms and said: "Mother of pity, show me a sign that you have heard my prayers." Then she closed her eyes and waited. It seemed an eternity that she knelt there, her head bowed in her hands.

Slowly she was aware of a feeling of peace and great comfort, as if the place were sanctified by the presence of something holy. She felt that if she opened her eyes she would look upon a vision. Yet she was afraid to obey her impulse, lest the thing she would see should blind her with its beauty. The longing grew stronger and stronger within her, until she was forced to give way. Unconscious of her surroundings, unconscious of what she was doing, Marie opened her eyes. The low window beside the altar was filled with the pale light of the moon, and just outside she saw the vision.

She saw Jean kneeling upon the grass, gazing at something, and there was a smile on his face, and slowly from the ground rose a figure which Marie could not see distinctly, for it was in shadow, but it was the figure of a woman. She watched her place two hands on Jean's shoulders, as if she were blessing him, and he buried his head in the folds of her gown. Only for a moment they remained like this, and then a cloud passed over the face of the moon, and the chapel was filled with darkness.

Marie closed her eyes and sank to the ground in worship. She had seen the blessed vision of the Sainte-Vierge. She had prayed for a sign, and it had been given her, Notre Dame des Bonnes Nouvelles had appeared unto her, and with her own hands had blessed Jean, and assured him of her love and protection. There was no longer fear in Marie's heart; she felt she would never be afraid again. She had put all her faith in the Sainte-Vierge, and her prayers had been answered.

She rose unsteadily from the ground and found her way to the door. Once more she turned, and looked for the last time at the figure on the altar. It was in shadow now, and the crown was no longer gold. Marie smiled and bowed her head; she knew that no one else would ever see what she had seen. In the chapel the Sainte-Vierge still smiled her painted smile, and the vacant blue eyes gazed into nothing. The faded wreath slipped a little over the ear of the infant Jesus.

Marie stepped out into the evening. She was very tired and could scarcely see where she was going, but her heart was at peace and she was filled with a great happiness.

In the corner of the narrow field, sheltered by the chapel window, Jean whispered his desire to the sister of Jacques the fisherman.

# INDISCRETION

I WONDER how many people's lives are ruined by a moment's indiscretion? The wrong word at the wrong time—and then finish to all their dreams. They have to go on living with their tongues bitten a second too late. No use calling back the spoken word. What's said is said.

I know of three people who have been made to suffer because of a chance sentence flung into the air. One of them was myself; I lost my job through it. The other fellow lost his illusions. And the woman . . . well, I guess she did not have much left to lose, anyway. Maybe she lost her one chance of security. I have not seen either of them since. The curt, typewritten letter came from him a week later. I packed up then and came away from London, leaving the shreds of my career in the waste-paper basket. In less than three months I read in a weekly rag that he was claiming a divorce. The whole thing was so needless, too. A word from me—a word from her. And all through the sordid little street that runs between Shaftesbury Avenue and Leicester Square.

We stood at the door of the office, he and I. It was icy, it was December. I had a cold in the head, and I did not want to think about Christmas. He came out of his private office and gave me a genial clap on the shoulder.

"You're no advertisement for the time of the year," he said. "Come out and have a bite of lunch."

I thanked him. It is not every day, or every Christmas for

that matter, that one's chief broadcasts his invitations. We went to his favourite restaurant in the Strand. I felt better once I had a plateful of beef before me, listening to his easy laugh, watching his familiarity with the waiter. He had the audacity to place a sprig of holly in his button-hole.

"Look here, Chief," I said. "What's the big idea? Are you going to play Santa Claus at a kids' party?"

He laughed loudly, a spot of gravy at the corner of his mouth.

"No," he said, "I am going to be married." I made the usual retort.

"I'm not joking," he went on. "I'm telling you the truth. They all know at the office. I told 'em before I left this morning. Kept it a secret up till now because I didn't want a scene. Aren't you going to congratulate me?"

I watched his smug, self-satisfied expression.

"Hell!" I said. "You don't know what I think about women."

He laughed again, his mood was ridiculous.

"This is different," he told me, "this is the real thing. I've found her at last—the only girl. You know, I'm fond of you, my dear fellow, I'm glad you came along to lunch."

I made some sort of noise of sympathy.

"It's all very sudden, of course," he said, "but I believe in that. I like everything cut and dried. None of your hanging about. We're going to Paris this evening, while this afternoon there will be a short ceremony at a registry office." He pulled out his watch. "In exactly an hour's time," he said, "I shall be a married man."

"Where's your bride?" I asked.

"Packing," he smiled foolishly. "I only decided on this trip yesterday evening. You'll have a tremendous amount of work at the office, I'm afraid, with the Christmas rush."

He leant forward, patronising, confidential. "I have a great deal of faith in you," he said. "I've watched you these few months. You're going to do big things. I don't mind saying..."

he lowered his voice as though people listened and cared... "I don't mind saying that I shall depend on you in the future to work like blazes. You'd like a rise, wouldn't you? Might think of getting married yourself?"

I saw his friendly beam without emotion, and remembered with cynicism a proverb about "a little something makes the whole world kin." I thought of a word that would fit. "That's extremely good of you," I said, "but I shan't marry."

"You're a cynic," he said. "You've no illusions. You see all women in the same pattern. I'm twice your age and look at me—the happiest man alive."

"Perhaps I've been unlucky," I said. "Maybe I've struck the wrong type."

"Ah!" he said. "A bad picker. That's fatal. I flatter myself"— he opened his mouth to admit a fork-load of food—"that I have chosen well. You young men are so bitter about life," he went on, "no romance."

Romance! The word conjured a vision in my mind of a dark night, with the rain falling, and a small face turned to me, weeping, her hat pulled over her eyes. The last taxi driving away from the Empire Cinema; men and women in evening dress, hurrying, bent under umbrellas.

"Romance!" I said. "That's funny." Funnier still the way I caught hold of one word. It would have been so easy to let it go.

I thought for a moment, turning it over in my head. "The last time I heard that word," I said, "was from the lips of a girl. I'm not likely to forget it in a hurry."

He glanced at me inquiringly, surprised at the note in my voice.

"More bitterness?" he suggested. "Why don't you tell me about it? You're such a silent fellow, you never give yourself away."

"Oh! It's a dull story," I said, "scarcely worth listening to! Besides, you're going to be married in an hour's time."

"Come on," he laughed, "out with it."

I shrugged my shoulders, yawning slightly, and reached for a cigarette.

"I ran up against her in Wardour Street," I said. "Queer sort of place for an adventure, if you come to think of it. Almost too obvious, perhaps. It's scarcely a beat of mine, anyway. I'm a retiring sort of a chap, as you know, don't go out much. Hate meeting people, and that kind of thing. Never go to theatres, never go to parties. Can't afford it, for that matter. My life is spent between the office and my rooms in Kensington. I read a lot, hang around museums on Saturdays. Let's admit it, I'm damn dull! But the point is I scarcely know the West End at all. So Wardour Street was unfamiliar to me. About six months ago I came back from the office feeling fed up with the world. You know how one gets, nervy, irritable, thoroughly dissatisfied with life in general.

"I hated my rooms suddenly, and I felt that any moment my landlady would come in and tell me about her sister who was 'expecting' again. It occurred to me out of the blue, then, this idea to go to the West End. I took the tube to Leicester Square.

"There's an organ that throbs a sentimental tune, and when you're soaked with this and rubbing knees with your next-door neighbour, they fling a picture on the screen calculated to send you soft inside. That night I was in the right mood. They kept on giving close-ups of the blonde heroine; she seemed to be staring right at me. The usual theme, of course. Lovely innocent girl in love with handsome hero, and the dark blackguard stepping in and trying to ruin her. You're kept on tenterhooks as to whether he ruins her or whether he doesn't. He doesn't, of course, and she finishes with the handsome hero. But even then it leaves you unsatisfied. I sat through the show twice, and stumbled out of my seat at twelve o'clock still living in a land of make-believe.

"When I got outside it was raining. Through a haze I saw

people crouching under umbrellas, whisking into taxis. I saw all this as a dream; in my mind I was watching the blonde heroine shut the opening of that tent in the desert. Turning up my collar I began to walk, my head low, hating the rain.

"So I found myself in Wardour Street. I remember glancing up at the name on the corner. A few minutes later somebody bumped into me. It was a girl. Thinly dressed, I noticed, not carrying an umbrella.

"'I beg your pardon,' I said. She looked up at me, a little white face under a hat pulled low over her brow. Then to my horror she burst into tears. 'I'm most frightfully sorry,' I began. 'Have I hurt you? Is there anything I can do?' She made as if to brush past me, and put her hands to her eyes. 'It's nothing,' she said, choking over her words, 'it was stupid of me.' She looked to the right and left, standing on the edge of the pavement, apparently in some hesitation as to which way she should go. The rain was streaming down, and her little black coat was clinging to her. Half-consciously I remembered the blonde heroine of the picture I had just seen. The tears were still running on her cheeks. I saw her make some attempt to brush them away.

"'Gosh! How pathetic,' I thought, 'how utterly rotten. And here am I dissatisfied with my life for no reason.' Acting on an impulse I touched her arm. 'Look here,' I said, 'I know it's no business of mine. I've no right to speak to you at all. But—is anything the matter? Can I help you? It's such a filthy night...' She pulled out a wretched little end of handkerchief and began to blow her nose.

"'I don't know what to do,' she said, 'I don't know what to do.' She was crying again. 'I've never been to London before,' she said, 'I've come up from Shropshire. I was to be married—and there's no address. There's nothing—he's left me. I don't know where to go. There's a man been following me,' she went on timidly, glancing over her shoulder, 'he tried to speak to me twice. He was horrid. I didn't understand...'

"'Good heavens!' I thought, she was scarcely more than a child.

"'You can't stand here,' I said. 'Don't you know of any-where? Have you no friends? Isn't there a Home you could go to?' She shook her head, her mouth worked queerly at the corners. 'It's all right,' she said, 'don't bother.' It was no use, I couldn't let her go, not with that frightened gleam in her eyes, in the pouring rain.

"'Listen,' I said. 'Will you trust me to look after you—just for the moment? Will you come and have something to eat? Then we will try to find a place for you to go.' She looked up at me for a moment, straight in my eyes, and then she nodded her head gravely. 'I think I can trust you,' she said. She said this in such a way—I don't know, it seemed to go straight to my heart. I felt very old and very wise, and she was such a child.

"She put her hand on my arm, still a little scared, a little doubting. I smiled at her. 'That's the way,' I said. We turned back again down Wardour Street. There was a crowd of people in Lyons. She clung tight to my arm, bewildered by them. She chose eggs and bacon and coffee. She ate as though she was starving.

"'Is this your first meal today?' I asked. She flushed and bit her lips, ashamed.

"'Yes,' she said. I could have cut my tongue out.

"'Supposing you tell me,' I said, 'just what it is that has hap-pened.'

"The food had pulled her together, she had lost some of her shyness; she was no longer tearful, hysterical.

"'I was to be married,' she told me. 'Back in Shropshire he seemed to be so fond of me, so attentive to me and my mother. Why, he was quite a gentleman. We live on a little farm, mother and I, and my sister. It's quiet, you know, away from the big towns. I used to take the produce to Tonsbury on mar-ket days. That's where I met him. He was a traveller from a firm in London. He had a little car, too. Nothing poor or shabby about him—constantly with his hand in his pocket. He was always coming to Tonsbury for his firm, and then he would visit me. Then he started courting me—he was ever so handsome. It was all so proper, too. He asked my mother for her consent, and the date and everything was arranged.

" 'Last Sunday he was up at home as usual, laughing and teasing, saying how soon we would have a home of our own. He was to give up travelling, and get a settled job in the firm, and we were to live in London. He insisted on the wedding being in London, too, which was the one upsetting thing, as my mother and sister couldn't leave home.

" 'Yesterday was to have been my wedding day.' I saw she was ready to burst into tears again. I leant across the table and patted her hand.

" 'There, there,' I said stupidly.

" 'We motored up on Tuesday in his little car,' she went on, 'and we came to London yesterday. He had taken rooms at some hotel.' Her words trailed off; I saw she was looking at her plate.

" 'And the blackguard's left you,' I said gently.

" 'He said we were to be married,' she whispered. 'I thought it was all right.' The tears sprang in her eyes. 'He went this morning, early, before I was awake. The people at the hotel were cruel—I found out then that it was a bad place.' She fumbled for her handkerchief, but I gave her mine.

" 'I couldn't go back there, I daren't ask them for a thing,' she told me, 'and I've been looking for him all day, but I know it's no use now. How can I go home? What will they say? What will they think?' She buried her face in her hands. Poor little thing! She couldn't have been more than eighteen. I tried to keep my voice as gentle as possible.

" 'Have you any money?' I said.

" 'I've seven-and-eightpence,' she said. 'He told me I wouldn't need much.'

"I felt that this was the most impossible situation that had ever happened to anyone at any time. And there she sat looking at me, the tears in her eyes, waiting for me to suggest something.

"Suddenly I became very matter of fact. 'You had better make shift at my lodgings for tonight,' I said, 'and in the morning I'll buy you a ticket and pack you off to Shropshire.'

" 'Oh, I couldn't,' she said awkwardly, 'I don't know you.'

" 'Nonsense,' I said firmly. 'You will be perfectly safe with me.'

"We had some slight argument, of course, but finally I persuaded her.

"She was tired, too. I took her home in a taxi—she nearly fell asleep with her head on my shoulder. My landlady had gone to bed; nobody saw us come in. There was a bit of fire left in the grate. The girl crouched in front of it, spreading her hands to the feeble flame. I remember looking down on her and wondering how I should explain her presence to the landlady in the morning.

"It was then that she looked up at me from the fire, and she smiled without fear for the first time. 'If I wasn't so unhappy,' she said, 'this would be like a romance, wouldn't it?'

"Romance! Funny. It was you saying the word romance just now, chief, that brought this story back to me."

I squashed my cigarette in the ash-tray.

"Well, go on," he said. "It's not finished yet, is it?"

"That was the finish of the romance," I said.

"How d'you mean?" he said. "Did she go back to Shropshire?"

I laughed. "That girl never saw Shropshire in her life," I told him. "I woke next morning and she had gone, of course. She had my pocket-book with all my worldly goods."

He stared at me in amazement. "Good Lord." He whistled, blowing out his cheeks. "Then you mean to say she was deceiving you the whole time? There wasn't a word of truth in her story?"

"Not a word!"

"But didn't you put the police on her tracks? Didn't you do something, make some effort?"

I shook my head. "Even if they had found her, I doubt if I could have legitimately retrieved my worldly goods."

"You mean you suspected her story before you left Lyons?" he asked.

"No," I said. "I didn't suspect her once."

"I don't understand," he said. "If she was nothing but a common swindler, why not inform the police?"

I sighed wearily. "You see, chief, the point is I didn't walk the streets all night, nor did I sleep on the sitting-room sofa..."

For a few minutes we sat in silence. He looked thoughtful, he stroked his chin. "You were a damn fool, and that's all there is to it," he said. "Ever go back to Wardour Street?"

"No," I answered, "never before and never again. My only visit."

"Extraordinary how you were so easily mistaken," he said. "I can spot that type of girl a mile off. Of course, it's the sort of thing to make you steer clear of women, I agree. But they're not all like that, my dear fellow—not all." He smiled. "Sometimes you find a really genuine case of a young, unsophisticated girl, with no money, let down by some blackguard."

"For instance?" I inquired.

"As a matter of fact, I was thinking of my own girl," he confessed, "the girl who has consented to become my wife this afternoon. When I met her six weeks ago she was quite new to London. Left an orphan quite suddenly, poor kid, without a bean. Very good family, she's shown me letters and photos and things. She was making a wretched living as a typist in Birmingham, and her swine of an employer made love to her. She ran away, scared to death. Thank heaven I came along. Someone would have got hold of her. First time I met her she had twisted her ankle going down that filthy moving stairway on the Piccadilly tube. However, that's not the point." He broke off in the middle of his speech and called for the bill. "If you could see her," he began again. "She's the loveliest thing."

Into his eyes crept that blue suffused haze of the man who has not yet loved, but will have loved by midnight.

"I guess I'm the happiest man alive," he said, "she's far too good for me." The bill was paid, we rose and left the room.

"Tell you what," he said, "come and see us off by the four o'clock train at Victoria. The good old Christmas spirit, eh?"

And because I was idle, because I was bored, because there was no reason to do it at all, I consented.

"I'll be there," I said.

I remember taking the tube to Victoria, and, not finding a seat, swinging from side to side, clinging to a strap.

I remember standing in a queue to buy a platform ticket, and being jostled by a crowd of pushing, feverish people. I remember walking senselessly up and down a platform, peering into the windows of first-class carriages, yelled at by porters. I remember wondering why I had come at all. Then suddenly I saw him, his big, red, cheerful face, smiling at me from the closed window of a Pullman car. He put up his hand and waved, shouting something through the glass I could not hear. He turned and moved down the car, coming to the open door, at the entrance.

"Thought you'd given us the miss," he shouted. "Good boy—turned up after all."

He pulled the girl forward, laughing self-consciously, scarlet with pride and satisfaction.

"Here's the bride," he said. "I want you two to be great friends. Show yourself, my darling."

I stood motionless with my hat in my hand. "A happy Christmas to you," I said. She leant from the window staring at me.

Her husband gazed at us both with a quick, puzzled frown. "I say, have you two met before?" he said.

Then she laughed affectionately, and, putting her arms round his neck, she flung into the air her silly little gesture of bravado, mistress of the situation, but speaking without forethought, reckless, a shade too soon. The guard waved his little green flag.

"But, of course, I know your face," she said. "Didn't we run up against each other once in Wardour Street?"

# MONTE VERITÀ

THEY TOLD me afterwards they had found nothing. No trace of anyone, living or dead. Maddened by anger, and I believe by fear, they had succeeded at last in breaking into those forbidden walls, dreaded and shunned through countless years—to be met by silence. Frustrated, bewildered, frightened, driven to fury at the sight of those empty cells, that bare court, the valley people resorted to the primitive methods that have served so many peasants through so many centuries: fire and destruction.

It was the only answer, I suppose, to something they did not understand. Then, their anger spent, they must have realized that nothing of any purpose had been destroyed. The smouldering and blackened walls that met their eyes in the starry, frozen dawn had cheated them in the end.

Search parties were sent out, of course. The more experienced climbers amongst them, undaunted by the bare rock of the mountain summit, covered the whole ridge, from north to south, from east to west, with no result.

And that is the end of the story. Nothing more is known.

Two men from the village helped me to carry Victor's body to the valley, and he was buried at the foot of Monte Verità. I think I envied him, at peace there. He had kept his dream.

As to myself, my old life claimed me again. The second war churned up the world once more. Today, approaching seventy,

I have few illusions; yet often I think of Monte Verità and wonder what could have been the final answer.

I have three theories, but none of them may be true.

The first, and the most fantastic, is that Victor was right, after all, to hold to his belief that the inhabitants of Monte Verità *had* reached some strange state of immortality which gave them power when the hour of need arrived, so that, like the prophets of old, they vanished into the heavens. The ancient Greeks believed this of their gods, the Jews believed it of Elijah, the Christians of their Founder. Throughout the long history of religious superstition and credulity runs this ever-recurrent conviction that some persons attain such holiness and power that death can be overcome. This faith is strong in eastern countries, and in Africa; it is only to our sophisticated western eyes that the disappearance of things tangible, of persons of flesh and blood, seems impossible.

Religious teachers disagree when they try to show the difference between good and evil: what is a miracle to one becomes black magic to another. The good prophets have been stoned, but so have the witch-doctors. Blasphemy in one age becomes holy utterance in the next, and this day's heresy is tomorrow's credo.

I am no great thinker, and never have been. But this I do know, from my old climbing days: that in the mountains we come closest to whatever Being it is that rules our destiny. The great utterances of old were given from the mountain tops: it was always to the hills that the prophets climbed. The saints, the messiahs, were gathered to their fathers in the clouds. It is credible to me, in my more solemn moods, that the hand of magic reached down that night to Monte Verità and plucked those souls to safety.

Remember, I myself saw the full moon shining upon that mountain. I also, at midday, saw the sun. What I saw and heard and felt was not of this world. I think of the rock-face, with the moon upon it; I hear the chanting from the forbidden walls; I see the crevasse, cupped like a chalice between the twin peaks of the mountain; I hear the laughter; I see the bare bronzed arms outstretched to the sun.

When I remember these things, I believe in immortality...

Then—and this is perhaps because my climbing days are over, and the magic of the mountains loses its grip over old memories, as it does over old limbs—I remind myself that the eyes I looked into that last day on Monte Verità were the eyes of a living, breathing person, and the hands I touched were flesh.

Even the spoken words belonged to a human being. "Please do not concern yourself with us. We know what we must do." And then that final, tragic word, "Let Victor keep his dream."

So my second theory comes into being, and I see nightfall, and the stars, and the courage of that soul which chose the wisest way for itself and for the others; and while I returned to Victor, and the people from the valley gathered themselves together for the assault, the little band of believers, the last company of those seekers after Truth, climbed to that crevasse, between the peaks, and so were lost.

My third theory is one that comes to me in moods more cynical, more lonely, when, having dined well with friends who mean little to me, I take myself home to my apartment in New York. Looking from the window at the fantastic light and colour of my glittering fairy-world of fact that holds no tenderness, no quietude, I long suddenly for peace, for understanding. Then, I tell myself, perhaps the inhabitants of Monte Verità had long prepared themselves against departure, and when the moment came it found them ready, neither for immortality nor for death, but for the world of men and women. In stealth, in secret, they came down into the valley unobserved, and, mingling with the people, went their separate ways. I wonder, looking down from my apartment into the hub and hustle of my world, if some of them wander there, in the crowded streets and subways, and whether, if I went out and searched the passing faces, I should find such a one and have my answer.

Sometimes, when travelling, I have fancied to myself, in coming upon a stranger, that there is something exceptional in the turn of a head, in the expression of an eye, that is at once compelling and strange. I want to speak, and hold such a person instantly in conversation, but—possibly it is my fancy—it is as though some instinct warns them. A momentary pause, a hesitation, and they are gone. It might be in a train, or in some crowded thoroughfare, and for one brief moment I am aware of someone with more than earthly beauty and human grace, and I want to stretch out my hand and say, swiftly, softly, "Were you among those I saw on Monte Verità?" But there is never time. They vanish, they are gone, and I am alone again, with my third theory still unproven.

As I grow older—nearly seventy, as I have said, and memory shortens with the lengthening years—the story of Monte Verità becomes more dim to me, and more improbable, and because of this I have a great urge to write it down before memory fails me altogether. It may be that someone reading it will have the love of mountains that I had once, and so bring his own understanding to the tale, his own interpretation.

One word of warning. There are many mountain peaks in Europe, and countless numbers may bear the name of Monte Verità. They can be found in Switzerland, in France, in Spain, in Italy, in the Tyrol. I prefer to give no precise locality to mine. In these days, after two world wars, no mountain seems inaccessible. All can be climbed. None, with due caution, need be dangerous. My Monte Verità was never shunned because of difficulties of height, of ice and snow. The track leading to the summit could be followed by anyone of sure and certain step, even in late autumn. No common danger kept the climber back, but awe and fear.

I have little doubt that today my Monte Verità has been plotted upon the map with all the others. There may be resting camps near the summit, even an hotel in the little village on the eastern slopes, and the tourist lifted to the twin peaks by electric cable. Even so, I like to think there can be no final desecration, that at midnight, when the full moon rises, the mountain face is still inviolate, unchanged, and that in winter, when snow and ice, great wind and drifting cloud make the climb impassable to man, the rock-face of Monte Verità, her twin peaks lifted to the sun, stares down in silence and compassion upon a blinded world.

We were boys together, Victor and I. We were both at Marlborough, and went up to Cambridge the same year. In those days I was his greatest friend, and if we did not see so much of each other after we left the Varsity it was only because we moved in rather different worlds: my work took me much abroad, while he was busily employed running his own estate up in Shropshire. When we saw each other, we resumed our friendship without any sense of having grown apart.

My work was absorbing, so was his; but we had money enough, and leisure too, to indulge in our favourite pastime, which was climbing. The modern expert, with his equipment and his scientific training, would think our expeditions amateur in the extreme—I am talking of the idyllic days before the First World War—and, looking back on them, I suppose they were just that. Certainly there was nothing professional about the two young men who used to cling with the hands and feet to those projecting rocks in Cumberland and Wales, and later, when some experience was gained, tried the more hazardous ascents in southern Europe.

In time we became less foolhardy and more weather-wise, and learnt to treat our mountains with respect—not as an enemy to be conquered, but as an ally to be won. We used to climb, Victor and I, from no desire for danger or because we wanted to add mountain peaks to our repertoire of achievement. We climbed from desire, because we loved the thing we won.

The moods of a mountain can be more varying, more swiftly-changing, than any woman's, bringing joy, and fear, and also great repose. The urge to climb will never be explained. In olden days, perhaps, it was a wish to reach the stars. Today, anyone so minded can buy a seat on a plane and feel himself master of the skies. Even so, he will not have rock under his feet, or air upon his face; nor will he know the silence that comes only on the hills.

The best hours of my life were spent, when I was young, upon the mountains. That urge to spill all energy, all thought, to be as nothing, blotted against the sky—we called it mountain-fever, Victor and I. He used to recover from the experience more quickly than I did. He would look about him, methodical, careful, planning the descent, while I was lost in wonder, locked in a dream I could not understand. Endurance had been tested, the summit was ours, but something indefinable waited to be won. Always it was denied to me, the experience I desired, and something seemed to tell me the fault was in myself. But they were good days. The finest I have known ...

One summer, shortly after I returned to London from a business trip to Canada, a letter arrived from Victor, written in tremendous spirits. He was engaged to be married. He was, in fact, to be married very soon. She was the loveliest girl he had ever seen, and would I be his best man? I wrote back, as one does on these occasions, expressing myself delighted and wishing him all the happiness in the world. A confirmed bachelor myself, I considered him yet another good friend lost, the best of all, bogged down in domesticity.

The bride-to-be was Welsh and lived just over the border

from Victor's place in Shropshire. "And would you believe it," said Victor in a second letter, "she has never as much as set foot on Snowdon! I am going to take her education in hand." I could imagine nothing I should dislike more than trailing an inexperienced girl after me on any mountain.

A third letter announced Victor's arrival in London, and hers too, in all the bustle and preparation of the wedding. I invited both of them to luncheon. I don't know what I expected. Someone small, I think, and dark and stocky, with handsome eyes. Certainly not the beauty that came forward, putting out her hand to me and saying, "I am Anna."

In those days, before the First World War, young women did not use make-up. Anna was free of lipstick, and her gold hair was rolled in great coils over her ears. I remember staring at her, at her incredible beauty, and Victor laughed, very pleased, and said, "What did I tell you?" We sat down to lunch, and the three of us were soon at ease and chatting comfortably. A certain reserve was part of her charm, but because she knew I was Victor's greatest friend I felt myself accepted, and liked into the bargain.

Victor certainly was lucky, I said to myself, and any doubt I might have felt about the marriage went on sight of her. Inevitably, with Victor and myself, the conversation turned to mountains, and to climbing, before lunch was half-way through.

"So you are going to marry a man whose hobby is climbing mountains," I said to her, "and you've never even gone up your own Snowdon."

"No," she said, "no, I never have."

Some hesitation in her voice made me wonder. A little frown had come between those two very perfect eyes.

"Why?" I asked. "It's almost criminal to be Welsh, and know nothing of your highest mountain."

Victor interrupted. "Anna is scared," he said. "Every time I suggest an expedition she thinks out an excuse."

She turned to him swiftly. "No, Victor," she said, "it's not that. You just don't understand. I'm not afraid of climbing."

"What is it, then?" he said.

He put out his hand and held hers on the table. I could see how devoted he was to her, and how happy they were likely to become. She looked across at me, feeling me, as it were, with her eyes, and suddenly I knew instinctively what she was going to say.

"Mountains are very demanding," she said. "You have to give everything. It's wiser, for someone like myself, to keep away."

I understood what she meant, at least I thought then that I did; but because Victor was in love with her, and she was in love with him, it seemed to me that nothing could be better than the fact that they might share the same hobby, once her initial awe was overcome.

"But that's splendid," I said, "you've got just the right approach to mountain climbing. Of course you have to give everything, but together you can achieve that. Victor won't let you attempt anything beyond you. He's more cautious than I am."

Anna smiled, and then withdrew her hand from Victor's on the table.

"You are both very obstinate," she said, "and you neither of you understand. I was born in the hills. I know what I mean."

And then some mutual friend of Victor's and my own came up to the table to be introduced, and there was no more talk of mountains.

They were married about six weeks later, and I have never seen a lovelier bride than Anna. Victor was pale with nerves, I remember well, and I thought what a responsibility lay on his shoulders, to make this girl happy for all time.

I saw much of her during the six weeks of their engagement, and, though Victor never realized it for one instant, came to love her as much as he did. It was not her natural charm, nor yet her beauty, but a strange blending of both, a kind of inner radiance, that drew me to her. My only fear for their future was that Victor might be a little too boisterous, too light-hearted and cheerful—his was a very open, simple nature—and that she might withdraw into herself because of it. Certainly they made a handsome pair as they drove off after the reception—given by an elderly aunt of Anna's, for her parents were dead—and I sentimentally looked forward to staying with them in Shropshire, and being godfather to the first child.

Business took me away shortly after the wedding, and it was not until the following December that I heard from Victor, asking me down for Christmas. I accepted gladly.

They had then been married about eight months. Victor looked fit and very happy, and Anna, it seemed to me, more beautiful than ever. It was hard to take my eyes off her. They gave me a great welcome, and I settled down to a peaceful week in Victor's fine old home, which I knew well from previous visits. The marriage was almost definitely a success, that I could tell from the first. And if there appeared to be no heir on the way, there was plenty of time for that.

We walked about the estate, shot a little, read in the evenings, and were a most contented trio.

I noticed that Victor had adapted himself to Anna's quieter personality, though quiet, perhaps, is hardly the right definition for her gift of stillness. This stillness—for there is no other word for it—came from some depth within her and put a spell upon the whole house. It had always been a pleasant place in which to stay, with its lofty rambling rooms and mullioned windows; but now the peaceful atmosphere was somehow intensified and deepened, and it was as though every room had become impregnated with a strange brooding silence, to my mind quite remarkable, and much more than merely restful, as it had been before.

It is odd, but looking back to that Christmas week I can

recollect nothing of the traditional festivity itself. I don't remember what we ate or drank, or whether we set foot inside the church, which surely we must have done, with Victor as the local squire. I can only remember the quite indescribable peace of the evenings, when the shutters had been fastened and we sat before the fire in the great hall. My business trip must have tired me more than I realized, for sitting there, in Victor and Anna's home, I had no desire to do anything but relax and give myself up to this blessed, healing silence.

The other change that had come upon the house, which I did not fully take in until I had been there a few days, was that it was much barer than it had been before. The multiple odds and ends, and the collection of furniture handed down from Victor's forebears, seemed to have disappeared. The big rooms were now sparse and the great hall, where we sat, had nothing in it but a long refectory table and the chairs before the open fire. It seemed very right that it should be so, yet, thinking about it, it was an odd change for a woman to make. The usual habit of a bride is to buy new curtains and carpets, to bring the feminine touch into a bachelor house. I ventured to remark upon it to Victor.

"Oh yes," he said, looking about him vaguely, "we have cleared out a lot of stuff. It was Anna's idea. She doesn't believe in possessions, you know. No, we didn't have a sale, or anything like that. We gave them all away."

The spare room allotted to me was the one I had always used in the past, and this was pretty much as it had been before. And I had the same old comforts—cans of hot water, early tea, biscuits by my bed, cigarette box filled, all the touches of a thoughtful hostess.

Yet once, passing down the long corridor to the stair-head, I noticed that the door of Anna's room, which was usually closed, was open; and knowing it to have been Victor's mother's room in former days, with a fine old four-poster bed and several pieces of heavy solid furniture, all in keeping with the style of the house, ordinary curiosity made me glance over my shoulder as I passed the open door. The room was bare of furniture. There were no curtains to the windows, and no carpet on the floor. The wooden boards were plain. There was a table and a chair, and a long trestle bed with no covering upon it but a blanket. The windows were wide open to the dusk, which was then falling. I turned away and walked down the stairs, and as I did so came face to face with Victor, who was ascending. He must have seen me glance into the room and I did not wish to appear furtive in any way.

"Forgive the trespass," I said, "but I happened to notice the room looked very different from your mother's day."

"Yes," he said briefly, "Anna hates frills. Are you ready for dinner? She sent me to find you."

And we went downstairs together without further conversation. Somehow I could not forget that bare sparse bedroom, comparing it with the soft luxury of my own, and I felt oddly inferior that Anna should consider me as someone who could not dispense with ease and elegance, which she, for some reason, did so well without.

That evening I watched her as we sat beside the fire. Victor had been called from the hall on some business, and she and I were alone for a few moments. As usual I felt the still, soothing peace of her presence come upon me with the silence; I was wrapped about with it, enfolded, as it were, and it was unlike anything I knew in my ordinary humdrum life; this stillness came out of her, yet from another world. I wanted to tell her about it but could not find the words. At last I said, "You have done something to this house. I don't understand it."

"Don't you?" she said. "I think you do. We are both in search of the same thing, after all."

For some reason I felt afraid. The stillness was with us just the same, but intensified, almost overpowering.

"I am not aware," I said, "that I am in search of anything."

My words fell foolishly on the air and were lost. My eyes, that had drifted to the fire, were drawn, as if compelled, to hers.

"Aren't you?" she said.

I remember being swept by a feeling of profound distress. I saw myself, for the first time, as a very worthless, very trivial human being, travelling here and there about the world to no purpose, doing unnecessary business with other human beings as worthless as myself, and to no other end but that we should be fed and clothed and housed in adequate comfort until death.

I thought of my own small house in Westminster, chosen after long deliberation and furnished with great care. I saw my books, my pictures, my collection of china, and the two good servants who waited upon me and kept the house spotless always, in preparation for my return. Up to this moment my house and all it held had given me great pleasure. Now I was not sure that it had any value.

"What would you suggest?" I heard myself saying to Anna. "Should I sell everything I have and give up my work? What then?"

Thinking back on the brief conversation that passed between us, nothing that she said warranted this sudden question on my part. She implied that I was in search of something, and instead of answering her directly, yes or no, I asked her if I must give up all I had? The significance of this did not strike me at the time. All I knew then was that I was profoundly moved, and whereas a few moments before I had been at peace, I was now troubled.

"Your answer may not be the same as mine," she said, "and anyway, I am not certain of my own, as yet. One day I shall know."

Surely, I thought to myself in looking upon her, she has the answer now, with her beauty, her serenity, her understanding.

What more can she possibly achieve, unless it is that up to the present she lacks children, and so feels unfulfilled?

Victor came back into the hall, and it seemed to me his presence brought solidity and warmth to the atmosphere; there was something familiar and comfortable about his old smoking jacket worn with his evening trousers.

"It's freezing hard," he said. "I went outside to see. The thermometer is down to thirty. Lovely night, though. Full moon." He drew up his chair before the fire and smiled affectionately at Anna. "Almost as cold as the night we spent on Snowdon," he said. "Heavens above, I shan't forget that in a hurry." And turning to me with a laugh he added, "I never told you, did I, that Anna condescended to come climbing with me after all?"

"No," I said, astonished. "I thought she had set herself against it."

I looked across a Anna, and I noticed that her eyes had grown strangely blank, without expression. I felt instinctively that the subject brought up by Victor was one she would not have chosen. Victor, insensitive to this, went prattling on.

"She's a dark horse," he said. "She knows just as much about climbing mountains as you or I. In fact, she was ahead of me the whole time, and I lost her."

He continued, half-laughing, half-serious, giving me every detail of the climb, which seemed hazardous in the extreme, as they had left it much too late in the year.

It seemed that the weather, which had promised well in the morning for their start, had turned by mid-afternoon, bringing thunder and lightning and finally a blizzard; so that darkness overtook them in the descent, and they were forced to spend the night in the open.

"The thing I shall never understand," said Victor, "is how I came to miss her. One moment she was by my side, and the next she had gone. I can tell you I had a very bad three hours, in pitch darkness and half a gale."

Anna never said a word while he told the story. It was as though she withdrew herself completely. She sat in her chair, motionless. I felt uneasy, anxious. I wanted Victor to stop.

"Anyway," I said, to hasten him, "you got down all right, and none the worse for it."

"Yes," he said ruefully, "at about five in the morning, thoroughly wet and thoroughly frightened. Anna came up to me out of the mist not even damp, surprised that I was angry. Said she had been sheltered by a piece of rock. It was a wonder she had not broken her neck. Next time we go mountain climbing, I've told her that she can be the guide."

"Perhaps," I said, with a glance at Anna, "there won't be a next time. Once was enough."

"Not a bit of it," said Victor cheerfully, "we are all set, you know, to go off next summer. The Alps, or the Dolomites, or the Pyrenees, we haven't decided yet on the objective. You had better come with us and we'll have a proper expedition."

I shook my head, regretfully.

"I only wish I could," I said, "but it's impossible. I must be in New York by May and shan't be home again until September."

"Oh, that's a long way ahead," said Victor, "anything may happen by May. We'll talk of it again, nearer the time."

Still Anna said no word, and I wondered why Victor saw nothing strange in her reticence. Suddenly she said good night and went upstairs. It was obvious to me that all this chatter of mountain climbing had been unwelcome to her. I felt an urge to attack Victor on the subject.

"Look here," I said, "do think twice about this holiday in the mountains. I am pretty sure Anna isn't for it."

"Not for it?" said Victor, surprised. "Why, it was her idea entirely."

I stared at him.

"Are you sure?" I asked.

"Of course I'm sure. I tell you, old fellow, she's crazy about mountains. She had a fetish about them. It's her Welsh blood, I suppose. I was being light-hearted just now about that night on Snowdon, but between ourselves I was quite amazed at her courage and her endurance. I don't mind admitting that what with the blizzard, and being frightened for her, I was dead beat by morning; but she came out of that mist like a spirit from another world. I've never seen her like it. She went down that blasted mountain as if she had spent the night on Olympus, while I limped behind her like a child. She is a very remarkable person: you realize that, don't you?"

"Yes," I said slowly, "I do agree. Anna is very remarkable."

Shortly afterwards we went upstairs to bed, and as I undressed and put on my pyjamas, which had been left to warm for me before the fire, and noticed the thermos flask of hot milk on the bedside table, in case I should be wakeful, and padded about the thick carpeted room in my soft slippers, I thought once again of that strange bare room where Anna slept, and of the narrow trestle bed. In a futile, unnecessary gesture, I threw aside the heavy satin quilt that lay on top of my blankets, and before getting into bed opened my windows wide.

I was restless, though, and could not sleep. My fire sank low and the cold air penetrated the room. I heard my old worn travelling clock race round the hours through the night. At four I could stand it no longer and remembered the thermos of milk with gratitude. Before drinking it I decided to pamper myself still further and close the window.

I climbed out of bed and, shivering, went across the room to do so. Victor was right. A white frost covered the ground. The moon was full. I stood for a moment by the open window, and from the trees in shadow I saw a figure come and stand below me on the lawn. Not furtive, as a trespasser, not creeping, as a thief. Whoever it was stood motionless, as though in meditation, with face uplifted to the moon.

Then I perceived that it was Anna. She wore a dressing-gown, with a cord about it, and her hair was loose on her shoulders. She made no sound as she stood there on the frosty lawn, and I saw, with a shock of horror, that her feet were bare. I stood watching, my hand on the curtain, and suddenly I felt that I was looking upon something intimate and secret, which concerned me not. So I shut my window and returned to bed. Instinct told me that I must say nothing of what I had seen to Victor, or to Anna herself; and because of this I was filled with disquiet, almost with apprehension.

Next morning the sun shone and we were out about the grounds with the dogs, Anna and Victor both so normal and cheerful that I told myself I had been overwrought the previous night. If Anna chose to walk bare-foot in the small hours it was her business, and I had behaved ill in spying upon her. The rest of my visit passed without incident; we were all three happy and content, and I was very loath to leave them.

I saw them again for a brief moment, some months later, before I left for America. I had gone into the Map House, in St. James's, to buy myself some half-dozen books to read on that long thrash across the Atlantic—a journey one took with certain qualms in those days, the *Titanic* tragedy still fresh in memory—and there were Victor and Anna, poring over maps, which they had spread out over every available space.

There was no chance of a real meeting. I had engagements for the rest of the day, and so had they, so it was hail and farewell.

"You find us," said Victor, "getting busy about the summer holiday. The itinerary is planned. Change your mind and join us."

"Impossible," I said. "All being well, I should be home by September. I'll get in touch with you directly I return. Well, where are you making for?"

"Anna's choice," said Victor. "She's been thinking this out

for weeks, and she's hit on a spot that looks completely inaccessible. Anyway, it's somewhere you and I have never climbed."

He pointed down to the large-scale map in front of them. I followed his finger to a point that Anna had already marked with a tiny cross.

"Monte Verità," I read.

I looked up and saw that Anna's eyes were upon me.

"Completely unknown territory, as far as I'm concerned," I said. "Be sure and have advice first, before setting forth. Get hold of local guides, and so on. What made you choose that particular ridge of mountains?"

Anna smiled, and I felt a sense of shame, of inferiority beside her.

"The Mountain of Truth," she said. "Come with us, do."

I shook my head and went off upon my journey.

During the months that followed I thought of them both, and envied them too. They were climbing, and I was hemmed in, not by the mountains that I loved but by hard business. Often I wished I had the courage to throw my work aside, turn my back on the civilized world and its dubious delights, and go seeking after truth with my two friends. Only convention deterred me, the sense that I was making a successful career for myself, which it would be folly to cut short. The pattern of my life was set. It was too late to change.

I returned to England in September, and I was surprised, in going through the great pile of letters that awaited me, to have nothing from Victor. He had promised to write and give me news of all they had seen and done. They were not on the telephone, so I could not get in touch with them direct, but I made a note to write to Victor as soon as I had sorted out my business mail.

A couple of days later, coming out of my club, I ran into a man, a mutual friend of ours, who detained me a moment to ask some question about my journey, and then, just as I was going down the steps, called over his shoulder, "I say, what a tragedy about poor Victor. Are you going to see him?"

"What do you mean? What tragedy?" I asked. "Has there been an accident?"

"He's terribly ill in a nursing-home, here in London," came the answer. "Nervous breakdown. You know his wife has left him?"

"Good God, no," I exclaimed.

"Oh, yes. That's the cause of all the trouble. He's gone quite to pieces. You know he was devoted to her."

I was stunned. I stood staring at the fellow, my face blank.

"Do you mean," I said, "that she has gone off with somebody else?"

"I don't know. I assume so. No one can get anything out of Victor. Anyway, there he has been for several weeks, with this breakdown."

I asked for the address of the nursing-home, and at once, without further delay, jumped into a cab and was driven there.

At first I was told, on making inquiry, that Victor was seeing no visitors, but I took out my card and scribbled a line across the back. Surely he would not refuse to see me? A nurse came, and I was taken upstairs to a room on the first floor.

I was horrified, when she opened the door, to see the haggard face that looked up at me from the chair beside the gas-fire, so frail he was, so altered.

"My dear old boy," I said, going towards him, "I only heard five minutes ago that you were here."

The nurse closed the door and left us together.

To my distress Victor's eyes filled with tears.

"It's all right," I said, "don't mind me. You know I shall understand."

He seemed unable to speak. He just sat there, hunched in his dressing-gown, the tears running down his cheeks. I had never felt more helpless. He pointed to a chair, and I drew it up beside him. I waited. If he did not want to tell me what had happened I would not press him. I only wanted to comfort him, to be of some assistance.

At last he spoke, and I hardly recognized his voice.

"Anna's gone," he said. "Did you know that? She's gone."

I nodded. I put my hand on his knee, as though he were a small boy again and not a man past thirty, of my own age.

"I know," I said gently, "but it will be all right. She will come back again. You are sure to get her back."

He shook his head. I had never seen such despair, and such complete conviction.

"Oh no," he said, "she will never come back. I know her too well. She's found what she wants."

It was pitiful to see how completely he had given in to what had happened. Victor, usually so strong, so well-balanced.

"Who is it?" I said. "Where did she meet this other fellow?"

Victor stared at me, bewildered.

"What do you mean?" he said. "She hasn't met anyone. It's not that at all. If it were, that would be easy..."

He paused, spreading out his hands in a hopeless gesture. And suddenly he broke down again, but this time not with weakness but with a more fearful sort of stifled rage, the impotent, useless rage of a man who fights against something stronger than himself. "It was the mountain that got her," he said, "that God-damned mountain, Monte Verità. There's a sect there, a closed order, they shut themselves up for life—there, on that mountain. I never dreamed there could be such a thing. I never knew. And she's there. On that damned mountain. On Monte Verità..."

I sat there with him in the nursing-home all afternoon, and little by little had the whole story from him.

The journey itself, Victor said, had been pleasant and

uneventful. Eventually they reached the centre from which they proposed to explore the terrain immediately below Monte Verità, and here they met with difficulties. The country was un-known to Victor, and the people seemed morose and un-friendly, very different, he said, to the sort of folk who had welcomed us in the past. They spoke in a patois hard to under-stand, and they lacked intelligence.

"At least, that's how they struck me," said Victor. "They were very rough and somehow undeveloped, the sort of people who might have stepped out of a former century. You know how, when we climbed together, the people could not do enough to help us, and we always managed to find guides. Here, it was different. When Anna and I tried to find out the best approach to Monte Verità, they would not tell us. They just stared at us in a stupid sort of way, and shrugged their shoulders. They had no guides, one fellow said; the mountain was—savage, unexplored."

Victor paused, and looked at me with that same expression of despair.

"You see," he said, "that's when I made my mistake. I should have realized the expedition was a failure—to that particular spot at any rate—and suggested to Anna that we turned back and tackled something else, something nearer to civilization anyhow, where the people were more helpful and the country more familiar. But you know how it is. You get a stubborn feel-ing inside you, on the mountains, and any opposition some-how rouses you.

"And Monte Verità itself..." he broke off and stared in front of him. It was as though he was looking upon it again in his own mind. "I've never been one for lyrical description, you know that," he said. "On our finest climbs I was always the practical one and you the poet. For sheer beauty, I have never seen anything like Monte Verità. We have climbed many higher peaks, you and I, and far more dangerous ones, too; but this was somehow... sublime."

After a few moments' silence he continued talking. "I said to Anna, 'What shall we do?' and she answered me without hesitation, 'We must go on.' I did not argue, I knew perfectly well that would be her wish. The place had put a spell on both of us."

They left the valley, and began the ascent.

"It was a wonderful day," said Victor, "hardly a breath of wind, and not a cloud in the sky. Scorching sun, you know how it can be, cut the air clean and cold. I chaffed Anna about that other climb, up Snowdon, and made her promise not to leave me behind this time. She was wearing an open shirt, and a brief kilted skirt, and her hair was loose. She looked... quite beautiful."

As he talked, slowly, quietly, I had the impression that it must surely be an accident that had happened, but that his mind, unhinged by tragedy, baulked at Anna's death. It must be so. Anna had fallen. He had seen her fall and had been powerless to help her. He had then returned, broken in mind and spirit, telling himself she still lived on Monte Verità.

"We came to a village an hour before sundown," said Victor.

"The climb had taken us all day. We were still about three hours from the peak itself, or so I judged. The village consisted of some dozen dwellings or so, huddled together. And as we walked towards the first one, a curious thing happened."

He paused and stared in front of him.

"Anna was a little ahead of me," he said, "moving swiftly with those long strides of hers, you know how she does. I saw two or three men, with some children and goats, come on to the track from a piece of pasture land to the right of us. Anna raised her hand in salute, and at sight of her the men started, as if terrified, and snatching up the children ran to the nearest group of hovels, as if all the fiends in hell were after them. I heard them bolt the doors and shutter the windows. It was the most extraordinary thing. The goats went scattering down the track, equally scared."

Victor said he had made some joke to Anna about a charming welcome, and that she seemed upset; she did not know what she could have done to frighten them. Victor went to the first hut and knocked upon the door.

Nothing happened at all, but he could hear whispers inside and a child crying. Then he lost patience and began to shout. This had effect, and after a moment one of the shutters was removed and a man's face appeared at the gap and stared at him. Victor, by way of encouragement, nodded and smiled. Slowly the man withdrew the whole of the shutter and Victor spoke to him. At first the man shook his head, then he seemed to change his mind and came and unbolted the door. He stood in the entrance, peering nervously about him, and, ignoring Victor, looked at Anna. He shook his head violently and, speaking very quickly and quite unintelligibly, pointed towards the summit of Monte Verità. Then from the shadows of the small room came an elderly man, leaning on two sticks, who motioned aside the terrified children and moved past them to the door. He, at least, spoke a language that was not entirely patois.

"Who is that woman?" he asked. "What does she want with us?"

Victor explained that Anna was his wife, that they had come from the valley to climb the mountain, that they were tourists on holiday, and they would be glad of shelter for the night. He said the old man stared away from him to Anna.

"She is your wife?" he said. "She is not from Monte Verità?"

"She is my wife," repeated Victor. "We come from England. We are in this country on holiday. We have never been here before."

The old man turned to the younger and they muttered together for a few moments. Then the younger man went back inside the house, and there was further talk from the interior. A woman appeared, even more frightened than the younger man. She was literally trembling, Victor said, as she looked out of the doorway towards Anna. It was Anna who disturbed them.

"She is my wife," said Victor again, "we come from the valley."

Finally the old man made a gesture of consent, of understanding.

"I believe you," he said. "You are welcome to come inside. If you are from the valley, that is all right. We have to be careful."

Victor beckoned to Anna, and slowly she came up the track and stood beside Victor, on the threshold of the house. Even now the woman looked at her with timidity, and she and the children backed away.

The old man motioned his visitors inside. The living-room was bare but clean, and there was a fire burning.

"We have food," said Victor, unshouldering his pack, "and mattresses too. We don't want to be a nuisance. But if we could eat here, and sleep on the floor, it will do very well indeed."

The old man nodded. "I am satisfied," he said, "I believe you."

Then he withdrew with his family.

Victor said he and Anna were both puzzled at their reception, and could not understand why the fact of their being married, and coming from the valley, should have gained them admittance, after that first odd show of terror. They ate, and unrolled their packs, and then the old man appeared again with milk for them, and cheese. The woman remained behind, but the younger man, out of curiosity, accompanied the elder.

Victor thanked the old fellow for his hospitality, and said that now they would sleep, and in the morning, soon after sunrise, they would climb to the summit of the mountain.

"Is the way easy?" he asked.

"It is not difficult," came the reply. "I would offer to send someone with you, but no one cares to go."

His manner was diffident, and Victor said he glanced again at Anna.

"Your wife will be all right in the house here," he said. "We will take care of her."

"My wife will climb with me," said Victor. "She won't want to stay behind."

A look of anxiety came into the old man's face.

"It is better that your wife does not go up Monte Verità," he said. "It will be dangerous."

"Why is it dangerous for me to go up to Monte Verità?" asked Anna.

The old man looked at her, his anxiety deepening.

"For girls," he said, "for women, it is dangerous."

"But how?" asked Anna. "Why? You told my husband the path is easy."

"It is not the path that is dangerous," he answered; "my son can set you on the path. It is because of the . . ." and Victor said he used a word that neither he nor Anna understood, but that it sounded like *sacerdotessa*, or *sacerdozio*.

"That's priestess, or priesthood," said Victor. "It can't be that. I wonder what on earth he means?"

The old man, anxious and distressed, looked from one to the other of them.

"It is safe for you to climb Monte Verità, and to descend again," he repeated to Victor, "but not for your wife. They have great power, the *sacerdotesse*. Here in the village we are always in fear for our young girls, for our women."

Victor said the whole thing sounded like an African travel tale, where a tribe of wild men pounced out of the jungle and carried off the female population into captivity.

"I don't know what he's talking about," he said to Anna, "but I suppose they are riddled with some sort of superstition, which will appeal to you, with your Welsh blood."

He laughed, he told me, making light of it, and then, being confoundedly sleepy, arranged their mattresses in front of the fire. Bidding the old man good evening, he and Anna settled themselves for the night.

He slept soundly, in the profound sleep that comes after climbing, and woke suddenly, just before daybreak, to the sound of a cock crowing in the village outside.

He turned over on his side to see if Anna was awake.

The mattress was thrown back, and bare. Anna had gone...

No one was yet astir in the house, Victor said, and the only sound was the cock crowing. He got up and put on his shoes and coat, went to the door and stepped outside.

It was the cold, still moment that comes just before sunrise. The last few stars were paling in the sky. Clouds hid the valley, some thousands of feet below. Only here, near the summit of the mountain, was it clear.

At first Victor felt no misgiving. He knew by this time that Anna was capable of looking after herself, and was as sure-footed as he—more so, possibly. She would take no foolish risks, and anyway the old man had told them that the climb was not dangerous. He felt hurt, though, that she had not waited for him. It was breaking the promise that they should always climb together. And he had no idea how much of a start she had in front of him. The only thing he could do was to follow her as swiftly as he could.

He went back into the room to collect their rations for the day—she had not thought of that. Their packs they could fetch later, for the descent, and they would probably have to accept hospitality here for another night.

His movements must have roused his host, for suddenly the

old man appeared from the inner room and stood beside him. His eyes fell on Anna's empty mattress, then he searched Victor's eyes, almost in accusation.

"My wife has gone on ahead," Victor said. "I am going to follow her."

The old man looked very grave. He went to the open door and stood there, staring away from the village, up the mountain.

"It was wrong to let her go," he said, "you should not have permitted it." He appeared very distressed, Victor said, and shook his head to and fro, murmuring to himself.

"It's all right," said Victor. "I shall soon catch her up, and we shall probably be back again, soon after midday."

He put his hand on the old fellow's arm, to reassure him.

"I fear very much that it will be too late," said the old man. "She will go to them, and once she is with them she will not come back."

Once again he used the word *sacerdotesse*, the power of the *sacerdotesse*, and his manner, his state of apprehension, now communicated itself to Victor, so that he too felt a sense of urgency, and of fear.

"Do you mean that there are living people at the top of Monte Verità?" he said. "People who may attack her, and harm her bodily?"

The old man began to talk rapidly, and it was difficult to make any sense out of the torrent of words that now sprang from him. No, he said, the *sacerdotesse* would not hurt her, they hurt no one; it was that they would take her to become one of them. Anna would go to them, she could not help herself, the power was so strong. Twenty, thirty years ago, the old man said, his daughter had gone to them: he had never seen her again. Other young women from the village, and from down below, in the valley, were called by the *sacerdotesse*. Once they were called they had to go, no one could keep them back. No one saw them again. Never, never. It had been so for many years, in his father's time, his father's father's time, before that, even.

It was not known now when the *sacerdotesse* first came to Monte Verità. No man living had set eyes upon them. They lived there, enclosed, behind their walls, but with power, he kept insisting, with magic. "Some say they have this from God, some from the Devil," he said, "but we do not know, we cannot tell. It is rumoured that the *sacerdotesse* on Monte Verità never grow old, they stay forever young and beautiful, and that it is from the moon they draw their power. It is the moon they worship, and the sun."

Victor gathered little from this wild talk. It must all be legend, superstition.

The old man shook his head and looked towards the mountain track. "I saw it in her eyes last night," he said, "I was afraid of it. She had the eyes they have, when they are called. I have seen it before. With my own daughter, with others."

By now the rest of the family had woken and had come by turn into the room. They seemed to sense what had happened. The younger man, and the woman, even the children, looked at Victor with anxiety and a strange sort of compassion. He said the atmosphere filled him not so much with alarm as with anger and irritation. It made him think of cats, and broomsticks, and sixteenth-century witchcraft.

The mist was breaking slowly, down in the valley, and the clouds were going. The soft glow in the sky, beyond the range of mountains to the eastward, heralded the rising sun.

The old man said something to the younger, and pointed with his stick.

"My son will put you on the track," he said, "he will come part of the way only. Further he does not care to go."

Victor said he set off with all their eyes upon him; and not only from this first hut, but from the other dwellings in the little village, he was aware of faces looking from drawn shutters, and faces peering from half-open doors. The whole village was astir now and intent upon watching him, held by a fearful fascination.

His guide made no attempt to talk to him. He walked ahead, his shoulders bent, his eyes on the ground. Victor felt that he went only on command of the old man, his father.

The track was rough and stony, broken in many places, and was, Victor judged, part of an old water-course that would be impassable when the rains came. Now, in full summer, it was easy enough to climb. Verdure, thorn, and scrub they left behind them, after climbing steadily for an hour, and the summit of the mountain pierced the sky directly above their heads, split into two like a divided hand. From the depths of the valley, and from the village even, this division could not be seen; the two peaks seemed as one.

The sun had risen with them as they climbed, and now shone in full upon the south-eastern face, turning it to coral. Great banks of clouds, soft and rolling, hid the world below. Victor's guide stopped suddenly and pointed ahead, where a jutting lip of rock wound in a razor's edge and curved southward out of sight.

"Monte Verità," he said, and then repeated it again, "Monte Verità."

Then he turned swiftly and began scrambling back along the way that they had come.

Victor called to him, but the man did not answer; he did not even bother to turn his head. In a moment he was out of sight. There was nothing for it but to go on alone, round the lip of the escarpment, Victor said, and trust that he found Anna waiting for him on the further side.

It took him another half-hour to encircle the projecting shoulder of the mountain, and with every step he took his anxiety deepened, because now, on the southward side, there was no gradual incline—the mountain face was sheer. Soon further progress would be impossible.

"Then," Victor said, "I came out through a sort of gully-way, over a ridge about three hundred feet only from the summit; and I saw it, the monastery, built out of the rock between the two peaks, absolutely bare and naked; a steep rock wall enclosing it, a drop of a thousand feet beneath the wall to the next ridge, and above, nothing but the sky and the twin peaks of Monte Verità."

It was true, then. Victor had not lost his mind. The place existed. There had been no accident. He sat there, in his chair by the gas-fire, in the nursing-home; and this had happened, it was not fantasy, born out of tragedy.

He seemed calm, now that he had told me so much. A great part of the strain had gone, his hands no longer trembled. He looked more like the old Victor, and his voice was steady.

"It must have been centuries old," he said, after a moment or two. "God knows how long it must have taken to build, hewn out of the rock-face like that. I have never seen anything more stark and savage, nor, in a strange way, more beautiful. It seemed to hang there, suspended, between the mountain and the sky. There were many long narrow slits, for light and air. No real windows, in the sense we know them. There was a tower, looking west, with a sheer drop below. The great wall encircled the whole place, making it impregnable, like a fortress. I could see no way of entrance. There was no sign of life. No sign of anyone. I stood there staring at the place, and the narrow window slits stared back at me. There was nothing I could do but wait there until Anna showed herself. Because now, you see, I was convinced the old man had been right, and I knew what must have happened. The inhabitants had seen Anna, from behind those slit windows, and had called to her. She was with them now, inside. She must see me, standing outside the wall, and presently would come out to me. So I waited there, all day..."

His words were simple. Just a plain statement of fact. Any husband might have waited thus for a wife who had, during their holiday, ventured forth one morning to call upon friends. He sat down, and later ate his lunch, and watched the rolling banks of cloud that hid the world below move, and disperse, and form again; and the sun, in all its summer strength, beat down upon the unprotected face of Monte Verità, on the tower and the narrow window-slits, and the great encircling wall, from whence came no movement and no sound.

"I sat there all the day," said Victor, "but she did not come. The force of the sun was blinding, scorching, and I had to go back to the gully-way for shelter. There, lying under the shadow of a projecting rock, I could still watch that tower and those window slits. You and I in the past have known silence on the mountains, but nothing like the silence beneath those twin peaks of Monte Verità.

"The hours dragged by and I went on waiting. Gradually it grew cooler, and then, as my anxiety increased, time raced instead. The sun went too fast into the west. The colour of the rock-face was changing. There was no longer any glare. I began to panic then. I went to the wall and shouted. I felt along the wall with my hands, but there was no entrance, there was nothing. My voice echoed back to me, again and again. I looked up, and all I could see were those blind slits of windows. I began to doubt everything, the old man's story, all that he had said. This place was uninhabited, no one had lived there for a thousand years. It was something built long ago in time, and now deserted. And Anna had never come to it at all. She had fallen, on that narrow lip-way where the track ended and the man had left me. She must have fallen into the sheer depths where the southern shoulder of the mountain ridge began. And this is what had happened to the other women who had come this way, the old man's daughter, the girls from the valleys; they had all fallen, none of them had ever reached the ultimate rock-face, here between the peaks."

The suspense would have been easier to bear if the first strain and sign of breakdown had come back into Victor's voice. As it was, sitting there in the London nursing-home, the room impersonal and plain, the routine bottles of medicines and pills on the table by his side, and the sound of traffic coming from Wigmore Street, his voice took on a steady monotonous quality, like a clock ticking; it would have been more natural had he turned suddenly, and screamed.

"Yet I dared not go back," he said, "unless she came. I was compelled to go on waiting there, beneath the wall. The clouds banked up towards me and turned grey. All the warning evening shadows that I knew too well crept into the sky. One moment the rock-face, and the wall, and the slit windows were golden; then, suddenly, the sun was gone. There was no dusk at all. It was cold, and it was night."

Victor told me that he stayed there against the wall until daybreak. He did not sleep. He paced up and down to keep warm. When dawn came he was chilled and numb, faint, too, from want of food. He had brought with him only the rations for their midday meal.

Sense told him that to wait now, through another day, was madness. He must return to the village for food and drink, and if possible enlist the help of the men there to form a search-party. Reluctantly, when the sun rose, he left the rock-face. Silence enwrapped it still. He was certain now there was no life behind the walls.

He went back, round the shoulder of the mountain, to the track; and so down into the morning mist, and to the village.

Victor said they were waiting there for him. It was as though he was expected. The old man was standing at the entrance of his home, and gathered about him were neighbours, mostly men and children.

Victor's first question was, "Has my wife returned?" Somehow, descending from the summit, hope had come to him again—that she had never climbed the mountain track, that she had walked another way, and had come back to the village by a different path. When he saw their faces his hope went.

"She will not come back," said the old man, "we told you she would not come back. She has gone to them, on Monte Verità."

Victor had wisdom enough to ask for food and drink before entering into argument. They gave him this. They stood beside him, watching him with compassion. Victor said the greatest agony was the sight of Anna's pack, her mattress, her drinking bottle, her knife; the little personal possessions she had not taken with her.

When he had eaten they continued to stand there, waiting for him to speak. He told the old man everything. How he had waited all day, and through the night. How there was never a sound, or a sign of life, from those slit windows on the rock-face on Monte Verità. Now and again the old man translated what Victor said to the neighbours.

When Victor had finished the old man spoke.

"It is as I said. Your wife is there. She is with them."

Victor, his nerves to pieces, shouted aloud.

"How can she be there? There is no one alive in that place. It's dead, it's empty. It's been dead for centuries."

The old man leant forward and put his hand on Victor's shoulder. "It is not dead. That is what many have said before. They went and waited, as you waited. Twenty-five years ago I did the same. This man here, my neighbour, waited three months, day after day, night after night, many years ago, when his wife was called. She never came back. No one who is called to Monte Verità returns."

She had fallen, then. She had died. It was that after all. Victor told them this, he insisted upon it, he begged that they would go now, with him, and search the mountain for her body.

Gently, compassionately, the old man shook his head. "In the past we did that too," he said. "There are those among us who climb with great skill, who know the mountain, every inch of it, and who have descended the southern side even, to the edge of the great glacier, beyond which no one can live. There are no bodies. Our women never fell. They were not there. They are in Monte Verità, with the *sacerdotesse*."

It was hopeless, Victor said. It was no use to try argument. He knew that he must go down to the valley, and if he could not get help there go further yet, back to some part of the country that was familiar to him, where he could find guides who would be willing to return with him.

"My wife's body is somewhere on this mountain," he said. "I must find it. If your people won't help me, I will get others."

The old man looked over his shoulder and spoke a name. From the little crowd of silent spectators came a child, a small girl of about nine years old. He laid his hand upon her head.

"This child," he said to Victor, "has seen and spoken with the *sacerdotesse*. Other children, in the past, have seen them too. Only to children, and then rarely, do they show themselves. She will tell you what she saw."

The child began her recitation, in a high sing-song voice, her eyes fixed upon Victor; and he could tell, he said, that it was a tale she had repeated so many times, to the same listeners, that it was now a chant, a lesson learnt by heart. And it was all in patois. Not one word could Victor understand.

When she had finished the old man acted as interpreter; and from force of habit he too declaimed as the child had done, his tone taking that same sing-song quality.

"I was with my companions on Monte Verità. A storm

came, and my companions ran away. I walked, and lost myself, and came to the place where the wall is, and the windows. I cried; I was afraid. She came out of the wall, the tall and splendid one, and another with her, also young and beautiful. They comforted me and I wanted to go inside the walls with them, when I heard the singing from the tower, but they told me it was forbidden. When I was thirteen years old I could return to live with them. They wore white raiment to the knees, their arms and legs were bare, the hair close to the head. They were more beautiful than the people of this world. They led me back from Monte Verità, down the track where I could find my way. Then they went from me. I have told all I know."

The old man watched Victor's face when he had finished his recital. Victor said the faith that must have been put in the child's statement astounded him. It was obvious, he thought, that the child had fallen asleep, and dreamt, and translated her dream into reality.

"I am sorry," he told his interpreter, "but I can't believe the child's tale. It is imagination."

Once again the child was called and spoken to, and she at once ran out of the house and disappeared.

"They gave her a circlet of stones on Monte Verità," said the old man. "Her parents keep it locked up, in case of evil. She has gone to ask for it, to show you."

In a few moments the child returned, and she put into Victor's hand a girdle, small enough to encompass a narrow waist, or else to hang about the neck. The stones, which looked like quartz, were cut and shaped by hand, fitting into one another in hollowed grooves. The craftsmanship was fine, even exquisitely done. It was not the rude handiwork of peasants, done of a winter's evening, to pass the time. In silence Victor handed the circlet back to the child.

"She may have found it on the mountain side," he said.

"We do not work thus," answered the old man, "nor the

people in the valley, nor even in the cities of this country, where I have been. The child was given the circlet, as she had told us, by those who inhabit Monte Verità."

Victor knew then that further argument was useless. Their obstinacy was too strong, and their superstition proof against all worldly sense. He asked if he might remain in the house another day and night.

"You are welcome to stay," said the old man, "until you know the truth."

One by one the neighbours dispersed, the routine of the quiet day was resumed. It was as though nothing had happened. Victor went out again, this time towards the northern shoulder of the mountain. He had not gone far before he realized that this ridge was unclimbable, at any rate without skilled help and equipment. If Anna had gone that way she had found certain death.

He came back to the village, which, situated as it was on the eastern slopes, had already lost the sun. He went into the living-room, and saw that there was a meal there prepared for him, and his mattress lay on the floor before the hearth.

He was too exhausted to eat. He flung himself down on the mattress and slept. Next morning he rose early, and climbed once more to Monte Verità, and sat there all the day. He waited, watching the slit windows, while the hot sun scorched the rock-face through the long hours and then sank down into the western sky; and nothing stirred, and no one came.

He thought of that other man from the village who some years ago had waited there three months, day after day, night after night; and Victor wondered what limitation time would put to his endurance, and whether he would equal the other in fortitude.

On the third day, at that moment of midday when the sun was strongest, he could bear the heat no longer and went to lie in the gully-way, in the shadow and blessed coolness of the projecting rock. Worn with the strain of watching, and with the despair that now filled his entire being, Victor slept.

He awoke with a start. The hands of his watch pointed to five o'clock, and it was already cold inside the gully. He climbed out and looked towards the rock-face, golden now in the setting sun. Then he saw her. She was standing beneath the wall, but on a ledge only a few feet in circumference, and below her the rock-face fell away sheer, a thousand feet or more.

She waited there, looking towards him, and he ran towards her shouting "Anna...Anna..." And he said that he heard himself sobbing, and he thought his heart would burst.

When he drew closer he saw that he could not reach her. The great drop to the depths below divided them. She was a bare twelve feet away from him, and he could not touch her.

"I stood where I was, staring at her," said Victor. "I did not speak. Something seemed to choke my voice. I felt the tears running down my face. I was crying. I had made up my mind that she was dead, you see, that she had fallen. And she was there, she was alive. Ordinary words wouldn't come. I tried to say "What has happened? Where have you been?'—but it wasn't any use. Because as I looked at her I knew in one moment, with terrible blinding certainty, that it was all true, what the old man had said, and the child; it wasn't imagination, it wasn't superstition. Though I saw no one but Anna, the whole place suddenly became alive. From behind those window slits above me there were God knows how many eyes, watching, looking down on me. I could feel the nearness of them, beyond those walls. And it was uncanny, and horrible, and real."

Now the strain had come back into Victor's voice, now his hands trembled once again. He reached out for a glass of water and drank thirstily.

"She was not wearing her own clothes," he said. "She had a kind of shirt, like a tunic, to her knees, and round her waist a circlet of stones, like the one the child had shown me. Nothing on her feet, and her arms bare. What frightened me most was that her hair was cut quite short, as short as yours or mine. It altered her strangely, made her look younger, but in some way terribly austere. Then she spoke to me. She said quite naturally, as if nothing had happened, 'I want you to go back home, Victor darling. You mustn't worry about me any more.'"

Victor told me he could hardly credit it, at first, that she could stand there and say this to him. It reminded him of those so-called psychic messages that mediums give out to relatives at a spiritualistic séance. He could hardly trust himself to answer. He thought that perhaps she had been hypnotized and was speaking under suggestion.

"Why do you want me to go home?" he said, very gently, not wanting to damage her mind, which these people might have destroyed.

"It's the only thing to do," she answered. And then, Victor said, she smiled, normally, happily, as if they were at home discussing plans. "I'm all right, darling," she said. "This isn't madness, or hypnotism, or any of the things you imagine it to be. They have frightened you in the village, and it's understandable. This thing is so much stronger than most people. But I must have always known it existed, somewhere; and I've been waiting all these years. When men go into monasteries, and women shut themselves up in convents, their relatives suffer very much, I know, but in time they come to bear it. I want you to do the same, Victor, please. I want you, if you can, to understand."

She stood there, quite calm, quite peaceful, smiling down at him.

"You mean," he said, "you want to stay in this place always?"

"Yes," she said, "there can be no other life for me, any more, ever. You must believe this. I want you to go home, and live as you have always done, and look after the house and the estate, and if you fall in love with anyone to marry and be happy. Bless you for your love and kindness and devotion, darling, which I shall never forget. If I were dead, you would want to think of me at peace, in paradise. This place, to me, is paradise. And I would rather jump now, to those rocks hundreds of feet below me, than go back to the world from Monte Verità."

Victor said he went on staring at her as she spoke, and he said there was a radiance about her there had never been before, even in their most contented days.

"You and I," he said to me, "have both read of transfiguration in the Bible. That is the only word I can use to describe her face. It was not hysteria, it was not emotion; it was just that. Something—out of this world of ours—had put its hand upon her. To plead with her was useless, to attempt force impossible. Anna, rather than go back to the world, would throw herself off the rock-face. I should achieve nothing."

He said the feeling of utter helplessness was overwhelming, the knowledge that there was nothing he could do. It was as if he and she were standing on a dockway, and she was about to set foot in a ship, bound to an unknown destination, and the last few minutes were passing by before the ship's siren blew, warning him the gangways would be withdrawn and she must go.

He asked her if she had all she needed, if she would be given sufficient food, enough covering, and whether there were any facilities should she fall ill. He wanted to know if there was anything she wanted that he could send to her. And she smiled back at him, saying she had everything, within those walls, that she would ever need.

He said to her, "I shall return every year, at this time, to ask you to come back. I shall never forget."

She said, "It will be harder for you if you do that. Like putting flowers on a grave. I would rather you stayed away."

"I can't stay away," he said, "with the knowledge you are here, behind these walls."

"I won't be able to come to you again," she said, "this is the last time you will see me. Remember, though, that I shall go on looking like this, always. That is part of the belief. Carry me with you."

Then, Victor said, she asked him to go. She could not return inside the walls until he had gone. The sun was low in the sky and already the rock-face was in shadow.

Victor looked at Anna a long time; then he turned his back on her, standing by the ledge, and walked away from the wall towards the gully, without looking over his shoulder. When he came to the gully he waited there a few minutes, then looked out again towards the rock-face. Anna was no longer standing on the ledge. There was nothing there but the wall and the slit windows, and above, not yet in shadow, the twin peaks of Monte Verità.

I managed to spare half an hour or so, every day, to go and visit Victor in the nursing-home. Each day he appeared stronger, more himself. I spoke to the doctor attending him, to the matron and the nurses. They told me there was no question of a deranged mind; he came to them suffering from severe shock and nervous collapse. It had already done him immense good to see me and to talk to me. In a fortnight he was well enough to leave the nursing-home, and he came to stay with me in Westminster.

During those autumn evenings we went over all that had happened again and again. I questioned him more closely than I had done before. He denied that there had ever been anything abnormal about Anna. Theirs had been a normal, happy marriage. Her dislike of possessions, her spartan way of living, was, he agreed, unusual; but it had not struck him as peculiar—it was Anna. I told him of the night I had seen her standing with bare feet in the garden, on the frosted lawn. Yes, he said, that was the sort of thing she did. But she had a fastidiousness, a certain personal reticence, that he respected. He never intruded upon it.

I asked him how much he knew of her life before he married her. He told me there was very little to know. Her parents had died when she was young, and she had been brought up in Wales by an aunt. There was no peculiar background, no skeletons in the cupboard. Her upbringing had been entirely ordinary in every way.

"It's no use," said Victor, "you can't explain Anna. She is just herself, unique. You can't explain her any more than you can explain the sudden phenomenon of a musician, born to ordinary parents, or a poet, or a saint. There is no accounting for them. They just appear. It was my great fortune, praise God, to find her, just as it is my own personal hell, now, to have lost her. Somehow I shall continue living, as she expected me to do. And once a year I shall go back to Monte Verità."

His acquiescence to the total break-up of his life astounded me. I felt that I could not have overcome my own despair, had the tragedy been mine. It seemed to me monstrous that an unknown sect, on a mountain side, could, in the space of a few days, have such power over a woman, a woman of intelligence and personality. It was understandable that ignorant peasant girls could be emotionally misled and their relatives, blinded by superstition, do nothing about it. I told Victor this. I told him that it should be possible, through the ordinary channels of our embassy, to approach the government of that country, to have a nationwide inquiry, to get the Press on to it, the backing of our own government. I told him I was prepared, myself, to set all this in motion. We were living in the twentieth century, not in the Middle Ages. A place like Monte Verità should not be permitted to exist. I would arouse the whole country with the story, create an international situation.

"But why," said Victor quietly, "to what end?"

"To get Anna back," I said, "and to free the rest. To prevent the break-up of other people's lives."

"We don't," said Victor, "go about destroying monasteries or convents. There are hundreds of them, all over the world."

"That is different," I argued. "They are organized bodies of religious people. They have existed for centuries."

"I think, very probably, Monte Verità has too."

"How do they live, how do they eat, what happens when they fall ill, when they die?"

"I don't know. I try not to think about it. All I cling to is that Anna said she had found what she was searching for, that she was happy. I'm not going to destroy that happiness."

Then he looked at me, in a way half puzzled, half wise, and said, "It's odd, your talking in this way. Because by rights you should understand Anna's feelings more than I do. You were always the one with mountain fever. You were the one, in old climbing days, to have your head in the clouds and quote to me—

> The world is too much with us; late and soon,
> Getting and spending, we lay waste our powers."

I remember getting up and going over to the window and looking out over the foggy street, down to the embankment. I said nothing. His words had moved me very much. I could not answer them. And I knew, in the depths of my heart, why I hated the story of Monte Verità and wanted the place to be destroyed. It was because Anna had found her Truth, and I had not...

That conversation between Victor and myself made, if not a division in our friendship, at least a turning-point. We had reached a half-way mark in both our lives. He went back to his home in Shropshire, and later wrote to me that he intended making over the property to a young nephew, still at school, and during the next few years intended having the lad to stay with him in the holidays, to get him acquainted with the place. After that, he did not know. He would not commit himself to plans. My own future, at this time, was full with change. My work necessitated living in America for a period of two years.

Then, as it turned out, the whole tenor of the world became disrupted. The following year was 1914.

Victor was one of the first to join up. Perhaps he thought this would be his answer. Perhaps he thought he might be killed. I did not follow his example until my period in America was over. It was certainly not my answer, and I disliked every moment of my army years. I saw nothing of Victor during the whole of the war; we fought on different fronts, and did not even meet on leave. I did hear from him, once. And this is what he said:

In spite of everything, I have managed to get to Monte Verità each year, as I promised to do. I stayed a night with the old man in the village, and climbed on to the mountain top the following day. It looked exactly the same. Quite dead, and silent. I left a letter for Anna beneath the wall and sat there, all the day, looking at the place, feeling her near. I knew she would not come to me. The next day I went again, and was overjoyed to find a letter from her in return. If you can call it a letter. It was cut on flat stone, and I suppose this is the only method they have of communication. She said she was well, and strong, and very happy. She gave me her blessing, and you also. She told me never to be anxious for her. That was all. It was, as I told you at the nursing-home, like a spirit message from the dead. With this I have to be content, and am. If I survive this war, I shall probably go out and live somewhere in that country, so that I can be near her, even if I never see her again, or hear nothing of her but a few words scrawled on a stone once a year.

Good luck to yourself, old fellow. I wonder
where you are.

Victor

When the Armistice came, and I got myself demobilized and
set about the restoration of my normal life, one of the first
things I did was to inquire for Victor. I wrote to him, in
Shropshire. I had a courteous reply from the nephew. He had
taken over the house and the estate. Victor had been wounded,
but not badly. He had now left England and was somewhere
abroad, either in Italy or Spain, the nephew was not sure
which. But he believed his uncle had decided to live out there
for good. If he had news of him, he would let me know. No
further news came. As to myself, I decided I disliked post-war
London and the people who lived there. I cut myself loose
from home ties too, and went to America.

I did not see Victor again for nearly twenty years.

It was not chance that brought us together again. I am sure of
that. These things are predestined. I have a theory that each
man's life is like a pack of cards, and those we meet and sometimes love are shuffled with us. We find ourselves in the same
suit, held by the hand of Fate. The game is played, we are discarded, and pass on. What combination of events brought me
to Europe again at the age of fifty-five, two or three years before
the Second World War, does not matter to this story. It so happened that I came.

I was flying from one capital city to another—the names of
both are immaterial—and the aeroplane in which I travelled
made a forced landing, luckily without loss of life, in desolate
mountainous country. For two days the crew and passengers,
myself amongst them, held no contact with the outer world.
We camped in the partially wrecked machine and waited for

rescue. This adventure made headlines in the world Press at the time, even taking precedence, for a few days, over the simmering European situation.

Hardship, for those forty-eight hours, was not acute. Luckily there were no women or children passengers travelling, so we men put the best face on it we could, and waited for rescue. We were confident that help would reach us before long. Our wireless had functioned until the moment of the forced landing, and the operator had given our position. It was all a matter of patience, and of keeping warm.

For my part, with my mission in Europe accomplished and no ties strong enough back in the States to believe myself anxiously awaited, this sudden plunging into the sort of country that years ago I had most passionately loved was a strange experience. I had become so much a man of cities, and a creature of comfort. The high pulse of American living, the pace, the vitality, the whole breathless energy of the New World, had combined to make me forget the ties that still bound me to the Old.

Now, looking about me in the desolation and the splendour, I knew what I had lacked all these years. I forgot my fellow-travellers, forgot the grey fuselage of the crippled plane—an anachronism, surely, amid the wilderness of centuries—and forgot too my grey hair, my heavy frame, and all the burden of my five-and-fifty years. I was a boy again, hopeful, eager, seeking an answer to eternity. Surely it was there, waiting, beyond the further peaks. I stood there, incongruous in my city clothes, and the mountain fever raced back into my blood.

I wanted to get away from the wrecked plane and the pinched faces of my companions; I wanted to forget the waste of the years between. What I would have given to be young again, a boy, and, reckless of the consequences, set forth towards those peaks and climb to glory. I knew how it would feel, up there on the higher mountains. The air keener and still more cold, the silence deeper. The strange burning quality of ice, the penetrating strength of the sun, and that moment when the heart misses a beat as the foot, momentarily slipping on the narrow ledge, seeks safety; the hand's clutch to the rope.

I gazed up at them, the mountains that I loved, and felt a traitor. I had betrayed them for baser things, for comfort, ease, security. When rescue came to me and to my fellow-travellers, I would make amends for the time that had been lost. There was no pressing hurry to return to the States. I would take a vacation, here in Europe, and go climbing once again. I would buy proper clothes, equipment, set myself to it. This decision taken, I felt light-hearted, irresponsible. Nothing seemed to matter any more. I returned to my little party, sheltering beside the plane, and laughed and joked through the remaining hours.

Help reached us on the second day. We had been certain of rescue when we had sighted an aeroplane, at dawn, hundreds of feet above us. The search party consisted of true mountaineers and guides, rough fellows but likeable. They had brought clothing, kit, and food for us, and were astonished, they admitted, that we were all in condition to make use of them. They had thought to find none of us alive.

They helped us down to the valley in easy stages, and it took us until the following day. We spent the night encamped on the north side of the great ridge of mountains that had seemed to us, beside the useless plane, so remote and so inaccessible. At daybreak we set forth again, a splendid clear day, and the whole of the valley below our camp lay plain to the eye. Eastward the mountain range ran sheer, and as far as I could judge impassable, to a snow-capped peak, or possibly two, that pierced the dazzling sky like the knuckles on a closed hand.

I said to the leader of the rescue expedition, just as we were starting out on the descent, "I used to climb much, in old days, when I was young. I don't know this country at all. Do many expeditions come this way?"

He shook his head. He told me conditions were difficult. He

and his companions came from some distance away. The people in the valley to the eastward there were backward and ignorant; there were few facilities for tourists or for strangers. If I cared about climbing he could take me to other places, where I should find good sport. It was already rather late in the year, though, for expeditions.

I went on looking at that eastward ridge, remote and strangely beautiful.

"What do they call them," I said, "those twin peaks, to the east?"

He answered, "Monte Verità."

I knew then what had brought me back to Europe...

We parted, my fellow-travellers and I, at a little town some twenty miles from the spot where the aeroplane had crashed. Transport took them on to the nearest railway line, and to civilization. I remained behind. I booked a room at the small hotel and deposited my luggage there. I bought myself strong boots, a pair of breeches, a jerkin, and a couple of shirts. Then I turned my back upon the town and climbed.

It was, as the guide had told me, late in the year for expeditions. Somehow I did not care. I was alone, and on the mountains once again. I had forgotten how healing solitude could be. The old strength came back to my legs and to my lungs, and the cold air bit into the whole of me. I could have shouted with delight, at fifty-five. Gone was the turmoil and the stress, the anxious stir of many millions; gone were the lights, and the vapid city smells. I had been mad to endure it for so long.

In a mood of exaltation I came to the valley that lies at the eastern foot of Monte Verità. It had not changed much, it seemed to me, from the description Victor gave of it, those many years ago before the war. The little town was small and primitive, the people dull and dour. There was a rough sort of inn—one could not grace it by the name of hotel—where I proposed to stay the night.

I was received with indifference, though not discourtesy. After supper I asked if the track was still passable to the summit of Monte Verità. My informant behind his bar—for bar and café were in one, and I ate there, being the only visitor—regarded me without interest as he drank the glass of wine I offered him.

"It is passable, I believe, as far as the village. Beyond that I do not know," he said.

"Is there much coming and going between your people in the valley here and those in the village on the mountain?" I asked.

"Sometimes. Perhaps. Not at this time of year," he answered.

"Do you ever have tourists here?"

"Few tourists. They go north. It is better in the north."

"Is there any place in the village where I could sleep tomorrow night?"

"I do not know."

I paused a moment, watching his heavy sullen face, then I said to him, "And the *sacerdotesse*, do they still live on the rockface on the summit of Monte Verità?"

He started. He turned his eyes full upon me, and leant over the bar. "Who are you, then? What do you know of them?"

"Then they do exist still?" I said.

He watched me, suspicious. Much had happened to his country in the past twenty years, violence, revolution, hostility between father and son, and even this remote corner must have had its share. It may have been this that made reserve.

"There are stories," he said, slowly. "I prefer not to mix myself up in such matters. It is dangerous. One day there will be trouble."

"Trouble for whom?"

"For those in the village, for those who may live on Monte Verità—I know nothing of them—for us here in the valley. I do not know. If I do not know, no harm can come to me."

He finished his wine, and cleaned his glass, and wiped the bar with a cloth. He was anxious to be rid of me.

"At what time do you wish for your breakfast in the morning?" he said.

I told him seven, and went up to my room.

I opened the double windows and stood out on the narrow balcony. The little town was quiet. Few lights winked in the darkness. The night was clear and cold. The moon had risen and would be full tomorrow or the day after. It shone upon the dark mountain mass in front of me. I felt oddly moved, as though I had stepped back into the past. This room, where I should pass the night, might have been the same one where Victor and Anna slept, all those years ago, in the summer of 1913. Anna herself might have stood here, on the balcony, gazing up at Monte Verità, while Victor, unconscious of the tragedy so few hours distant, called to her from within.

And now, in their footsteps, I had come to Monte Verità.

The next morning I took my breakfast in the café-bar, and my landlord of the night before was absent. My coffee and bread were brought to me by a girl, perhaps his daughter. Her manner was quiet and courteous, and she wished me a pleasant day.

"I am going to climb," I said, "the weather seems set fair. Tell me, have you ever been to Monte Verità?"

Her eyes flickered away from mine instantly.

"No," she said, "no, I have never been away from the valley."

My manner was matter-of-fact, and casual. I said something about friends of mine having been here, some while ago—I did not say how long—and that they had climbed to the summit, and had found the rock-face there, between the peaks, and had been much interested to learn about the sect who lived enclosed within the walls.

"Are they still there, do you know?" I asked, lighting a cigarette, elaborately at ease.

She glanced over her shoulder nervously, as though conscious that she might be overheard.

"It is said so," she answered. "My father does not discuss it before me. It is a forbidden subject to young people."

I went on smoking my cigarette.

"I live in America," I said, "and I find that there, as in most places, when the young people get together there is nothing they like discussing so well as forbidden subjects."

She smiled faintly but said nothing.

"I dare say you and your young friends often whisper together about what happens on Monte Verità," I said.

I felt slightly ashamed of my duplicity, but I felt that this method of attack was the most likely one to produce information.

"Yes," she said, "that is true. But we say nothing out loud. But just lately..." Once again she glanced over her shoulder, and then resumed, her voice pitched lower, "A girl I knew quite well, she was to marry shortly, she went away one day, she has not come back, and they are saying she has been called to Monte Verità."

"No one saw her go?"

"No. She went by night. She left no word, nothing."

"Could she not have gone somewhere quite different, to a large town, to one of the tourist centres?"

"It is believed not. Besides, just before, she had acted strangely. She had been heard talking in her sleep about Monte Verità."

I waited for a moment, then continued my inquiry, still nonchalant, still casual.

"What is the fascination in Monte Verità?" I asked. "The life there must be unbearably harsh, and even cruel?"

"Not to those who are called," she said, shaking her head. "They stay young always, they never grow old."

"If nobody has ever seen them, how can you know?"

"It has always been so. That is the belief. That is why here, in the valley, they are hated and feared, and also envied. They have the secret of life, on Monte Verità."

She looked out of the window towards the mountain. There was a wistful expression in her eyes.

"And you?" I said. "Do you think you will ever be called?"

"I am not worthy," she said. "Also, I am afraid."

She took away my coffee and offered me some fruit.

"And now," she said, her voice still lower, "since this last disappearance, there is likely to be trouble. The people are angry, here in the valley. Some of the men have climbed to the village and are trying to rouse them there, to get force of numbers, and then they will attack the rock. Our men will go wild. They will try to kill those who live there. Then there will be more trouble, we shall get the army here, there will be inquiries, punishments, shooting; it will all end badly. So it is not pleasant at the moment. Everyone goes about afraid. Everybody is whispering in secret."

A footstep outside sent her swiftly behind the bar. She busied herself there, her head low, as her father came into the room.

He glanced at both of us, suspiciously. I put out my cigarette and rose from the table.

"So you are still intent to climb?" he asked me.

"Yes," I said. "I shall be back in a day or two."

"It would be imprudent to stay there longer," he said.

"You mean the weather will break?"

"The weather will break, yes. Also, it might not be safe."

"In what way might it not be safe?"

"There may be disturbance. Things are unsettled just now. Men are out of temper. When they are out of temper, they lose their heads. And strangers, foreigners, can come to harm at such a time. It would be better if you gave up your idea of climbing Monte Verità and turned northwards. There is no trouble there."

"Thank you. But I have set my heart on climbing Monte Verità."

He shrugged his shoulders. He looked away from me.

"As you will," he said, "it is not my affair."

I walked out of the inn, down to the street, and crossing the little bridge above the mountain stream I set my face to the track through the valley that led me to the eastern face of Monte Verità.

At first the sounds from the valley were distinct. The barking of dogs, the tinkle of cow bells, the voices of men calling to one another, all these rose clearly to me in the still air. Then the blue smoke from the houses merged and became one misty haze, and the houses themselves took on a toy-town quality. The track wound above me and away, ever deeper into the heart of the mountain itself, until by midday the valley was lost in the depths and I had no other thought in my mind but to climb upwards, higher, always higher, win my way beyond that first ridge to the left, leave it behind me and gain the second, forget both in turn to achieve the third, steeper yet and overshadowed. My progress was slow, with untuned muscles and imperfect wind, but exhilaration of spirit kept me going and I was in no way tired, rather the reverse. I could have gone on for ever.

It was with a shock of surprise that I came finally upon the village, for I had pictured it at least another hour away. I must have climbed at a great pace, for it was barely four o'clock. The village wore a forlorn, almost deserted appearance, and I judged that today there were few remaining inhabitants. Some of the dwellings were boarded up, others fallen in and partly destroyed. Smoke came only from two or three of them, and I saw no one working in the pasture-land around. A few cows, lean-looking and unkempt, grazed by the side of the track, the jangling bells around their necks sounding hollow somehow in the still air. The place had a sombre, depressing effect, after the stimulation of the climb. If this was where I must spend the night I did not think much of it.

I went to the door of the first dwelling that had a thin wisp of smoke coming from the roof and knocked upon the door. It was opened, after some time, by a lad of about fourteen, who after one look at me called over his shoulder to somebody within. A man of about my own age, stupid-looking and heavy, came to the door. He said something to me in patois, then staring a moment, and realizing his mistake, he broke, even more haltingly than I, into the language of the country.

"You are the doctor from the valley?" he said to me.

"No," I replied, "I am a stranger on vacation, climbing in the district. I want a bed for the night, if you can give me one."

His face fell. He did not reply directly to my request.

"We have someone here very sick," he said, "I do not know what to do. They said a doctor would come from the valley. You met no one?"

"I'm afraid not. No one climbed from the valley except myself. Who is ill? A child?"

The man shook his head. "No, no, we have no children here."

He went on looking at me, in a dazed, helpless sort of way, and I felt sorry for his trouble, but I did not see what I could do. I had no sort of medicines upon me but a first-aid packet and a small bottle of aspirin. The aspirin might be of use, if there was fever. I undid it from my pack and gave a handful to the man.

"These may help," I said, "if you care to try them."

He beckoned me inside. "Please to give them yourself," he said.

I had some reluctance to step within and be faced with the grim spectacle of a dying relative, but plain humanity told me I could hardly do otherwise. I followed him into the living-room. There was a trestle bed against the wall and lying upon it, covered with two blankets, was a man, his eyes closed. He was pale and unshaven, and his features had that sharp pointed look about them that comes upon the face when near to death. I went close to the bed and gazed down upon him. He opened his eyes. For a moment we stared at one another, unbelieving. Then he put out his hand to me, and smiled. It was Victor...

"Thank God," he said.

I was too much moved to speak. I saw him beckon to the fellow, who stood apart, and speak to him in the patois, and he must have told him we were friends, for some sort of light broke in the man's face and he withdrew. I went on standing by the trestle bed, with Victor's hand in mine.

"How long have you been like this?" I asked at length.

"Nearly five days," he said. "Touch of pleurisy; I've had it before. Rather worse this time. I'm getting old."

Once again he smiled, and although I guessed him to be desperately ill, he was little changed, he was the same Victor still.

"You seem to have prospered," he said to me, still smiling, "you have all the sleek appearance of success."

I asked him why he had never written, and what he had been doing with himself for twenty years.

"I cut myself adrift," he said. "I gather you did the same, but in a different way. I haven't been back to England since I left. What is it that you're holding there?"

I showed him the bottle of aspirin.

"I'm afraid that's no use to you," I said. "The best thing I can suggest is for me to stay here tonight, and then first thing in the morning get the chap here, and one or two others, to help me carry you down to the valley."

He shook his head. "Waste of time," he said. "I'm done for. I know that."

"Nonsense. You need a doctor, proper nursing. That's impossible in this place." I looked around the primitive living-room, dark and airless.

"Never mind about me," he said. "Someone else is more important."

"Who?"

"Anna," he said, and then as I answered nothing, at a loss for words, he added, "She's still here, you know, on Monte Verità."

"You mean," I said, "that she's in that place, enclosed, she's never left it?"

"That's why I'm here," said Victor. "I come every year, and have done, since the beginning. I wrote and told you, surely, after the war? I live in a little fishing port all the year round, very isolated and quiet, and then come here once in twelve months. I left it later this year, because I had been ill."

It was incredible. What an existence, all these years, without friends, without interests, enduring the long months until the time came for this hopeless annual pilgrimage.

"Have you ever seen her?" I asked.

"Never."

"Do you write to her?"

"I bring a letter every year. I take it up with me and leave it beneath the wall, and then return the following day."

"The letter gets taken?"

"Always. And in its place there is a slab of stone, with writing scrawled upon it. Never more than a few words. I take the stones away with me. I have them all down on the coast, where I live."

It was heart-rending, his faith in her, his fidelity through the years.

"I've tried to study it," he said, "this religion, belief. It's very ancient, way back before Christianity. There are old books that hint at it. I've picked them up from time to time, and I've spoken to people, scholars, who have made a study of mysticism and the old rites of ancient Gaul, and the Druids; there's a strong link between all mountain folk of those times. In every instance that I have read there is this insistence on the power of the moon and the belief that the followers stay young and beautiful."

"You talk, Victor, as if you believe that too," I said.

"I do," he answered. "The children believe it, here in the village, the few that remain."

Talking to me had tired him. He reached out for a pitcher of water that stood beside the bed.

"Look here," I said, "these aspirins can't hurt you, they can only help, if you have fever. And you might get some sleep."

I made him swallow three, and drew the blankets closer round him.

"Are there any women in the house?" I asked.

"No," he said, "I've been puzzled about that, since I've been here this time. The village is pretty much deserted. All the women and children have shifted to the valley. There are about twenty men and boys left, all told."

"Do you know when the women and children went?"

"I gather they left a few days before I came. This fellow here—he's the son of the old man who used to live here, who died many years ago—is such a fool that he never knows anything. He just looks vague if you question him. But he's competent, in his own way. He'll give you food, and find bedding for you, and the little chap is bright enough."

Victor closed his eyes, and I hoped that he might sleep. I thought I knew why the women and children had left the village. It was since the girl from the valley had disappeared. They had been warned that trouble might come to Monte Verità. I did not dare tell Victor this. I wished I could persuade him to be carried down into the valley.

By this time it was quite dark, and I was hungry. I went through a sort of recess to the back. There was no one there but the boy. I asked him for something to eat and drink, and he understood. He brought me bread, and meat, and cheese, and I ate it in the living-room, with the boy watching me. Victor's eyes were still closed and I believed he slept.

"Will he get better?" asked the boy. He did not speak in patois.

"I think so," I answered, "if I can get help to carry him to a doctor in the valley."

"I will help you," said the boy, "and two of my companions. We should go tomorrow. After that, it will be difficult."

"Why?"

"There will be coming and going the day after. Men from the valley, much excitement, and my companions and I will join them."

"What is going to happen?" He hesitated. He looked at me with quick bright eyes.

"I do not know," he said. He slipped away, back to the recess. Victor's voice came from the trestle bed.

"What did the boy say?" he asked. "Who is coming from the valley?"

"I don't know," I said casually, "some expedition, perhaps. But he has offered to help take you down the mountain tomorrow."

"No expeditions ever come here," said Victor, "there must be some mistake." He called to the boy, and when the lad reappeared spoke to him in the patois. The boy was ill at ease, and diffident; he seemed reluctant now to answer questions. Several times I heard the words Monte Verità repeated, both by him and Victor. Presently he went back to the inner room and left us alone.

"Did you understand any of that?" asked Victor.

"No," I replied.

"I don't like it," he said, "there's something queer. I've felt it, since I've lain here these last few days. The men look furtive, odd. He tells me there's been some disturbance in the valley, and the people there are very angry. Did you hear anything about it?"

I did not know what to say. He was watching me closely.

"The fellow in the inn was not very forthcoming," I said, "but he did advise against coming to Monte Verità."

"What reason did he give?"

"No particular reason. He just said there might be trouble."

Victor was silent. I could feel him thinking there beside me.

"Have any of the women disappeared from the valley?" he said.

It was useless to lie. "I heard something about a missing girl," I told him, "but I don't know if it's true."

"It will be true. That is it, then."

He said nothing for a long while, and I could not see his face—it was in shadow. The room was lit by a single lamp, giving a pallid glow.

"You must climb tomorrow and warn Anna at Monte Verità," he said at last.

I think I had expected this. I asked him how it could be done.

"I can sketch the track for you," he said, "you can't go wrong. It's straight up the old water-course, heading south all the while. The rains haven't made it impassable yet. If you leave before dawn you'll have all day before you."

"What happens when I get there?"

"You must leave a letter, as I do, and then come away. They won't fetch it while you are there. I will write, also. I shall tell Anna that I am ill here, and that you've suddenly appeared, after nearly twenty years. You know, I was thinking, just now, while you were talking to the boy, it's like a miracle. I have a strange sort of feeling Anna brought you here."

His eyes were shining with that old boyish faith that I remembered.

"Perhaps," I said. "Either Anna, or what you used to call my mountain fever."

"Isn't that the same thing?" he said to me.

We looked at one another in the silence of that small dark room, and then I turned away and called the boy to bring me bedding and a pillow. I would sleep the night on the floor by Victor's bed.

He was restless in the night, and breathed with difficulty. Several times I got up to him and gave him more aspirin and water. He sweated much, which might be a good thing or a bad, I did not know. The night seemed endless, and for myself, I barely slept at all. We were both awake when the first darkness paled.

"You should start now," he said, and going to him I saw with apprehension that his skin had gone clammy cold. He was worse, I was certain, and much weaker.

"Tell Anna," he said, "that if the valley people come she and the others will be in great danger. I am sure of it."

"I will write all that," I said.

"She knows how much I love her. I tell her that always in my letters, but you could say so, once again. Wait in the gully. You may have to wait two hours, or even three, or longer still. Then go back to the wall and look for the answer on the slab of stone. It will be there."

I touched his cold hand and went out into the chill morning air. Then, as I looked about me, I had my first misgiving. There was cloud everywhere. Not only beneath me, masking the track from the valley where I had come the night before, but here in the silent village, wreathing in mist the roofs of the huts, and also above me, where the path wound through scrub and disappeared upon the mountain side.

Softly, silently, the clouds touched my face and drifted past, never dissolving, never clearing. The moisture clung to my hair and to my hands, and I could taste it on my tongue. I looked this way and that, in the half light, wondering what I should do. All the old instinct of self-preservation told me to return. To set forth, in breaking weather, was madness, to my remembered mountain lore. Yet to stay there, in the village, with Victor's eyes upon me, hopeful, patient, was more than I could stand. He was dying, we both knew it. And I carried in my breast pocket his last letter to his wife.

I turned to the south, and still the clouds came travelling past, slowly, relentlessly, down from the summit of Monte Verità.

I began to climb...

Victor had told me that I should reach the summit in two hours. Less than that, with the rising sun behind me. I had also a guide, the rough sketch map that he had drawn.

In the first hour after leaving the village I realized my error. I should never see the sun that day. The clouds drove past me, vapour in my face, clammy and cold. They hid the winding water-course up which I had climbed five minutes since, down which already came the mountain springs, loosening the earth and stones.

By the time the contour changed, and I was free of roots and scrub and feeling my way upon bare rock, it was past midday. I was defeated. Worse still, I was lost. I turned back and could not find the water-course that had brought me so far. I approached another, but it ran north-east and had already broken for the season; a torrent of water washed away down the mountain-side. One false move, and the current would have borne me away, tearing my hands to pieces as I sought for a grip among the stones,

Gone was my exultation of the day before. I was no longer in the thrall of mountain fever but held instead by the equally well-remembered sense of fear. It had happened in the past, many a time, the coming of cloud. Nothing renders a man so helpless, unless he can recognize every inch of the way by which he has come, and so descend. But I had been young in those days, trained, and climbing fit. Now I was a middle-aged city dweller, alone on a mountain I had never climbed before, and I was scared.

I sat down under the lee of a great boulder, away from the drifting cloud, and ate my lunch—the remainder of sandwiches packed at the valley inn—and waited. Then, still waiting, I got up and stamped about for warmth. The air was not penetrating yet but seeping cold, the moist chill cold that always comes with cloud.

I had this one hope, that with the coming of darkness, and with a fall in temperature, the cloud would lift. I remembered it would be full moon, a great point to my advantage, for cloud rarely lingers at these times, but tends to break up and dissolve. I welcomed, therefore, the coming of a sharper cold into the atmosphere. The air was perceptibly keener, and looking out towards the south, from which direction the cloud had drifted all the day, I could now see some ten feet ahead. Below me it was still as thick as ever. A wall of impenetrable mist hid the descent. I went on waiting. Above me, always to the south, the distance that I could see increased from a dozen feet to fifteen, from fifteen to twenty. The cloud was cloud no longer, but vapour only, thin, and vanishing; and suddenly the whole contour of the mountain came into view, not the summit as yet, but the great jutting shoulder, leaning south, and beyond it my first glimpse of the sky.

I looked at my watch again. It was a quarter to six. Night had fallen on Monte Verità.

Vapour came again, obscuring that clear patch of sky that I had seen, and then it drifted, and the sky was there once more. I left my place of shelter where I had been all day. For the second time I was faced with a decision. To climb, or to descend.

Above me, the way was clear. There was the shoulder of the mountain, described by Victor; I could even see the ridge along it running to the south, which was the way I should have taken twelve hours before. In two or three hours the moon would have risen and would give me all the light I needed to reach the rock-face of Monte Verità. I looked east, to the descent. The whole of it was hidden in the same wall of cloud. Until the cloud dissolved I should still be in the same position I had been all day, uncertain of direction, helpless in visibility that was never more than three feet.

I decided to go on, and to climb to the summit of the mountain with my message.

Now the cloud was beneath me my spirits revived. I studied the rough map drawn by Victor, and set out towards the southern shoulder. I was hungry, and would have given much to have back the sandwiches I had eaten at midday. A roll of bread was all that remained to me. That, and a packet of cigarettes. Cigarettes were not helpful to the wind, but at least they staved off the desire for food.

Now I could see the twin peaks themselves, clear and stark against the sky. And a new excitement came to me, as I looked up at them, for I knew that when I had rounded the shoulder and had come to the southern face of the mountain, I should have reached my journey's end.

I went on climbing; and I saw how the ridge narrowed and how the rock steepened, becoming more sheer as the southern slopes opened up to view, and then, over my shoulder, rose the first tip of the moon's great face, out of the misty vapour to the east. The sight of it stirred me to a new sense of isolation. It was as though I walked alone on the earth's rim, the universe below me and above. No one trod this empty discus but myself, and it spun its way through space to ultimate darkness.

As the moon rose, the man that climbed with it shrank to insignificance. I was no longer aware of personal identity. This shell, in which I had my being, moved forward without feeling, drawn to the summit of the mountain by some nameless force which seemed to hold suction from the moon itself. I was impelled, like the flow and ebb of tide upon water. I could not disobey the law that urged me on, any more than I could cease to breathe. This was not mountain fever in my blood, but mountain magic. It was not nervous energy that drove me, but the tug of the full moon.

The rock narrowed and closed above my head, making an arch, a gully, so that I had to stoop and feel my way; then I emerged from darkness into light, and there before me, silver-white, were the twin peaks and the rock face of Monte Verità.

For the first time in my life I looked on beauty bare. My mission was forgotten, my anxiety for Victor, my own fear of cloud that had clamped me through the day. This indeed was journey's end. This was fulfilment. Time did not matter. I had no thought of it. I stood there staring at the rock-face under the moon.

How long I remained motionless I do not know, nor do I remember when the change came to the tower and the walls; but suddenly the figures were there, that had not been before. They stood one behind the other on the walls, silhouetted against the sky, and they might have been stone images, carved from the rock itself, so still they were, so motionless.

I was too distant from them to see their faces or their shape. One stood alone, within the open tower; this one alone was shrouded, in a garment reaching from head to foot. Suddenly there came to my mind old tales of ancient days, of Druids, of slaughter, and of sacrifice. These people worshipped the moon, and the moon was full. Some victim was going to be flung to the depths below, and I would witness the act.

I had known fear in my life before, but never terror. Now it came upon me in full measure. I knelt down, in the shadow of the gully, for surely they must see me standing there, in the moon's path. I saw them raise their arms above their heads, and slowly a murmur came from them, low and indistinct at first, then swelling louder, breaking upon the silence that hitherto had been profound. The sound echoed from the rock-face, rose and fell upon the air, and I saw them one and all turn to the full moon. There was no sacrifice. No act of slaughter. This was their song of praise.

I hid there, in the shadows, with all the ignorance and shame of one who stumbles into a place of worship alien to his knowledge, while the chanting rang in my ears, unearthly, terrifying, yet beautiful in a way impossible to bear. I clasped my hands over my head, I shut my eyes, I bent low until my forehead touched the ground.

Then slowly, very slowly, the great hymn of praise faded in strength. It sank lower to a murmur, to a sigh. It hushed and died away. Silence came back to Monte Verità.

Still I dared not move. My hands covered my head. My face was to the ground. I am not ashamed of my terror. I was lost between two worlds. My own was gone, and I was not of theirs. I longed for the sanctuary of the drifting clouds again.

I waited, still upon my knees. Then furtive, creeping, I lifted up my head and looked towards the rock-face. The walls and the tower were bare. The figures had vanished. And a cloud, dark and ragged, hid the moon.

I stood up, but I did not move. I kept my eyes fixed upon the tower and the walls. Nothing stirred, now that the moon was masked. They might never have been, the figures and the chanting. Perhaps my own fear and imagination had created them.

I waited until the cloud that hid the moon's face passed away. Then I took courage and felt for the letters in my pocket. I do not know what Victor had written, but my own ran thus:

Dear Anna,

Some strange providence brought me to the village on Monte Verità. I found Victor there. He is desperately ill, and I think dying. If you have a message to send him, leave it beneath the wall. I will carry it to him. I must warn you also that I believe your community to be in danger. The people from the valley are frightened and angry because one of their women has disappeared. They are likely to come to Monte Verità, and do damage.

In parting, I want to tell you that Victor has never stopped loving you and thinking about you.

And I signed my name at the bottom of the page.

I started walking towards the wall. As I drew close I could see the slit windows, described to me long ago by Victor, and it came to me that there might be eyes behind them, watching, that beyond each narrow opening there could be a figure, waiting.

I stooped and put the letters on the ground beneath the wall. As I did so, the wall before me swung back suddenly and opened. Arms stretched forth from the yawning gap and seized me, and I was flung to the ground, with hands about my throat.

The last thing I heard, before losing consciousness, was the sound of a boy, laughing.

I awoke with violence, jerked back into reality from some great depth of slumber, and I knew that a moment before I had not been alone. Someone had been beside me, kneeling, peering down into my sleeping face.

I sat up and looked about me, cold and numb. I was in a cell about ten foot long, and the daylight, ghostly pale, filtered through the narrow slit in the stone wall. I glanced at my watch. The hands pointed to a quarter to five. I must have lain unconscious for a little over four hours, and this was the false light that comes before dawn.

My first feeling now, on waking, was one of anger. I had been fooled. The people in the village below Monte Verità had lied to me, and to Victor too. The rough hands that had seized me, and the boy's laugh that I heard, these had belonged to the villagers themselves. That man, and his son, had preceded me up the mountain track, and had lain in wait for me. They knew a way of entry through the walls. They had fooled Victor through the years, and thought to fool me too. God alone knew their motive. It could not be robbery. We neither of us had anything but the clothes we wore. This cell into which they had thrust me was quite bare. No sign of human habitation, not even a board on which to lie. A strange thing, though— they had not bound me. And there was no door to the cell. The entry was open, a long slit, like the window, but large enough to permit the passage of a single form.

I sat waiting for the light to strengthen and for the feeling, too, to come back to my shoulders, arms and legs. My sense of caution told me this was wise. If I ventured through the open-ing now, I might in the dim light stumble, and fall, and be lost in some labyrinth of passage-way or stair.

My anger grew with the daylight, yet with it also a feeling of despair. I longed more than anything to get hold of the fellow and his son, threaten them both, fight them if necessary—I would not be thrown to the ground a second time unawares. But what if they had gone away and left me in this place, with-out means of exit? Supposing this, then, was the trick they played on strangers, and had done so through countless years, the old man before them, and others before him, luring the women from the valley too, and once inside these walls leaving the victims to starvation and death? The uneasiness mounting in me would turn to panic if I thought too far ahead, and to calm myself I felt in my pocket for my cigarette case. The first few puffs steadied me, the smell and the taste of the smoke belonged to the world I knew.

Then I saw the frescoes. The growing light betrayed them to me. They covered the walls of the cell, and were drawn upon the ceiling too. Not the rough primitive efforts of uncultured peasants, nor yet the saintly scrawling of religious artists, deeply moved by faith. These frescoes had life and vigour, colour and intensity, and whether they told a story or not I did not know, but the motif was clearly worship of the moon. Some figures knelt, others stood; one and all had their arms up, raised to the full moon traced upon the ceiling. Yet in some strange fashion the eyes of the worshippers, drawn with uncanny skill, looked down upon me, not upwards to the moon. I smoked my cigarette and looked away, but all the time I felt their eyes fasten on me, as the daylight grew, and it was like being back outside the walls again, aware of silent watchers from behind the slit windows.

I got up, stamping on my cigarette, and it seemed to me that anything would be better than to remain there in the cell, alone with those figures on the painted walls. I moved to the opening, and as I did so I heard the laughter once again. Softer this time, as though subdued, but mocking and youthful still. That damned boy...

I plunged through the opening, cursing him and shouting. He might have a knife upon him but I didn't care. And there he was, flattened against the wall, waiting for me. I could see the gleam of his eyes, and I saw his close-cropped hair. I struck at his face, and missed. I heard him laughing as he slipped to one side. Then he wasn't alone any more; there was another just behind, and a third. They threw themselves upon me and I was borne to the ground as though I had no strength at all, and the first one knelt with his knee on my chest and his hands about my throat, and he was smiling at me.

I lay fighting for breath, and he relaxed his grip, and the three of them watched me, with that same mocking smile upon their lips. I saw then that none of them was the boy from the village, nor was the father there, and they did not have the faces of village people or of the valley people: their faces were like the painted frescoes on the wall.

Their eyes were heavy-lidded, slanting, without mercy, like the eyes I had seen once long ago on an Egyptian tomb, and on a vase long hidden and forgotten under the dust and rubble of a buried city. Each wore a tunic to his knees, with bare arms, bare legs and hair cropped close to the head, and there was a strange austere beauty about them, and a devilish grace as well. I tried to raise myself from the ground, but the one who had his hand upon my throat pressed me back, and I knew I was no match for him or his companions, and if they wanted to they could throw me from the walls down to the depths below Monte Verità. This was the end, then. It was only a matter of time, and Victor would die alone, back in the hut on the mountain-side.

"Go ahead," I said, "have done with it," resigned, caring no longer. I expected the laughter again, mocking and youthful, and the sudden seizing of my body with their hands, and the savage thrusting of me through the slit window to darkness and to death. I closed my eyes, and with nerves taut braced myself for horror. Nothing happened. I felt the boy touch my lips. I opened my eyes and he was smiling still, and he had a cup in his hands, with milk in it, and he was urging me to drink, but he did not speak. I shook my head but his companions came and knelt behind me, supporting my shoulders and my back, and I began to drink, foolishly, gratefully, like a child. The fear went as they held me, and the horror too, and it was as though strength passed from their hands to mine, and not only to my hands but to the whole of me.

When I had finished drinking the first one took the cup

from me and put it on the ground, then he placed his two hands on my heart, his fingers touching, and the feeling that came to me was something I had never experienced in my life before. It was as if the peace of God came upon me, quiet and strong, and, with the touch of hands, took from me all anxiety and fear, all the fatigue and terror of the preceding night; and my memory of the cloud and mist on the mountain, and Victor dying on his lonely bed, became suddenly things of no importance. They shrank into insignificance beside this feeling of strength and beauty that I knew now. If Victor died it would not matter. His body would be a shell lying there in the peasant hut, but his heart would be beating here, as mine was beating, and his mind would come to us too.

I say "to us" because it seemed to me, sitting there in the narrow cell, that I had been accepted by my companions and made one of them. This, I thought to myself, still wondering but bewildered, happy, this is what I always hoped that death would be. The negation of all pain and all distress, and the centre of life flowing, not from the quibbling brain, but from the heart.

The boy took his hands from me, still smiling, but the feeling of strength, of power, was with me still. He rose to his feet and I did the same, and I followed him and the two others through the gap in the cell. There was no honeycomb of twisting corridors, no dark cloisters, but a great open court on to which the cells all gave, and the fourth side of the court led upwards to the twin peaks of Monte Verità, ice-capped, beautiful, caught now in the rose light of the rising sun. Steps cut in the ice led to the summit, and now I knew the reason for the silence within the walls and in the court as well, for there were the other ones, ranged upon the steps, dressed in those same tunics with bare arms and legs, girdles about the waist, and the hair cropped close to the head.

We passed through the court and up the steps beside them.

There was no sound: they did not speak to me or to one another, but they smiled as the first three had done; and their smile was neither courteous nor tender, as we know it in the world, but had a strange exulting quality, as if wisdom and triumph and passion were all blended into one. They were ageless, they were sexless, they were neither male nor female, old or young, but the beauty of their faces, and of their bodies too, was more stirring and exciting than anything I had ever seen or known, and with a sudden longing I wanted to be one of them, to be dressed as they were dressed, to love as they must love, to laugh and worship and be silent.

I looked down at my coat and shirt, my climbing breeches, my thick socks and shoes, and suddenly I hated and despised them. They were like grave clothes covering the dead, and I flung them off, in haste to have them gone, throwing them over my shoulder down to the court below; and I stood naked under the sun. I was without embarrassment or shame. I was quite unconscious how I looked and I did not care. All I knew was that I wanted to have done with the trappings of the world, and my clothes seemed to symbolize the self I had once been.

We climbed the steps and reached the summit, and now the whole world lay before us, without mist or cloud, the lesser peaks stretching away into infinity, and far below, concerning us not at all, hazy and green and still, were the valleys and the streams and the little sleeping towns. Then, turning from the world below, I saw that the twin peaks of Monte Verità were divided by a great crevasse, narrow yet impassable, and standing on the summit, gazing downwards, I realized with wonder, and with awe as well, that my eyes could not penetrate the depths. The ice-blue walls of the crevasse descended smooth and hard without a break to some great bottomless chasm, hidden for ever in the mountain heart. The sun that rose to bathe the peaks at midday would never touch the depths of that crevasse, nor would the rays of the full moon come to it, but it seemed to me, between the peaks, that the shape of it was like a chalice held between two hands.

Someone was standing there, dressed in white from head to foot, on the very brink of the chasm, and although I could not see her features, for the cowl of the white robe concealed them, the tall upright figure, with head thrown back and arms outstretched, caught at my heart with sudden tense excitement.

I knew it was Anna. I knew that no one else would stand in just that way. I forgot Victor, I forgot my mission, I forgot time and place and all the years between. I remembered only the stillness of her presence, the beauty of her face, and that quiet voice saying to me, "We are both in search of the same thing, after all." I knew then that I had loved her always, and that though she had met Victor first, and chosen him, and married him, the ties and ceremony of marriage concerned neither of us, and never had. Our minds had met and crossed and understood from the first moment when Victor introduced us in my club, and that queer, inexplicable bond of the heart, breaking through every barrier, every restraint, had kept us close to one another always, in spite of silence, absence, and long years of separation.

The mistake was mine from the beginning in letting her go alone to find her mountain. Had I gone with them, she and Victor, when they asked me that day in the Map House long ago, intuition would have told me what was in her mind and the spell would have come upon me as well. I would not have slept on in the hut, as Victor had slept, but would have woken and gone with her, and the years that I had wasted and thrown away, futile and misspent, would have been our years, Anna's and mine, shared here on the mountain, cut off from the world.

Once again I looked about me and at the faces of those who stood beside me, and I guessed dimly, with a sort of hunger near to pain, what ecstasy of love they knew, that I had never known. Their silence was not a vow, condemning them to darkness, but a peace that the mountain gave to them, merging their minds in tune. There was no need for speech, when a smile, a glance, conveyed a message and a thought; while laughter, triumphant always, sprang from the heart's centre, never to be suppressed. This was no closed order, gloomy, sepulchral, denying all that instinct gave the heart. Here Life was fulfilled, clamouring, intense, and the great heat of the sun seeped into the veins, becoming part of the blood stream, part of the living flesh; and the frozen air, merging with the direct rays of the sun, cleansed the body and the lungs, bringing power and strength—the power I had felt when the fingers touched my heart.

In the space of so short a while my values had all changed, and the self who had climbed the mountain through the mist, fearful, anxious, and angry too, but a little while ago, seemed to exist no more. I was grey-haired, past middle age, a madman to the world's eyes if they could see me now, a laughing-stock, a fool; and I stood naked with the rest of them on Monte Verità and held up my arms to the sun. It rose now in the sky and shone upon us, and the blistering of my skin was pain and pleasure blended, and the heat drove through my heart and through my lungs.

I kept my eyes fixed on Anna, loving her with such intensity that I heard myself calling aloud, "Anna...Anna..." And she knew that I was there, for she lifted her hand in signal. None of them minded, none of them cared. They laughed with me, they understood.

Then from the midst of us came a girl, walking. She was dressed in a simple village frock, with stockings and shoes, and her hair hung loose on her shoulders. I thought her hands were folded together, as though in prayer, but they were not. She held them to her heart, the fingers touching.

She went to the brink of the crevasse, where Anna stood.

Last night, beneath the moon, I should have been gripped by fear, but not now. I had been accepted. I was one of them. For one instant, in its space of time above us in the sky, the sun's ray touched the lip of the crevasse, and the blue ice shone. We knelt with one accord, our faces to the sun, and I heard the hymn of praise.

"This," I thought, "was how men worshipped in the beginning, how they will worship in the end. Here is no creed, no saviour, and no deity. Only the sun, which gives us light and life. This is how it has always been, from the beginning of time."

The sun's ray lifted and passed on, and then the girl, rising to her feet, threw off her stockings and her shoes and her dress also, and Anna, with a knife in her hand, cut off her hair, cropping it close above the ears. The girl stood before her, her hands upon her heart.

"Now she is free," I thought. "She won't go back to the valley again. Her parents will mourn her, and her young man too, and they'll never discover what she has found, here on Monte Verità. In the valley there would have been feasting and celebration, and then dancing at the wedding, and afterwards the turmoil of a brief romance turning to humdrum married life, the cares of her house, the cares of children, anxiety, fret, illness, trouble, the day-by-day routine of growing old. Now she is spared all that. Here, nothing once felt is lost. Love and beauty don't die or fade away. Living's hard, because Nature's hard, and Nature has no mercy; but it was this she wanted in the valley, it was for this she came. She will know everything here that she never knew before and would not have discovered, below there in the world. Passion and joy and laughter, the heat of the sun, the tug of the moon, love without emotion, sleep with no waking dream. And that's why they hate it, in the valley, that's why they're afraid of Monte Verità. Because here on the summit is something they don't possess and never will, so they are angry and envious and unhappy."

Then Anna turned, and the girl who had thrown her sex away with her past life and her village clothes followed barefoot, bare armed, cropped-haired like the others; and she was radiant, smiling, and I knew that nothing would ever matter to her again.

They descended to the court, leaving me alone on the summit, and I felt like an outcast before the gates of heaven. My brief moment had come and gone. They belonged here, and I did not. I was a stranger from the world below.

I put on my clothes again, restored to a sanity I did not want, and remembering Victor and my mission I too went down the steps to the court, and looking upwards I saw that Anna was waiting for me in the tower above.

The others flattened themselves against the wall to let me pass, and I saw that Anna alone amongst them wore the long white robe and the cowl. The tower was lofty, open to the sky, and characteristically, with that same gesture I remembered when she used to sit on the low stool before the fire in the great hall, Anna sat down now, on the topmost step of the tower, one knee raised and elbow on that knee. Today was yesterday, today was six-and-twenty years ago, and we were alone once more in the manor house in Shropshire; and the peace she had brought to me then she brought me now. I wanted to kneel beside her and take her hand. Instead I went and stood beside the wall, my arms folded.

"So you found it at last," she said. "It took a little time."

The voice was soft and still and quite unchanged.

"Did you bring me here?" I asked. "Did you call me when the aircraft crashed?"

She laughed, and I had never been away from her. Time stood still on Monte Verità.

"I wanted you to come long before that," she said, "but you shut your mind away from me. It was like clamping down a receiver. It always took two to make a telephone call. Does it still?"

"It does," I answered, "and our more modern inventions need valves for contact. Not the mind, though."

"Your mind has been a box for so many years," she said. "It was a pity—we could have shared so much. Victor had to tell me his thoughts in letters, which wouldn't have been necessary with you."

It was then, I think, that the first hope came to me. I must feel my way towards it, though, with care.

"You've read his letter," I asked, "and mine as well? You know that he's dying?"

"Yes," she said, "he's been ill for many weeks. That's why I wanted you to be here at this time, so that you could be with him when he died. And it will be all right for him, now, when you go back to him and tell him that you've spoken to me. He'll be happy then."

"Why not come yourself?"

"Better this way," she said. "Then he can keep his dream."

His dream? What did she mean? They were not, then, all-powerful here on Monte Verità? She understood the danger in which they stood.

"Anna," I said, "I'll do what you want me to do. I'll return to Victor and be with him at the last. But time is very short. More important still is the fact that you and the others here are in great danger. Tomorrow, tonight even, the people from the valley are going to climb here to Monte Verità, and they'll break into this place and kill you. It's imperative that you get away before they come. If you have no means of saving your-selves, then you must allow me to do something to help you. We are not so far from civilization as to make that impossible. I can get down to the valley, find a telephone, get through to the police, to the army, to some authority in charge..."

My words trailed off, because although my plans were not clear in my own mind I wanted her to have confidence in me, to feel that she could trust me.

"The point is," I told her, "that life is going to be impossible for you here, from now on. If I can prevent the attack this time, which is doubtful, it will happen next week, next month. Your days of security are numbered. You've lived here shut away so long that you don't understand the state of the world as it is now. Even this country here is torn in two with suspicion, and the people in the valley aren't superstitious peasants any longer; they're armed with modern weapons, and they've got murder in their hearts. You won't stand a chance, you and the rest, here on Monte Verità."

She did not answer. She sat there on the step, listening, a remote and silent figure in her white robe and cowl.

"Anna," I said, "Victor's dying. He may be already dead. When you leave here he can't help you, but I can. I've loved you always. No need to tell you that, you must have guessed it. You destroyed two men, you know, when you came to live on Monte Verità six-and-twenty years ago. But that doesn't matter any more. I've found you again. And there are still places far away, inaccessible to civilization, where we could live, you and I—and the others with you here, if they wished to come with us. I have money enough to arrange all that; you won't have to worry about anything."

I saw myself discussing practicalities with consuls, embassies, going into the question of passports, papers, clothing.

I saw too, in my mind's eye, the map of the world. I ranged in thought from a ridge of mountains in South America to the Himalayas, from the Himalayas to Africa. Or the northern wastes of Canada were still vast and unexplored, and stretches of Greenland. And there were islands, innumerable, countless islands, where no man ever trod, visited only by sea-birds, washed by the lonely sea. Mountain or island, scrubby wilderness or desert, impenetrable forest or Arctic waste, I did not care which she chose; but I had been without sight of her for so long, and now all I wanted was to be with her always.

This was now possible, because Victor, who would have claimed her, was going to die. I was blunt. I was truthful. I told her this as well. And then I waited, to hear what she would say.

She laughed, that warm, much loved, and well-remembered laugh, and I wanted to go to her and put my arms round her, because the laugh held so much life in it, and so much joy and promise.

"Well?" I said.

Then she got up from the step and came and stood beside me, very still.

"There was once a man," she said, "who went to the booking office at Waterloo and said to the clerk eagerly, hopefully, "I want a ticket to Paradise. A single ticket. No return." And when the clerk told him there was no such place the man picked up the ink-well and threw it in the clerk's face. The police were summoned, and took the man away and put him in prison. Isn't that what you're asking of me now, a ticket to Paradise? This is the mountain of truth, which is very different."

I felt hurt, irritated even. She hadn't taken a word of my plans seriously and was making fun of me.

"What do you propose, then?" I asked. "To wait here, behind these walls, for the people to come and break them down?"

"Don't worry about us," she said. "We know what we shall do."

She spoke with indifference, as if the matter was of no importance, and in agony I saw the future, that I had begun to plan for us both, slip away from me.

"Then you do possess some secret?" I asked, almost in accusation. "You can work some miracle, and save yourself and the others, too? What about me? Can't you take me with you?"

"You wouldn't want to come," she said. She put her hand on my arm. "It takes time, you know, to build a Monte Verità. It isn't just doing without clothes and worshipping the sun."

"I realize that," I told her. "I'm prepared to begin all over again, to learn new values, to start from the beginning. I know that nothing I've done in the world is any use. Talent, hard work, success, all those things are meaningless. But if I could be with you..."

"How? With me?" she said.

And I did not know what to answer, because it would be too sudden and too direct, but I knew in my heart that what I wanted was everything that could be between a woman and a man; not at first, of course, but later, when we had found our other mountain, or our wilderness, or wherever it was we might go to hide ourselves from the world. There was no need to rehearse all that now. The point was that I was prepared to follow her anywhere, if she would let me.

"I love you, and have always loved you. Isn't that enough?" I asked.

"No," she said, "not on Monte Verità."

And she threw back her cowl and I saw her face.

I gazed at her in horror...I could not move, I could not speak. It was as though all feeling had been frozen. My heart was cold...One side of her face was eaten quite away, ravaged, terrible. The disease had come upon her brow, her cheek, her throat, blotching, searing the skin. The eyes that I had loved were blackened, sunk deep into the sockets.

"You see," she said, "it isn't Paradise."

I think I turned away. I don't remember. I know I leant against the rock of the tower and stared down into the depths below, and saw nothing but the great bank of cloud that hid the world.

"It happened to others," Anna said, "but they died. If I survived longer, it was because I was hardier than they. Leprosy can come to anyone, even to the supposed immortals of Monte Verità. It hasn't really mattered, you know. I regret nothing. Long ago I remember telling you that those who go to the mountain must give everything. That's all there is to it. I no longer suffer, so there's no need to suffer for me."

I said nothing. I felt the tears run down my face. I didn't bother to wipe them away.

"There are no illusions and no dreams on Monte Verità," she said. "They belong to the world, and you belong there too. If I've destroyed the fantasy you made of me, forgive me. You've lost the Anna you knew once, and found another one instead. Which you will remember longer rather depends upon yourself. Now go back to your world of men and women and build yourself a Monte Verità."

Somewhere there was scrub and grass and stunted trees; somewhere there was earth and stones and the sound of running water. Deep in the valley there were homes, where men lived with their women, reared their children. They had firelight, curling smoke and lighted windows. Somewhere there were roads, there were railways, there were cities. So many cities, so many streets. And all with crowded buildings, lighted windows. They were there, beneath the cloud, beneath Monte Verità.

"Don't be anxious or afraid," said Anna, "and as for the valley people, they can't harm us. One thing only..." She paused, and although I did not look at her I think she smiled. "Let Victor keep his dream," she said.

Then she took my hand, and we went down the steps of the tower together, and through the court and to the walls of the rock-face. They stood there watching us, those others, with their bare arms and legs, their close-cropped hair, and I saw too the little village girl, the proselyte, who had renounced the world and was now one of them. I saw her turn and look at Anna, and I saw the expression in her eyes; there was no horror there, no fear and no revulsion. One and all they looked at Anna with triumph, with exultation, with all knowledge and all understanding. And I knew that what she felt and what she en-

dured they felt also, and shared with her, and accepted. She was
not alone.

They turned their eyes to me, and their expression changed;
instead of love and knowledge I read compassion.

Anna did not say goodbye. She put her hand an instant on
my shoulder. Then the wall opened, and she was gone from
me. The sun was no longer overhead. It had started its journey
in the western sky. The great white banks of cloud rolled upward from the world below. I turned my back on Monte Verità.

It was evening when I came to the village. The moon had
not yet risen. Presently, within two hours or less, it would top
the eastern ridge of the further mountains and give light to the
whole sky. They were waiting, the people from the valley. There
must have been three hundred or more, waiting there in groups
beside the huts. All of them were armed, some with rifles, with
grenades, others, more primitive, with picks and axes. They
had kindled fires, on the village track between the huts, and
had brought provisions too. They stood or sat before the fires
eating and drinking, smoking and talking. Some of them had
dogs, held tightly on a leash.

The owner of the first hut stood by the door with his son.
They too were armed. The boy had a pick and a knife thrust in
his belt. The man watched me with his sullen, stupid face.

"Your friend is dead," he said. "He has been dead these
many hours."

I pushed past him and went into the living-room of the hut.
Candles had been lit. One at the head of the bed, one at the
foot. I bent over Victor and took his hand. The man had lied to
me. Victor was breathing still. When he felt me touch his hand,
he opened his eyes.

"Did you see her?" he asked.

"Yes," I answered.

"Something told me you would," he said. "Lying here, I felt
that it would happen. She's my wife, and I've loved her all these

years, but you only have been allowed to see her. Too late, isn't it, to be jealous now?"

The candlelight was dim. He could not see the shadows by the door, nor hear the movement and the whispering without.

"Did you give her my letter?" he said.

"She has it," I answered. "She told you not to worry, not to be anxious. She is all right. Everything is well with her."

Victor smiled. He let go my hand.

"So it's true," he said, "all the dreams I had of Monte Verità. She is happy and contented and she will never grow old, never lose her beauty. Tell me, her hair, her eyes, her smile—were they still the same?"

"Just the same," I said. "Anna will always be the most beautiful woman you or I have ever known."

He did not answer. And as I waited there, beside him, I heard the sudden blowing of a horn, echoed by a second and a third. I heard the restless movement of the men outside in the village, as they shouldered their weapons, kicked out the fires and gathered together for the climb. I heard the dogs barking and the men laughing, ready now, excited. When they had gone I went and stood alone in the deserted village, and I watched the full moon rising from the dark valley.

# TITLES IN SERIES